a NOVEL

# Congo

SPIRIT OF DARKNESS

# ALLAIN NGWALA
## and MAYI NGWALA

**GENET PRESS**

# Congo
## SPIRIT OF DARKNESS

PUBLISHER'S NOTE

This book is a work of fiction. Names, characters, places, and incidents either are the product of the author's imagination or are used fictitiously, and any resemblance to actual persons, living or dead, business establishments, events, or locales is entirely coincidental.

Library of Congress Control Number: 2012937279
ISBN 978-0-9846663-0-0 (Paperback)
ISBN 978-0-9846663-1-7 (ebook)
Fiction.
Printed in the United States of America
NOVEMBER 2012 – First Edition

Cover and Interior Design by Rachel Lopez
www.r2cdesign.com

Published by:
GENET PRESS, Ltd. Liability Co.
For information address Genet Press,
Post Office Box 530
Lanham, Maryland 20703-0530 U.S.A.
www.genetpress.com

# PUBLISHER'S NOTE

BOOKS ARE AVAILABLE AT QUANTITY DISCOUNTS WHEN USED TO PROMOTE PRODUCTS, SERVICES OR FUND RAISING, OR FOR EDUCATIONAL USE. A PORTION OF THE PROCEEDS FROM ALL BOOK SALES IS DONATED TO HUMANITARIAN CAUSES AND CHARITIES. FOR MORE INFORMATION PLEASE CONTACT GENET PRESS.

# DEDICATION

*We dedicate this book*
*to the people of the Congo, and*
*to victims of past and modern-day slavery;*
*the daily struggle to survive and to be free.*
*May you find peace in a renewed*
*life beyond the walls of the wicked*
*world of human trafficking.*

*Thank you My lovely Friend for your great support*

# DEAR READERS

According to the Christian Bible, Jesus of Nazareth spoke of a mysterious parable, a lesson from a lamp. "Is a lamp brought to be put under a basket or under a bed? Is it not to be set on a lampstand? For there is nothing hidden which will not be revealed, nor has anything been kept secret but that it should come to light." (Mark 4:21-22, New Testament)

Men and women not only need light to see, but also for their minds and souls. Jesus said, "Walk while you have the light, lest darkness overtake you..."

We believe this book to carry a lot of facets that deal with the world; issues that cause all sorts of awareness. This narrative is for those who are willing to learn of the mysteries of the far-side world: people, cultures, societies, religions, beliefs, and civilisations of Ancient times. This alternate history novel is a reflection of the ancient African way of life, the tribal traditions and historical events that formed the basis of their cultural beliefs, joys, faith, hopes and dreams, and their living harmony with nature. It is an acknowledgement of their solidarity, their love for each other, their sense of belonging, and their respect for their elders and ancestors and their people—from the older to the younger generation.

We believe this book may also be a tool of education, whilst mostly entertaining. The renowned Greek philosopher Posidonius (ca. 135 BCE - 51 BCE), said, "A single day among the learned lasts longer than the longest life among the ignorant." Furthermore, a Greek proverb states, "If you love learning, you shall be learned."

This book is written in honour of those who struggled and those who continue to struggle for peace and spiritual and physical freedom. Since the exploration of the African continent by the Europeans, the establishments of the slave trade by Arab and European trades have created conflict and division between tribes, leaving the Kingdoms of Central Africa shattered and forever gone.

We hope this tale will captivate your imagination, touch your hearts, and offer a newfound understanding of Africa. We believe this narrative to be a source of immense adventure: through it, explore and discover the degree of risk and danger people took in exchange for their birth right to live; discover the way of life, culture, and beliefs of other world civilisations.

We hope this narrative shall give light to your mind and soul in your journey through life. As written in the Christian Bible, "For as the rain comes down, and the snow from heaven, and do not return there, but water the earth, and make it bring forth and bud, that it may give seed to the sower and bread to the eater, so shall My word be that goes forth from My mouth; it shall not return to Me void, but it shall accomplish what I please, and it shall prosper in the thing for which I sent it." (Isaiah 55:10–11, Old Testament)

"A great book remains eternally in one's memory as today's legend." (Ngwala brothers, 2012)

# PREFACE

*London, United Kingdom*
*Saint Bartholomew's Hospital*
*December 18, 1938*

I am on my death bed.

Physicians declare I have less than one week to live; perhaps a few days more, perhaps less, and I have a sense of the afterlife looming.

*Not yet*, I beseech. *Not just yet.*

My name is Susan Bailey Dawson. I'm 100 years of age, a lifelong abolitionist. Prior to embracing this existence, I had been a retired British journalist. Yet my story commences neither now nor then; it did so much earlier, almost eight decades past, as a dyed-in-the-wool member of the press for *The Times* in England...

The door to my room opens.

Elizabeth Smith, a white nurse, returns from fetching clean linen. She has been my caregiver for as long as I can remember. I have been here for twelve moons, with no family or children to call my own. All that is mine is flesh, soon to be departed, but it was not always so.

In the recent past, I had taken notice of Elizabeth's curiously full lips; a pair that I'd undoubtedly never seen on a pasty woman. Except Elizabeth had revealed to me her most guarded secret.

She was not entirely white.

She had revealed to me that her forefather had been a slave from *Wene wa Kongo*, Kingdom of the Kongo, who had come to have a child with a white woman and then, generations thereafter, all descendants had children with white mates. That was how she came to be: in my eyes, the whitest-looking black Caucasian I had ever seen.

At the close of this revelation, a tear had rolled down from the edge of my eye. Elizabeth knew not why; only I did.

The wheels had turned.

It was time for me to reveal to her my deepest secret, the secret of how I once came to meet and fall in love with a man, a Belgian-Dutch by the name of Bison Van Lanterman—a henchman for slave traders and a devotee of the King of the Belgians.

Elizabeth lays fresh linen on the dresser. She looks to me.

I nod.

She digs in my valise and withdraws a thick, aged tome.

I nod again.

She moves before me and pulls a chair by my bedside.

I had wished to tell her the tale myself, but my memory had been lapsing, part of my malady. "Read it, Liz," I say. "It will help me remember."

Elizabeth sets the bulky paperback on her lap. Her finger lifts the first page. She is reading my story, my memoir, a journey to the heart of darkness…

*Death does not sound a trumpet.*

—Congo proverb

PART ONE:

# THE NATIVES

# PROLOGUE

*Zulu Kingdom*
*December 16, 1838*

A t twilight, on the banks of the Ncome River, dense, humid mist blinded their eyes, leading into sunrise, *Impis* blood pounding in their chests, scorching from built-up angst over a wakeful night as they hung in silence, awaiting a dawn of bloodshed.

*Impis*, armed Zulu warriors, were fearless men.

"*Azife izitha!*" roared an indigenous fighter, armed with a stabbing spear, charging towards the laager of the enemy. A hailstorm of bullets from hundreds of shooters demolished his skull as he caved into the ground to die.

Some 10,000 Zulu combatants scaled the steep incline of the riverbank, striking assegais with no regard of the hundreds of gathered *Voortrekkers*. Thousands of men were fighting for land, dignity, and freedom; it was the Battle of Blood River.

"Kill them!" barked a Zulu commandant, wielding a bulky combat shield.

"Fire," came the angry reply from Bison Van Lanterman, a youngster, fit with the bluest eyes, behind the laager, pointing to the lashing horde of Zulu warriors.

There was a continuous crescendo of gunshots. A powerful explosion thundered, and *Ou Grietjie* blasts battered the air.

Many died, and the *Impis* retreated. The river transformed into a crimson stream, flowing with their blood and the blood of their slain brethren.

The charged air had turned eerily still; the only sound was the sobs of the wounded. Dust and smoke settled.

Now, 3,000 Zulus lay dead on the Ncome riverbank, whilst the surviving *Voortrekkers* and the young Van Lanterman praised the will of their god and hailed their victory.

By age fifteen, Bison Van Lanterman had killed more Negroes than his father had killed men at the Battle of Leuven. Yet, with the larger demand on the black market for cheap human labour from the west coast of Africa, there was always more killing to be done in the pursuit of money, power, and glory.

# CHAPTER I

# FAMILY

*Kingdom of the Kongo*
*Dry Season, 1860s*

Drifting weather had been timely with each new era and then vanished with stifling blowing winds, marking Van Lanterman's triumphant battle some decades past. A new day had dawned in a distant land; a land distinct in its verdant lavishness from the unvarnished fields of the Ncome territory.

In the early morning, the blood-red sunrise inspired the birds to perform a concert of twittering and singing. The sun shimmered on the still waters of the river, glittering like a sea of diamonds.

Flitting and jutting above the surface of the water were the tilapia, distinguishable by their characteristic fins and red hue, seemingly enjoying lazing, exerting their much-savoured energy only to catch and consume any insect unfortunate enough to wander onto the water surface.

Freshwater *Nzombo* could also be found, encircling the bottom and feeling their way with their long barbells, sailing upwards, only to take a lazy but much-needed breaths of air.

The vegetation and the flora in its exquisite beauty encompassed all hues of the rainbow. The riverbanks were crowded by the inspiring heads of the blooms, dabbing colourful drops of natural paint on the tall, dense backdrop of the tropical rainforest. The sun lit up the scene magnificently, inspiring even the smallest shrubs and blossoms to stretch skyward, searching out the precious beams.

Upon the rising of the sun on a new day, the greenery was fresh and dew-covered; nature's beasts—both small and large—awoke. Tree branches provided the fruits of nature, offering breakfast to all wildlife—bird, mammal, and human.

The riverbanks were home to a number of different rocks and stones, which provided the local women with a means of washing and cleaning. The rocks seemed to be waiting patiently, resting on the many layers of sand, mud, and grain, undisturbed for countless centuries.

Not long after the rise of the sun, clothes would be rubbed and washed—a sound musical to the ears of the women and their babes, who would gather to carry out their chores with joy.

When it was time to leave, the mothers would call the children to wash their feet. They would sit on the large stones and rub their feet on the rough surface; when they were gone, the cool water would continue to slowly flow through each new day.

One day, like every day, the women and children arrived. They were the Kongo women who lived within *Wene wa Kongo*, deep in the untarnished heart of Central Africa, north of the Pende and west of the Kuba Kingdom, yet isolated enough that they were sheltered from the outside world. Young and old women, children, and grandmothers gathered on the banks of the river in the early morning. They arrived, carrying belongings, ready to delve into their work.

A muscular, dark-skinned man, Ombe, with a long, sharp-edged spear clamped in his left hand, rubbed the belly of a pregnant woman, Mpende. The woman would bear his first child.

Mpende was so heavily pregnant that her casual breathing sounded like that of a panting leopard. She lovingly smiled at Ombe, then tightly held on to a dried, half-broken log and Ombe's arm, and, with great effort, heaved herself up and released a heavy sigh. Once up, she leant herself onto his open chest to a rewarding, loving embrace. Her expanding belly made for a somewhat uncomfortable contact, but they settled for it. A moment later, he joined his fellow hunters, who insisted on teasing him.

"Must be a boy!" shouted one of the hunters in Kongo language.

"Perhaps it will be a girl. He's getting a little soft," said another, laughing.

"Let's go hunting," exclaimed Ombe, dismissing their taunts.

The men laughed, then disappeared deeper into the forest, a trek that kept them away from their loved ones through several sunrises.

High up on a hill, peeping down, was Ndoki, a sorcerer, pitching cowrie shells on the earth. He consulted them, shifting the shells around, when dismay and trepidation crossed his face. A foreboding—one he had never felt for as long as he had lived—swept over him. Fear stained his eyes as he rose and stared up at the blue skies. Reminiscent of a madman, he repeatedly muttered, "The devil lures. You must run… Take your children…and run…" He then retreated, akin to a spectre, into a cluster of leafy shrubs.

Down below by the pool, the elder women cleaned clothes. The younger girls helped with the washing of dishes. Some were cleaning children, whilst others cleansed their own bodies or their babes. Children filled bottles, and women filled large jugs with water to carry to villages for cooking and drinking.

The river, like a meeting pool, came to life with chatter and laughter, like a marketplace where people gathered to exchange news and stories.

Children played in the water, splashing and jumping. Women were deep in conversation, oblivious to their surroundings, absorbed by their work and the stories of the day. They dipped and squeezed clothes, rubbing them with papaya sap to clean; they splashed like a chorus until the clothes were clean and the tune of their chores was complete.

That day, a group of young mothers from the Yombe tribe arrived late, singing the old songs their grandmothers had sung before them. The rhythmic melodies motivated the group to work hard together. They chatted loudly and finally greeted the other women.

Amongst the group was Nsala, a calm, strong woman, tall and slim. She was not easily overexcited, and when she spoke, everyone listened. She greeted her friends, Mpende and Yambi, and sat on the grass by their side.

Mpende, heavily pregnant, walked awkwardly for such a small woman, but her broad shoulders supported her plump frame. She was lively and loud, with a hearty laugh, always teasing and telling stories.

Yambi had soft, big eyes that were vigilant and watchful. Though she had a slightly nervous disposition, she was a kind, caring woman, one the others could rely upon.

Although Mpende and Yambi were descendants of the Wabembe tribe in a distant village, all three women were the closest of friends.

They had agreed that Yambi would look after Mpende. It was traditional for women to protect each other in this way; in case of an emergency, she would not be alone.

"*Mbote.*"

"Good morning to you also."

"Why are you so late today?"

"Nsimba was sick all night," Nsala answered, referring to her youngest girl, who was just two years old. "Her stomach was painful. I took her to see

Mlozi." Mlozi was the medicine man whom the women relied upon when their children were ill.

"Did he give her something?"

"Yes. She took *nkisi*." Nsala spoke of the medicine Mlozi had made by carefully grinding selected herbs into a paste. The paste would be carefully mixed with water to form a fluid substance, crafted by expert hands and years of knowledge. That would then be squeezed until the juice poured out, ready to be consumed by the patient—a historical tradition to treat and cure a number of ailments. The juice would be taken from a wooden cup believed to hold power. "Poor child. I did not sleep for the rest of the night. I wanted to watch over her. I need a little rest." Nsala eased her body slowly down onto the grass, glancing over to her daughter.

"She must be feeling better now. Look at how she's running with the other children," said Yambi, smiling reassuringly at her friend.

Mpende chimed in, "Well, you know how sickness passes quickly in children."

Nsala turned to Yambi. "Where is your child?"

"Oh, he's hunting with his father. He's getting older now and wants to be with his father more and more. His interest is in hunting. He's tired of being with the women and the younger children."

"Yes, and as his virility develops, he will chase the girls," said Mpende mischievously.

The three friends laughed aloud. They were happy their children were well, and they felt comforted by each other's support.

Mpende lay down on the bare grass, for her bloated stomach made it hard for her to sit comfortably. She rubbed her belly tenderly. The thought of the birth of her first child brought forth all her maternal instincts. She was content, ready to have the baby, although it was not due for several suns and moons.

Boali, her sister-in-law, about thirteen, came to kneel in front of her. She had flourished into a young woman whose perky breasts were the main attraction for young bachelors, but she was already claimed and would soon be with child herself. She was keen to learn about pregnancy. "Mama, how is your belly today?" she asked.

"You remember, don't you, in the early stages, I was tired and wanted to sleep all the time? I didn't know what to eat. Everything made me feel sick. My stomach could only hold cow's milk. Now, my husband claims I can eat a whole goat!" Mpende threw back her head and laughed heartily, encouraging the other women to cackle with her. "I don't feel sick anymore," she continued, "just heavy. My back and legs hurt, and I can't walk for long distances. I need to rest often." She sighed and rubbed her belly again.

"But can you feel the baby moving? Does it kick?" asked Boali.

"Oh yes—always at night," Mpende said with a giggle, "and always low." The thought interrupted her laugh as she recalled the discomfort of carrying her unborn.

Nsala joined the exchange. "You know, when I was pregnant with my first child, Layila, I was tired right until the end."

"Really?" Boali's eyes were wide, eager to learn more from her elders.

"Yes. Every time is different. The first was calm, but the second with the twins, Nsimba and Nzuzi, was harder. Those girls kicked all night and came early. It was as if they were in a rush to see the world. They never stay still now. They are always active." Nsala beamed at the thought of her children, whom she loved dearly.

Mpende moaned. "Now that my baby is kicking so much, do you think it is time? Please! I want it to be time." She turned and looked imploringly at her older friends.

Yambi comforted her. She knew the kicking was normal in the latter stages of pregnancy. "Well, we can see your belly is stretching every day. The baby will be here soon. Be patient," she said reassuringly.

Mpende lay back, closed her eyes, and groaned. "I can't wait any longer."

"What have you been eating lately?" Boali asked, searching for more information.

"In the early stages, my mouth had a bitter taste and, for some reason, I felt like eating bland food. My mother used to tell me the story every night before I slept. I can still hear her voice now… My father dug out greyish mud found on the riverbank, dried it, and burned it in charcoal. He was making *mabele*. He gave it to my mother, who was expecting me. Now I eat *mabele* and *safu*," said Mpende.

"*Mabele?* Awful!" Yambi wrinkled her nose and stuck out her tongue. "That dreadful food! You're right about it having no taste. I just can't eat it."

"*Safu* is not so bad. During my last pregnancy, I craved it in the morning. I had my husband pick it at dawn, before hunting. He used to hate that," reflected Nsala.

When unripe, the *safu* was a pale colour, but ripening brought forth a distinct violet-blue shade. The women did not doubt it was good for the development of their babes.

"Is it what I'm going to eat? Really? Will my taste really change?" asked Boali.

Nsala smiled at her. "That's nothing," she said. "When I was pregnant with Layila, I ate green mango, not ripe, mixed with salt and red peppers."

Everyone laughed except Boali, who continued to be amazed. "That can't be true!" she cried.

"Of course! You must have heard of this before. My grandmother ate the same. Be careful, because your taste *will* change. You never know what to expect from a pregnancy," said Nsala.

"And I can tell you more." Mpende propped herself up on one elbow, slightly letting it sink into the sand, as if searching better comfort. "Since I have been eating *safu*, my husband has the same passion—and he's not even pregnant!"

The women fell about, laughing so hard that tears began streaming down their cheeks.

Mpende continued, happy to entertain her friends. "Really! He likes to eat them so much that, when he is due home from the evening hunt, Boali rushes to boil the *safu* in the water for him."

Boali was hunter Ombe's youngest sister; she'd come to live with them some weeks prior, whilst Mpende was pregnant, to help with the heavier chores. She was shy in the company of her elders, yet she had a strong, determined character.

"When the water is hot enough, I clean the fruit and put them in the water," Boali advised in a serious tone, hoping to impress her elders, "and when the colour changes to a light blue, I remove them. They are ready for my dear brother to enjoy."

Mpende began to struggle to her feet, and Boali jumped to hold her arm. Mpende placed her hand on her hip, enjoying the mischief. By now, she had the attention of the group, and they turned to listen for more. "It's true. When he has eaten the first half of the fruit, he turns to me, with the juice streaming from his mouth, and whispers, 'I love you, mama.'"

The women screamed with laughter that ricocheted off the rocks all about.

"It's true," said Boali. "When Ombe is happy, everyone is happy."

The women clapped their hands.

"Ombe is excited to have his first child. He thinks the baby will be a girl because it is kicking." She smiled, exhibiting more mischief. For a moment, she had forgotten about her discomfort. "This is what he thinks, but I'm not so sure. You know what the elders say. When the pregnant mother eats *mabele* or *safu*, the baby is likely to be a boy."

Yambi argued. "Have you forgotten the old saying that if a pregnancy is calm, it is a girl?"

Mpende's mischief subsided, and she looked serious. "My baby's been kicking for days now."

"Ah yes, but you remember how calm the baby was before? It's only recently that the baby has been kicking," Yambi reminded her.

"Yes, that's true." Mpende recollected. She called to Boali to help her lie down again. "Anyway, I'm too hot to care. I just want a healthy baby now. Boali, please fetch me a leaf. I'm so hot."

Boali ran to cut a banana leaf.

The other women carried on their discussion about the sex of the baby. A girl or a boy, they agreed, would be a blessing.

The children were playing and had made a rope from small branches of the palm tree. They skipped rope, chanting songs in time. A few yards from the water's edge, the bush thinned, and the forest floor expanded.

Layila, Nsala's daughter, a single-minded eleven-year-old, had walked back in that direction to look for ripe mangoes that had fallen to the ground. She had heard the women's conversation and couldn't bear the thought of Mpende eating them green with salt.

Nsala called to her, "Stubborn you! Be careful of snakes."

# CHAPTER II

# FEAR

Far ahead in the distance was *Mayombe* land—the largest forest in the kingdom, stretching either side of the Congo River.

Here, where the forest was most dense and the sunrays were prevented from filtering by umbrella leaves, with merely a fraction able to touch the earth below, a young native ran.

He was sweating; his eyes wide open. Saliva ran from the edge of his lips. He panted, tired and struggling. He pressed his legs forward as his feet dragged in the undergrowth beneath him.

The forest was dark, thick, and humid; conditions in which only the strongest, most durable of seedlings would survive, leaving the weaker to perish without the much-craved sunshine. Those that had learned to survive with only a glimpse of sunshine flourished. Within the conflicting atmosphere— hot, then cold, and always damp—monkeys screeched and danced amongst the treetops whilst frogs croaked, poison swelling from their throats.

The man's breath was hot, yet his skin was cold. Sweat trickled in beads down his lean body.

He couldn't see where he was going, but he knew he had to move fast. The ground was wet, and he kept slipping and sliding, almost falling. Whenever he fell, he quickly scrambled back up on his feet. He fumbled with the bow and arrows and the dead, black-cheeked, white-nosed monkey on his back, pulling them away from his body and throwing them down to the ground so he was free to run faster.

He stomped the undergrowth and kicked at small bushes, jumping over some of them. Leaves and branches whipped his face and scratched his arms, but he kept pushing himself to run faster, zigzagging down his own precarious path. His arms and legs bled from stabbing, stinging plants, but he paid no attention to his pain, for his fear was too great. He simply, absolutely couldn't stop.

Although he knew not why or who, something—someone—was chasing after him in the darkness, and so he ran, his thoughts begging the gods to grant him that one desperate, final wish: life! He wanted to live, so he was forced to run. Thus, he hastened until he found himself in a place he had never been before. He never had to cross to the other side of the jungle— never for anything—but now he had no choice.

He had to run.

He was confused, afraid. *Why me?* he asked himself.

*Why now?* He hurried further.

His chest was bare, as were the soles of his feet. He was naked except for a piece of cloth strung between his muscular legs, tied to his waist with bark string. When the loincloth became caught in the bushes, the man was forced to halt.

He couldn't move, and he was petrified.

"Help," the man hissed to himself in the darkness. "What do you want from me?" His voice was rasping, breathless. He looked desperately in every direction, hoping for an answer, but now there was only a sense of something or someone—or many—moving; maybe a lion, maybe many;

maybe cheetahs. *How can this be? The animals surely would have caught me by now*, he thought in desperation.

As the man tugged the branch that had snared his loincloth, he began to pray, fearing for his life. He could only hope *Bakulu*, spirits of ancestors, would protect him from such a fate.

Then he heard voices, men's voices, speaking in strange tongues. He was befuddled and frightened; he had never heard anything remotely like those voices in his life.

Terrified, he tugged desperately at his loincloth. By the grace of *Bakulu*, he broke free. His loincloth slipped away, left hanging on the branch, and he ran naked.

As long as he was free, he would run.

As long as there was life, he would run.

He felt neither the scratches to his skin or the itching from the bushes. Fear had left him numb and senseless.

He had nothing to give; he was just a poor village-dweller. *Why*, he thought, *do they continue to chase after me?* All that he had left behind—the monkey, his weapons, and even his small shred of cloth… *And what now?*

In his race, he sped through the mass of thick vegetation covered in moss, trees with bark of many years' growth, thick, gummy layers of vines. He could see the sunlight through the trees in the distance, and as he neared, he could hear the voices of women and children; laughter, water splashing.

"Help!" he screamed.

Everyone was busy with their chores: washing, cleaning, splashing, and talking. Much activity buzzed, both beneath and above the surface of the river water; birds, fish, insects, and people alike enjoying the cool water on the hottest of days.

Only Yambi's eyes were drawn to the other side of the river. The sight of flocks of pelicans, herons, and water birds exploding up and out of the top branches of a tree from the forest captured her attention. She looked questioningly, peering and frowning far into the distance.

The birds fluttered higher up into the blue sky. The forest remained thick and dark below. There was no way she could see what had startled the birds.

Yambi thought it peculiar and momentarily, her heart lurched. She had a sudden urge to warn her friends, but she hesitated. *Is there something happening on the other side of the river, deep in the jungle?* she wondered. The anxiety rose inside her, like that of a mother whose child is out of sight. "Look! Over there. Do you see what I see? The birds. They flew in a hurry." Yambi nudged Nsala, who followed the direction of Yambi's pointing finger.

"Yes, I see the birds. It could be nothing," replied Nsala calmly.

"Don't you think it's strange for birds to fly out abruptly like that?" questioned Yambi. "Something is wrong."

"It must be hunters from the neighbouring village," said Nsala.

Yambi was not easily persuaded; she turned to Mpende. "Look! Don't you see? It looks as though the birds were startled. They're used to hunters. This is something different."

"You're scaring me," said Mpende. "Stop it."

Now, a black cloud formed over the treetops, thick, like a swarm of bees.

Mpende tilted her chin and looked questioningly. "What is that?" Her voice was tinged with anxiety.

The hairs on Nsala's arms rose, and goose bumps tingled on her skin. "Come. Children, come here." She signalled her children, who were still playing by the river, Nsimba and Nzuzi. Her throat felt tight, and her stomach twisted into a knot. She knew to be cautious.

Something peculiar was indeed happening, something deep within the jungle. It was not the hunters they knew so well, for they had gone the other way, deep into the jungle behind them. When she was a child, her mother had warned her many times to always trust her intuition, her gut instinct. *Mama was right*, she thought. *Something is not right.*

Back in the forest, like a runner nearing the finishing line, the man was relieved at the sight of the women and children. He was not alone. He had run for so long, and momentarily, his fear subsided.

Still trembling and out of breath, he reached the soft grass on the riverbank. He saw the women and the children on the far banks. He was frantic once again.

"Run!" he shouted.

He threw himself into the river and swam forcefully towards the other side. The current was strong, forcing him backwards, but he fought, plunging his large hands through the water and kicking ferociously.

The water felt cool on his body, but the current contended with his strength; at the same time, every wave of water drenched his face. He could not forget his peril, and he dared not look back. His eyes remained focused on the other side of the river.

The women and children watched the naked man throw himself into the river like a madman. They were frightened. There was no one around to protect them because their brave, strong, valiant men were hunting, far away from there.

"Why is this bushman so frantic?" Nsala frowned, perplexed by the crazed man swimming towards them.

The man waved his hands, screaming and begging the gathering of women and children to run, but they couldn't hear his warnings in order to heed them, for he was too far away. The flow of the river was rapid, and the majestic expanse doused the poor man's voice. Their instinct was to help him, but fear froze them to the spot. The crazed man knew why the birds scattered in such a panicked flurry.

"Swim! Swim to us," Nsala shouted bravely, struck with compassion for the struggling man.

A sharp blast bellowed from deep within the jungle, like a crack of lightning during the rainy season, overshadowing the surge of the river. A displeasing silent moment passed and unnerved the women. All that was audible was the swimmer's tamed voice. The women looked up at the sky with uncertainty. There was no thunder, no lightning; they saw only blue skies and bright sunshine. They had never heard thunder in the dry season. They clung to each other in fear. Traditional beliefs had taught them that thunder and lightning were expressions of anger by the spirits of the dead.

The women believed in the strong, ever-present link between the earth and the spirit world, with power—good and evil—felt by the living. Whenever the spirits were believed to be angry, not only would people flee, but also the birds, monkeys, reptiles, and rodents; not only the weak, but also the strong. All creation would take cover and hide, awaiting the inevitable wrath.

At times, when the village felt the presence of the spirits' anger, there would be a gathering of the influential leaders—the chief of the tribe, the heads of the family, the medicine man—who would discuss and offer sacrifice animals to appease the anger and illustrate the respect held by the villagers. Sacrifice and death would be emphasized through dress, red and black adorning the people.

Another blast echoed.

All hushed. Doubts travelled through the minds of the women. Should lightning strike, they knew how to act. They would gather the infants and children and head back towards their village, wherein the umbrella huts would provide shelter until the stormed had passed.

*Maybe a ritual will appease the angry spirits.* The thought passed fleetingly through Nsala's mind, but there was no time. The fear was still imminent. The spirits had never before manifested themselves so early in the day.

The women stood still, chilled by the thunder, their eyes drawn back to the man in the river, yet consciously aware of the black clouds billowing higher. The man continued to swim hard, though hardly making any advance. The women, taking Nsala's lead, began to wail and plead for him to keep going.

The man reached a branch caught in the midst of the river and clung to it. He could barely shout, barely fight. He was weak—very weak.

There was another blast, this time from somewhere within the bushes close by the river. As if he were a ragdoll, the man's head fell to one side. His strong arms dropped their hold on the branch. He slipped into the water silently. The muddy water became a pool of red, swirling, crimson and, driven by the current, he flowed almost gracefully downstream.

Yambi wailed. "He's dead! The man is dead."

The water lifted the man like pallbearers carrying a coffin. His corpse swept in the current like driftwood, floating further and further away from the stunned women.

The realisation that the man was running from the thunder-like noise slowly entered their minds. *What evil spirit could this be?* they wondered, in utter disbelief that a brave man had sacrificed his life to try and warn them.

Another blast pierced the air. The women screamed. Fear and panic crept in. Children ran to hold their mothers. Their shock was evident in every eye.

Nsala instinctively reacted first. "We need to run," she warned the other women. As was her character, she issued the instruction in a low, calm voice, but the women heard the urgency in her voice.

All abandoned their clothes, dishes, and buckets. Their only thought was to grab their children. Sap buckets were brushed aside, their clean clothes dropped and left behind.

Nsala quickly spun 'round to the undergrowth where she'd last seen her daughter. "Layila! Layila, where are you?"

Layila cried, "Here! I'm here!"

Nsala was gripped with fear. *I must save my children.* She grabbed the twins' hands and shouted to Layila to follow her into the sea-green, dense Congo forest. As she reached a dark, dense area of bushes, she turned back to make sure the others were behind her, only to see Mpende had barely made it a few steps away from the grassy edge. She bawled in agony whilst Boali, still by her side, held her arm, both stricken with fear, unable to move.

"My belly! My belly," the pregnant one groaned.

"Get up. Get up, Mpende!" shouted Boali. "We must leave."

"My water has broken."

"Nsala, we must help Mpende." Yambi turned to her friend, pleading. They stared into each other's eyes, searching for a solution and knowing they had to make a decision quickly.

Nsala spoke first and shouted to Boali, "Come! Take the children back to the village. We will help Mpende."

Boali ran and clutched the hands of Nsimba and Nzuzi. "Come, Layila," she shouted to Nsala's eldest. She looked back at the women only once, then proceeded straight along the trail towards the village.

"Tell the men what has happened," instructed Nsala. "And hurry!"

Layila turned away from Boali, as she didn't want to leave her mother. She went back to embrace her. "Ma, I am not going without you. I won't leave without you," the girl cried. "Father says I must always stay by your side."

"No!" instructed Nsala. "Go quickly and tell your father what has happened." Her mother's voice was firm; there would be no negotiation.

Layila knew not to argue; she'd been taught to obey her elders. She scanned her mother's face in desperation, tears streaming down her dark cheeks.

"I love you so much," said Nsala. "Go now. I must help Mpende."

"Mama, no," begged Layila.

"*Bakulu*, the spirits of our ancestors, will protect you," stressed Nsala. Nsala watched Layila back away, encouraged that her child had summoned the vigour to leave her. She prayed for the ancestral spirits to protect her.

Boali pulled on Layila's arm, and together they began to run, frightened for their lives, along the dusty, well-trodden path towards their village.

Nsala turned away, hot tears suddenly stinging her eyes. She dared not look back at her children, even when her daughter's cry echoed through the darkness of the forest. She forced her maternal instincts, demanding that she protect her children, out of her mind.

Only the three women were left on the riverbank now. Wrought with anguish for their children walking alone, as their mothers before them, they knew what they had to do for their pregnant friend.

Yambi knelt at the back of Mpende, serving as a pillow to support her head. She scanned the jungle across the river. It was still, not echoing a sound. *Maybe the spirits' rage has subsided,* she thought for a second, *but right now a baby is to be born, and I must help the best way I know how.*

Mpende groaned with the beginning of the next contraction. A desperate panic contorted her face as searing pain travelled in waves up and down her belly. She cried out as she bore down, "I need to…I must push!"

Nsala watched her friend being overtaken by the familiar, uncontrollable primal urges to deliver her child. Mpende let out an expulsive cry from deep within herself and firmly grabbed on to Yambi's folded knees, who felt the grip like a set of nails going through her limbs.

Nsala intuitively looked down between Mpende's legs. Another gush of water, followed by the pulsating umbilical cord wrapped around a tiny foot that rushed out of Mpende's body.

"Just breathe and let the baby come," implored Yambi, unaware of what had just presented itself.

Nsala tried to remain focused and disguise any uncertainty whilst she thought of what to do. Nsala knew she only had minutes to deliver the baby before the cord went into spasm and stopped pulsating. Nsala spoke firmly with an authority that caught the attention of the distressed Mpende. "Mpende, you cannot push now. You must resist the urge. Your baby's string is out, and I have to cut you, or the baby will die."

Mpende stared, wide-eyed with silent hysteria, at Nsala and then at Yambi. She trusted them. She wanted her baby to live.

"Lay her down here," ordered Nsala, now completely aware of what she had to do.

While another blast travelled through the smoky atmosphere, Yambi helped Mpende to lie flatter, using her own knees supporting her head. The contractions were spacing and gave welcome relief to Mpende. That was just as well, because the pain she was about to endure would be beyond her imagination.

Nsala opened Mpende's clothes, exposing her perspiring dark abdomen, tattooed by numerous stretch marks. She took a sharp blade from her pouch, one commonly used for de-scaling fish. There was no time for the usual ritual cleansing she had witnessed before such a procedure, nor was there time for the administration of intoxicating wine to numb the pain for the patient. Nsala had only to remember what she had seen, and she had to be quick about it; there was no time to be afraid.

Yambi, anticipating Nsala's next move, reached for something nearby for Mpende to grip between her teeth. That was all she could do.

Nsala pressed the tip of the cold blade between pendulous breasts and darkened nipples. Mpende's hot skin flinched as a burning line ran down her belly. She bit down hard on the bark as the pain intensified. Involuntary convulsions caused her body to spasm violently, and her head lolled from one side to the other. Nsala stopped and waited for her friend to pass into unconsciousness, and then there was stillness.

Nsala reached both hands into Mpende's bloody womb and removed the infant. Nsala, now back to herself, knelt in statue-like fashion, unable to think, while the child lay limp and lifeless in her hands.

"Nsala. Dry him," yelled Yambi, aware that her friend was frozen in some kind of shock. When she saw that Nsala couldn't move, Yambi hurried over to the child, placed him on a cloth, and rubbed his small frame vigorously.

CHAPTER III

# WARNING

Aways down the riverbank were two boys. Inga was twelve, and Kimoko was ten, and the boys were from the same village. They were bored with the younger children but too young to begin hunting with their fathers.

Boredom had driven them away on their own small adventure. When the first blast had come, they had jumped.

"What was that?"

Their first instinct was to run back up the riverbank along the dirt track, towards the women and children.

Inga was the more athletic of the two boys and raced easily in front of Kimoko, who was shorter and plump.

As Kimoko ran, he was quickly out of breath, gasping for air. "Slow down!" he yelled to Inga.

"Come on, Kimoko," shouted Inga. "Is your potbelly weighing you down?" he teased. "Come on. We've got to keep running."

"It's…it's not my fault," he panted. Breathing heavily, he bent over and rested his palms on his knees, sweat seeping from his forehead.

"You eat too much," said Inga. "Now you can't keep up. Come. We must go back to the river to collect the gourds." The gourds were made from Calabash plants, dried and used as containers for palm oil. The boys had left the gourds down by the river earlier in the day, and their job was to wash them.

Their banter was suddenly silenced by a second blast, which echoed high in the air. The boys stared at each other.

Not wanting to appear frightened, Inga beckoned his friend. "Follow me, quickly, back up the river."

They could hear the women's voices now. Inga dared not look at his friend. Kimoko would have wanted to run away, but he trusted Inga, who always protected him from dangers in the wild. A snake had once attempted an attack on Kimoko, but Inga had promptly smashed its head with a large tree branch. To Kimoko, Inga was like a god. He had saved him on many occasions.

Inga bent down on his knees behind the bushes near the river. He pulled apart the masses of flowers and tender undergrowth for a clearer view. "Look," encouraged Inga. "Take a look."

Kimoko wasn't sure. He had never heard such a blast without the tropical rain he was accustomed to. *Maybe we ought to run*, he thought, but then he looked at his potbelly. The thought of resting on his knees a while longer seemed like a much better idea, so Kimoko stooped down beside Inga and peered through the bushes.

The boys saw men, but they were unlike any men they'd ever seen before. Their skin was light, and they had thick straight hair that curled upward on their top lips.

"*Kimbindi*, spirit of darkness. *Kimbindi*," Kimoko repeated, trying to sound knowledgeable.

"No, they are white—like pigs."

The boys looked stunned.

"And look at their clothes! They all wear the same, and everything is covered." Kimoko looked at the short beige tunics the men wore over trousers with shiny black boots that went up to their knees.

"Look at the coconut heads," added Inga, in disbelief at the sight of their helmets.

Kimoko pointed a second time. "Look!" he said. "Their spears are not like my father's. How come they don't have broad heads on the tip?"

"I don't know, but I think we should leave," said Inga. Inga had always been the tough one, the protector, the one to look after Kimoko. Alone, his instinct would have been to jump out of the bushes and charge towards the intruders, but this time, it felt wrong. *These are not friendly men from a village nearby,* he thought. *These are like no other people.*

"Maybe they are gods," said Kimoko. "Maybe they have fallen from the sky, sent by the angry spirits."

"I don't want to wait to find out. Come, fat boy. Let's go," replied Inga.

"Wait…wait!" said a curious Kimoko. "Maybe they made the thunder we heard. I want to see how they do it." Kimoko had always been a curious boy, and the idea of witnessing the so-called 'gods' making lightning was a good enough reason for any ten-year-old boy to stay.

Inga nodded, admitting his interest.

The boys crouched together behind bushes and broken stems, watching. Curiosity overcame their fear for a minute or two, but not for long.

Inga suddenly grabbed Kimoko and pulled him to his feet. "They are not gods," he said. "They want to hurt us. We must go now."

That was the Inga Kimoko knew—the warrior. Kimoko did not hesitate to rise to his feet this time, for he trusted his friend. Whatever was going through Inga's mind, he would go with him.

The boys ran back down the track, the adrenalin pumping through their veins as they tried to get out of sight. As they ran, blasts echoed, and this time, they did not stop. Repeating echoes filled the air like a chorus of endless drums. The cracking sound was loud enough to frighten even the most robust of African warriors.

# CHAPTER IV

# SOLDIERS

A Flemish soldier stepped forward to face his brigade. He was a distinguished-looking man in his early forties, with light brown, whispery hair and an imperial-style moustache, whiskers soaring from above his lip to caress his cheeks. His name was Captain Bison Van Lanterman. He viewed his troops with a lofty air of authority, barking his orders in a manner that conveyed urgency. "You," he signalled, "go left and follow those natives. Sergeant Lekens, take your men to the right. I will go straight forward with the rest of the men. Capture all of them—even the women and the children. Kill any who resist," he said, forthright, cool, and unemotional.

"Yes, Captain. Follow me." Sergeant Lekens motioned to his men. They were hot, sweaty, and exhausted in the midday heat of the Congo forest.

Captain Van Lanterman was unmoved. He had been given strict instructions to bring back as many slaves as humanly possible. The belief was that many would die en route, and only the strongest, most valuable would survive until they reached Port Banana.

Succeeding in such a treacherous mission was one of the captain's strengths. For years now, he had travelled across the Dark Continent, capturing slaves for the Arabs and Europeans. Business had been booming. There was ample money to be made trading slaves, so it was an easy decision for him. He was good at it and was paid well for his troubles.

Van Lanterman was strong in his convictions. After all, he had been hired by Belgian nobles and the prime subjects of King Leopold II himself. The trading of slaves on the black market was a lucrative enterprise, and the expansion and ownership of plantations throughout the Americas brought about riches to those who traded in cheap human labour. Although the king never met with the captain in person, Van Lanterman knew well that the King of the Belgians had his hand in it; the uniform they wore was proof enough. Van Lanterman cared not, though, for his mission was clear: capture the natives and deliver them to designated locations throughout the West Coast of Africa and the Americas.

The mission brought the captain a sense of self-empowerment and authority that he could never replicate as a lawful businessman—a little king in the land of the natives—so he took pleasure in pursuing the quest in exchange for money, glory, and all that came with it.

The soldiers trudged out of the dense forest until they came upon the river. The bright sunlight caused them to shield their eyes for a second or two. Then, in an excited frenzy of activity, hundreds of soldiers plunged their boots into the river, whilst others ran along the bank, chasing after terrified women and children.

"Those Negroes won't stop running, Captain," hollered one of the frustrated troops.

"Shoot at their ankles then!" ordered the captain.

Blasts from their rifles emitted smoke that wafted into the air and obliterated their vision. They heard women screaming. As the smoke cleared, they saw three women at the riverbank.

Nsala, stricken with fear, flew to her feet. "*Mvumbi! Mvumbi!* Dead spirit," she screamed at Yambi.

"They are coming. They are coming!" Yambi yelled. "Mpende! Mpende? Oh, Mpende!"

"We must save the baby. Hold the baby, Yambi. Hold her tight. Never let her go. No matter what happens, the child must survive. Do you hear me, Yambi? Do you hear me?"

"Yes, yes, Nsala," Yambi said between heavy, terrified sobs. "I hear you. I will hold this baby as if it were my own." She fell to her feet, exhausted and terrified. Too terrified to move, she clutched the infant in cloth from her own back.

Nsala plunged herself forward, on top of Mpende. She held Mpende, burying her head into her neck, screaming, "Mpende? Mpende. wake up! I beg you to wake up."

It was to no avail, because the soldiers were upon them, drenched and sodden, followed closely by Van Lanterman and his soldiers.

"Don't shoot!" he ordered.

Van Lanterman's brigade gazed at the women. Their ebony skin shone. The few clothes they wore hung softly over their dark, womanly curves, ragged and torn. Salty tears trickled from their dark eyes, and their bodies trembled with fear as they mumbled incoherently.

"*Nzazi, Nzazi,*" Nsala wailed. "Don't take baby, *Nzazi.*" She had named her *Nzazi* meaning 'for the day the gods descended from Heaven.' *Nzazi* was their redeemer. If they were to die now, they would die happy, for they, if nothing else, had brought a child safely into the world of the living.

Captain Van Lanterman jammed his pistol back into his holster. He removed his hat, reached for his handkerchief, and wiped the sweat from his face. The equatorial sun beat down on him relentlessly and burned his pale, fair skin to a blotchy pink. His shirt was saturated and reeked with the stench of sweat and muddy water. He and his men had been trekking for days in the dense, verdant forest; they would have given anything in exchange for a cool bath.

The dark eyes of the Congo women stared into the blue, cold eyes of the captain.

Van Lanterman shifted the weight on his feet. "*Wij doen u geen kwaad, als u doet wat ik zeg.*"

But the women understood nothing.

Nsala, now kneeling, lowered her head into her lap and muttered, "*Mvumbi. Mvumbi.*" Nsala prayed for the bad spirits to leave them. "Leave us. Go, go," she hissed. She wished with all her heart that she could tell them to leave them alone and let them go back to their village and their men, but she could say nothing. The men who stood before them were like none she had ever encountered, and they spoke words she had never heard.

Captain Van Lanterman stuffed his handkerchief back into his pocket. His expression was stern. He had a job to do, and even for women hanging on to a newborn, pity never entered his mind; if it did, he never showed. The instructions were simple: take men, women, and children, and kill any who dared to resist. The wounded were not mentioned.

At that moment, Mpende spluttered and coughed.

Nsala and Yambi turned to her. Nsala had bound a cloth over Mpende's stomach, which was now drenched with blood.

Mpende was still bleeding heavily. She tried to draw her legs up to her stomach and let out a wail. "My belly."

Nsala had no more cloth to soak up the blood.

There was a chilled silence during which a communication of a kind occurred—not a verbal communication, because neither party could comprehend the language spoken by the other, but a nonverbal understanding.

"Soldier!" called the captain. "That one…stitch her up."

A young man stepped forward immediately. "Yes, sir," he said, fumbling in a bag he had slung over his shoulder, from which he withdrew a small tin.

As he approached, Nsala and Yambi recoiled, looking on and clutching at each other, but allowing the strange white man to be near their friend.

He knelt down by Mpende. The ground was sticky red, sodden with the Negress's blood. Flies hovered in a concentrated, dark swarm, hopeful for a share of the sun-baked coagulation soaking into the ground.

Beside her, he opened the tin and laid out some instruments. The metallic, salty stench of blood permeated his nostrils. The women sensed these unfamiliar objects would complete what Nsala would have finished before the interruption. Taking a length of gut suture, he ordered an idle soldier to hold her legs down and another to remove the bloodied tourniquets.

Mpende let out a howl in agony and rolled to one side. Nsala and Yambi fell to their knees and held her arms. Yambi whispered words into Mpende's ears, trying to soothe her.

The soldier was conscious of the captain looking over his shoulder and trembled slightly, as he took a needle and began. With the apex to the longitudinal gaping wound visualised, he began to stitch, taking large bites with the needle and ligating bleeding uterine vessels. The mercenary, a medical brain, knew his craft well, for the bleeding began to cease.

"*Mlozi*," Nsala whispered to Yambi, referring to the soldier as a medicine man.

Captain Van Lanterman stood, watching silently, trying to hide his discomfort at the sight of the black woman and the surgical procedure being performed upon her. He shifted from one foot to another uneasily. "Hurry up, for heaven's sake," he ordered. Then he turned to the soldiers behind him.

"Don't just stand there! You two," he ordered. "prepare something on which to carry this creature."

Mpende let out another high-pitched scream, pulling away. "No! No!"

The men sniggered. "Savages," said one. Officers aimed their rifles, ready to shoot.

Captain Van Lanterman raised his hands. "No, we need them alive. They will fetch a good price," insisted the captain.

"What about the baby, sir?"

Captain Van Lanterman squatted and grabbed the baby as the women wailed, fighting back. He retreated to a bush and laid the child down whilst the women begged for mercy. The captain then rose to his feet and stared coldly at *Nzazi*. Without wavering, he fired.

"The baby!" cried Nsala.

The blast resounded as the women wept, too weak and shaken to put up a fight.

"Devil," barked Nsala. "Cursed is the day you set foot in our kingdom."

Two soldiers grabbed the arms of Nsala and Yambi and jerked them to her feet. He dragged them roughly, clipping chains to their writhing wrists.

Mpende was then dumped on a carrier the soldiers had fashioned out of bamboo and palm leaves. She writhed in pain, barely conscious, mostly delirious, mumbling and crying alternately. "Ombe…Ombe… Where is my husband?" She was unaware that her baby lay dead.

Other than a morbid silence, slaves' hums echoed in the hot air. Nsala and Yambi looked to see other women and children in chains, who'd been brought from far and wide by the same white-skinned soldiers.

The soldiers pulled and tugged at their wrists. The women stared back in the direction of the bush, where baby *Nzazi* had been killed, angered yet saddened at the same time. For the first time, they realised that the soldiers had tricked them. They may have saved Mpende, but they had killed her firstborn. These men were evil spirits, they were sure—*Nduki*.

They trudged along the riverbank until they saw more soldiers dragging natives systematically chained together, those who had tried to escape into the dark *Mayombe* jungle. Some were women and children from the *Kisúndi* clan. Children, crying for their mothers, were chained like animals, the catch of the day.

They walked forever—for what seemed like miles—deep within the impenetrable and deepest maze of the Congo. Sometimes they stumbled on each other's feet. Thick, rusty chains weighed heavily on their wrists and, after a while, rubbed, cutting into the flesh. They bled around their necks, wrists, legs, and arms.

Their steps became heavier and heavier, their march slower and slower. The sun was fierce, never discerning amongst natives and alien. Sunlight heated up the metal chains, burning their flesh. Each of their steps took great effort.

Soldiers counted heads and were pleased with themselves at their terrific catch. *Well done*, they thought, but it was never enough. Many had died along the trek.

They rested for a while by a pool.

"We'll send these back to the ship," ordered the captain as he strode alongside the sergeant. "Master Corporal…"

"Aye, sir?" answered the man.

"Take a few men and take these slaves back to the coast. The ship is ready and waiting," said Van Lanterman. "Sergeant and the rest will join me in securing more from the next village."

"*Kapitein*," saluted the master corporal before marching to his duly appointed crew.

"Sergeant, inform the regiment to gear up. We're leaving," said Van Lanterman, turning to face a third group of resting soldiers, hungry for more. "Soldiers, let's move!"

The men respected their captain and had pledged allegiance to him and to the mission: the capture of Congo slaves. Although they were pleased to rest and light a coffin nail that they took turns puffing, they were happy to know there were more Negroes to capture. That meant more riches. For them, life was rosy. They got to their feet and, in a formation, tailed the captain.

Headed for the coast, the other soldiers pushed and prodded their captives with the nuzzles of their guns, forcing them to their stiff and swollen feet.

The women held each other's hands, silently fearing the worst. Those who couldn't keep up were lashed with *chicottes*, whips made of rhinoceros hide.

# CHAPTER V

# ALONE

In order to save time, Boali, Layila, and Nsala's young twins, Nsimba and Nzuzi, took the shortcut to the nearest village. Boali was used to that trail, as she'd been travelling that way every since she was a small child, following her mother and the other women to wash and clean at the river.

Thick bushes and undergrowth encroached upon the narrow trail, which meant they had to keep turning sideways to push their way through. Even so, it was a well-used path, having felt the steps and witnessed the journeys of countless villagers. The children were used to walking long distances, and their bare feet were hardened to it. Dry dust covered them, clear up to their ankles.

The constant chatter of wildlife surrounded them; a heady fusion of sounds emanating across the treetops and deep in the shrubs, dancing in every crevasse. The flora and fauna smelt beautiful to them. The tall trees towered over their heads, creating shade for a cool walk.

When Boali grew old enough to leave her mother, she was fond of strolling alone there, picking fruits and tiny berries from the low-hanging branches. She would wrap the fruits in a cloth and carry them back to her mother for cooking.

Today, they had to walk fast, but it did not stop the girls from conversing along the way.

"We must not think about what happened at the river," offered Boali.

"We must think good thoughts. That's how we will keep our strength."

"Tell me a story," said Layila. "I can't stop thinking about it."

"Layila, you know, walking this way takes me back. I have so many memories of my childhood here," said Boali.

"Oh? *Ya nkulutu*," said Layila, indicating a sign of respect to her elder. "Boali, will you tell me about it please?"

"I remember when I was about three or four years old. I was very afraid of walking this path. I remember holding Mama's hand very tight and closing my eyes," said Boali.

"Really?" said Layila.

"Oh, yes! I had to wait until we were deep inside the forest, until I could open my eyes. Everything was sea green. I was scared to face the giant trees. I thought this was where the spirits lived. It was only in time that I came to realise the forest was not any danger to me. Now I see the trees are always still, as if they are watching me, watching over me," said Boali.

Boali's thoughts seemed so mature to Layila, who was younger than her friend. She wished she could be more like her.

"Have you heard the elders talking about the travellers who reported seeing strange things on this path? As a child, I was scared I might see what they saw, and the forest noise is so loud when you are afraid. When you are little, you cannot explain what you hear," said Boali. "At early dawn, we joined the other women bound for the riverbank. It was still quite dark, and sometimes the clouds would lie low. It was cold, and we could barely see two steps in front of us. I remember feeling so scared. There was a day when I was walking with a friend, and we made the wrong turn and got lost," said Boali.

"What happened? Did you manage to find your way again?" asked Layila, wanting to know more. "It must have been hard for you all alone."

"We had no choice but to wait for the next group of women walking along the path to the river. It was frightening, and it took us by surprise. We often got to talking and fell behind the others, but we could hear them ahead, singing. Even if we couldn't see them, we could follow their songs."

"You were anxious to get to the river," Layila said, feeling herself that the walk was too far.

"You're right. I wanted to reach the end of the path. Once we were at the riverbank, I was so happy. I always wished the days were longer. I hated the anticipation of the long walk home through the forest. I used to wish the women would use the old pathway because there was more sunlight there. That was where I felt safer," Boali replied.

"*Ya nkulutu*, Boali. I remember Mama sometimes waking us up early in the morning, when the sun had not risen and the cockerel had not sung. We quickly took what we had prepared the day before—dirty garments, dishes, bottles, and buckets. I remember I was still half-asleep," said Layila.

Boali was uncertain whether chatting about her fear helped. She looked around at the tall, grizzly trees, their height seemingly overpowering her, leaving her feeling helpless and inferior. Boali turned to Layila. "Come on, let's run."

She grabbed the hands of the younger children, and they ran as one. Their pace seemed to propel them faster and faster, until they believed they were running for their lives. The two older girls wanted to run faster, but they could not, for the small children's feet could not keep up. They panted so hard they could no longer speak.

One of the twins needed to urinate. Layila led the twin behind the greenery and helped the girl to squat down.

Silence fell over them whilst they paused. Within the momentary quiet, a man's voice, in a language unknown to them, could be heard.

The twin eyed Layila. "Who is—"

"Shhh! Quiet," Layila hissed. "Listen."

Then another man's incomprehensible voice could be heard, followed by the heavy stomping of running boots.

"Are those strange men following us?" Layila whispered fiercely to Boali.

"Layila, we have to run again. Quickly, children! We must go." Boali knew she had to keep calm, but fear twisted in her stomach. Layila responded quickly, but the twins pulled against her as she grabbed their hands.

"I'm tired."

"I can't run anymore," they protested.

"Come on! It's not too far," encouraged Layila.

"Just run until we reach the bushes. We will find a place to hide," Boali spoke in a hushed tone, despite her belly twisting into tighter knots.

The girls grabbed the children and darted along the path until they reached an area with tall fruit trees and broad leaves—an ideal place to hide.

"Come on," Layila encouraged the children. "We can pick fruits to eat."

They trod carefully through the dense undergrowth. A frog croaked suddenly, making them jump, but they carried on further into the shrubbery, until they found a fallen tree. They crouched down beneath it, breathing heavily, their hands clammy.

Heavy pounding of boots continued, seemingly coming closer.

They held each other, crouching lower, wishing they could shrink and make themselves invisible. They peered between the bushes.

A faction of Belgian soldiers proceeded along the very path they had just departed.

The children held their breath as they watched the brigade rush past them, ushering more Negro captives.

Nsimba, one of the twins, wanted to sneeze. Layila hastily clasped her hand over his nose and mouth. They shivered from the dampness and clung to each other like baby monkeys clinging to their mothers.

Soon, the pounding footsteps grew fainter, until silence enveloped them and they could at last move.

"It will be all right. Hold on to us," said Boali. "They're gone."

The long, lifeless log provided a natural, beautiful seat for the girls. A shiny morph—a large, blue butterfly—took flight from its position on a branch and fluttered away, deep into the forest and its mysteries.

"I'm afraid to go along the path now. What if we come across the men again?" asked an anxious Layila.

"You're right, but there's only one path," countered Boali.

They sat for a while, pondering their journey, until the children became restless.

"I'm hungry," said Nzuzi.

"We will go through the forest," announced Boali.

"*Ya nkulutu*, Boali, are you sure? Won't we get lost?" worried Layila. "Remember, we were always warned against venturing in these parts of the forest. We are alone. How can we possibly survive the forbidden jungle?"

"We have no choice," Boali insisted. "We must try. Let the children eat some fruit before we go."

The two young women encouraged the children to pick the yellow, star-shaped fruits from the ground under the *pakapaka* tree. The juice from the fruit was cool and refreshing. The children ate anxiously, as fruit juice ran down their hands and dusty legs. All around was a hive of activity now. The birds sang, the insects buzzed, and the monkeys chattered.

"Are those voices of the forest?" asked Nsimba as he took another bite from the star-fruit.

"Yes, just harmless animals," said Boali.

"Mmm! It's good," said Nzuzi, sucking the fruit dry. "Can we have more?"

"Yes. Eat plenty now so we can walk for longer without stopping." Boali smiled at the twins, even though she knew not what they may encounter next.

"I want Mama," Nsimba cried.

"Remember what Mama said? We must try and get them help. *Kimbindi* are close by. We must carry on," Boali said firmly.

"What do you think has happened to them?" asked Layila.

"I don't know," said Boali pensively, staring in the distance. "I can only trust that the spirits will protect them from evil."

"Yes, and the spirits have spared us," added Layila.

"That's good, Layila," said Boali. "They're with us."

Nsimba and Nzuzi curled up into their arms, exhausted. Their eyes were heavy. They gazed at the butterflies that were fluttering and circling one another in delicate dances, before taking rest on vine leaves.

"They want to sleep," motioned Layila.

The children watched with curiosity as colourful wings fluttered from branch to branch. "Come on. It's time to move now. We must hurry, before it's too late," Boali said gently.

She picked up one of the children and placed her on her back whilst the other reached out for Layila's hand. They continued more slowly now, but they had to make progress. They wanted to sing to make the walking easier, but they knew they had to be quiet.

A long while later, after endless walking, just as they felt they could go no further, Boali spotted an opening in the trees ahead. The setting sun was shining through.

"Is that a village?" Layila asked, pointing ahead.

Boali squinted and peered ahead. "I think so." She smiled. "See? The spirits are with us!"

Buoyant, their steps quickened until they emerged from the forest into a clearing, where a cluster of simple mud thatched-roof huts sat amongst the forest land. But there was no sign of life.

"Where is everyone?" asked Nsimba.

They moved towards the mud huts and called out, but there were no answers—not a sound and just a spine-chilling silence.

"There's no one here. It's deserted. It must be a ghost village." Boali stated.

She had heard of a village that had been stricken down by fever, causing the villagers to suffer terribly. Some of their people had abandoned their huts as death rang its toll. The deathly curse was only avoided by a few, who left their village to seek refuge elsewhere, only to be stricken down again. Their fate was later remembered as the Congo Basin *pariah*.

Weather had destroyed some of the huts, leaving straw roofs loose and broken, whilst some had been completely torn away by the winds, leaving nothing but dust as a reminder of what had once been there.

Stagnant water filled the buckets where rainwater had collected; it would have been used as drinking water for the cows. Now it was infested, green and mouldy and undrinkable.

When the children peered into the buckets, they could see their reflections in the dark, dank water. Clouds of mosquitoes hung low, as if defending the water from predators with their lethal bite.

Boali remembered tribal elders telling stories about the ghost village and how the spirits of those taken by the disease remained, angry, seething, and seeking revenge on the living. One such story told of a group of villagers who had become lost at night.

Exhaustion took over after many hours' walking, with fear overwhelming them that they would be stalked and hunted by starving beasts—a fear so wild they were forced to take rest in the ghost village.

Unearthly sounds awoke the villagers as the night slowly passed, creating a presence of life in the darkness. Sounds of voices humming, and the beating of drums could be heard, but the sources of such noises could not be found. People were nowhere to be seen, but the flames of torches nevertheless danced and blazed. Shadows of beings were seen and appeared to be dancing in a circle. As the weary villagers watched, terrified, faces began to appear from dark bushes one by one, surrounding the huts: white-painted faces without bodies. The faces circled the villagers; they were the ghosts of the past.

No one knew what had happened to those villagers. Only one escaped to tell half the tale. He had died in the most atrocious way; his hands and feet severed, leaving him to slowly bleed to death. There were no footprints leading up to his door, and the cone-shaped hut remained closed.

Recalling this tale, Boali was afraid. She spoke quietly in hushed tones to Layila, worried her fear would scare the children.

They stood at the edge of the village. Boali was frightened of waking the spirits and motioned to Layila to go no further.

Her fear was realised when suddenly, shrieks of natives could be heard, mostly women, children, and babes crying in agony.

The hairs on Boali's neck stood up.

A dreadful stench filled the air.

"What is that?" Layila asked.

"I don't know, but it's bad," said Boali.

The children covered their noses in the palms of their hands.

Layila had the curiosity of 10,000 mice in search of rotten goat's milk. She darted inside one of the huts.

Boali reached to pull her back, but it was too late.

Inside, the hut was dark, but daylight was just enough for her to see. She gasped. "Ya, Boali! Boali, come in quickly, but leave the children outside."

Boali motioned for the children to stay still and then crept inside the hut. She saw the outline of a body lying on a straw mat. As her eyes scanned the darkness, she saw more bodies lying around.

Layila fearfully whispered to Boali, pointing a trembling finger to the mass of dead bodies. "*Kimbindi, Kimbindi,*" she pressed with insistence.

"Layila…yes, it's the same Kimbindi we saw at the river," whispered Boali thoughtfully. She paused for a while, stupefied by the cadaveric ordeal in sight. She then very slowly advanced to a corpse, ready to retreat at any given moment. She continued to slowly approach the corpse, which by its position appeared to be awkwardly rolled to its back and on its right arm. Seemingly, the arm had been broken before it had been dumped.

As Boali moved closer, almost within touching distance, Layila, fully aware of what her friend was about to do, glanced at the door, as if to make sure nothing would stand in the way of a necessary escape. She briefly smiled at the children, who caught her eyes, perhaps feeling reassured that the adults had not forgotten them. Layila turned back to Boali, whose outstretched hand touched the exposed and cold soldier's arm.

In realisation, Boali stood up sharply and momentarily startled Layila. "They are not *Kimbindi*, Layila," she uttered, trying to contain her shock. "*Kimbindi* never dies. These are just white men. They are just white men, Layila…and they are dead. Oh, Layila, what is happening to us?"

The bodies belonged to soldiers, like the men who had ambushed them at the river. They had died that day during the hottest part of the day, and the stench overwhelmed the confined space. The bodies had been brutally mutilated, as if they had been in a battle. They bore gashes and wounds, and some had missing limbs. Dried blood caked the dust that surrounded them. Flies and mosquitoes hovered over the corpses, sucking the fetid fluid from the dead men's bodies.

"Who could have done this?" Layila was horrified.

The hush draped across them once more, and they stood, still fearful to move even another inch.

Suddenly, the haunting chants returned, loud and angry.

The girls ran out of the hut and back to the twins, who were wailing in terror; all heard distinct voices shouting clearly.

"No, you evil! No. Evil, no!" she screamed in dialect tongue.

"Shut up, Negro. Shut up, whore!"

*What are these sounds?*

They sank to their knees behind the bushes on the edges of the village, holding the twins tightly between them. Boali and Layila peered between the bushes, stretching to see.

Gunfire exploded, with bullets and shells assaulting the ground, causing a whirlwind of dust to blind their sight.

"Run! Children, run! Layila, go!" Boali pushed Layila and the children in front of her.

Layila fled, grasping the children's hands, knowing she mustn't let them go and that, even if they fell or tripped, she would simply have to pull them. With Boali following, they ran as fast as they could, afraid to stop, afraid to listen for fear of what they might hear, for fear of who might see them.

The ground was slippery, and their feet were trapped in the undergrowth as night fell over the forest. Their fear propelled them further and further, until they fell exhausted, straining to fill their lungs with fresh air. Their limbs ached, and their skin was scratched and bloodied. Wild vegetation surrounded them; deep ferns, shining leaves, and moss. The dank humidity settled on the leaves with droplets of condensation.

Once they'd caught their breath, they strained to hear if the sounds continued. All remained still, and they dared not move. They waited, like tiny creatures of the night, under the towering trees.

"We are going to be all right. The angry men are gone," said Boali, wiping the children's faces with the rim of her rag and hugging them. "Just rest a while. Here...put your head on my lap."

Nsimba willingly did as he was told.

Layila searched Boali's face for reassurance.

"Take Nzuzi, and we will sleep."

Layila held Nzuzi, hugging her tightly. When the child slept, Layila could hold her fear no longer, and tears streamed down her cheeks. She wished she could be as strong as Boali. She lay against a strong, large trunk to provide support for her weary back—one of many strong, majestic trees in the deep, dense forest. Layila listened to rustling in the trees high above them. Strong winds came during the night, shaking leaves from the branches. They fell like small parachutes, fluttering to the ground. She heard movements, rustling in the bushes, howls of night-time predators, and she reached for Boali's hand. *Will we be safe for the night?*

There was no answer.

They slept fitfully, waking to every sound, then drifting off again.

Whilst awake in the dead of the night, Boali anxiously thought of their journey in the morning, when they would cross into *Mayombe* land—the most treacherous of lands in the kingdom. Men, hunters, and even warriors had lost their lives to wild animals. Lions, leopards, and other brutish animals had long roamed the jungle, preying on men as they would any other warm-blooded kill. She feared for witchcraft and demons that were known to inhabit those parts; day and night they wandered in search of souls.

*What's coming?* she wondered as she clung to Layila. *Is this the way one feels just before death?* She prayed to the ancestral spirits to guide them on their journey the next day and for peace throughout the night.

# CHAPTER VI

# SURVIVAL

Inga and Kimoko were running down the track as fast as their legs would carry them. They had been running for what seemed like miles and miles, without ever letting up or looking back. Panic and adrenalin had set in, driving them onwards.

Their chore for the day before had been to clean the gourds, but that chore had long since left their minds, and dread and terror had taken over. The pain in their feet went unfelt; their hunger unnoticed. They simply ran.

This was more urgent, perhaps even life-threatening. It was imperative that they run. They had to run as far away as they could from what they had witnessed. There had been men, so many of them, carrying the strangest flat-head spears, not the broad heads of their hunter fathers' spears.

The men were *Mundele buna ngulu tsala*, white men, though to the two Negro boys, they were "white—like pigs." The boys had never before seen men with such Pale-faces; they had only ever heard of Pale-faces in stories of the dead spirits. To them, these were not dead spirits; these men were real. They could walk like men on forest land, and the boys knew spirits did not walk the land. They were not *Mvumbi*, but white men who walked the Earth, like them.

*Who were they? And what do they want? Where are they from?* The boys' thoughts were fast as they moved as swiftly as they were able. *Maybe they are the gods personified.*

The boys were clever, if not a little naïve; after all, they were still only young, and their judgment was clouded by inexperience. They had never been on their own and had never hunted like their fathers and forefathers; their orders were to care for the gourds, except now, disobedience had forced them to shirk that responsibility, and fear had them on the run.

The river was far away in the distance. Now, deep in the Congo basin forest, they ran like they had never run in their lives. This was serious, a matter of life or death.

When they finally slowed down sufficiently to look each other in the eye, they agreed they should rest. They scanned the dense forest and saw a gathering of bushes that seemed the best place to hide, so they pushed through and threaded their way into the thickness to escape the more visible trail.

They sank to the ground, panting, their chests throbbing.

"I…can't…I can't breathe," Inga finally managed to gasp.

Kimoko could still not talk. He lay with his arms outstretched, his chest heaving.

They were focused so entirely on their own exhausted condition that when they heard a sound like a girl's voice, they could not quite comprehend it. *Was that a girl…or an animal?* They sat up, instantly alert.

"Inga!" exclaimed Boali.

The boys leapt to their feet and searched for the direction from which the voice had come.

Boali stepped past the bushes under which they had been hiding, pushing the vines and thin branches out of her way. She smiled broadly at the boys.

"Ya, Boali!" rejoiced Kimoko, running to embrace his friend. As he looked over Boali's shoulder, he saw Layila, who was equally as joyful to see the boys.

"Ya, Layila!" Inga exclaimed, hardly able to contain his pleasure.

The group embraced.

"We heard you running. We thought you were leopards or some other wild animal," explained Layila. "Thanks be to the gods."

They embraced each other again.

"Did you see what we saw…by the river?" asked Inga.

"White men," bawled Kimoko.

"Quiet," hissed Boali. "I know. We saw them too."

"Our mothers sent us home to our village. We've been so frightened all alone in the forest, but we must do what our mamas have asked of us. We must find the hunters. Father Ombe will know what to do."

"I see," said Inga solemnly. "May we come with you? We are too frightened to go back to the river. We left our gourds and ran."

"You must come with us. Of course you must," agreed Layila.

"But this land here is as mysterious and as dangerous as they claim. I've been here once, and I have seen things. I hardly made it back home safe. This place is cursed," added Inga.

"Enough, Inga," said Boali. "You're scaring the children. We must go now. I'll lead the way to *Kisúndi*, then you must take us to Father Ombe."

The group gathered themselves and began their march onwards into *Mayombe* land. The elder girls held the twins' hands and, with Boali leading, the rest followed close behind. They knew they had a long journey ahead of them if they were to make it to Father Ombe and the huntsmen. The only way was forward. They began their trek together, further into the depths of the forest.

They hadn't been walking for very long before they came upon yet another forsaken village. They could see the sunlight shining in front, and they knew it was a village, but they feared what they might find there.

Boali warned the boys. She didn't want to frighten them, but her worst fears were realised, for underneath a tree, a group of children lay, slumped lifelessly. Boali held her hands out and her palms wide to prevent the group from passing her. "Don't go any further," she whispered.

Layila drew the twins' faces close into her skirt to protect their young eyes from the dreadful sight.

Boali, Inga, and Kimoko peered between the bushes to take a closer look.

The lifeless bodies lay in the dust with their mouths open, as if they had been screaming in torture just before their demise. Salty tracks of white, dried tears plastered their ashen faces.

"White men." Inga could find no other explanation.

"Where are the elders? Did they only kill the children?" Boali whispered, unable to explain the scene before them.

They were silent.

"I don't like it. It's not good," ventured Kimoko.

A cry rang out of the silence. With a simultaneous sharp intake of breath, the group turned to look in the direction of the cry. There was a survivor!

From behind the mud huts ran a child. That child was Bikoro, Yambi's niece.

"Bikoro. Bikoro," implored Boali to the child. "Look! It's us. We are here for you."

Bikoro was hysterical. She ran, waving her arms, ranting uncontrollably, clearly in shock. Her arms, legs, and face were swathed in dust and streaked with blood. Her lips were dry and cracked. Her eyes were red and swollen, and it was clear that she'd been crying. She suddenly caught sight of the other children and ran, waving in the direction behind her.

Boali reacted as any human being would: She ran to her, reaching for her hands. Bikoro grabbed her, dragging her behind mud huts. Boali's anxiety was making her stomach roll, but she knew she had to be brave and follow Bikoro. She looked behind her briefly and signalled to the others to stay where they were. As they turned the corner, Boali flinched at the sight of two dead bodies lying in the dust.

"My brothers! My brothers! Help them, Boali," implored Bikoro.

Boali was speechless. She knelt by the dead boys and beckoned to Bikoro to kneel by her side. The stench of death filled the air. Boali laid her hand on the lifeless bodies. She then gently took Bikoro's hand and did the same and whispered quietly, "They have passed, Bikoro. Feel their bodies. There's nothing more to be done."

Bikoro flung herself over her dead brothers, crying hysterically. "No, no, NO! Help me," she pleaded, sobbing uncontrollably.

Inga was behind them now. He looked on, shaking his head.

The burden of grief and loss lay heavy in the air. The atmosphere was thick with sorrowful helplessness.

"There's nothing you can do. Let them go, Bikoro," the boy said. He took her hand and led her gently whilst she continued to mumble incoherently, unable to comprehend the irrevocable sting of death or the fact that her brothers were gone.

The three walked back to where Layila was sitting with the twins on arid ground. The twins stared at Bikoro with wide, terrified eyes.

Layila whispered to the twins, "Come." She stood and took their hands. "We'll find some fruit to make Bikoro feel better."

Kimoko summoned his strength and spoke in his strongest voice. "We must leave this place."

"There's something we must do first," said Boali. "We must lay the bodies to rest. Inga, Kimoko, go get some banana leaves. We can cover the bodies and say a prayer."

Inga and Kimoko obediently did as they were asked. They soon came back with enough to cover the brothers.

As they placed them, silent tears streamed from Bikoro's eyes.

Boali knelt first and beckoned Bikoro to do the same. She laid her hand on the covering, whispered a small prayer, and kissed the leaves.

Bikoro buried her face in the leaves and mumbled her final words. She cried for several hours after they left the village. Finally, she clutched Boali's hand firmly and never once looked back. She clung to Boali as they walked along the damp path that led the group away from the forsaken village.


As they pressed forward, the children tried to avoid the clusters of mosquitoes that hung in weightless clouds by shaking their heads and waving them away. Even so, the mosquitoes constantly bit the children, causing red welts to erupt on their skin and terrible itching to ensue. The twins wailed when a fog-like cloud engulfed them. They ran, trying to escape them, the boys in front, stomping and kicking the undergrowth with their feet so the girls could follow. Finally, they turned and headed up a slight incline, until they had outrun the insects and they could stop for a moment to gather their breath.

"Do you hear anything?" Kimoko asked hesitantly.

They listened. All was quiet, and even the birds had stopped singing and the frogs had ceased croaking. Only a disturbing silence descended across the land. All wildlife was still.

The group looked fearfully all around them.

"Look!" Inga pointed to dark, ill-omened clouds gathering high above in the distant sky.

It was as if a storm was brewing, but as they waited, no thunder could be heard in the distance; no lightning could be seen in the sky; and only an eerie silence encompassed them.

"Bad spirits!" Boali's eyes were wide with fear.

Bikoro began to mumble prayers under her breath, still disturbed by earlier events.

Boali's grip tightened around the twins' hands. She could contain her fear no longer. Petrified, she jumped to her feet. "Run," she roared, pulling Nsimba and Nzuzi to their feet.

The shocked twins immediately jumped up. Inga and Kimoko took her instruction and began to run ahead, with the others in close pursuit. The children covered the ground quickly, never daring to stop, back down the incline and towards the densest part of the forest, where they knew no one would come. It was difficult to venture forward through the low-growing shrubs. Thorny branches tore at their arms and bare feet, but they knew they had to keep to trails that soldiers would not dare to go.

They halted finally, out of breath. The sky above was blue once more, and they were clear of the dark clouds.

Breathing heavily, Inga stood with his hands on his hips, peering around him, scanning the bushes.

Layila followed his eyes, noticing at once that Boali and the twins were not with them.

"Ya, Boali?" asked Inga. "The twins? Where are they?"

"I thought they were behind us. Did we run too fast? I didn't hear them call for us to stop."

"Nsimba!" Layila called as loudly as she dared. "Nzuzi!"

But they were nowhere in sight. The damp path they had trodden behind them was desolate.

Bikoro shook her head sadly.

Layila again shouted, "Ya, Boali!"

But there was not a sound. They gazed around them for a sign, but there was nothing. They pulled at leaves and vines, desperately trying to see further.

Inga ran back down the path and reappeared alone.

Boali and the twins had completely disappeared, and they were nowhere to be found. The group listened for any sound, just the smallest cry, but no human voice could be heard. Only the birds sang, the wildlife chattered, and frogs croaked between sodden branches.

Layila reached for Bikoro's hand in disbelief. After some minutes of contemplation, Layila looked up brightly. "Boali knows her way. She told us, didn't she?"

"Yes, she did," Inga agreed.

Kimoko nodded. He wasn't sure, but he knew he had to follow Inga's lead and remain positive for Layila's sake.

"Come," she announced. "We can find our way too." She headed off, with the boys quickly following behind her. She stopped almost as suddenly as she'd started and stared around her. With a sudden sense of déjà vu, she cried, "We've been here before. This is where we met you, Inga and Kimoko."

Kimoko stood and looked around too, but everywhere looked the same. He couldn't be sure. "What do you think, Inga? Have we been here before?"

Inga rubbed his head and nodded. "We have come back to the same place!"

"What are we going to do?" Bikoro was forlorn. The tears swelled in her eyes again.

"We will stay strong and find Boali and the twins," said Inga sternly.

Layila looked at Bikoro and wiped her tears with the back of her hand.

Boali had known the way to *Kisúndi* land. She had suggested taking the shortcut, but now she and the twins had vanished within that perilous jungle.

*How are we going to find Kisúndi?* thought Inga, now feeling a sense of responsibility as the elder to the hungry and exhausted children. He was only too aware that *Mayombe* land was the territory known as 'the devil's ground.' Dark thoughts crossed his mind. *Either white men or a wild animal will take our lives. I must find…* "That way!" said Inga, taking a decisive step on the dirt path.

The pack marched on without question. Wherever they were going, it was better to be away from that place than dead.


Hours passed as their weary feet moved forward, one step after another, with breaks taken only to sip at a spring of clear water.

Layila marvelled at the wondrously beautiful butterflies as they danced and fluttered from branch to branch flirtatiously. She remembered watching similar butterflies at the riverbank. She gazed at them, just for a moment, glad to escape her reality for a few brief seconds.

"Come on. We must hurry," Inga commanded impatiently. "The sun is setting."

Bikoro, ever vigilant, spotted an opening in the trees ahead where sunlight shone through. "There!" she exclaimed. "Look."

The boys, whose eyes had been focused on the ground, intent on beating a path with sticks, looked up. Their eyes widened as they peered ahead.

"A village!" said Kimoko

"No," said Layila. "We cannot enter another village. We have found nothing but death so far today."

Bikoro spoke. "I've seen the dead in my dreams. This must be the place. It is cursed."

"Ya, Bikoro, but there might be people who can help us this time. We have to try," Kimoko urged.

"We must try and get help. Don't be afraid," reasoned Inga.

Their steps were cautious until they emerged from the forest into a clearing with several mud huts.

"The smell is bad," said Bikoro, covering her nose. "It is the smell of the dead—again." She knew the smell only too well. "It's lifeless, and it frightens me."

It was true: There was no sign of life, only empty huts. The cold ashes of a fire remained in the centre. The odd bowl or gourd lay empty on the ground, but there were no voices. The village was barren and deserted.

"Let's leave," Layila pleaded.

Inga and Kimoko looked at each other with disappointment. If only there had been some elders who could help them. They shook their heads sadly and turned to walk away.

Almost instantly, a swarm of *Iboco* circled all around their heads again. The jungle was teeming with clouds of flies, but these were particularly lethal. They seemed to appear from nowhere and were suddenly upon them. They were large, like hornets, and they darted quickly in all directions, biting at the children, piercing their clothes with their sharp teeth. The children waved erratically to get them away, screaming with pain, blood oozing from the spiked bites.

Bikoro was the first to succumb. She was weak, for she'd been alone for hours in her home village, nursing her brothers until their demise. She hadn't eaten for some time. She could barely lift her arms to wave the ferocious flies away. They bit her bare arms and legs mercilessly. She wanted to cover her face, but they were everywhere. Bikoro's small body fell to the ground, victim to a thousand tiny stabs.

The others ran to her defence, waving wildly, desperate to disperse the myriad.

By the time the *Iboco* receded, Bikoro's face was severely bitten. She moaned, rolling from side to side in pain. The children watched in anguish as Bikoro scratched and rubbed at her skin to relieve the itch, blood smeared over her blotchy skin.

Layila fell to her knees, pulling Bikoro's hands away. "Oh, my child, let me help you!" Layila took damp leaves to dab on her face, arms, and legs in an attempt to soothe the girl's distress. She dabbed at injured skin. She knew the swelling would reduce in time, but poor Bikoro's face would be scarred, probably forever.

Exhausted, Bikoro laid her head on Layila's lap and closed her eyes.

"We must wait. We cannot go further whilst Bikoro is like this." Layila spoke to the boys, who were anxious to move on.

They knew it was impossible to carry Bikoro, so they squatted, facing outwards to keep watch, with their sticks in their hands, ready for whatever may come their way.

Right away, they were startled by a blast that echoed above treetops. The boys were immediately on their feet. By now, this sound was becoming familiar to them. The gunshot ricocheted across the treetops some distance from them.

"Shhh!" said Inga.

"White men," whispered Kimoko.

The children knew they had to move deeper into the forest, away from the blasts. They had to escape to safety.

Layila touched Bikoro's arm to wake her. She pulled her body to help her stand, motioning to Inga to help her. Together they held Bikoro between them and made their escape to a nearby bush inside the opening of large 100-foot Baobab tree, one of the jungle's tallest trees, sometimes with a trunk as wide as 40 feet. The tree trunk was hollow, like a cave.

Layila and Inga lay Bikoro down inside the tree, then sat near to the opening, peering from within and scanning the surrounding area.

In the distance, they could see white men, Belgian soldiers, on a dirt path. They sat as silently as they could, not daring to make a sound, stunned by the sight before them. The white men were guiding natives, chained together one behind the other.

"They have our people," ventured Inga.

"They are *taking* our people," Kimoko concurred. "Now we know why the villages are empty."

The children watched in horror as the soldiers stopped and unchained a woman. As the chains were released, she slumped to the ground. She was clearly ill or injured, and they let her fall roughly to the floor. One soldier pushed his boot against her shoulder, as if to force her to show her face.

"Is she dead?" Layila hardly dared ask the question.

She covered her face with her hands as the soldier raised his gun and fired a shot directly into the woman's head. The shot resounded through the trees. He shoved her again with his foot; this time her body fell limply backwards, revealing her face. Her eyes were closed, and blood trickled down the side of her face. The soldier had killed the woman in cold blood. He continued to kick her body roughly, shoving her lifeless corpse to the side of the path.

The boys stared, wide-eyed, at the callous act in disbelief.

Layila held her hand over her mouth to stifle her sobs.

The soldiers then ordered the women, men, and children to move forward again. The queue shuffled, muted by the death of their friend. From behind the trees, more natives appeared in a long line.

The boys stared hard, fearing the worst—that they might recognise someone.

Sure enough, the faces of two familiar women came around the corner.

"Look!" Kimoko urged Layila.

Layila held both hands over her mouth. Her face was screwed up, and she was blinking the tears away from her eyes. It was her mother, Nsala, and Yambi. She wanted to scream. Her mother trudged wearily, her head down, clearly exhausted, walking in step with the other chained prisoners. Layila let a tiny whimper escape.

"Shhh!" demanded Inga. "They will take us too."

Layila turned away. She could no longer bear to look. *My mama!* She cried silently to herself. *I want my mother.* Her pain was unbearable. She rolled on her side and brought her legs up to her chest in a foetal position, hugging herself in the absence of her mother. *Don't let my mother die.*

Only Inga and Kimoko continued to watch the spectacle. Just hours before, the boys had been playing by the river. Like all little boys, they had played innocently, absorbed in their own imagination, but those happy, carefree times were now only a distant memory now. They had been brutally forced into a world of unknown cruelty.

The soldiers were calling and shouting to each other in words the children could not understand.

Soldiers counted heads. "Captain, 400 women," hollered one.

"I count 500 men and 40 children," yelled another.

Captain Van Lanterman stepped forward, heaved a sigh, and rested his hand over Sergeant Lekens's shoulder. "We can't fall short. We are contracted for 10,000, and we've got half. We need more. Children won't fetch as much, for they're much too weak. We need men—strong men that can survive the long voyage." His voice was harsh. He was unemotional in his assessment of the situation, simply counting heads, as coldly and heartlessly if they were sheep. "Take 100 men. Stick up competing convoys. Bribe village chiefs if you have to. If any resist, you know what to do. The rest of the platoon will join me, and I'll take these back to the ship."

"*Kapitein,*" replied Lekens, saluting. "You and your regiment come with me," said Sergeant Lekens, turning to face his brigade.

The regiment was comprised of Belgian and Dutch individuals from all walks of life. They were younger and middle aged, some simply seeking adventures and others mercenaries who, by word of mouth, were told of opportune bounty good enough for retirement; if, by the grace of God, they could reach their ship once more and return to Europe. Many had deserted their previous military companies and were considered undesirables; however, they had served in various forts along the coastline of North African counties. How they were still in the king's legion was mostly subjectively due to the fact that some of them, if not most, delighted in working together. They were well-formed soldiers with good ground combat experience and the meanest of attitudes; men whom any wise king would mercifully keep on his side.

"Let's move!" roared Sergeant Lekens.

The faction trooped forward as commanded, flanking the sides of the chained captives.

Towards the rear, a woman lay delirious on bamboo sticks, carried by weary, emotionless captives; carrying the sick woman made their journey more arduous. The sticks had been hastily bound together to form a travel mat. The woman's blood-covered right hand was holding on to the ringed joints of the bound bamboo, and she had slid her left hand under her belly in hopes of relaxing the insurmountable pain from the primitive surgery. The irregular terrain caused her much discomfort, forcing her left hand to tighten her grip over the wound and prevent the stitches from opening. She frequently emitted grievous moans. She could hear the heavy chains clanking in time to the movement of their bodies as they shuffled, dragging their tired, swollen feet through the dust. The exhausted, half-dead woman was Mpende.

Van Lanterman waved his company onwards. They continued on the path, disappearing into the jungle.

Layila wiped tears from her eyes with the back of her hand. "We're all going to die," she said desperately, almost resigned to the inevitable. Her own mother was chained, being dragged somewhere unknown; that was almost too much for the child to contemplate.

"Don't say that," said Inga. "Don't ever say that. We leave now, right this moment."

Layila searched Inga's face for a sign of emotion. He was strong, she thought, and she trusted him. She was sure he would make a good hunter one day.

They all stood, except for Bikoro, who lay motionless on the tree floor.

Layila dropped to her knees again and shook the insect-bitten girl. "Wake up, Bikoro," she demanded desperately. "Please wake up!" Her voice trailed off as she realised that Bikoro wasn't asleep. Her body was inert, unmoving. Layila touched her head and found it cold. She shook her again in misery, but Bikoro's body was limp, yielding to her pulling. "Oh, Mama! Mama, help us," Layila wept.

Inga and Kimoko frowned.

*Is it possible that Bikoro is…dead?* Inga crouched and lowered his right ear to Bikoro's nose. The stench of sweat and dirt emanated from her clothes. He moved his head closer to her nostrils to listen for breath but he heard none. He looked at Layila, who searched his face desperately for a positive answer. Inga shook his head.

Bikoro was dead. Her natural defences had been too weak to withstand the infestation the *Iboco* caused, and her body had succumbed.

Layila drew away and held her knees in her arms, weeping quietly.

"This will be her resting place," Inga spoke softly.

The friends huddled together within the cavity of the Baobab tree until they could summon the energy to once again perform the ceremonial ritual and prayer.

Now just three, they were more united than ever. Their desire to reach home had only been strengthened by their fear of dying like Bikoro or being taken by bad spirits like Boali and the twins. They marched with fierce determination. The hollow of the large Baobab tree, grave to their dear friend, was soon far behind them.

They walked, following each other in single file, parted by a few paces from each other. They naturally kept that distance, as Inga instinctively recalled some of the elders' advice on forest-trekking about allowing the leader to remain several paces in front. This was necessary, should there be an urgent or sudden need to wield a spear in response to an imminent predatory assault or the like.

Inga led, Layila followed, and Kimoko tailed. The soles of their feet were numb from exhaustive walking; as numb as their immunity to the sight of lifeless bodies that floored each burnt village they encountered. Inga, for lack of better equipment, did his best, pushing with his hands and raking open narrowed passages as he advanced through thick hedges of dead leaves. He frequently snapped obtrusive limbs of branches and untangled ramified vines and saplings. He worked hard to create a pathway for his friends. They needed to avoid all existing pathways for fear of encountering white men.

Inga was forced to pause often. He would bend down, resting his hands on his knees to catch his breath, his body sorely exhausted. His throat was dry, his gaze very alert, and his breathing laboured. Thoughts of home flashed through his mind, and he wondered if his suffering was similar to the initiation of the young men from his tribe into to adulthood on their virgin hunting excursions.

He tried to swallow but instead choked, desperate for a sip of cool water. He anxiously wondered how he was to lead the children home when he was barely old enough for the initiation into manhood.

His eyes rapidly scanned the terrain before him; left to right, up and down, and then in front. His gaze rested on some red-orange woody vines, nearly sliced in half. It was certainly his doing, seeing that they were freshly cut, but he could not remember having sliced them. It didn't really matter. He looked intently at them, gently moved one hand, and slightly lifted one end of the broken vines. It was dripping honey-coloured nectar, glistening in the sunlight. The liquid flowed, inviting him to satisfy his intense thirst. He was hot, and he could feel every porous opening in his dry mouth. *I need this*, he thought. *Let me just …*

"Inga! Inga!" screamed Layila from just behind him. She ran the short distance and tugged at Inga's torn and dirty garment, motioning him to immediately turn around.

Inga, somewhat startled, gazed at her. "What is it, Layila?" he questioned, tossing the vine away.

Her eyebrows frowned inwardly in panic. "It's Kimoko. Look at Kimoko!" In fear, she held Inga's arm tightly.

Inga straightened and stood up, struggling for a moment to release his arm from Layila's grip. He couldn't see Kimoko, the narrow passages he'd worked so hard to clear were closing in again. The forestation around them was so compact that their meagre efforts could not undo the years of natural, wild growth. Closely followed by a confused Layila, he sped through the passage.

Finally, he spotted Kimoko. He was on his knees. One arm was stabbing the air with a bunch of dried twigs and broken stilt roots, which he'd randomly grasped from the base of a large mangrove. He had somehow formed them into the shape of a torch and kept rigorously waving and flinging them with spearing force.

"Kimoko! Kimoko!" shouted Inga as he rushed towards him.

He seized him and tried to pull him up, but Kimoko reacted suddenly with extreme rage and impetuously pushed Inga, who was caught off guard and in shock tumbled onto a clump of hairy brown-yellow epiphytes. Before he got back to him, Kimoko was stomping and flattening the moist surroundings for no apparent reason. From a distance, he looked like someone engaged in a fight, inflicting repeated blows on his opponent.

Layila desperately screamed, "No, Kimoko! No! STOP!"

Kimoko, now standing and beating the air with his wooden arsenal, abruptly paused. His eyes were of a lighter reddish tone, and his face was covered in small fragments of leaves. He quickly bent slightly forward, awaiting an attack, his breath rapid, short, and nasal. His body was boiling and throbbing with the occasional involuntary shiver. He struck the air twice from side to side in vicious movements with his hastily formed weapon, stopping to look intently in Inga and Layila's direction. Kimoko saw two forms. "*Sengula. Kadi kiese sengula!*" he screamed.

One was a tall statue that came to life, surrounding him with aggressive chants. It had arisen from tombs to his left and was moving forward to assault him.

Kimoko smashed the wide-eyed statue with his broad wooden sticks, desperately defending himself.

The second form, a nail-studded torso, took hold of his ankle.

He shook his leg to rid the evil, but he couldn't. The grip was cold and pulling him hard. He fell and rolled over onto his back to fight his attackers. His fury increased, and he was screaming at the top of his voice.

The grotesque statues crowded him, constricting his body, until he shook violently, as if possessed by the devil. The shaking released him from their tight grip for a time, during which he broke his weapon in two and began slicing wildly at anything close by.

He became weak and rolled over on his back once more. His strength was subsiding, and he could now hardly lift his wooden sticks. His hope of survival began to fade. At this, the enemy surrounded him and vehemently pulled him backwards, over to the base of the tree. He was disbanded of his weapons and was tied by both ankles with lianas. He screamed, kicking his feet wildly.

Now, settling in the pocket of the buttress root to where he had been pulled, Inga desperately kept a strong grasp of his beloved friend, securing him in his arms. He uttered to Layila, "Keep holding. Keep holding the lianas. Keep holding!"

Layila had gathered the lianas; that deciduous biome was full of them. She had slipped them around Kimoko's ankles in a bid to tackle him to ground. She had pulled as if ringing a toll bell, unbalancing the poor child.

Inga had caught him in his fall with both hands, resting his head on his chest. He had then dragged him through the muddy decomposed grove to a corner of the fifteen-foot buttress. The root wall formed a perfect support for Inga's back whilst he wrestled to control a semi-convulsive Kimoko.

They lay exhausted, and Kimoko's body was rigid. His muscles were tense. His breath had tightened as he remembered his mutterings about Sengula.

They remained in their position for a while, Inga trying to understand what had happened and Layila twisting the ropes.

When Kimoko appeared to have calmed down, awakened from the deep, trance-like, feverish state, Layila recognised his joyful face and approached, glad to embrace him.

Inga, realising that his friend was returning to his former self again, kindly rubbed his head. "We thought we had lost you. You fought Sengula, the demon."

Kimoko was half-conscious, but he heard what Inga said. "Sengula?" repeated an anxious Kimoko. Kimoko felt heavy, like forty sacks of cassava-root flour. He looked at the vines around his ankles. He then got up and gave them a gentle toss. He slowly looked around him, slightly bewildered, until he found the remnant of the red-orange vine whose slimy nectar—unlike Inga—he had so succulently consumed. "I-I did not see Sengula, Inga. I was thirsty, and I drank this," admitted a defeated Kimoko, falling on his knees, covering his face in both hands. He sobbed in regret, and his friends joined him consolingly.

An eerie silent moment of sadness passed while only the noises of the forest could be heard afar.

Inga realised that he would have suffered the same fate had he not been interrupted by Layila. It appeared that the nectar contained a mild hallucinogenic ingredient, provoking an altered state of mind for a short period. The hallucination of statuesque forms were none other than his friends, Kimoko ultimately realised. The elders would have recognised the nectar, but the children were too inexperienced to notice and too thirsty to care.

After they had composed themselves, Kimoko asked, "Where is her body?"

"Whose body?" Inga queried, confused.

Layila quickly realised that Kimoko had lost all sense of time and place. She put her hand on his shoulder, like an affectionate sister, consoling her brother for the loss. "We prayed for her, remember? Come now. We have to go."

Suddenly the frown vanished from Kimoko's face, as if reality had just crept back into his consciousness. Layila touched his arm, recognising his pain.

Kimoko gave her a weak smile.

Inga was vigilant again, searching for direction. He was straining to look over and above the dense bushes.

"Wait," Layila suddenly exclaimed. "My father once told me if you get lost in the Mayombe, look for the Okoume. They are the tallest of all the trees, second only to the majestic Kapok and Baobab. Come! Let's find such a tree."

Choosing which tree to climb first was not obvious. The smooth, grainy trees were numerous, but not one was the correct tree. The most ramified trees had plentiful branches were good for climbing, but not all were tall. They walked on to the place where Inga had first stopped for a break. This time, they kept closer proximity to each other and worked together until they could find the right tree. The forest floor was undulating; there were lows and highs, and Inga dissected more thick, narrow paths.

Finally, they reached an opening of loose bushes and clustered trees. While some were strong, others were thin, short, or tall. Importantly, some tall ones had a great amount of branches and peeked through the top dome of the forest.

The children studied the trees to see which one might offer direction to Okoume.

"Let's go for that one," Inga said, pointing.

Layila and Kimoko ran towards it eagerly, but they quickly stopped when they realised what they were running into; a thin layer of stagnating water lay at their feet. It remained invisible due to the large nonporous and parasite-filled leaves that covered it. Lame and wet bushes emerged and were submerged by this water.

"Water!" exclaimed Layila.

"Don't drink it," Inga immediately intervened. "It's not flowing, and many things die in it." He was referring to the natural decomposition of fallen materials and organisms. "Look there, near the tree…bromeliads," Inga added. "We can drink from them. Come."

The wise Inga led the children to it, splashing through the water on their way. They reached the tree they needed to climb. It was large and intimidating. Its base had roots the size of young palms. They curved inside out, above ground and down deep. It was surrounded by long, distinct strangler fig shoots; they were so thick they could accommodate rafts of bird nests.

They looked at the neighbouring bromeliads that could have easily been mistaken for pineapples; their welcoming long green leaves overlapped one another to form a vase shape that gathered rain.

They waded through each, looking for one that did not contain dead insects, earthworms, larvae, or uninspiring woodlice. They stopped at the only one that had a very deep and hollow sole and had only caught a few layers of wind sand. A tiny, small amount of water trickled there.

Inga indicated first, "Dip your finger through the hole, wet it, and slowly pull it out and drink." He showed them how he collected a single drop of water, moistened his lips with it, and wiped his tongue.

The others followed and repeated for a little while, until the plant base was disturbed and leaked, mixing the rest of the water with muddy sediment and debris from their fingers.

It clearly wasn't enough to quench their thirst, but they had to move on.

Layila hitched up her sarong, held with both hands on one of the fig long shoots and heaved up off the base of the tree whilst the boys watched patiently. Momentarily, she thought she had forgotten how well she could climb and peeped down at the boys for encouragement. She saw the anxiety in their faces and carried on upwards with agility and dexterity.

"Hurry! We cannot stay here," said Inga.

Layila scrambled several feet high and stretched, but she still could not see. The tree was uninviting, with many dry branches, dying from the numerous suffocating roots. It would eventually die, as so often happened to many trees.

"Can you see anything?" asked an anxious Kimoko.

"Nothing on this side of the jungle," she said, shading her face with her left hand.

"We will never get out of here," Kimoko mourned in a desolate tone.

"We will find a way." Inga remained determined and positive.

Layila looked down again one more time. At that height, Inga and Kimoko appeared tiny in size, smaller than her thumb. She looked up again and peered into the distance. She had risen above the broadleaf treetop. Her heart raced.

Once at the top, she reeled another liana around her waist to make sure she would not fall to her inevitable death. Most treetops, visible into far unreachable distances, were covered with old nests, where some kind of feathered colony must have bred for a while. She could see where some of her lianas had taken root, just under those nests, which contained fish bones and broken eggshells. Spiders had taken over, but they did not look poisonous.

"Oh there! The Okoume! They're so far away. They are so, so far away. It is a long, long journey—so long I can hardly see, but we've got to go that way," she spoke, though the others could not hear. She pointed further east, deeper into the jungle.

Treetops were covered in mist, the sky was clear, and the weather promised a temperate climate. Sunrays were flickering through the open flora, broken into patches of green and dark shades of light by the foggy mist. The trees formed a natural barrier to the invisible horizon and stretched far out in any direction that she could view.

*What a sight*, she thought to herself, *but how evil is the lower ground.* "I must return and tell the others," she whispered.

Inga and Kimoko sighed in relief to see her jump back through the undercover. They were impressed at Layila's wits.

She grinned, confident and ready for the journey ahead, determined to find the territory that would lead them to Father Ombe and the hunters. When she descended, she told them how far they were from the Okoume, and it was good news.

With anticipation, they penetrated deeper into the heart of Congo's tropical maze. They remembered how their fathers were sometimes gone for two or three sunrises, only to proudly carry a kill home on their return. There was always plenty for the whole village. Today, they summoned their energy, preparing for a venture such as a hunt, as if with their fathers.

"It's that way," Layila said, pointing.

"Okay," said Inga. "That way we go."

They departed, jogging like the hunters they sought.

"How did your father know about the Okoume?" asked Kimoko.

"He was attacked by a lion whilst hunting. He escaped the wild animal and found himself lost in the forest. The Okoume led him to *Kisúndi*. I am only doing what he has told me," said Layila, "but we still have a long way to go."

The children walked for many hours. The sun had set, and they had slept, taking turns to stay awake, ever watchful for predators.

The following day, they reached a fork in the path. They spent some time deliberating over which path to take.

Whilst the boys argued, Layila sat on a log to catch her breath, too tired to argue. It seemed to her that both paths led in the general direction of Okoume. *Why do the boys have to argue?* She had often watched boys reaching manhood, desperate to be initiated as a hunter, argue in such a manner, and it tired her. She lay on the log and closed her eyes in complete and utter exhaustion. She experienced what could only be described as an overwhelming desire to sleep.

# CHAPTER VII

# SPIRITS

Out of nowhere, a wind passed slowly, rising over Layila's body; it was cold—very cold. She shivered. She felt a hand on her shoulder. She was inert; her neck felt heavy, and she hurt immensely.

As she turned to look, expecting to see someone behind her, she was immediately thrust with great force into the air, her feet leaving the ground all at once. She landed with a *thud* on the soft, dense forest floor several feet ahead. Small leaves and twigs had scratched her bare arms and legs and torn the clothes she wore. She screamed hysterically.

"What's happening?" Kimoko was panic stricken.

He and Inga searched for something, anything that would help them understand, but there was nothing.

Layila tried standing shakily but fell back to the ground, her face contorted in agony.

"Lay still," said Inga. "Someone's here."

"I'm cold," she whispered, panting heavily.

"Listen," said Inga, staring in the direction of nearby bushes, where whispers and mumbling emerged.

"Who's there?" ordered Kimoko, tears welling up in his eyes.

"Shhh!" said Inga.

It was so quiet that even the smallest sound could not be heard.

Layila couldn't feel her fingers; they were numb.

"Someone is here," said Inga. "I heard whispers."

"I'm so cold. I can't feel my arms," said Layila. "I want to sleep."

"Don't. You must stay up," said Inga.

"Is it a spell, Inga?" whispered Kimoko. "Is it spirits?"

Inga looked blank but nodded. There was no other explanation.

"What do we do?" asked Kimoko nervously.

"I don't know," admitted Inga hesitantly.

The boys stood, watching the shivering body of Layila stretched out on the ground. *Is it possible that spirits lifted her body?* They stood motionless, struck with fear. *Are they bad spirits?*

Inga crouched and held his head in his hands, searching for answers.

"Is she going to die too? Can you see?" said Kimoko.

"Layila, you must keep talking," urged Inga.

"I'm cold. I can't get up. I'm so cold!" said Layila. "I-I heard a voice," continued Layila.

"Keep talking. I am about to move slowly towards you," said Inga.

"What are you doing?" said Kimoko. "Are you mad?"

Kimoko nervously retreated under a canopy of large leaves. Inga took one step at a time, slowly, watching his surroundings.

"I will leave. I will leave you two here. Ya, Inga. If you don't come back, I will leave," said Kimoko.

Inga stopped, taking notice of a warm, gentle wind passing over his left shoulder.

"Do you feel that?" asked Inga, gazing back at Kimoko.

"Feel what?" said Kimoko. "Please! Let's leave. I beg you."

"Someone is holding me," said Inga.

"There is no one here but us. It's the spell. She has brought the spell on you. Come back."

Inga quickly scanned the area and saw no one. He felt another touch, this time on his left hand. "Wh-who are you?" stuttered the boy, nervousness etching his face. Then he tried moving his right hand. Again, he felt a warm touch. A sense of peace overcame his body. Somehow, he was not afraid anymore. He let the wave of heat touch his hands. He felt a presence around him. Both of his hands were warm. The touch was gentle and soft. He had never felt anything even remotely like it. The warmth spread up his arms and through his chest, finally reaching his head. He felt a sense of serenity, calm, and tranquillity flow over his body. Never before had he felt such a presence, but he was not afraid.

He felt the urge to walk. The pain in the soles of his feet had faded away into a distant memory. He did not know why, but he moved slowly forward, until he saw strange lights, like stars, dancing from the trees and bushes.

Kimoko's eyes lit up in amazement and wonder.

Layila's vision followed the lights too.

All around them were tiny little stars, appearing brightly—so many that they brightly lit up the forest, compelling the young group towards them with magnetic quality, drawing them closer, into the whirl of light. Inga allowed his whole body to be encompassed by the lights, turning slowly, as if held by them. Their shapes slipped in and out of focus, translucent like the water of the river, where fishes could be seen swimming beneath the surface.

One flew over Layila and, in an instant, she exhaled heavily and coughed. Kimoko rushed to her side.

She smiled. "I-I saw her."

"Saw who, Layila?" urged Kimoko, all the time watching Inga in amazement as the illuminations encircled them. One neared Kimoko, and he cautiously extended his hand. The light rubbed against it. It was surreal.

Layila and Kimoko smiled. They were not afraid. Their hearts lifted with joy.

"*Mvumbi*...dead spirits," said Inga. He spoke of them now effortlessly, as if in a trance.

Like chameleons, the lights turned into different colours, blending in with their surroundings; sea-green and emerald, glistening like the plume of peacock feathers. They took the shape of trees and leaves, blending in with nearby vegetation, gold and aurous.

Another light neared Kimoko, slowly transforming into the deep, sea-green hue of the Venus flytrap before subsequently illuminating in an array of dazzling colours, then dulling into a grey-brown shade, imitating the buttress roots.

Layila moved her hands towards one. The beings took the shape of her face. Inga and Kimoko's jaws dropped open. Layila was aware of herself in the glowing light, thrilled and unafraid.

Although the light was radiant, it was never blinding; it could be looked upon directly without hurting their eyes. Perhaps they were the gods' spirits, or perhaps they were not.

*I want to see my mother again*, Layila thought, the joy of the lights lifting her spirits. The lights, now white and golden shapes, had brought them hope.

"Who are you?" asked Inga. "What do you want from us?"

The lights circled around, taking their turn to touch the children's outstretched hands. One connected with Inga's upper body, and a brighter light emerged out of his body. Inga floated effortlessly. He felt as light as a cloud, as soft as a feather, as he wafted higher and higher in midair. *I am flying!* he thought in wonder, watching his friends below staring up into the lights. *Am I dead?* He saw himself above. Suddenly, he rolled over and was whisked towards two wooden sculptures. They appeared very ancient but were filled with life, as if they would move at any second and flourish like the living animals within the forest.

Inga watched a light that seemed to grow brighter and brighter, until its brilliance had completely encircled them, as if their souls had been transformed and enveloped in love. It was stunning, beautiful, and surreal. He had the glorious sense of being gathered up and held like a newborn child, nestling in the warmth of his mother's loving embrace. He knew now that nothing could ever harm them again: Whether they lived or died, he knew they had been given the strength to pursue their journey.

Beforehand, these beings had simply been peculiar lights. He had been so amazed he could not fathom them. Now, he knew who they were and what they wanted: *Bakulu*, spirits of ancestors, helping them to find their way to *Kisúndi*. It was clear to Inga that the *Bakulu* had shown them the way, the second path. The spirits had given them the strength they so badly needed to travel homewards, south of where they had journeyed.

He saw the trail so clearly. It stretched across the forest from way above as he descended back into his own flesh. He sighed with pleasure and caressed the lights. *Thank you.*

Slowly, one at a time, the spirits drifted upwards, vanishing one by one, second by second. Only a pied crow sat observing, its beautiful breast and collar seemingly emanating light and colour as it stood tall and strong, perched on a branch of the tallest tree. The bird looked down, raised a black foot, and scratched its neck.

The brighter lights remained close to Layila, hovering longer, but gradually drifting upwards and vanishing into the blue sky beyond the canopy of branches above their heads. Layila had a faraway look in her eyes. She held her right hand gently on the spirit, refusing to let it fade away.

Softly, the spirit moved and turned to face her, and that was when a face appeared visible to Layila, one she recognised in awe.

She clasped her palms across her mouth as tears filled her eyes. "Don't leave us! Don't leave us."

The face turned and moved further away.

"We have to let them go, Layila," said Inga. "They have shown us the way. We have to let them go."

Amazingly, the light stopped and turned once more and took the humanly shape of Boali with the twins, Nsimba and Nzuzi, shimmering and translucent, yet crystal clear.

"Oh! Ya, Boali," said Kimoko, falling to his knees. "Peace be upon you."

Boali's spirit smiled serenely, her eyes shining with pleasure.

"Praise be unto the gods," said Layila, wiping her tears.

Then, as quickly as they had first appeared, Boali and the twins vanished into thin air.

The children embraced each other, overcome with emotion, joyful, delighted, and ecstatic, yet at the same time peaceful and relieved.

*Were they spirits? Have they...passed on?*

They could not be sure, but their light pointed them to *Kisúndi* land. The road was still far ahead and dangerous, but for now, the trio appreciated and counted their blessings.

"You knew it was Boali, didn't you?" asked Kimoko, looking to Inga.

"Yes. She took me up in the skies, and I saw you both below. I smelled the *yombo* cream," said Inga. "You know that smell, don't you? Coconut milk?

It tickled my nose. Boali always uses that cream. That was how I could be certain. I knew it was her. Maybe the *Bakulu* will care for her soul and that of the children? Have a safe journey, Boali."

The pied crow alighted on a nearby branch. Its glossy head and shiny white chest feathers glinted. The crow was soon joined by other birds.

Kimoko turned to watch curiously, wondering if they, too, were bringing a message.

The birds danced from one tree to the next, circling and crowing, forming a black and white cloud amongst the deep green of the forest. The birds reminded him of Boali; his childhood; and a time far in the past, when Boali fed and talked to them. He remembered her kindness and how she spoiled him with goat's milk, like the big sister for whom he had longed as a child.

Then he was reminded of the monkey story his mother had told him time and again. When Kimoko was just a baby, he remembered the sunlight shining brightly on the women's journey back to the village from the riverbank. His mother and the other women used to have a rest under the Baobab tree. Whilst resting, they would unearth the food they had left underground, well wrapped with banana leaves, to keep the provisions cool. On that particular day, they decided to pick fruits for a change.

Boali and a group of younger girls were left to care for Kimoko. She was the elder of the children. She had fallen asleep in warm sunshine and was awakened by the jarring chorus of a plumed guinea fowl. She turned quickly to look for Kimoko. To her horror, a troop of *Nkewa*, red-head monkeys, had passed by and taken baby Kimoko up into the trees. They spread out on branches and tossed him between them like a mango.

When his mother and the women returned, they saw Boali and the girls shouting up into trees, encouraging the monkeys to bring Kimoko safely down.

Kimoko's mother, alarmed, feared the worse. She gazed up and begged the shrieking monkeys to return her child safely into her arms. She understood they meant no harm and they'd surely come down from high up above.

But Boali had something better in mind. She plunged her hands in the women's baskets and pulled out all the fruits. She threw some fruits temptingly onto the ground, right under the trees where the red-heads enjoyed their play. At the sight of delicious tropical fruits, the monkeys scaled down the branches, laying Kimoko gently on the ground and scampering away with fruits in their possession.

Kimoko was gurgling happily, unaware of the danger of being tossed high up in the trees. Later, when the scare had passed, the women sat together and cackled about what had happened that day. Days when the women laughed were good days in the Congo kingdom.

With those warm memories in mind, Kimoko was spurred into action, ready to run again. He turned to Layila and Inga, who were smiling broadly too. They held each other's hands and almost skipped joyfully onwards.

## CHAPTER VIII

# DEATH

On the trio marched with renewed vigour. The going was tough, but they brought down vines and bushes with energised strength as they headed down the southern path that the spirits had outlined so vividly.

They continued on, farther and farther into the *Mayombe*, deeper and deeper, until they finally reached a giant log that was covered by a steady current of army ants, all marching regimentally, searching for food, surging in one direction like an angered blood river. For a moment, they examined the ants in pursuit of prey, one touching the next in front, and thought, *Like us, they will not be deterred.*

By now, the sun had reached its peak in the sky, its rays beating down with burning, unforgiving heat through the umbrella of treetops above their heads. A breeze whispered across the children's faces but brought no resolve from the warmth of the sun carried in its wisps. Sweat poured from the group, their lips chapped and their mouths parched.

They had been battling an ever-worsening thirst for some time but had fought against their thoughts in the absence of a spring from which to drink. The *Mambala*, although hydrated, was swampy and marshy, and the water was undrinkable. The children knew to avoid that stagnant water for fear of infection. There were signs of wildlife amongst the dense vegetation that had been unable to survive the swampy marshes. Fishes were seen to struggle the most, many dying in vain in shallow pools, unable to gain any depth in which to swim, instead succumbing to anguish and eventually dying.

As they approached a stream, the children found a larger fish in torment, trapped without deeper water, becoming meals for smaller creatures and snakes. Inga called Kimoko's attention to the way in which snakes digested their prey whole; it was not an image Kimoko relished.

Despite sadness and clear anguish at witnessing life ebbing away from lack of water, Layila reminded the boys how the dry season was nevertheless welcome by some species. For some birds, the shallow puddles with their finned captives provided a delicious meal. Such birds would land and feast beneath the glorious, sweltering *Mayombe* sunshine.

Soon, all puddles would cease to exist. The children watched abandoned animal carcasses across the landscape.

"Let's keep going," said Inga. "We'll find water elsewhere."

"Wait," said Kimoko.

"What?" said Layila.

"Do you hear that? Listen."

Rhythmic, repetitive, measured sounds, like those of an axe chopping logs, were coming from somewhere in the distance.

"Yes, I hear," said Inga, moving in the direction of the thudding.

"If they are hunters, we may be lucky," whispered Layila.

"Let's see," said Kimoko.

"We must be careful," warned Inga to Layila and Kimoko, trailing right behind him.

The *thud* sounded nearer.

"How do we know it's not white men?" asked Kimoko, concerned.

"We don't," said Inga, "but we have to see."

"Cutting trees? It may just be villagers," said Layila.

"You think so?" said Kimoko.

"I *hope* so," said Layila. "Listen."

The sounds were growing louder. To Kimoko, they were worrying, and Inga agreed with him. Layila dismissed their morbid thoughts, for these were somewhat familiar sounds they had not heard for some time.

In the jungle, Inga had a gift of distinguishing sounds. His hearing was acute. He could distinguish monkeys shifting from treetop to treetop, from the distinct knock of a hornbill to the breathing of a starved lion. Nonetheless, at this point, he had no clue.

There suddenly came a loud bellow.

Inga listened carefully whilst they stood still and silent. He sought out the sound; ears more alert than ever, eyes scouring the surroundings for any sign of movement. The sounds were unique, individual, and distinctive—high-pitched sounds descending into hushed thuds before entirely fading. Dull, repetitive drones followed. The location was difficult to pinpoint.

They moved cautiously forward, treading quietly, pushing the dense bush to one side rather than hacking through it with sticks.

As the forest cleared, a graveyard stretched out before them. The bright sunlight blinded them momentarily, until they could clearly distinguish wooden statues. The children agreed the graveyard may not have been safe, so they knelt amongst the plant life some distance away.

Inga's eyebrows raised and drew together.

Kimoko's eyes widened.

Layila's heart raced. Turning to look at the boys, she saw that Kimoko's lips were firmly closed with fear, holding his desire to scream.

The dull, thudding, repetitive sound came closer with each passing moment.

Still hidden, they waited, but they saw no one. They were so quiet in their confined hiding space that they could hear each other's breathing.

No longer able to control herself, Layila leapt to her feet and began shouting frantically. "Enough! Stop it. That's enough." As she ran from their hiding place, Inga and Kimoko were unable to grab her quickly enough to hold her back. She ran through the graveyard, shouting for the noise to stop.

Out of the bushes, an enormous brown tortoise slowly emerged, crossing the pathway heading to the other side of the bushes.

Layila sighed, relieved. She stood there, watching the animal take a bite from a violet and white fungus before continuing on its route.

"A tortoise," announced Kimoko, rising from their den.

"Just a silly animal," said Inga.

"It will be killed if caught by the nearby hunters," said Layila.

"One blow of a sharp blade," added Kimoko, marching towards the creature.

Inga sighed. "They'll destroy it, gut it, and roast it on a spit inside its shell—a meal like no other…" His voice trailed off as he became conscious of hunger pangs in his stomach.

"Maybe we can cook it," said Layila, attempting to pick up the animal as it withdrew its leathery head and flattened itself to the ground.

"It looks torn on top of its shell. The skin has been squashed down," said Kimoko.

"And it's missing a foot," Inga noticed.

"Maybe a crocodile bite or an elephant foot," said Layila.

The thudding sound had stopped momentarily but had now returned and seemed to be approaching the pathway where they stood.

"The sound!" said Kimoko.

"I know. It's still here," acknowledged Inga.

"We should have stayed in our hideout," said an anxious Kimoko.

"Hurry up! Back to the bushes," ordered Inga.

They dashed across the graveyard and back into the bushes, where they hoped they might be safe. The thudding and tapping was closing in on them. The louder it became, the more the sounds echoed.

Kimoko moved closer to Layila, somehow feeling safer there, holding on to her waist tightly. Perhaps he needed the safety that only mothers offer. And Layila, being a woman, could offer that, if only for a moment. Layila and Inga said nothing; it was understood.

The children scrutinised the direction from which the ruckus emerged, their limbs stiff with fear, aching from running and hiding from sunrise to sunset.

Inga was distracted by a tiny ant that had bitten his ankle. He slapped it to its death, regretting taking its life whilst knowing it had to be done. When his eyes returned to the dirt road ahead, what he saw made his heart sink deep into his stomach.

A never-ending line of native men, women, children, and babes were chained together. There were many young girls among the shuffling captives, exhausted and emaciated from starvation. Women of all ages had large, heavy iron bars on their necks, which dragged them helplessly down to a stooping position.

Inga and the children immediately grasped the situation, having seen Layila's mother, Nsala, with Yambi and Mpende earlier. They understood why the people were chained together and knew they were captives.

Every area was filled with white men, all herding, lashing *chicottes* on any of their natives considered to be lagging behind, flailing, or progressing too slowly. Children were made to lug heavy items on their heads, secured to their bodies with belts made from bark. Some of the women were dying on their feet, attacked by flies that were seeking out any flesh they could find while their bodies were still warm.

The white men shouted. They held weapons that the natives called 'lightning' for their power to take lives. They shoved the children and women with the tips of their lightning. The men mocked them, even the dying, claiming them to be weak, whilst lashing harder at their backs.

As Kimoko held on to Layila, his heart never stopped racing.

Two men, who acted like chiefs, barked at each other.

Inga and the children understood nothing of the men's talk, yet they knew their intent was malicious.

The men's voices grew louder and louder. An argument ensued between two soldiers. Without warning, one of the men threw a punch and hit the other man full on in his face, sending him flying backwards, right into the chain of captives.

His colleagues began spitting profanities at the man. The rage in the other man's eyes was evident. Like a bull, he leapt up, struggling free, and in no time, the exchange fell into a full-fledged fight, with fists and kicks being thrown in all directions.

Now the men crowded 'round, encouraging the battle and cheering the man who had fallen to the ground.

"Boudewijn!"

"Get from under him."

"Flemish bastard. Fight him!"

"Hit him in the jaw, Dietger."

Soldiers crowded the fighters, yelling and shouting.

Inga peered further behind the line of natives and watched a white man rushing to the fighting men.

Layila and Kimoko continued to stare ahead quietly, bemused at what was unfolding, wondering if the men had been playing with each other or battling like those they remembered between tribes, the bouts that had claimed many of their kin.

Spectating officers doubled up hysterically and applauded, booing and shoving fighters back into the brawl when they withdrew or standing them up again whenever they fell to the dusty ground.

A chief surged forward angrily, fired two rounds in the air from his lightning, and then jammed it back into his holster.

Inga and the others jumped back in fright, realising that the white men had an innate gift: They could make thunder. Inga closed his eyes, praying to the gods. Kimoko held on tightly to Layila.

"*Soldaten!*" shouted Sergeant Lekens with a stabbing stare. "We've lost many men. Is this your idea of honouring their memories? I am appalled. Get these Negroes on their feet, and let's march. Is it understood?"

The brawl halted. All men stood to attention and saluted Sergeant Lekens.

"You heard the sergeant!" said a superior officer. "Pick up your weapons and get back in line. We march now."

The fighters regained their composure quickly, brushing aside their bruised and battered faces, fearing the wrath of the officers. They marched on, quickly resuming their lashing at trailing women and children.

Inga watched the spectacle of them leaving. He had wanted to save those chained people, but he knew he wasn't strong enough.

Kimoko began wheezing, and Inga rushed to cover his nose to prevent the noise from drawing attention to them. Even so, his hand never made it in time, and Kimoko let out a loud sneeze.

Layila stared back at the marching regiment.

"We're dead," said Inga with the palm of his hand still hovering over Kimoko's mouth.

"We are going to be dead if we don't leave now," said Layila, pointing to two Belgian mercenaries, lagging behind, who dashed across the graveyard in the direction of Layila and the children.

"Into the bushes!" hissed Inga.

"Right behind you!" Layila and Kimoko hissed back.

They moved fast, their small, athletic legs finding a way through dense wild plants and the graveyard. Their swift escape meant the men were left far behind, scratching their heads, wondering if they had indeed heard a sneeze.

The children quickly moved to thicker bushes, which were difficult to penetrate and dark to the naked eyes of the soldiers, who were used to the blinding glare of the sunshine. Darkness loomed around them. They quivered in fear, hanging on to each other, afraid to move. They saw nothing, but they heard the men's footsteps. The men's body odour was potent and putrid.

Inga's heart banged against his chest and felt as though it would explode out of his body. At any moment, the angry soldiers might stumble upon them and take them as captives.

They hardly dared to breathe, rigid with terror as the men stabbed with their lightning at the bushes, unable to find anything. Another sneeze surely would have put the children in grave danger.

Inga felt sharp pains in his chest, and Layila wanted to vomit.

One of the men turned to the other. "Find anything?"

"No. There's nothing here."

"Come on. Let's leave it. May have been an animal," said the defeated soldier. "Van Lanterman will have our heads if we fall too far behind. Let's get out of here."

Inga and Layila watched them leave the graveyard. *By the gods!* They felt they had escaped the worst. Kimoko stretched his legs out on the ground and propped himself up with his hands.

"Be careful, Kimoko. The white pigs may still see you," hissed Layila.

They continued to watch the procession of slaves trudging onwards. At the far end of the captives' line, the children saw an elderly woman, walking slowly, with Belgian soldiers on each side of her.

"Look!" said Kimoko. "Elder Ngoma."

Kimoko and Layila recognised her immediately.

"Why her?" Layila gasped.

Inga shook his head. "There's nothing we can do. We cannot go to her. We cannot risk our own lives. We must find Father Ombe."

Layila covered her face with her hands, not wanting to show her tears of sadness for the elder woman. *She's a grandmother. Why would they take a grandmother?* she thought despairingly.

"It will be all right," whispered Inga, shaking Layila slightly. "We cannot do anything. We must stay alive. Do you understand me?"

"Yes, yes," Layila agreed, but she sobbed.

"It will be all right. Ya, Layila," Kimoko tried to reassure Layila, even though he felt tears stabbing at the ducts of his own eyes. "But Inga is right. We must stay alive."

"Remember, she lives near Kisúndi. We can't be too far now," said Inga, squeezing Layila's shoulder. Layila looked up at Inga with a pained expression.

"People say she has been here since the making of our kingdom."

"Yes, she's a mother to our tribe," said Kimoko.

"And she wouldn't want us to risk our own lives. Trust me. Be brave, Layila," encouraged Inga. "We'll look after one another. That's what she would want us to do."

"You are the elder, Inga. We will do as you say," Layila said, resigned to Grandmother Ngoma's fate. With the heavy chains around her neck and hands, she would surely die.

The children watched helplessly as the blind old woman, exhausted, debilitated, and bruised trudged behind the others.

"March!" ordered one of the two men, shoving her by the nose of his gun. Two more lashes brought her to her knees.

The children wept, watching fluid spew from her mouth as she coughed.

"*Vertrekt*," squealed the sentry.

"March, old woman," said another, lashing his *chicotte* on the old lady's back.

Ngoma collapsed on the ground, her life fading, draining out of her lungs. She did not move again but lay panting, gasping her last breath on the ground, like cadavers before her.

"Is the old wench finally dying?" asked one.

"She's been slowing us down," said the other. "Do it."

The soldier fired one round that Ngoma never felt, for she was already dead.

The two white soldiers marched away, cold and unemotional, paying no mind to their dreadful, murderous deed.

The children waited patiently, until the road became quiet and the danger had disappeared out of sight, and then they rushed to Ngoma. There was nothing they could do but mourn her gruesome passing. The lightning had penetrated her chest.

Layila stood still. It was customary that, upon the death of an elder, a gathering of tribesmen and women would flock from all corners of the kingdom to attend a burial ceremony. Such a ceremony took sunrises and sunsets to organise. But there was no possibility of a traditional ceremony there, alone, in the forest.

Inga felt part of his heritage lost to the blowing wind, his roots slowly being compromised, but he was unable to do anything. He felt a pain he had never experienced and was unable to digest.

It was time to bestow their last farewell.

As they stood facing Ngoma, who rested on the ground like a beaten animal, Kimoko and Inga laid banana leaves over another corpse and bade her well. As Layila looked up, she watched as little winds swirl and circle around them. They felt Ngoma's presence amongst them, her spirit manifesting itself. She was leaving them.

"Farewell, mother of our kingdom, mother of our land," said Inga.

The swirling winds gently blew away and finally disappeared into the trees above their heads.

The children felt intense remorse as they left the elderly woman behind. They began to walk back into the forest, the horrifying image planted for ever in their memories.

Layila wished with all her heart that somehow, she could have interred Ngoma with honour following her people's customs. She longed to bless Ngoma in her tribe's traditional manner. She remembered the warning words of her mother, who emphasised that, during a ceremonial burial, the souls of the weak would be taken by death. Her desire to find the hunters was accentuated with the thought that she was young and strong. She reflected on the ways of her people. Children and infants were not permitted to attend funerals. Once, when she was a child, the rules were broken, although the secret was kept so as to avoid punishment. Now she recalled one fine, most glorious funeral. The ceremony was for Mama Pfumu Maseti, the first wife of one of the chiefs. Layila recalled the woman's kind heart, full of power, just like Ngoma.

A great deal of preparation was necessary not only for the burial ceremony, but also for the funeral. All the women were called upon, including Layila's mother, to attend to the elaborate ceremonial rituals.

Curiosity had been rife amongst Layila and her companions. They wanted to see it all with their own eyes. So, at dawn, Layila and her friends crept into the shrine, hiding behind the large statues or under a table, holding a pile of holy textiles only used at such important events. In a hushed silence, they waited.

At first, Layila was thrilled to be in the room, but slowly her excitement subsided. She had the full view and watched in awe. The *nganga*, a powerful spiritual healer, worked in that room. He used herbs to formulate medicinal concoctions to aid the sick and the dying.

The room was adorned with basketwork and mats, axes and jugs, decorated with ancient symbolic patterns, even on the smallest of tools and instruments. Layila remembered being completely transfixed and fascinated by the beautiful room. Her wide-eyed gaze was full of incredulity and awe as she took in every detail.

The spiritual healer's room was home to a number of different leaves, herbs, roots, and seeds, some recently harvested, some dried and stored. Some could be seen hanging upside down from ceilings, and others were kept in giant gourds, whilst others contained a mixture of herbs and oils, acting as a preservative.

From her hiding place, Layila had spotted a number of small *Basundi* tribal boxes, all beautifully crafted. Some were plain, some adorned with individual patterns and animal-like depictions. When opened, a wondrous scent escaped. A combination of the oils and herbs were applied to the corpse, prior to wrapping it in textile.

"Shhh! Shhh!" Layila whispered.

"Quiet! They're coming," said the girl under the table.

The girls listened intently as footsteps grew nearer. They tried not to fidget, but they were very nervous. Layila wished she could stand up and leave. She regretted her curiosity and wished she'd not broken the rules, but it was too late. She watched as her mother and the other women entered the room and laid the dead body of the chief's wife on the table. They carefully uncovered the body. One of the women took a sharp instrument. The women made a deliberate and precise incision in the top of the woman's head, causing blood to pour to the floor and seep into the linen of the women's clothes, some even flowing down to where Layila's friend hid beneath the table. Trembling, the little girl had simply met the gaze of her friend Layila, not daring not to move, even though she felt like screaming as the crimson oozed towards her.

As Layila looked to her left, she saw another of her friends. She pinched her nose with her fingers, for the smell was potent. Layila wanted to vomit. She was lucky to be near the door. She crept away from the gathering, feeling guilty for leaving her friends behind. She had no choice but to gasp for fresh air.

There were other huts such as those that housed cadavers. Without doubt, the bodies had been stored for long periods of time; others awaiting cleansing, still comprising their internal organs, Layila guessed, judging by the smell of death. Bile flooded Layila's mouth, the smell sickening her stomach, forcing her to cup her nose in her hand.

One of the huts contained bodies wrapped in white cloth; the walls were decorated with motifs, symbols of animals and *mizumu*, evil spirits.

Peace and tranquillity washed over Layila when she picked up the scent of perfume and blossoms, coming across bodies that were cleansed and laid on straw beds. At some stage, she'd become lost and panicked after venturing into the sacred huts. She couldn't call for help for fear of being caught, so she kept moving and proceeded to a grinding room, where seeds and dry herbs were crushed and to be used.

She fainted.

Sometime later, she found herself back in her own hut, in the company of the other young girls. They talked about their experience and swore amongst each other that their secrets would never be shared with their parents or with anyone.

Layila never forgot how sick and terrified she was after that, for a very long time. At times, she was unable to sleep in the dark; when she did sleep, she dreamt only of the dead. In particular, she had many nightmares about Mama Maseti waking from the dead to rip her soul. She would wake up screaming in the middle of the night. In the end, it forced her parents to take her to the *nganga* for healing and break whatever curse they thought she had.

Layila wished she could faint like in her past and awaken in the company of her loved ones. Her reality was different now: The white men were real, as were the mysteries of the *Mayombe* land, so she cautioned Inga and Kimoko, telling them that they should continue south as planned.

# CHAPTER IX

# TRAPPED

The forest was full of life, maddening buzzing insects, and the echoes of birds in the treetops. Once in a while, Kimoko ran against the web of the great yellow spider, and occasionally the trio heard the distinctive cry of birds above others. They were near *Kisúndi*. Soon, they would reach its territory.

On the way, they came across more dead bodies; many children and older women could not make the hard journey. The bodies scared them every time they saw one lying motionless. They kept their distance out of respect, gripped with fear. Some of the deceased still had chains around their wrists and ankles. Some looked emaciated from lack of food and water. Some bore the wounds of torture at the hands of the Belgian soldiers. It was chilling. The sight hit them sharply, yet the children continued, spurred on by their eagerness to reach *Kisúndi*.

At last, Kimoko could run no longer. The plump boy's legs were obviously shorter than Inga's, and he had grown tired. "I cannot run any further," he said with pant. "My legs are trembling. They hurt."

"We cannot stop," said Inga. "We must go on."

"Perhaps we should rest, Elder Inga," said Layila. "Yes, we must reach *Kisúndi* as soon as we can, but we are tired. We have been walking and running forever."

"It's so hot…and I'm so thirsty," said Kimoko.

As they spoke, once more, the stillness of the forest made the children worry. There was not a single sound—not even from maddening insects. A hushed stillness encompassed the forest. The children searched for signs of what the stillness might mean.

"Look!" Kimoko pointed his right index finger upward.

The hot sun disappeared behind dark clouds that moved across the sky, making the forest darker than ever. The air was cool. A leopard roared in the distance, each roar moving further away from the children, as if the creature sensed some imminent danger. When the roar ceased, darkness covered the *Mayombe* forest, and a strong wind arose, ripping trees, intense and fierce, swirling the treetops above their heads.

"Quick! In the bushes," said Inga.

They quickly hid amongst the greenery and undergrowth, waiting once again to see what danger lurked.

"What now?" asked Kimoko.

"I don't know," said Inga.

"Don't be afraid," encouraged Layila, as her own body broke out in a cold sweat.

"We have to hide until their anger passes," said Kimoko, trying to rid himself of his fear.

"We wait," said Inga.

Heavy rainstorms and lightning intermittently streaked the sky, causing the forest to light up for an instant before gloom fell again.

"I can't see anything," Layila whispered.

It continued to get darker. All was still except for the terrorizing flashes of lightning.

*Why are the spirits of the ancestors so angry?* Layila wondered anxiously.

And then it rained. The downpour drenched their faces, and their feet sank into the cold mud, until their swollen ankles were covered. Tired and starving, they shivered, blinking up at the canopy above. The wetness and dampness chilled them to the bone.

Kimoko became increasingly agitated. He stood up and began to pace.

"What are you doing, Kimoko?" whispered Layila.

"I can't stay here any longer. I must get out," said Kimoko.

"Don't," said Inga, clasping Kimoko's ankle.

Kimoko spun around and punched him square in the face, causing Inga to fall back, with blood trickling from his nose.

Layila was quick to tend to Inga, pressing down on the bridge of his nose with wet leaves to suppress the pain.

"He's going to get us all killed," Inga hissed angrily.

"Shush!" appeased Layila. "He's frightened. He's just a little boy."

Kimoko stepped forward, away from their hiding place, and sat with his head buried in his knees. He knew he should not have punched his elder, and he was so ashamed that he could not look back at the damage he had caused his friend. Despite the rain, the hush across the forest was unusual. Kimoko glanced around, his vision obscured by the pelting rain.

He heard a call: "Kimoko! Kimoko!"

Kimoko stared back. *Have I ventured too far?* He could no longer see Inga and Layila, but he knew it was not Layila's voice.

"Kimoko! Kimoko!"

Kimoko stared into the darkness a second time. He still could not see anything. He stepped cautiously further, into the shadows. He heard a roar. *Was that thunder?* He kept on moving, galloping and jumping over shrubs.

"Kimoko! Come here! Help me."

Kimoko suddenly recognised the voice: It was that of his mother. Kimoko was thrilled. He couldn't believe his mother was alive, calling to him for help, possibly free from the shackles of white man. He spontaneously ran, sprinting ahead as the rain pounded down on him. Nothing would stop him from reaching his mother.

"Kimoko!" called Inga and Layila from their hideout, into a grassy clearing, but Kimoko was too far ahead to hear their calls.

Kimoko bolted beyond a grassy terrain and felt a cold wind passing through his face. He slid to a halt on the damp ground and turned to look. His mother's words were still resounding in his ears. He could not resist the temptation to run. Longing to feel her loving, consoling arms around him, he rushed into the gloom.

He heard another voice behind him, whispering, "Look behind you."

He turned and screamed.

Inga and Layila, far behind, could just about make out his cry.

Layila was gripped with fear. She dared not think of what danger  might have befallen their young friend.

"Something has happened to Kimoko. We must help him," said Inga.

"Don't go," pleaded Layila. "I'm afraid. I'm begging you not to go, Inga." Layila's cold hands took hold of Inga's arm. She was shaking, imploring him to stay.

Inga was in a quandary: He could leave Layila and hide her in the bushes, but the place was eerie and dangerous, and they knew nothing of the hazards ahead. He shouted desperately, "Kimoko? Kimoko!"

There came no reply.

"I'm sorry, Layila, but I must find him and help him," said Inga.

"Don't go," said Layila, holding Inga's arms with tiger claws that nearly cut into his flesh. "I-I don't want to die," said Layila.

"We cannot leave him behind," said Inga. "He needs our help."

Another cry pierced the forest. This was not a human cry, but that of the *gbuku*, a black bird.

"Witchcraft!" said Layila. "A witch, blowing her magic whistle."

"I'm sorry," apologised Inga, walking away.

"Then I'm coming with you," said Layila, wiping the rain from her face.

Once again, they heard the *gbuku*'s cry.

"Wait," said Layila. "We need sticks to protect ourselves."

They quickly searched the undergrowth and collected damp but sturdy, then headed towards where they had last heard Kimoko's call for help. They walked carefully on the wet ground.

"Kimoko! Kimoko!" called out Inga and Layila in the dark. Their voices echoed in the deep *Mayombe*. Somehow, they were no longer afraid: They had each other and their sticks.

Once more they heard the *gbuku*'s cry.

They took cover, scanning the forest, and what they saw sent a chill up their spines.

They knew of witches and sorcerers that, at times, lived amongst them, but the *nkuyu*, death envoys, were little creatures their people rarely talked about. They were a taboo because it was believed that they brought wickedness and death. They were the persona of evil, living beyond the forest where no one had ever set foot, or so their people believed.

It was dark. There was a strong, pungent smell of gas, one that forced Layila and Inga to shield their noses whilst they called out, "Kimoko! Kimoko!"

Layila trembled. She felt as if she wanted to retch from the putrid smell. She wondered if it was the gas or the white man's witchcraft or the making of *nkuyu* that caused her sick feeling. She feared the worst as she fell backwards and blacked out.

"Wake up!" Two boys were yelling at her. "Wake up!"

"They're gone," said one of the boys. "Are you all right?"

Layila wearily held herself up on one arm. She couldn't focus properly, and her head hurt. She remembered the pungent smell and quickly moved her hand to guard her nose. She tried to focus and peered curiously at the two boys before her. They were natives, so her fear was not intense, but she wondered where they had come from.

"They're gone," said the other boy. "You're safe."

"Who do you speak of?" said Layila, confused.

"*Nkuyu*," said the boy. "We came just in time and found you here."

The two boys smiled victoriously at each other, proud of their accomplishment.

"Where is Kimoko? Where's Inga?" demanded Layila.

"We haven't seen anyone but you. They must have been taken away by *nkuyu*," said one of the boys. "You're the only one here, but we must leave now."

Layila was baffled. She looked closer at the boys, not recognising them, although realising through her muddled thoughts that they had to be from a village, though she had no idea which one. "Who are you?" she queried.

They explained that they were brothers who had escaped their village when soldiers had taken over, savagely capturing many of the men, women, and other children.

"We were lucky. We had been sent to the river to collect water and heard the screams from our people. When smoke poured above the roofs of our huts, we were frightened and ran for our lives."

Layila's heart softened, for she understood the boys' plight all too well. "We are Wene and Nimi."

Both were skinny boys, about fourteen and fifteen years of age. Nimi could be distinguished by his lighter complexion. They stood tall, looking down at her, with sticks in their hands, ready for their own venture through the forest.

"We must go," said Wene. "We cannot stay here. It is too dangerous."

"No," said Layila. "I cannot go until I find my friends."

Nimi, the gentler of the boys, looked into Layila's face and said solemnly, "They are gone."

Layila's heart lurched. *No! No! I beg you, don't let them be gone*, she screamed silently to herself. The agony she felt was excruciating. She stood covering her head with her hands. The terror and agitation she felt was too much. She turned around and around, clutching her head and bending over and over. She covered her face with her hands, desperately trying not to cry.

Wene, the stronger of the two boys, stepped forward to take charge. "Listen," he cried, "if you stay, you die. It was *nkuyu*. Trust us. We know."

It was true, and Inga and Kimoko were nowhere in sight. Layila sat down and buried her head in her knees. *Was it nkuyu, a Mayombe myth, or white men who took my friends?* She knew waiting could put her in great danger; after all, they were on treacherous grounds. "What is that smell?" she asked.

"Here," said one of boys. "This is what chased *nkuyu* away. They can't stand the strong scent. Rub it all over."

He produced a small gourd full of paste that he called *smilage*. He explained that it was made from celery seeds and was used to protect people from witches and evil, particularly children.

"Come with us. You will be safe. *Nkuyu* never give up. They will pursue if they know that the paste has worn off. With us, you will be safe."

"All right. I will go with you," said Layila, resigned to her fate, though she was still curious about that of her friends. She trailed after the boys, who marched on a path where Inga and Kimoko had been with Layila just hours before. Layila desperately scanned the bushes, hoping for a sign of Inga and Kimoko, before they moved further away from the area in which they had been lost. Finally, she gazed back, wishing adieu to her vanished friends before she hurried to join her new travelling companions.

Soon, the dark clouds above cleared, giving way to sunlight peeping through the canopy above their heads. It was as though *nkuyu*'s gloom had never roamed the land.

*But are dark clouds truly nkuyu's curse or angered spirits of my ancestors? Perhaps they're even the making of white men!* Layila's thoughts wondered as she hurried along the dirt path with her new friends.

"They have left us," said Nimi, staring up to the heavens. "The paste must have worked."

"Yes, but I remember what my mother said. We must never stay on the same path. There!" said Wene, pointing. "Let's take that one."

"You're a great listener, my brother," said Nimi. "You've learned well. Come on. This way."

Layila followed the boys to the adjacent path. They asked her for her name, and she kindly introduced herself: "I am Layila."

Nimi talked to Layila while they walked, while Wene remained in front. He explained that he and his brother were from the village of Mpemba. Layila had never heard of it. Nimi went on to explain that his people had been preparing for their sister's wedding. There was great excitement amongst his people until the men with Pale-faces ransacked their village.

Layila sighed and uttered in reply that the same white men had taken her mother.

"They have taken our father, mother, and sister." Nimi shook his head sadly. "So we ran away. My brother and I ran for our lives."

Wene looked back and said over his shoulder, "Before we left, we went back into the village when all was quiet and took the paste and other provisions for our escape." Wene spoke in a matter-of-fact manner, but Layila could see his anger in every line of his face. "As soon as we saw these things happening, we knew from our father that we had to go towards the neighbouring kingdom," he added. Wene spat bile from his mouth in disgust at the thought of the men with Pale-faces. "They're not men. They're evil. Men don't harm men the way they do. They are not from the skies. They're from beneath the ground."

Silence fell amongst them as they tried to absorb the story and the harsh reality.

Nimi spoke first, as he preferred the sound of their voices to the painful silence. It calmed him and distracted him from the thought of his family. "We got lost in the *Mayombe*, trying to run from them," he said. "We found we were running in circles, not knowing where we were going. We were lost, until we heard you calling for help. We rubbed the paste on ourselves first. After that, we made flame torches." He was glad to talk and ask Layila questions.

Layila explained that her mother had told her and friends to run from the river before the men with Pale-faces reached them. She spoke of her need to reach *Kisúndi*, her Uncle Ombe, and the other village hunters. She spoke sadly of losing Boali, the twins, Bikoro, and now Inga and Kimoko. "Why are the gods so angry?" A single tear rolled down her cheek when she asked the question for which none of them had an answer.

"We will help you safely find your way. Then Wene and I will march further, near the neighbouring kingdom, away from the great river. You are welcome to come with us. It will be much safer if we are together."

Layila was grateful. She imagined a terrible fate for herself if she'd have been left alone in the heart of the forest.

They marched onwards. The forest was damp and humid, as it often was after a torrential rain the night before. Nimi was reminded of the sudden lightning and the blasts that had emanated through the forest. They had hidden, frightened, just as Layila, Inga, and Kimoko had done.

"It was not thunder. The blasts were an attack by the white men," Wene suddenly exclaimed angrily, clearly thinking aloud.

Aware that the boys had fallen victim to the same fate as she, Layila was at ease with them and sympathized with their sorrow. She could not forget her anguish, but for the moment, she'd found some semblance of peace.

Farther into the forest they ventured. Layila stumbled across the trees of the weaverbirds—yellow and black—located on what had once been a stream, but after being trampled and trodden by a family of warthogs, there was nothing left but mud and bog. The warthogs' future was insecure, considering their numerous adversaries; danger was part of their day-to-day battle to live in *Mayombe*.

Layila watched as warthog families foraged for food around the water hole, desperate for any morsel, happy to consume anything, including mashed vegetation and any trace of water they could find. The younger ones, on the other hand, were able to suckle from their mothers, who would consume as much grass as possible, converting her food into milk for the young; the young subsequently changed the milk into vigour for play.

Lost in the deep and dark *Mayombe*, Layila and Nimi continued on in conversation, talking about happier times, if only to fill up the empty, dead, eerie space between them. They occasionally stopped to eat fruits from the trees and sip water from springs. It was enough to distract them from the reality surrounding them.

Wene walked in front, alone, vigilant for danger, priming himself for an attack at any moment. He ignored the conversation behind him.

Layila suddenly remembered something and spoke up. "We came across many dead bodies in villages and on dirt paths." She spoke sadly, but Nimi was undeterred in his brightness.

"Remember, Wene, when we were sitting under some large leaves, trying to figure our way to the neighbouring kingdom?"

Wene ignored him.

"We saw a leopard cub walking past the edge of the fallen tree," Nimi continued, regardless of his brother's attitude. "We were both surprised to see a leopard cub alone and abandoned in the forest."

Layila gasped.

"It was frightening to be so close to a dangerous animal," Nimi continued excitedly. "We were terrified because we didn't know what the young leopard cub was up to. We knew at any time, the cub's mother could have been anywhere."

Layila nodded, understanding.

"We left the cub alone and stormed off to the forest," said Nimi. "A while later, just when we were to continue on our journey, we saw the same leopard cub again."

Layila admired Nimi's enthusiasm, especially under such terrible circumstances.

"It was very surprising," added Nimi.

"What do you mean the leopard cub wasn't alone? Surely he was with his mother!" Layila asked.

"Well…" said Nimi. "With great surprise, we saw a pied crow with the leopard cub."

"A pied crow? With a leopard?" Layila was amazed. "That's not possible."

"It's true! We saw a pied crow with that leopard cub," said Nimi. "Even Wene was mesmerised."

"By the living forces!" said Layila. "A crow with a cub."

"Yes," said Nimi. "Both bird and beast, side by side, walking down the pathway together—like best friends. I was in disbelief myself," said Nimi, "The cub was not chasing the crow, but they were side by side."

"I've never heard of anything like that in my whole life," said Layila.

"The bird and the young beast must have been friends by a miracle of the *Bakulu*."

"That's not all," said Wene, now grinning widely, since his brother's enthusiasm was infectious. "Tell her."

"Tell me what?" prompted Layila.

"Well," said Nimi, "it seemed the cub was starving. We were worried it might starve to death."

Wene burned in anticipation, waiting for his brother to unveil the big *voila* moment.

"What? What?" shouted Layila, hungry for more.

"I tried to feed the cub," said Nimi.

"You did what?" asked Layila, dumbfounded.

"Yes," he said with a proud grin. "I tried to feed it with my bare hands!"

"No!" exclaimed Layila. "And did it eat? Right out of your hands?"

"Not exactly," said Nimi. "In fact, it did not eat at all."

"Tell her," pressed Wene. "Please tell her the exciting part."

Layila was puzzled, and she asked, "How did the cub manage to eat then?"

Nimi smiled broadly, like the teacher he had always wanted to be. "The pied crow."

"The pied crow?" said Layila.

"Yes," confirmed Nimi. "The cub was cared for by the pied crow, which led it to fresh water, made sure it ate, and did everything it would do for its own fledgling."

"It was a miracle!" said Wene.

The three relished in the story for some time. It was a wonderful story that captured their imaginations and kept their minds busy for quite a while.

After a while, the trio came upon a large stream. Layila raced the boys to drink and cool their faces and hands. Whilst they stooped to fill their hands with water, Wene noticed that some dense shrubs had begun to shake, and there was crackling of branches as something or someone approached.

To the children's stunned amazement, out came a great *kudu*, an antelope. Its horns emerged from the bushes first, long, strong, and twisted. The children froze, but despite its power, it simply eyed the children thoughtfully, considering the potential threat, before proceeding to join them at the stream, quietly and peacefully—likely his usual drinking hole. The beautiful brown and white beast stood proud.

Layila had never seen one so close. When she was growing up, her grandmother had taught her about the great antelope and its inclination to establish itself as the most dominant in a group: illustrating its strength; discouraging and intimidating rivals; exhibiting its power and authority.

Whilst the great antelope continued to lap water, from behind dense bushes emerged a female, who came and stood beside the *kudu* bull.

The children held back their desire to speak, knowing the slightest noise would scare the creatures away. To their utter amazement, one after another, females began to emerge, joining the bull in the water. Lacking the intimidating horns of their male counterparts, the females sought the protection of the bulls. It seemed that was their nature.

At the other end of the water hole, the bull rose to watch one of the females eating grass and then continued to drink.

When the females felt secure, certain that their calves would not be endangered, they drank.

Soon the antelope left the water hole and wandered lazily back from where they'd come, deep in the forest.

Layila returned to refresh herself and splashed her face with water.

Wene called to her, "The route to *Kisúndi* is not far! We must hurry."

"Not again," Nimi complained. "We just got here. My feet are sore. Can't we rest a while longer?"

"If we are truly near, our journey will be over soon enough," encouraged Layila. "Then you can rest as long as you want. Come on."

Nimi was reluctant to move, but he knew that resting would take them nowhere. The sooner they got help, the better their chances of saving Layila's mother.

Wene called out to Nimi with a nod of his head, encouraging him that freedom was near and the cost was to press on.

Nimi heaved a sigh and then followed his brother. Soon after he continued talking, and his conversation ended up where it had begun. Perhaps the story was simply too miraculous to bury, so they spoke of the boys' unbelievable encounter with the crow and the leopard cub in the forest, recalling it all over again.

Nimi could talk endlessly, it seemed. One had to listen, and Layila could not afford to be rude to her elder. Out of respect, she listened and asked questions. Somehow, Nimi was always able to answer them in the context of his story.

Layila's mind wandered elsewhere though. She couldn't help thinking of her mother, Nsala, and of the other women. She thought of the white soldiers. *Where did they go? Are they still in the kingdom?* She thought of the hunters and Father Ombe. *Were our hunters hunted down too by the pale-faced men too?*

Nimi's voice intruded her concentration again, jolting her back to the moment.

She smiled as he continued with the same story.

"Well," commented Nimi, "the pied crow actually fed food directly into the mouth of the cub, beak to mouth. It was astounding and incredible! You'd have to be there to believe it, watching it with your own eyes. And another thing," he continued, "although the crow needed to eat himself, he always made sure the cub ate first and that he was okay."

As soon as Layila realised Nimi hadn't changed subjects, her mind wandered once more. She thought of Inga and Kimoko. Her stomach wrenched, so she shifted to positive thoughts, reminiscing about playing with the boys back at the village and how much fun they had. She thought of the great kingdom and how close-knit they were. She recalled her ancestors and those before them, how they had protected the land at all costs.

Nimi's voice interrupted her concentration again, bringing her back; she had unknowingly continued walking.

Nimi screamed, and then both boys were screaming.

"Help!"

"Layila!"

"Get help!"

Layila stopped and turned to look back. She gasped, her eyes wide. *What happened?* Terror raced through her mind as she saw both boys hanging upside down by their feet. Hastily, she dashed back. "Wait! Wait…I'm coming."

"It's a trap," shouted Nimi. "Stay back."

"No, Layila! Don't come. It's a trap!" screamed Wene, terrified and waving his hands "Go back."

But Layila could not, for her instinct was to protect. She was upon them, reaching her arms out, when her body suddenly fell, feet first, into a wide and deep hole, ingeniously covered with leaves and brush. Layila screamed, but all she heard was the echo of her own voice bouncing against the hollow of the confined space. Her body hurt, the pain severe as she crashed to the bottom. She felt the pain of the impact spread throughout her body. She held her knee, which began bleeding. She wiped it with her already filthy skirt and peered up at the light above her head.

*What is this? It must be a trap—perhaps for elephants. The boys were right!* Still, she was grateful to be alive, and she thanked *Bakulu*. She was fortunate that the trap had no poisonous spears in it. She remembered her father's talk of those hellish holes where elephants were captured by hunters, with spears left behind to help butcher the catch even quicker. Layila cried out, her voice rasping with fear.

She heard Nimi wail, "Layila? Layila, are you all right?"

"My legs," said Layila. "I-I can't walk." Layila had lost all hope. She was certain she would die like the animals before her in that forsaken ditch. Should help never materialise, hunger would claim her life in matter of hours.

She listened intently and heard the boys panting, struggling to break free of the vines, crying out in pain. "Nimi? Wene?" she whispered, but there was no answer.

Instead, she heard footsteps approaching from above. *Hunters?* she thought desperately. Her desire was to shout for help, but by now she knew better. Terror gripped her. *White men! Oh, help them. I beg you, don't let the white men take them too. Help!*

The footsteps seemed to be getting closer.

Layila shook with fear. With dreaded thoughts swirling in her mind, she trembled, grasping her knees in her hands, trying to make herself smaller, willing herself invisible.

The boys' screams suddenly pierced the hushed forest.

"*White men!*" yelled Nimi. "No! NO!"

"I beg you, no!" screeched Wene.

"Leave him alone," roared Nimi.

Layila's heart dropped to her stomach. She heard men's voices coming closer, speaking words she did not understand. She froze, motionless in the depths of the elephant trap. She searched her mind, desperate to help the boys, but she could think of nothing. Paralysed with fear that she could do nothing, tears silently rolled down her face. "*Ya Nkulutu*, Nimi," she whispered. "Answer me, Wene. Wene!" She knew they could not hear her, but she whispered as if in prayer, willing the boys to let her know they were free and safe.

But there was no answer—only an alien language, emerging from above, men immersed in conversation, speaking in gruff, brutish voices.

"*Nimi?*" Layila prayed helplessly. "*Wene?*"

The men's voices began to rise until they were shouting. She could hear struggling and the boys screaming. They were fighting. The men yelled at the boys, who must have been trying to fight the men off. Panting, grunting, shouting, and more struggling emerged from above, until Layila heard the clanking of chains.

She dared not look up, but she knew for sure that those men were clamping the chains around the boys' wrists, just as they had her mother's and all the other natives' before them.

She heard rasping, gruff panting above her head. Her face half-covered by her hands, she peered between her fingers and, to her horror she saw a burnt-faced man staring down at her. Layila fell back in and crawled around the hole, scratching the ground with her bare fingernails, desperately trying to escape, her thoughts confused by the terror, until she finally peered upwards at the man.

He stood with his hands on his hips, chuckling cruelly, certain that there was no escape for the girl. He severed a vine with a blade from his belt and threw it to her, yelling and gesturing for her to grab it.

"No! No! I beg you, no!" Layila screamed.

He took a gun from his belt and pointed the silver nose directly at her eyes, yelling with it like a starved animal, desperate to take its prey between its teeth.

Layila succumbed like a frightened mouse, envisaging its inevitable demise.

The man dragged the creeper. He was strong and pulled her up quickly.

She scrambled at the rough edges of the hole, until she fell on the ground above. She whimpered uncontrollably, curling into a foetal position. Her terror was so great that her vision was blurred, and she wretched as if to vomit. She groaned and curled herself tighter.

Like a hunter, the man kicked her roughly, trying to turn her over with his foot and shouting. She quivered, the palpitations beating against her chest, as she forced herself to stand.

She rubbed her eyes that were filled with grit and saw more of the burnt-face men. They were rugged and filthy, their chins covered with stubble. They had their sleeves rolled up and headdresses wrapped around their heads, knives jutting from their belts. They stood victorious, smug with their captures.

Layila and the boys were dragged roughly by their chained wrists to where a slave party stood, on its way to *Kianga*, near the Congo River.

One of the slave women turned to Layila. She spoke in hushed whispers, not wanting to attract the unwanted attention of the burnt-faces. They were not meat-hunters but slave-hunters, and Layila was later to learn they were Arabs.

# CHAPTER X

# ESCAPE

As the children trudged along with the other slaves, Layila noticed that the burnt-faces had left traps all over the forest floor, in hopes of capturing more natives. Layila saw many people; the eldest of them were women, but the majority were young boys and girls. They trooped endlessly along dusty paths, stepping occasionally in puddles, tripping over the undergrowth, as they could hardly see their own feet since they were so closely held together by chains.

The burnt-face people, the Arabs, were armed with rifles, bearing sabres, dirks, shields, and long daggers of Oman. They marched in front.

Layila looked in disbelief to see her own kind—tribesmen and chiefs who were not chained—talking in broken tongues to the Arabs. The horrible realisation that her own people were selling them into slavery slowly and painfully dawned on her.

The black drivers were equipped with a number of weapons—blades and spears—and adorned with the finest attire. They charged forward confidently, positioned in the middle and at the rear, some blowing triumphant tones through antelope horns.

A rifle shot followed, and another announced a short halt for a rest.

Layila and the boys watched as the Arabs knelt down and prayed to their *Bakulu*, spirits of the ancestors, only they weren't praying to *Bakulu*, but to Allah. They pulled out their Qur'an and beads and sprawled their praying carpet on the ground facing Qiblah and invoked all together in Arabic, "It is Allah, the Only God, the Everlasting and Outright. And none other compares to Him, the One."

The men then fell into a profound silence of personal prayers.

Layila and the other slaves were able to rest a while and took the opportunity to pray their own prayers.

A long time afterwards, following prayer, the group stacked their cargo and spent a while relaxing, drinking, and joking with each other in conversation. Some of them blew smoke from strange white tubes. They jeered mercilessly when the Negro children cried or whimpered in pain, exhaustion coursing through their veins.

Layila listened silently. She felt nothing. She was numb, even to the cries of her own people that emanated through the air; breathless cries as their feet pounded and rubbed the dusty earth.

Later, when they stopped to rest again, other unfamiliar sounds passed her ears: the pestle of the Arab cooks rubbing against the mortar, coffee being extracted. The strong smell of coffee was a new smell. She liked it but also feared it. The Arab's drank their coffee, offering none to the slaves and soon reformed in their marching lines alongside the black drivers, who continued in their air of achievement and victory, feeling proud and noble.

Layila stole a glance backwards over her shoulder and saw Wene walking behind her with his head down. She straightened herself, realising that head-down was no way to honour her ancestors who had fought for freedom and protected their fine kingdom. The pain of straightening her neck seared through her body, but she persevered, pushed along with the tide of prisoners. Their necks were bound with ties created from bark, binding the women captives, later turning as stiff as iron after exposure to the day, but she forced her head up, unwilling to submit.

As she marched, Layila heard a conversation amongst the captives about escaping; most of the plotters were men, *Yombe* tribesmen. Layila wanted to join in their conversation, but she felt too small; they were men and elders, and she was quite sure her young, female contribution wouldn't amount to anything. She had always been taught to keep quiet when elders engaged in a conversation. Besides, it was not the common conversation, but one of grave consequence. *I will keep my mouth shut*, she decided.

Layila hated the heavy chains that slowed them down. Each time her walk held up the line, she was whipped savagely, just like the others. She flinched with pain. She felt the blood roll down her back and seep through her filthy clothes. Nevertheless, she would not submit to their cruelty or give them the pleasure of her cries, so she suffered in silence.

She was beaten again and again, as if the men knew she was unwilling to admit defeat. The beating drained her strength, until she felt she could no longer hold her head up, but unlike the others, she stubbornly held her head high. As her wise mother had always said, she was a girl of vigour and determination. She repeated her mother's words to give her strength.

It was hot and humid. There was little time to rest and drink. There were casualties along the way, and many died along the path. Their bodies were left to rot or served as a meal to hungry beasts. No remorse or compassion was shown by the burnt-faces.

Layila was silent, numb, and exhausted. Some of the women wailed. Others chanted prayers. Layila stared into the distance, imagining her mother's face calling her, beckoning her to come home.

Earlier on in their journey, exhaustion and fatigue had overtaken a man, and he'd fallen to the ground. Layila had watched as he was murdered with an axe; brutal and without consideration. The massacre had shocked her, sent fright running through her, right to her core. This was part of the journey and something she would see often. Single, solitary tears flowed from her eyes over her expressionless face.

She soon came to realise that if she wept, she was whipped. She was powerless at their hands to even express grief. Each and every one of the captives suffered quietly in their powerlessness. She wished her mother were there to keep her safe in her embrace.

Nimi was far ahead, never allowed to come close. Burnt-faces knew to divide those who knew each other, those of the same tribes. In this way, they were able to guard against mutiny.

Wene, far behind her, was lashed till the black on his back turned purple and blood oozed from huge welts raised on his body. Nevertheless, he hung on to his last breath, trekking with whatever strength he had. Layila looked at his face and knew his end would soon be coming.

Despite Layila's sore feet, she had no choice but to press on in fear she would share Wene's fate at the hands of the burnt-faces. She wondered why her tribesmen were taken as slaves, something she was soon to find out if she was to make the journey alive.

Dead, she would never know.

"Where are they from?" Layila inquired of the woman ahead. "I have never seen so many of us in this way, other than when my tribe fought against intruders in my village. These captives are from all over the kingdom."

"My daughter," said the arthritic-legged, elderly woman, "the gods have left our kingdom."

"Why?" said Layila.

"Perhaps we have done something wrong. Who can be sure? Perhaps the blood of those we have enslaved through our tribal wars have declared vengeance upon their own kingdom."

"Is this what happened to your people?" asked Layila.

"I have been captured in war," the elderly woman spoke, as if resigned to her fate. "Burnt-face incited our village chief to attack another tribe, lending him their own armed slaves and rifles to ensure their victory, but most were sold to burnt-face for food and betrayal by their relatives."

"Our kingdom is in flame," whispered a young man. "Burnt-face raided my village, killing warriors, burning houses, and bleaching skeletons. They took children and women."

"But what will they do to us?" said Layila.

All around her, the slaves shook their heads, unwilling to contemplate their own cruel fate.

"Shut up!" barked a black driver. "Move and keep your mouths shut."

"It was not long ago that two women and four men were killed, simply for loosening the ties," whispered the young man as soon as the black driver looked ahead again. "It was a lesson to all of us, a teaching to show the consequences of any attempt at escape. Another woman, carrying her baby, could not manage her load, so the head of her infant was battered. Believe me, silence will keep your life."

Layila obeyed the young man and said nothing more, praying to the spirits of the ancestors for favour.


As the convoy trekked further, Layila could not avoid noticing one of the burnt-faces steadily gazing at her, watching her every move. The man never took his eyes from Layila, ensuring that she took notice, which made her uneasy. But she knew she had to remain calm and say nothing to avoid whatever ruse the man may have been scheming. Layila turned her face and focused her attention on the opposite side of the pathway for some distance, until she heard high-pitched screams up in front.

A struggling mother, fighting against the undergrowth, was lagging behind with her baby. Both she and her child were hauled from the chain of slaves and were cruelly axed to death; the body of the baby was callously thrown into the bushes. Much sobbing ensued from the natives. The shock made Layila's legs tremble. The sight was horrific. She thought she might fall, but she managed to remain upright. The trauma of the scene flashed through her mind over and over. It was unbearable to see her people treated so brutally.

A blast erupted, and this time Layila could not control herself. She fell to her knees. She had heard the sound before, and it sent chills of terror up her spine. She remembered it vividly from the riverbank. It was the pale-faces.

She could only watch, confused to hear the panic in burnt-faces' voices. At the sound of the blasts, they began yelling to each other as they readied their rifles.

Then, a second blast went off.

These were rifle shots, not lightning as she had once believed. Layila was certain, for she had learned from the riverbank. This was not the gods' angry spirits either. She was sure of that as well, but she did wonder what was going on up ahead. "What's happening?" Layila whispered to anyone who might hear.

She peered ahead to Nimi and back at Wene. They were both still alive, though Wene was lagging. The natives began to whisper, "Pale-faces" in hushed, timid tones.

Ahead, she caught a glimpse of the white men approaching the convoy. There was yelling and shouting amongst the black drivers, who jumped and fled, leaving all their possessions behind them. They dispersed in a frenzied panic into the forest, like red-head monkeys.

Burnt-faces and their chief, under a high red turban, remained alone now. They would not leave without a fight. They began shooting back at the enemy in a crescendo of fire. The white soldiers' rifles had immense power though, and soon the burnt-faces were falling one by one to the ground. They were clearly outnumbered and outmanoeuvred by the pale-faces. The natives could do nothing but watch, helplessly wailing in terror, fearing it may be their turn next. Some injured burnt-faces fled on foot into the forest, and others stayed to fight, angrily defending their prized prisoners. The pale-faces marched fearlessly towards the convoy, firing and shouting for victory.

Layila stared back at Wene, who was screaming in pain. She wished she could break free and run back to him. He lay on the dry ground, wounded and bleeding heavily. Layila had never seen so much fluid flowing so quickly from a body, except at Mama Maseti's burial preparation. She flinched at the thought.

She could hear Wene wailing in agony. A pale-face was marching towards him with a weapon at his side. He looked viciously at Wene and, without warning, began pulverising his chest with his weapon.

"Leave him alone!" screamed Nimi as he looked helplessly at his bleeding brother.

The natives sobbed aloud. Layila wanted to cry too, but when she opened her mouth, nothing emerged. Her tongue stuck to the roof of her mouth. Her eyes were dry like sand. All her emotions were numbed. The horror of what the men had done to Wene was too much to comprehend. The scene flashed through her mind, but she couldn't bear to look.

The chain began to moan louder in their mourning the death of another one of their own. The moaning gathered momentum until there was wailing.

As the men prodded them with their weapons and lashed them with whips, they screamed in agony. There was uproar. A massed frenzy ensued, with no one in control.

Layila turned away, sickened in the pit of her stomach, when she noticed something glinting in the bushes. She peered closer. There was still uproar as the pale-faces shouted and the natives screamed. The sound was but a faint echo as she realised what lay in the grass verge. It was a weapon—the kind she'd seen the burnt-faces carrying. It had a wide, sharp blade that they used for chopping the vegetation aside.

She slowly stooped and picked it up, not wanting to draw attention to herself. The man behind her had seen it too. She quickly and silently passed it to him. He grabbed it with both hands as Layila bent down and placed her wrists on the ground. With one fell swoop, the blade descended on the chain between her wrists; by the mercy of the gods, the chain broke free.

She quickly searched for Nimi, but he was far ahead. She couldn't risk calling him.

"Go!" hissed the man. "Go quickly!"

She did not look back. She scrambled quickly out of sight, into the bushes.

More and more blasts echoed behind her whilst the pale-faces and burnt-faces continued firing at each other relentlessly up in front.

As Layila scrambled through the vegetation, tearing at bushes and vines, her foot got caught. After seconds of quiet, she heard in the distance, "Run! Layila, RUN!" It was Nimi, shouting in native tongue.

She did not look back. She sensed that her only chance of survival was to run for her life. She couldn't look back, for the sight would be too painful. She felt guilty abandoning the boys who had saved her life, yet somehow she was grateful for their sacrifice. And, deep in her heart, she knew Nimi was right: She had to find Kisúndi and reach Father Ombe and the hunters before it was too late. Her fierce determination was an inspiration from the boys who had saved her life in the face of horrific adversity. *I will see you again*, she thought.

She scrambled as fast as her feet would carry her, panting breathlessly but not daring to stop. It was her chance, and she'd taken it like a frightened antelope escaping an attacking leopard.

In her haste, she fell for a second time. Footsteps were pounding behind her. She scrambled to her feet and was running again. Her legs stretched over bushes. She jumped over vines, too terrified to look back. Fallen branches and buttress roots lay in her way, but she jumped over them, determined she would not be slowed by the dense ferns and foliage.

Wildlife—rabbits, squirrels, and countless birds—frightened by her scrambling, scurried from the path she drove through the forest, leaving a disarray of vegetation in her wake like waves in the sea. *Danger!* Layila was in full flight, focused only on the sound of her footsteps, one after the other, carrying her further away from the death and chaos. Her heart raced, and she fought to breathe air into her lungs, inhaling and exhaling deeply, never stopping. Before her, images of Boali, Inga, and Kimoko flashed through her mind. She saw her mother's face clearly, Yambi and Mpende in front of her, as if beckoning her to safety.

Tears stung at the back of her eyes. The wind whistled in her ears. Her strength to run was simple. It was a primal instinct to flee in the face of danger.

Layila finally flung herself to the ground, gasping and wheezing for air, her lungs hurting, her heart pounding, until she could run no further. She hauled her tired body under a bush and rolled herself into a tiny ball, like a frightened bird.

*Mvumbi ba bibulu.*

She had to look back and make sure she had lost her pursuer. She peered from under the bush and saw no one. She waited and waited, for she could not risk being seen. She curled tighter, holding herself, comforting herself in her own embrace. She listened to the birds and wildlife all around her. She felt at one with nature, unnoticed by even the smallest creature. She was careful not to move until the wildlife resumed, loud and clear, across the forest.

Finally, she dared to edge from under the bush. She crouched, too frightened to stand for fear of being seen by anyone or anything. She listened as her father hunters would have, for the tiniest foreign sound that would give rise to danger. This time, she thought determinedly, *I will not walk out in the open. I will not speak nor even whisper. I will take one careful step at a time and will be constantly vigilant, like the creatures of the forest.* She dared only to breathe and creep slowly through the vegetation.

*Kisúndi!* Her heart had sensed it now.

As she took each careful step, avoiding the holes and the roots at her feet, Layila noticed the landscape changing. The forest grew thinner, and she could see vast hills growing nearer and nearer in the distance. Longing for home, she began to jog, spurred on by the sight, yet still vigilant.

The rainforest slowly opened up to reveal an array of new shrubbery and species of vegetation. She slowed to a walk again, too weak to run, carefully stepping over every root or vine underneath her, at the same time gazing forward. The canopy of trees above her head was loosening, revealing more and more of the cloudless skies. Layila continued to walk cautiously, almost limping sometimes, concentrating on moving forward and ignoring the pain searing through her bare feet.

Whilst she walked, many thoughts were flashing through her mind, including the burnt-face man who had been staring at her in the line of captives. She remembered that he, amongst others, had fled into the forest whilst being shot at by the pale-faces. She tried to put his face out of her mind, but it troubled her and kept flashing back into her consciousness. She was terrorized by the thought that he and other burnt-faces could be somewhere in the forest nearby.

She was quickly distracted, though, when she reached an area in the forest where the mist had thickened. She hastily covered her nose and mouth with her clothing, at all costs avoiding breathing in the ghastly mist. With her right hand over her nose, she was forced to move with care, lest she should lose her balance. She peered through the dense mist. She heard the roars of lions in the distance, so she trekked away. Further on, she spotted a dead young female leopard, its razor-sharp teeth clamped on a dead antelope. Further on, a zebra was trapped in the mist; it was alive, yet gasping as its lungs suffocated.

Layila was terrified. She knew the mist had taken lives. Her eyes ached from peering, trying to find her way through and taking care with every step. To her right was a large green reptile, fighting to breathe away from the mist. The beast raised its head but failed each time and again breathed in the mist, finally collapsing from exhaustion to a sure death.

Layila's eyes widened as she encountered so many carcasses of wild animals. They were still, white-cloaked, and scattered across the forest floor. It was a deathly trail. She was relieved when she eventually reached open space where the white mist lifted.

Layila at last lowered her hand. She sucked in a mass of fresh air that felt good and soothed her lungs. She rested for a moment. The humidity of the forest exhausted her, and alone, with no one to encourage her, she was overcome with fatigue.

She closed her eyes and almost immediately became aware of footsteps behind her. She was instantly alert. She scanned the forest surrounding her. From within the mist behind her, a tall, dark shadow emerged.

*Nkuyu. Evil spirits.*

The shadow was upon her., and she screamed.

*Burnt-face!*

He grabbed her roughly, growling and grunting. She tried to pull away, but he was too strong. He was pushing her hard. She fell to the ground, rolling and slipping over the wet grass and until suddenly, she was falling and it was dark. She dropped to the floor awkwardly, landing on her shoulder. It hurt. Her hand instinctively reached to touch the place where it hurt. All was dark. She was trembling. She looked up and saw light. She realised she had fallen into a deep hole, some sort of trap. There were bones and corpses scattered all over the ground.

*The abode of the dead! I have fallen into the abode of the dead.* These thoughts and others whirled through her mind. She was not thinking clearly. She couldn't. She could hardly breathe.

Layila dared to look up again. A dark shadow faced her. She screamed, but it was futile. She saw that the burnt-face was the same man who'd been watching her on the trek. She remembered him distinctly. She remembered the odour; the *kūfiyyah*—a headdress, in white, red, and dark blue; she remembered him watching her with glazed-over, hungry eyes. He was the ugliest man she had ever seen. His face sagged, and he had a broad, long, fat nose and a greasy black beard. His face was lined with the scars of war.

He roared at Layila in a language foreign to her ears. His eyes were bulging and bloodshot. He spoke fast and breathed deep. He was on his knees now, reaching into the hole. He grabbed Layila's arm and dragged her roughly out of the hole, so her legs scraped against the rough earth that lined it.

Layila cried, begging him to let go of her. He slapped her face when she screamed once more. She struggled to free herself, clawing at roots, scanning the area for any way to escape. She fought him, digging her fingernails into his flesh with all her might. Then she hit him and kicked him wildly, but he was too strong.

"Give it to me," he roared in Arabic, slapping Layila hard across the face. The force of the slap made her face smart with pain, and she felt blood drip from her nose. Before she could draw breath, he pulled her ebony legs apart and ripped her loincloth, forcing her naked. He stared at her with the lusty eyes of a brute, craving to claim her virginity. She begged him to stop, but her pleas fell on deaf ears, drowned in his lust. He leaned his full body over her, pinning one of her arms to the floor, grabbing his enormous, blood-red turban with the other. The turban draped with the tail over his left shoulder. Then he rubbed his huge, filthy, rough hand over her tiny breast, which had barely budded.

Layila fought wildly, scratching his face, digging her nails into his cheek this time, begging him to stop.

He roared, "Give it to me!" Sweat coated his face, the hairs on his broad chest bursting forth from his ripped shirt.

"I beg you, don't," pleaded Layila, her lips quivering. Layila was so weak. She was only eleven. She thought fleetingly of submitting, but she just couldn't. She would not let the brute hurt her. She summoned all her strength again and fought harder.

As she struggled, the man pulled out his dagger. He raised it into the air.

Layila forced her body away from him and rolled over onto her side. Her hand searched desperately over the ground for anything she might use to hit him. Her hand found something hard—a rock. She clamped her fingers around it and hurled the rock into the man's face.

Stunned, he fell backwards, releasing his grip on her other arm. Her eyes fixed on his dagger. She grabbed it, drew back her hand, and forced the blade into his stomach.

The blade was sharp, and it pierced his skin, sliding through his flesh like a knife through papaya fruit. The blood spewed from his ribs. He roared with pain, rolling over on the ground beside her. He gasped for breath, inhaling sharply, until his head fell to one side and he was still.

Layila lay shaking and trembling, staring at the man. *Is he dead?* She couldn't be sure. Once more, she plunged the dagger with both hands into his ribs.

His eyelids closed with his last gasp of breath.

Layila pushed the man's body away from her and climbed shakily to her feet. She needed to run more than she had ever needed to run, as far away from that brute of a man as she could possibly go. She grabbed what was left of her clothes, turned, and fled.

Further down the hill, she could hear water trickling over pebbles. She ran to the water's edge and sank her whole body in. She let the water run over her cut and bruised body. The water was cool, and she splashed her body and face with it. She was so tired she could barely lift herself out of the stream. She sat on the grass and let her body dry in the warm, humid air. Then she wrapped her clothes around her body. She took a vine and tied it around her waist to secure the already ripped cloth.

*I must reach Father Ombe. I must find the hunters, or my mother will surely die.*

Her feet began her march, despite the pain, turning into a jog that took her further south in the direction of the sunshine. It was a slow, painful jog, but the thought of her mother, Father Ombe, and her family, drove her on. She would not give up. Her determination drove her steadily forward.

As the sunlight grew brighter and the trees grew thinner, she saw something on the horizon. "Okoume!" She gasped, dashing across a clearing to stop in front of Okoume, the kapok tree, 115 feet high and 4 feet wide. She stared up at the tree in awe, yet not as stunned as when her father had first shown her the majestic kapok tree that had stood before them at 230 feet high and 10 feet wide—a picturesque view she would forever cherish.

She ran her hands gently over the bark of the huge trunk, stroking the sacred, tall, black hardwood. At last, she had made the landmark. She heaved a sigh of relief, knowing she was nearly home.

Layila could feel a presence: spirits, her ancestors. Security and confidence filled her. Strengthened by the magic in the air, the Okoume, tall and powerful, gave her strength.

She touched the tree with both hands, feeling the carvings in the wood. She reflected on the many stories of tribes and considered their tiny figures of gods. The inscriptions were clear and intense. Layila reflected, thoughts spiralling through her mind of the history of her people. She wept, realising she had found the way out of the forbidden forest. She remembered once more that the way to *Kisúndi* was found by following the shadow of the Okoume when the sun was at its highest, just above the sculptures. She smiled broadly when she looked up at the skies: The sun had reached its highest. She hurried, following the shadow.

And there, lo and behold, an opening to low grass gave way to *Kisúndi*. She fell to her knees and kissed the ground beneath, thanking the *Bakulu*. Her mother had been right: *Bakulu will always protect me.*

She rose and remembered her conversation with Inga, how he had told her a secret as they'd journeyed to *Kisúndi*—the proper way to track Father Ombe and the hunters. Having followed that advice, Layila had made it safely to the sought-after territory. She recognised that Inga had known the way all along.

And so she went...

# CHAPTER XI

# HOPE

High up in altitude, with its blood spilling at every wing flap, the great Congo serpent eagle desperately took large strokes in a bid to rid itself of the bronze, metallic arrow that pierced its right side. To the shaft of the arrow past the fletching was attached a thin rope. A moment earlier, several feet high, the Congo serpent eagle had been flying above the forest dome when the arrow struck it, but now its strength was draining out with blood flowing along the joined rope. Still, it found strength to stay up, but it could not fly away as a result of the fettering rope. The sudden attack on the bird was launched from underneath it at a forest clearing hardly obstructed by trees.

At that time of the year, the majestic bird was flying to southern counties, but an ostensibly dead corpse on the ground had caught its attention and seemed like a good meal before it could carry on with its journey. Now it was caught in midair, slowly dying and battering against opposing winds. Panicked in its measures, it began steering down and bracing itself high in last hope to free itself, but as it stretched higher, tension on the rope caused the arrowhead to sink deeper into its flesh, forcing the hawk to squeak and flap its flanks awkwardly, almost reeling itself around the rope. The choke was not bearable, thus it rolled back up. Its beak now wide open, its expression in pain and seeking freedom, it began losing feathers from excessive flapping. In a second attempt, it flew down in order to release the rope tension, then attempted to soar high with great speed.

Suddenly, a second arrow, this one ropeless, pierced through its body, perforating a bloodied red hole among the sets of its natural chesty black spots. It emitted a mournful and loud vocal scream and instantly died. The round-tailed mature bird spiralled down at a moderate speed and with its wingspan about a meter in length, resembling a primitive kite. It thudded through the tree branches, but at that open area of the forest with hardly any trees around, the bird landed on the top of a short hill and rolled down it.

Layila had seen all of this happening from her hiding place in a distance. Since trailing into that new territory and running for a time through open land, she finally came upon a clearing where she felt an urge to hide. Layila gazed at vast lowlands. She was extremely exhausted. She loved the low grass of the land and the traversable prairies. There was nowhere to hide: no caves, no crevasses, no ravines, but there was a hill.

Layila stopped and wondered. All in that environment had a reddish hue about it. Rocks and shrubs and a large adorning tree covered a part of the red-clayed incline, and she thought it wise to perhaps rest under it. A wide expanse of short, red-petal flowers covered the entire ground, clear to the horizon line. The flowers appeared as if they were emitting a red light.

She loved the place and decided to settle down. She sat under the tree for hours, occasionally recalling the last day's events and occasionally distracted by ants or bees at their usual activities on the floral banks. At times, an uncertain and emotional fear would attack her, but the countryside was beautiful and idyllic enough to help her forgo that fear. She panned her view from left to right. The usual cricketing noise of invisible insects could be heard here and there, the sun was cracking hot at its natural height, a terrain elevation to the far right was leading to a steep cliff, and all sorts of erosion landforms butted geologically upon vast expanses of rock columns. All was calm and brightly red and nothing moved except an excusable breeze.

From its height up in the sky, Layila, unaware, had appeared to the serpent eagle to be a dead corpse. It flew around the hill, circling a few times to catch a better view, examining its prey. It descended a few meters below, low enough to be struck by an arrow.

The bird's screams startled the young girl and, shocked, with her eyes wide open, she crawled out from under the shadowing tree. She could see the bird straining and struggling at the end of the rope, impaled by the arrows. She immediately recognised it as a hunting technique, for she'd seen it before, back home.

"Father Ombe?" she whispered quietly, muttering to herself. She then looked in the direction of the rope, but it faded at the horizon in the blazing light of the sun. When the second arrow flew and stabbed the raptor, her hopes were raised higher, but she waited. She knew the bird was going to come down, and all she had to do was go to it.

The spiralling bird came down almost in vertical drop a short distance from her hideout. All the more gladly, she heaved herself up, dusted the remnant of grassy bits off her tattered clothing, and with great excitement, ran to the landing site. Although dead, its claws seemed intimidating, and its large, sepia-brown thighs appeared intact from the crash. She gazed at the glorious bird. It was majestic. She wondered how many snakes, lizards, and rodents it had killed in its life. Now, it lay there lifeless. She looked at the rope. She didn't particularly recognise the threading, and it had blood coating all over. She waited.

A moment later, tension grew on the rope, and the bird began to be hauled. She had to think quickly before the bird was completely pulled over on open prairie. The rule from her home village in such a situation was that if she pulled before there was full tension on the rope, that would mean to the hunter that a rival huntsman was robbing the bounty, so more arrows would ensue to kill the thief. However, if she pulled *after* the tension had been first achieved, it would mean the bounty was ready and prepared for collection, but this latter rule was not de facto and could still mean intrusion. Therefore, her decision was a tricky dilemma, as she had no assurance whatsoever that Father Ombe was at the other end of the rope. She waited a bit longer.

Just before the bird was raised at the top of the hill, she took the risky gamble and pulled on the rope a number of times. Then she released her grip and waited. Auspiciously, no arrows spiralled wildly in her direction, which meant the hunters on the other end of the rope did not want her dead, even though this signal would be unexpected for them, considering that no one but her was there to prepare the bounty.

In glittering hope, she then began to follow the rope up the hill. She smiled to herself for a while, and the gentle, breezy wind felt like a reassuring caress on her face. The long, willowy grass was folding at her feet and felt like a fresh furry mat. She recalled the village chief had one made by his numerous concubines.

At top of hill, she looked in the rope direction. The sun was blazing into her eyes once again, but suddenly, at the other end of the rope, she saw a soldier avidly running in her direction, grasping the rope as if to make sure he would not lose it. More soldiers trailed behind him. When he had noticed and glanced at her, he stopped. He was still far away, but Layila recognised the soldier's uniform and smartly began to back down the hill in a panic, screaming her heart out. The soldier abandoned the rope and restarted his run, much faster and followed by others.

He barked, but Layila couldn't hear him, as her own cries and tears drowned her once more with anguish. This ordeal would never end. She was losing ground, falling down, and quickly getting up again. She ran past the hideout in sobs and was headed to the cliff. She thought she could jump off to a river, but there wasn't any. *Maybe I could pick up some stones and fight. If only I'd have taken the bloodied arrow to defend myself! The erosions! Not far now…not far now!*

She was crying in despair.

Before she could get away, the large man dived onto her, grabbing and rolling with her onto red soil. Her eyes instinctively closed. She was screaming to her gods and begging for mercy. Her screams were so loud—a plea to be free.

"Layila! Layila, open your eyes. It's me, Father Ombe."

In response, Layila stopped, turned, and looked. Her eyes opened wide, and sunrays travelled through her rolling tears, reflecting back the brown colour of her skin. She quickly scanned the interlocutor. She recognised him, yet was shocked, bewildered at his sight, especially since he was wearing a soldier's jacket. It was covered with knife cuts, scarlet bloodstains, sweat, and dried mud.

"Father Ombe, it's you! I thought you were one of them." She fell on his chest in lament. She was laughing and crying at the same time, contemplating him like a surprise, shedding tears of happiness.

"Calm now, child. Calm down," Ombe kept reassuring.

The rest of the hunters were just behind him, running and arriving one by one. As they noticed the child in Ombe's arms, they approached and touched her, spoke some words to her, rubbed her face gently, and removed sticky debris to reveal her beautiful childish chin. They were amazed that a single child had been brought forth through the dense forest. Then, without a word, using customary sign language, they indicated to each other to form a fairly large circle around Ombe and the child. They then crouched, pushing their spear bases firmly into the ground, each looking away in different direction for any enemy approach.

At the centre of this manmade, protective barrier, Ombe continued and explained to Layila that she was many days from home. She in turn explained all that had happened to her and her friends and many others.

Ombe then explained that they had not seen such people before either, but they had ravaged a lost faction of these soldiers with traps and ambushed them and had used their uniforms to camouflage themselves when necessary. They had then decided to immediately abandon the hunt, leave the territory, and journey back home, considering that such evil was spreading to all villages like cavernous disease.

Ombe then expressed his bewilderment at her survival, to which Layila responded that the spirit of the *Bakulu* must have been with her, but others were not as fortunate. She talked about her capture, her escape, her fears, and the dead.

"Do you know if anything happened to Mpende? And the hunters' families? Are they dead or alive?"

Layila illustrated that many were taken, killed, and left for dead on roads or littering the forest beds. Unreservedly, she related to him what she knew of Mpende and little about the rest.

Ombe paused and remained silent for a while, thinking about his pregnant wife. He embraced Layila as though she were his own, realising they might not make it in time to save their families. With Layila in their care, their home return would be slowed.

"You are strong. The spirits are with you, and they have allowed you to survive," said Ombe, rubbing red soil from her face. He then stood up, carrying the child firmly in his hands. For a long stretch, he gazed down the outline of the valley, the short mountain range peaks, and settled his gape at some distant red trees. Ombe then mentioned to the group. "Brothers, Layila needs rest. I propose to cast lots and see that two of us stay with her and set camp here. It is a nice place. Though the place is red, blood has not been spilled here. The rest of us will carry on the journey to rescue our people."

The proposal pleased them all. They then cast lots, and it fell on Munkanda and Yana, two valiant hunters, to stay back with the young girl.

The group then approached the two and shook their hands with honour, saying, "Protect her, protect her." They then thanked Bakulu and decided to call the place *Mbata Mbengi*, 'the hill of red trees.' That way, they knew where they could meet again, should spirits and providence allow their return.

A few hours later, before leaving, the men had built up a small wooden hut with basic necessities and aided Layila to sleep in after she had eaten stew with some of the bounty meat they had caught earlier.

They spoke about strategies, and then Ombe and the group made their last farewell to Yana and Munkanda.

Just then Yana, the older of the two, said, "Ombe, wait."

Yana had large sections of black-and-white-patched beard. He excelled in archery. He was hugely muscled and stout. He had once defeated an entire clan of about 500 warriors at the cultural seasonal village contest, but it was said that he lost the contest when the last opponent, a female maid, slapped him on his face for accidently tumbling over a cooking pot during the bout. She later became his wife.

While the men were busy building the hut, he had cut open the eagle and smoked it. Once it was all dried, he severed it at the neck, then cleaned the head in embalming liquid. The bird's eyes looked alive again. He then knitted a short lace through the beak from side to side and wrapped it firmly around Ombe's right bicep, near the shoulder, and told him, "See like the serpent eagle, but watch that your neck be not severed."

"*Dodokolo táta*," replied Ombe in thanking words. He then turned and addressed the rest of the group. "Men, before she went to sleep, Layila pointed in the direction away from the Congo River. They must be taking them to the river mouth. We will take shortcuts. Their convoys cannot go everywhere. Gear up."

In one motion, the men set out. They ran quickly. The bottom of their feet were like padded elephant feet: They felt nothing when they stepped on stones and broken spiked branches. They ran fast, like lions on a hunt. They tracked, they smelled, they moved, and they tracked again. Knowing as a group that they were not the hunted, they allowed themselves to rest during the night. They took turns to guard and were accommodated for it.

Two days later, they had travelled up to the highest elevation point of the jungle. Looking out to sea, Loanga exclaimed, "There!" He was pointing to a set of caravans of slaves in chains, just under half an hour journey away.

"We must cut through the gorge to get there much quicker," said Ombe.

The gorge rose approximately 120 feet in height and was about 8 miles in length. It had sharp rock cliffs, surrounded by layers of greenery, its soil was dark and grey, and the plunging cliffs on both sides of the gorge had marble-white walls.

"Cut some lianas off those trees. We will use them to swing over the higher ridges," said Ombe.

They then returned to a lower elevation point through the jungle, collecting best lianas on their way. They hurried through some rocky natural canals, which led them to the base of the gorge. It stood high and imposing. The black deposits on its surfaces had a staining effect, causing the men to leave imprints on them. In a way, it was helpful, as they somewhat served as a guide to the followers. Each of the men carried two of the ropes. They tied each liana end in a loop and cast them to hook onto selected solid rock extrusions.

Ombe went first, swinging to the end of his arc and landing high on a convenient platform. Then he swung his second one and moved on at the same level. He then waited for the next hunter to pass by, giving a little support here and there.

They all went through and by a good distance, occasionally needing to climb up or down looking for quasi-comfortable supportive platforms, sometimes they ran again at the very top of the gorge when the surface permitted it, jumping affordable obstacles, but across clusters and piles of racking rocks, the swing cycle restarted with Ombe. They had developed the mechanical journeying to resemble that of the noble orangutan, so they trailed the caravan until they were finally upon them.

# CHAPTER XII

# PRESAGE

*London, United Kingdom*
*Saint Bartholomew's Hospital*
*December 18, 1938*

A gentle knock sounded at the door. The hospital physiologist, an eminent Dr. Samuel Cones, walked in, accompanied by his assistant, and greeted us dearly well.

"G'day, Doctor," said Elizabeth. She then directed a smile to the assistant, whose clinical hat made her look like a young medical graduate. She was holding a small, strong, oak wooden stool, which the eminent doctor used on occasion to allow his patients to rest their legs.

"How are you today, Miss Dawson?" he kindly asked.

Before I could answer, Elizabeth eagerly and compassionately intervened. "Well, Miss Dawson has been very responsive today, sir. Her coughing is still congested, however. I cannot bear to imagine the pain her lungs must be going through. I so wish Susan would get well soon."

"Looking at her clipboard, my dear Elizabeth, I can see that his eminent, Dr. Redgrave, has prescribed some antibiotics for her. I should certainly trust that they will work in her favour," explained Dr. Samuel. He then continued, "I, rather, am here, as you know, to run awareness checks and perform physiotherapy on her."

"Would it been seen as an obstruction if Elizabeth were to stay in the room?" asked Susan.

"Not at all, miss—not even under my mother's intent," he replied. He then added and asked Susan, "I can see she is reading a book. Does it inspire to any belligerent article?"

Yet again, Elizabeth immediately replied, "Not at all, sir. Nothing that your eminent doctor would find interesting. Books are not always about war." She clearly said it to avoid sharing it with him, in case his intellectual mind might spur a fancy and corrupt me to lend it to him.

He looked at her as if insulted. "Fair enough. Susan. I need you to be aware at all times through my tests. We will get started right away," concluded the doctor, who then went on to indicate to his assistant to circle 'round the bed and leave the stool by the side.

As they continued with their duty, Elizabeth found comfort in her seat again and went on reading. She silently repeated the first word that she saw on the following page, written in old Baskerville traits; it read, "Vita."

# CHAPTER XIII

# VITA

The hunters were experienced in the ways of hunting, and they knew the Congo's terra firma like the back of their hands. Hence, tracking the white men's fleet had been child's play. At the highest point of the Katabangu gorge, they stood, numbering about thirty-eight. They had managed to pass the fleet unnoticed via the gorge riffs and posted themselves at the front, thereby cutting the way to sea. From this elevation, behind them, the large naval ships were just about visible, waiting for the return of the convoys so they could take them to far, unreachable lands; places the slaves had never been to and would never return from.

Ombe stepped up past his group's front line to the very edge of the cliff. He raised both hands, glittering in sweat and holding a cutting knife and an axe. He had long ago fashioned those items from overcooked wild boar skulls, which he ground and then mixed with dried rubber and resin oil for consistency. He looked up above into the sky, spread his legs, which were decorated in animal fur and skins, and loudly swore by the name of the only Mukulu who lived on high.

The thirty-seven responded in aggressive uproars, followed by short, coordinated war choreography. They then sharply stopped, disturbing dust, sediment, and rocks.

An alarmed Belgian soldier shouted with severely decayed teeth, spit spewing, "*Kapitein. Kapitein!* Negro warriors! There—over the gorge peaks."

The serpent convoy of marching captives and Belgian soldiers came to a halt.

"Line up immediately! Line up."

A young, firm, stern, and composed rider fiercely rode from the middle of convoy reservation area. Captain Bison Van Lanterman madly galloped to the front to get a better view of the situation.

Ombe, with an expression of anger and authority, turned to his men, some still wearing Belgian uniforms from previously defeated soldiers. He looked on both sides of his front line and said, "Your mother is in these cages. Your father is dishonoured and tied to these chains." As he spoke, he kept pointing back down to the convoy, and anger could be seen rising excessively in him. Only Belgian blood would satisfy him. He continued, "*Kimbindi* have enslaved your wives and children!" He finally turned around and in total wrath shouted, "Vita!"

The men then followed suit, resounding the same war cry, and charged down the Katabangu slopes. They knew exactly what they were up against, having been involved in a previous battle and survived. On the other hand, the soldiers had formed a single line as the hunters approached. Behind them, few soldiers were left to control the enslaved crowd. These began to get agitated, but none could find freedom.

The hunters ran with rage in their eyes, spears at the ready. They knew they had to take life; they had to slaughter the prowlers.

"Spears!" ordered Ombe as they kept running.

Those who held spears, ready to launch, dashed across the clearing. The ground was partly shaking at the weight of the stampede that was rapidly approaching.

Captain Van Lanterman reached the front line and realised what the hunters were about to do. He guided and vehemently rode his horse behind the long the line, roaring his heart out. "At my command."

The captain hastily raised his silver sword in his right arm; his eyes made contact with Ombe's, and the two great leaders faced off. Their stares burned with fire—fire for blood.

"Launch!" commanded Ombe.

"Fire!" charged Van Lanterman.

Spears spiralled into the air and slaughtered a number of soldiers. A continuous crescendo of gunshot blasts echoed, blocking the hunters' advances as they dropped like flies and died. Ombe, with a few others who had been missed in the first-fired pass, had rolled on and advanced, running like an enraged and possessed tiger. Ombe shouted with such fury, his nose flaring and his eyeballs protruded from their sockets.

"I'll handle this one," said Van Lanterman, firing away.

Ombe crumpled to the ground.

A second firing pass had resounded, and the Spirit of Darkness claimed more souls. Those in chains watch in horror as their loved ones fell at their feet.

"*Kapitein Van Lanterman!* Sir, do we check them?" inquired one of the soldiers.

"Leave them to rot," charged Van Lanterman, pointing west. "On we go."

The men resumed their crossing to the west coast of the Congo basin to surrender the captured slaves. As they passed by, some of the prisoners looked in disbelief at their fellow fallen. No sound came from them.

While looking, one of the prisoners would forever remember his name. She repeated, word by word, "*Kapitein Van Lanterman.*"

*War ends nothing.*

—Congo proverb

PART TWO:

# THE MISSION

# CHAPTER XIV

# DAWSON

*London, United Kingdom*
*Saint Bartholomew's Hospital*
*December 18, 1938*

"Miss Dawson, look!" said Elizabeth, interrupting her own reading. "Here's a set of detached pages, and they don't appear to follow the previous ones. Should I put them on the side so I may continue with the battle?"

"Wait…" All frail, I just managed to lay my hand on the pages before Elizabeth could move them over. "Wait…" I kindly repeated. The unbound pages were slightly darker and yellow-ochre in tone; they had soft, shredded tearing along their left edges and did not fit the original binding. I recognised them immediately. There were a number of them and had been inserted in that section of the book in groups. I looked at Elizabeth, then slowly wandered my eyes to the ceiling in wonder.

"What is it, Miss Dawson? Would you like me to stop reading?" asked the nurse, somewhat confused, thinking to herself that the unbound sections might contain very private information. Elizabeth stood up, tucked the book under her left shoulder, and helped me correct my bedding position.

"No, not at all," I replied as I went on coughing in the hopes of releasing congested trapped winds. I then allowed my body to sink into the large pillows on my back, once my position had been corrected. "Would you be so kind as to continuing the reading from those pages? My voyage features on them," I asked Elizabeth.

"Oh, ma'am! The hunters had bravely fought with the convoy, and I can anticipate some retaliation of some sort," said Elizabeth.

"I know, I know, but we can always come back to that later. Are you not interested in my voyage?" I cunningly asked her.

"Far from it, Miss Dawson!" replied Elizabeth. She took the hardcover tome, which, telling by its cover, might have been made in a steam-powered press. She opened it where she had left off, lifted the first pile of detached pages, and read on...

CHAPTER XV

# STRATAGEM

*Kingdom of Belgium*
*Late summer, 1880s*

pproximately twenty miles east of Tournai was the Beloeil, the moat chateau, known as the Belgian Versailles, located in Hainaut province, a region covering a vast arena; the post-industrial landscape through to the treasure chest of Tournai.

Four black horses drew a luxury private carriage, heading towards the castle. There were two gentlemen of some obvious importance seated inside the comfortable carriage, though they were hardly seen.

The drivers wore black, double-breasted Ulster coats, capes, and black hats and could be heard for long distances, chastising and commanding their horses. They were authoritarian in stance; their collars notched with a wide lapel, their clothes well fitting, down to the knees.

"*Ja. Ja. Komaan. Deuredoen,*" the voices of the chariot conductors boomed, their garments flowing behind them in the strong winds. One conductor relentlessly whipped at the horses, inducing improved velocity.

"Are we going to make it on time?" asked the driver of the coach, the one holding the rope.

"The horses are doing their best, believe me," said the other conductor. He yelled yet again at the horses, "Faster. Faster!"

The carriage travelled against the clock towards the little town of Beloeil— so fast that the lamps fastened to it rocked and flickered at the blowing wind.

Located in the very core of the city, the palace could be seen, positioned in the most picturesque of scenes, its beauty breathtaking.

At long last, the heavy chariot arrived at the main entrance of the Beloeil palace, which was guarded by four Royal Army guards, adorned in red and blue tunics.

A number of different sculptures and figurines were scattered occasionally and thoughtfully along the canals that ran through the classical gardens of Château de Beloeil. The magnificent gates comprised two incredible pillars, with two golden plaques reading, "*L'Association Internationale. Quartier Général, Bruxelles.*"

At the heavy, gold-plated gate, one of the guards approached the chariot conductors. Silently, one of the conductors handed a document to the guard.

A short while later, the soldier directed, "Open the gate."

Shortly thereafter, there was the opening of the gate, and the coach was permitted to enter the grounds of the palace. Summer breezed throughout the gardens; a vast array of flora and fauna and numerous aquatic gardens, all contained within almost 300 acres of park and meadow, home to countless birds and wildlife. In addition, a number of small, private grounds were set within the palace grounds, with ponds and lagoons. Essentially, the palace encapsulated all inherent and exquisite tableaux from the century's French classicism artists.

The coach made its way across the gardens. A flag could be seen, observed by the conductors: a blue background comprising a yellow star in the foreground. The flag waved in the breeze, a representation of enlightenment and prosperity.

The luxury carriage stopped at the main entrance of the castle. At the door, one of the conductors stepped down from the chariot, unfolded the stairs, and opened the door.

"*Messieurs*," said the stoic coachman, a dark man of about forty-six, strongly marked with smallpox scars.

"We are at the Château de Beloeil."

Two men in black military boots and formal military attire climbed out of the chariot. The taller man's blue eyes were distinctively recognisable, though his face had aged. Both men wore army uniforms.

At the door, a mulatto, freckle-faced butler welcomed them.

"*Messieurs*," said the butler. He wore a white waistcoat, complete with decoratively embellished buttons, and a tailored, single-breasted coat with large lapels. His pantaloons were ankle-length; his attire was representative of the current fashion and wealth.

"Could you please follow me?" said the butler.

The two men followed. Whilst heading to the main saloon, a long, magnificent corridor could be seen, the walls festooned with numerous paintings, all framed in gold. The images were all of spectacular beauty and royalty, including the Archduke of Austria, the German Emperor, King Leopold II, the King of Sweden, as well as acclaimed travellers and explorers, including Richard Burton and Dr. Livingstone. A number of other rooms were wealthily adorned, furnished with exquisite glasswork, Gobelin tapestries, and porcelain, all belonging to the De Ligne family. At the far end of the corridor was the door to the reception room.

The butler directed the men inside. "Kindly wait a moment please," said the butler in the waiting room. A while later the butler returned. "Messieurs," he said and allowed the two men to enter the Saloon of Ambassadors, where they admired the magnificent painting by Canaletto.

"Capitaine Bison Van Lanterman," greeted an elderly fellow with a cavalry moustache, who quickly took the captain's hands and held them in a firm shake.

"Monsieur Charleroi, bonjour," said the captain. He had a weathered face, yet youthful eyes, wielding greater confidence, and his physique represented that of a capable man.

"Sergeant Gérome Lekens," said the old man, offering Lekens a firm handshake.

"Enchanté, monsieur," greeted the sergeant.

"Gentlemen, would you care for refreshments? Tea? Coffee?" asked Sir Charleroi. "Capitaine?" said Charleroi.

"Well, a cup of tea will do me well," said the captain.

"And for you, Sergeant?" asked Charleroi.

"The same, if you please," said Sergeant Lekens.

Addressing the well-dressed black servant standing by, Sir Charleroi said, "Tea for the captain and sergeant."

"Oui, monsieur," said the servant, and he exited the room to fetch it.

"Capitaine, I would like to introduce to you my friends and colleagues," said Sir Charleroi. "My dear friend, Monsieur Antoine, the Vice President of The International Association, and also a member of Parliament in Brussels."

"Enchanté, Capitaine Bison Van Lanterman." He welcomed the man, a cup of tea in his hand. His hair was parted on the side, and he sported an imperial beard with a short moustache.

"Pleased to meet you, Monsieur Antoine," said the captain, shaking hands.

"Monsieur Louis-Maurice, Secretary of the Society, Monsieur Barbanneau who is our Treasurer and Commandant, Général Monsieur Bosco." As Sir Charleroi concluded his introductions of the Grand Central Committee, he further introduced the guests to two members. "Messieurs, this is Capitaine Bison Van Lanterman and Sergent Gérome Lekens."

Both officers nodded their heads in a gesture of greeting. Aristocracy in play, they bowed to society's most elite, with the largest gold holdings. Van Lanterman and Lekens knew this well, and they complied as any wise officers would.

"If you please, messieurs, let's all have a seat," said the president. "I would like to thank you for coming. As you probably know, Capitaine, L'Association Internationale is notably the outcome of the conference held during September of last year, chaired by His Majesty Leopold II," Sir Charleroi stated. "It is recognised that there was much muddle between the various European countries involved in the affairs of Africa, so there was the need for a conference to be held in order to address various issues concerning the exploration of the continent, the obliteration of the slave trade, and Africa's current civilisation."

Major General Bosco added, "It is understood that the main aim of society is to establish civilising stations across the country." He rose and walked to a wall that was covered by large curtains. He parted the curtains to reveal a hidden map of the Dark Continent. "As you can see, gentlemen," said the major, "our mission is to put into action a scheme for a belt of civilisatory mission across the width of Africa, from one ocean to the other." The major used a pointer to specify a position on the map. Next, he revealed a map of Central Africa. "The route adopted by Dr. Livingstone, spanning from Zanzibar, is the one the Association assembly and myself believe to be the best," he commented, "with the first of the stations to be positioned on Lake Tanganyika near Ujiji and the second to be established on Lualaba at Nyangwe.

In addition, there is the proposal that a third station be established in an area belonging to Muato-Yamvo, King of a small South Congo area. We know Lovett Cameron has had previous dealings with the man. Furthermore, we consider that feeder routes spanning north to the Nile, south to the Zambesi, and west to the Congo may be feasible."

"So, Commandant Général, if I am adding this up correctly, the main objective of such a mission is to establish commercial links and, accordingly, continue slantwise across Africa until emergence at the Nile?" queried Captain Van Lanterman.

"The main aim is not complex in the least. Africa is targeted to become a second America in regard to European power," said Sir Louis-Maurice, the secretary, sipping from a cup of coffee.

"I believe the Assembly wants Sergeant Lekens and myself to accomplish the task," said Captain Van Lanterman, keenly interested.

"Yes, Capitaine," said Sir Antoine, the vice president. "We'd like you to conduct the mission."

"If you don't mind me asking, sir, why us?" queried Sergeant Lekens, nervously shuffling his hat in his lap. "We pensioned off from military ranks long ago. We are no longer army men—"

"But businessmen," chimed in Van Lanterman.

"Precisely," said the vice president. "We need this to be done quietly. You are no longer on the army's rota, to be sure, but you are to don as army men, as you've done fittingly today at our request. There was a unanimous vote, following which you both emerged as best for the task."

"Even more so, the work done at the Congo basin a couple of years ago shows that you have valuable experience in Africa," interjected Sir Charleroi.

"In actual fact, the mission I described to you is the long-term strategy," said Major General Bosco.

Whilst the meeting was in deep conversation, a black female servant was walking through the same magnificent corridor that the captain and his sergeant had taken earlier. She carried a tray filled with insulated China teapots, miniature cups, some milk, and a set of small silver spoons. Her attention to the tray was more cautious than skilful; however, her firm walk helped her keep the garneted collection levelled and balanced.

As she entered the saloon to serve them tea, she waited at the door until Charleroi, finishing a lasting explanation, turned in her direction and greeted, "A-ha, Mpende! Gentlemen, I guess it is time for tea. *Viens nous servir.*"

Owing to *Bakulu*, Mpende had survived the deadly voyage from Port of Banana through the rough Atlantic and Celtic seas to the shores of the Kingdom of Belgium, where a peculiar language was unfamiliar to her virgin ears. She had heard such tongue widely spoken at l' Île de Gorée—one of the few course stops her hostage "slave" ship traveled, countless times, ahead of porting Antwerp in the most illicit manner.

André Peeters De Smet was a wealthy peer of the realm, with ties to the Belgian crown. He had been a slave proprietor like many nobles of his time, till recent times when the kingdom and its European allies, under political pressure, launched a series of historic discussions on the subject of declaring the wicked practice ruthless and unlawful. Nonetheless, above all, De Smet had developed an irresistible and profound lust for eye-catching Negresses. In particular, those originating from the Heart of Darkness, for he had fathered countless bastards that roamed the bleak streets of Brussels as filthy beggars. He'd been fond of deep, black-skinned—almost cerulean shade—resembling Mpende, whose fascination his eyes had settled on in the tavern of *Huis van Wouters*, whereby slaves incoming the constitutional monarch's Empire had been sold illegitimately to the highest bidder, only to be turned into justifiable servants by well-heeled landed gentries.

Unlike former concubines, De Smet had fallen deeply in love with Mpende. However, she did not return to him all the love he expected. Though unwilling to him, but for his lustful passion for her and those nightly indiscretions, he had taught her one of the lingos of the Belgians—*Français*—in the course of their private sessions. It was a language she believed would, in due course, serve her right if she were to find her way back to her beloved homeland and her dearly loved Ombe. De Smet had pledged to free her in a few short years because he cared deeply for her and wished for her true happiness.

Regrettably for her, André Peeters De Smet's fondness and chronic ingestion of fine wine, as his lust for blackamoors, claimed his life most untimely. He passed away of a failed liver a year short of fulfilling his promise. As a consequence, on account of debts owed to his colleague, Sir Charleroi, Mpende found herself servant to the new master. There, she reunited with her enslaved countrymen who had been living in custody as lawful servants.

Mpende had been well informed of the captain's arrival but had managed to conceal her anguish about him. Informing all servants about the guest list was standard protocol to ensure that they all were aware of the importance of an event. As she approached the sergeant, she moved slowly just before him and extended a plate with two cups, spoons, sugar, and milk. "*Du thé chaud, monsieur?*" she said to the sergeant. Now Mpende's face told of her anguish, and she trembled as she served.

"Oui, merci," said the sergeant, taking the cup of tea with sugar and milk.

A while later, Mpende had moved to serve Captain Van Lanterman. "Tea, sir?" asked the woman.

The captain momentarily stopped, as if impressed by the native's ability to speak two languages so well. Then he nodded positively in response to her query, took a cup of hot tea, and helped himself to some sugar and milk.

Meanwhile, Sergeant Lekens noticed Mpende's uneasiness. The woman stared dead at the captain. She began sweating, and her eyes grew wide.

Van Lanterman readied to sip his first cup, lifting it to his lips.

"Capitaine!" warned the sergeant.

Van Lanterman was known for his quick reflexes, and he swiftly chucked hot tea at Mpende. Whilst she squealed in agony and patted her face, a butcher knife collapsed to the base. One and all got flustered, and all of the gentlemen rose.

"What the devil?" reacted Sir Charleroi. "Guards!"

Notwithstanding her burning flesh, Mpende grappled the knife and swung at the captain. "I will kill you," barked the woman before the palace guards ran in and restrained her.

"Take her away from here. Quickly!" ordered Sir Charleroi.

"You killed my child!" she continued as she was ushered out.

"Assassin! Assassin!"

"I am awfully and deeply sorry for this incident, Capitaine," said Charleroi in utter disbelief, whilst extra hands neatened the mess.

"Just an accident," said the captain.

"A demon of the past?" asked Sir Antoine, a short, fat man.

"Surely," said Van Lanterman. "A face I now remember—and perhaps one I should never forget."

"I don't catch your meaning, Capitaine," said Sir Antoine.

"She was giving birth...captured amongst other slaves at a riverbank in the Congo basin. It had been a—shall we say—complicated birth. The child died. She never got to see it as she'd passed out, and though we carried her for a little while, in her coma, I expected she had died on the journey," said the captain, swabbing his uniform, sodden in tea.

"Demons never die, Capitaine. They're always haunting," guffawed Sir Antoine, along with his colleagues.

"Messieurs, can we get back to business please?" requested the president.

"By all means, Charleroi. Pardon my disruption. Carry on," said Sir Antoine.

"Very well, gentlemen. As Commandant Général Bosco alluded earlier, the station mission he described is the long-term strategy."

"The first immediate action is to organise expeditions to undergo some research projects on the Dark Continent," continued Sir Charleroi.

"What kind of research projects?" questioned Captain Van Lanterman.

"Well," said Sir Antoine, "in the Negro Congo, there will be both philanthropic and scientific initiatives comprising a number of studies, namely soil tests, weather records, and local language, in addition to the potential of establishing and accordingly navigating river-related hazards and risks so as to ensure that trade can be both induced and encouraged throughout the basin. Ultimately, of course, this will mean encouraging the native chiefs positioned along the banks of the river to cooperate."

The president further said, "We aim to implement the wide-ranging, all-encompassing penetration of the Congo, which is frankly propositioned to purchase or at least hire riverbank locations from the native chiefs with the aim of establishing trading post stand factories."

"Throughout the course of the journey, all explorers will be provided with all the necessary resources, such as trade goods, textiles, tools and foodstuffs," commented Sir Louis-Maurice.

"Furthermore," added Sir Barbanneau, "there will be an infirmary comprising modern medications and a collection of maps. The staff will have the capacity to take advantage of supplies and be able to rest and take leave if ever in danger or unwell."

"This is all intriguing, but I still cannot fathom my own role in this expedition. I am neither a scientific explorer nor an adventure traveller," responded the captain, a little uncertain.

Major General Bosco interjected, "Those involved in the voyage will not be armed but will be hand-selected and supervised by a commandant. With this in mind, Captain, we would like you to adopt the role of conducting, protecting, and ensuring the mission is completed in its entirety, to the standards of the Assembly. Essentially, you will be afforded with the role of governing several hundred soldiers, mercenaries, and engineer officers. All will be provided with weapons, military equipment, and munitions."

"What about compensation, Monsieur Charleroi? It sounds like this monumental mission will require us to spend a many few months deep in the jungle, even with a large number of officers and explorers. My concern is the funding of the mission for such a long period of time," said Sergeant Lekens.

"Realistically, this task is impossible to accomplish—even with the resources we can put into place," said the sergeant.

"Sergent Lekens, there has been much careful, meticulous planning for the past several months, all done with consideration to the experience of observers, trained engineers, and travellers. All issues have been taken into account, and all facts and details assessed and analysed," promised Sir Barbanneau.

"For instance, the Assembly will be paying 120,000 gold francs for materials alone, with stores equating to approximately 8 tons, in 2,000 different packing cases, to be distributed to Congo, including, amongst other things, clothing, munitions, portable huts, weapons, tools, tents, and even a specifically designed boat to be used for journeying across the river. Surely this demonstrates the level of our commitment and the degree of importance we assign to the mission. Importantly, success will be enjoyed by the entire Kingdom of Belgium—not only the Assembly."

"What's more," added Sir Antoine, "there is no need for you to be concerned with any funding, as a number of European countries are providing full sponsorship. There is the involvement of Austria, France, and Sweden, and furthermore, King Leopold II has also provided a somewhat substantial donation, with a notable 25,000 marks donated by the German Emperor. This should illustrate the attraction of so many to this mission."

"Hmm," said the captain, chafing his chin. "Well, it looks like the Assembly has thoroughly handled all preparation."

"So, Capitaine Van Lanterman and Sergent Lekens, you have listened to the exciting plan of this mission on the Dark Continent. Are you interested in taking the deal before we enter the final stage of this discussion?" inquired the president.

"Sir," said the captain, "with all due respect, I'd like to take a few moments away from the room to discuss this with my colleague, Officer Lekens."

"Certainly, Capitaine," said Sir Charleroi.

Van Lanterman and Lekens exited to the waiting room.

At the Salon Des Ambassadeurs, an almost tangible tension lurked amongst the members of the Assembly, with some discussions taking place. Some worried the officers would rescind the deal; others were sold on the fact that the captain would consent and take command of the mission.

Behind closed doors in the waiting room, however, Van Lanterman was seated with his legs crossed, while Sergeant Lekens paced about. "What do you think of this deal?" asked Van Lanterman. "Speak freely, Sergeant."

"His Majesty, Leopold II, has had his eye on the Congo for quite some time," said Sergeant Lekens.

"Indeed," said the captain.

"The good Lord has spared our lives plenty of times. The adventure could prove deadly again," offered Lekens. "There will be bloodshed—more village chief bribes, more demons, more deaths… Negroes will die."

"It sounds as if you care," said Van Lanterman.

"I am merely rationalising," offered Lekens.

"We're growing old, Lekens. Our ventures have all gone belly-up. Creditors and banks are at our throats, and you know that sergeant, don't you? We need this monetary lifeline, something to carry us well into our future. The only business we seem to excel in involves African affairs. There is high compensation here, Lekens. So? Are you with me on this?" asked Van Lanterman.

"Bearing in mind that King Leopold II has his dirty hands on this expedition, I guess it's a bloody good bargain of an investment," said Sergeant Lekens. They then both cachinnated and shook hands like old allies.

A while later, both men emerged from the waiting room and returned to the salon.

"It seems it took you both a good while to discuss the proposal," commented Sir Charleroi.

Captain Van Lanterman wiped the sweat from his temple. "Yes," said the captain. "Of course…and thank you for being patient."

"So? What have you decided?" asked Sir Charleroi with a nod.

"I'm pleased to inform you that we accept," said the captain. "I am willing to take command of this mission on the terms you have set forth."

A collective sigh of relief echoed from the men in the room.

"Thank you, Capitaine. I knew I could count on you. I'd like to ask you to sign this contract avowing your commitment to this mission, as well as the payment for the task," offered Sir Charleroi, beaming whilst members looked on, confident and relieved. Once the agreement was signed, Charleroi extended a large sealed envelope. "Capitaine Van Lanterman, please find in here your first payment in cash. The rest will be given to you upon full accomplishment of the task."

"Now, Capitaine, let me introduce you to Monsieur Le Renard Dechamps, who will be your second right-hand man on this mission," voiced the president. "He holds the key to the second immediate actions you will have to take once you arrive in the Congo basin. It is he who will provide you with a very important document there."

The man remained quiet, listening.

Once the president had completed the introduction, Le Renard offered his cold hand to the captain for a shake. "Pleased to meet you. I am more than happy to assist you on this journey."

The captain said nothing in return; his exchange with Le Renard was merely cold and brief. Le Renard was an odd-looking man in his mid-thirties, a grey-eyed ex-sergeant of the Belgian Army. He had a frightening façade that told he was a man of no faith, with a deep and dark past—perhaps a mercenary, a murderer, or even an assassin—but no one, not even in the Assembly, knew much about him. There was even little known about his recruitment for the mission; he was involved with the Foreign Legion, but that was the only fact everyone knew and agreed on. A lone traveller, he had been attacked, beaten, robbed, and left for dead several times in his wanderings through the North African desert. As a result, his left arm was shorter than the right, and he could no longer close the fingers of his right hand. In addition, he carried a long, distinctive scar across his face that travelled all the way to his left eye and down to his lip. Above his left eye was another noticeable scar, the result of a bullet wound. In the secretive and perilous world of the transatlantic slave trade, he had been known as 'Scarredface.'

"Captain, this evening I am organising a reception to commemorate the first year of the Assembly," said the president. "I would like to invite you to attend."

"I would be delighted, sir," responded the captain.

"I would like you to meet associates who will take part in the expedition, but for the moment, let's all have a glass of wine," said the president.

Satisfied with how things had been progressing, everyone lifted their glasses, anxious to share in a toast.

"Messieurs, let us toast to the success of the mission," Sir Charleroi exclaimed cheerfully. "Vive le Roi Leopold," he proclaimed as he clinked his glass against the captain's.

"Vive le Roi Leopold! Vive le Roi Leopold! Vive le Roi..."

That same evening, in celebration of the society's one-year anniversary in operation, a number of guests were invited to soirée at the Brussels headquarters. During the main reception, a number of the Assembly members, as well as Sir Charleroi, welcomed a number of academics, friends, travellers, scientists, and official government representatives. A number of important representatives attended from Austria-Hungary, France, Italy, Germany, and Great Britain, and hundreds more arrived en masse.

In an attempt to ensure that any suspicions concerning the presence of slave servants within the palace were circumvented, an order had been initiated by Sir Charleroi, whereby all Negro servants were to be banned from serving, with only whites to be present amongst them. This way, it was hoped that an event like that which happened to Captain Van Lanterman would be avoided.

Captain Bison Van Lanterman and Sergeant Gérome Lekens were the last of the guests to arrive at the palace. Their weapons—guns and swords—were taken from them upon entry to ensure safety in the rooms. The two men saw Sir Charleroi and moved towards him.

"Good evening, Captain and Sergeant," he greeted the expeditionists.

"Evening, Sir," replied Captain Van Lanterman.

"I am glad you are here. Let me introduce you to my wife, Chantal."

"Good evening, Capitaine," she said with a smile.

"Madame, enchanté," replied Captain Van Lanterman, ever the gentleman, bending forward to kiss her right hand.

"Chantal, this is Capitaine Van Lanterman, the man I spoke of. Capitaine, I entrust you for a moment with my dear wife. If you would kindly excuse me, Dr. Pascal Lapierre is waiting to meet Sergeant Lekens," said the president before whisking the sergeant away.

"My husband is quite fond of you," offered Madame Charleroi.

"You are too kind," replied Van Lanterman.

"Well, I only speak of what I see," she added.

"Thank you, madam," offered the captain. "I'm indeed very flattered."

"I heard you are a great officer. You've travelled into the deep forest of Africa, have you not? How is it in the jungle amongst the natives?" She wore her hair in a high fashion upon her head, adopting a catogan style, pinned low at her neck nape.

"Well, madam, the natives are not at all civilised, I'm afraid. This is partly the object of our mission," said the captain.

Beside Chantal Charleroi stood Comtesse Viviane, who took a sudden interest in their conversation. "Captain Van Lanterman, is it true the natives are wicked?"

"Comtesse, yes, indeed they are," confirmed the captain. "During the course of one mission, I was required to enter the territories of the western Nile in Niam-niam, the Azande, during which time I came across a strange people of cannibalistic nature. I had never before come across those who would willingly and happily eat the meat of other humans. I saw a number of dead bodies scattered. Some were cooked, others fully intact and awaiting their fate."

A disturbed expression flashed across the woman's face, and she curled her lip in disgust. "Captain, I think that is quite enough horror for me. I need a glass of wine," said Madame Charleroi.

"Oh no, Capitaine Van Lanterman. Don't stop. Tell us more about your adventures in the jungle," urged the comtesse. She was adorned in a Dolly

Varden dress, her bodice and skirt joining at her midriff, the material rich and bunched at the back and sides.

"I think Madam Charleroi is right, for we are here to celebrate and not to tell horror stories. Come…let us enjoy the party," said the captain.

The group moved into the main reception area, where Sergeant Lekens chatted with Dr. Pascal Lapierre.

"I understand, Doctor, that you have been selected by the Assembly to attend this expedition to Central Africa," said the sergeant.

"Yes," Dr. Lapierre confirmed. "I had taken a telegraphic message from L'Assemblée Internationale, inquiring as to whether I would be interested in partaking in a mission delving into the Congo's deep forests. Of course I accepted such a wild invitation, and was informed that Captain Van Lanterman would lead the expedition—notably a dear friend. I am delighted to go and, to be candid, I could not wait to come here and get ready to depart on this long journey," said the doctor, clearly enthused.

"Have you been to Africa before, Doctor?" asked Lekens, sipping his red wine.

"No, but I did spend some time in the Amazon jungle with the native Indians. There, I conducted intense research in tropical diseases and found ways to cure them. I believe that might be one of the reasons I was selected," said the doctor.

"Dr. Lapierre, I am forced to acknowledge that you are indeed one of the developers of the new detailed approaches to tropical disease," said Sergeant Lekens.

"I've come across a number of your publications, in addition to various articles about you, penned by others and printed in *The Daily Telegraph*. I believe your interest is essentially focused on the scientific aspects of the undertaking."

"Of course. My main role is to conduct scientific research, but I will also look after the health of the crew. I will make certain everyone is in good health—beginning tonight, with my advice that you do not drink so much," said Dr. Pascal Lapierre, and both men shared a laugh. "What about you, Sergeant? What brings you to this expedition?"

"Money," replied a tipsy Sergeant Lekens. "Beyond that, as king's men, we have the duty to serve our country and to serve His Grace King Leopold II."

Meanwhile, Captain Van Lanterman entertained guests, who crowded him. Ladies laughed, commenting on his adventurous stories.

Sir Antoine joined the captain and his giggling, flirting throng of beauties. "Capitaine, how are you doing with all these stunning ladies at your mercy?"

"What can I say? I'm head over heels," said the obliged captain.

"He is a complete gentleman, Sir Antoine," offered one lady.

"He is so passionate. May I take him home with me?" claimed another, flirting outrageously with the conversationalist.

"Oh, madam, that is too much of a compliment," replied Captain Van Lanterman, blushing faintly.

"But it's true, Captain. Is it not so, ladies?" asked Comtesse Viviane.

"Yes, yes, most certainly," said the ladies, fanning their faces with pleated paper fans.

"I am flattered," responded the captain.

"Ladies, I'm afraid I will have to take the capitaine away for a while, but I do promise to return him to you snappishly," said Sir Antoine in his slow, deliberate manner of speaking. "Excuse us, please."

"Sir Antoine, can we stay with him for a little longer? Just for a moment longer?" inquired Comtesse Viviane.

Captain Van Lanterman quickly held her right hand gently. "Patience, Madame la Comtesse, patience. I shall be back in next to no time."

The comtesse blushed all over her young, powdery face.

"Young women are all the same. They never change. They're all charming and attractive, flirting until they get what they want. Am I right, Capitaine?" offered Sir Antoine.

"Well, monsieur, I can't say more. That is precisely the way they are, I'm afraid," agreed the captain, and they both laughed.

"Sir Charleroi is to introduce you to Herr Jurgen Heinrich, a German who has agreed to contribute to the expedition. Unfortunately, he is not able to attend this festivity," said the vice president.

"However, allow me the honours to acquaint you to Mademoiselle Susan Bailey Dawson, a young British journalist," said Sir Antoine.

They moved towards Mademoiselle Dawson, who was chatting with company in the palace.

"Miss Dawson, allow me the honour of introducing you to Capitaine Bison Van Lanterman, the officer in charge of the expedition," said Sir Antoine.

"It is an honour to meet you, Capitaine," said Mademoiselle Dawson, shaking his hand and jingling her decorative bracelet.

"The pleasure is mine, mademoiselle," said the captain, who could not help but notice her beauty.

Dawson, on the other hand, had previously become aware of Van Lanterman's charm: his piercing blue eyes staring into the soul of her eyes, a stare she'd yearn from a proper man, except it was unlike her to seduce a chap. Still, she felt moved by this enormous character whom she knew so little about, despite having heard enough to remain curious about him.

As an equal in social stature, she maintained her composure as he took in her good looks. A pearly powder covered her face, creating an exquisite shine. She had the most wondrous scent: fragrant and natural. She wore flowers in her hair, which she wore in ringlets away from her face. Her attire was perfection: a satin ball dress, complete, with a velvet bow embellishing the front of her dress.

"Please excuse me. I will allow you your privacy, as other duties beckon me," said Sir Antoine, offering a departing nod as he left them alone. "Mademoiselle, Capitaine."

"So, is the captain jubilant to embark on this expedition?" asked Dawson.

"I wouldn't say *jubilant*. Frankly, the reward is of more prevalence," he answered. "And you, mademoiselle?"

"I'm a curious person, the kind who likes to know more. I like to report on the pragmatic truth, the facts. I suppose finding the truth is my real expedition. After all, I am a journalist," said Dawson.

"I see. So you want to know the real story behind the newspaper reports. Tell me something, how did you get mixed up in the expedition?" asked the captain.

"The National Committee of the United Kingdom was questioned by the Association whether or not they would be interested in participating in African affairs," commented Miss Dawson. "In consideration to their position in terms of Africa, it was felt by the British that they would actually prefer to deal with the International Association, although without direct involvement. As such, I was called upon to deal with the progress of the voyage, adopting the role of a reporter."

"Interesting. Who do you work for?" asked Captain Van Lanterman.

"*The Times*, in England," she said, fanning herself lightly with her hand. "Do you mind a walk to the outside garden? It is so warm in here. I'm fond of the breeze late at night."

"Of course not," confirmed the captain. "I believe *The Times* to be the most respected of His Majesty's newspapers. I believe the king goes to great lengths to ensure a copy each and every day."

"This is certainly true," said the young journalist. "We do take special care of His Majesty, and the journey is impossible to imagine. Look! Stunning, isn't it?" said Dawson as they stepped onto the patio in the outdoor garden.

"What?" said Van Lanterman.

"That star in the sky," replied Dawson.

"Certainly," said the captain. "Much the same shade as that of your eyes."

Dawson blushed, falling to the captain's charm. "I love the breeze coming in from the west."

"Indeed. It is calm, and the light from the lamp reflects the beauty of the garden, those flowers and wild plants," said Captain Van

Lanterman, sipping the tad bit of wine left in his glass.

"I'd like to hear your opinion," said the captain. "What's your take on the expedition? And is it worth doing?"

"It's difficult to comment," responded Dawson. "A special, dedicated African Exploration Fund was established by the British Committee under the patronage of the Prince of Wales, with much consideration to the approaches concerned with assisting The International Association initiative. I do believe that emphasises the degree of importance they have in regard to the realisation of such an expedition. However, I must state that, despite the support of so many gold francs, it is clear that a great deal more is required. Essentially, the task of opening up the Congo riverbank requires a great deal of strength."

"What makes you say that?" asked Captain Van Lanterman.

"An article," laughed Dawson. "Remember? I'm a journalist."

"Ah. That seems to have slipped my mind," Van Lanterman said, smiling.

"It was written about penetrating the Congo basin, and the critic—Stanley, whom you already know—argues that there will be a problem in opening the riverbank," said Dawson.

"How so?" said Van Lanterman. "We are well equipped."

"It is maintained by Stanley that the root of the issue is forcing the opening of the Congo gates, which can only be achieved through breaking past a number of lower falls said to hinder access to the river's middle basin," Miss Dawson commented. "Such lower falls, it has been stated by Stanley, are believed to be the most intimidating and hazardous of rapids, apparently surpassing the Nile's own cascades. Importantly, the river is known to flow through a somewhat narrow trench it has forged within the Crystal Mountains, one that is not even a quarter-mile wide, despite spanning some 200 miles long."

"I personally hold the belief that the main rationale behind such an endeavour is primarily to make profit and secondarily to maintain other interests. I do believe more than money is involved, such as gaining of additional advantages," emphasised the captain.

"I must acknowledge," added Dawson, "I have heard that the king does have a somewhat remarkable fascination with the Congo, and there have been a great many reports and gossip surrounding his objectives. I've come across a number of views regarding what Stanley had in mind, such as claiming the river."

"Is that so?" queried the captain.

"Yes. *The Daily Telegraph* received a letter, which I committed to memory," said Dawson. The beguiling, yet gifted journalist regurgitated Stanley's letter literally, citing the powerful stream becoming of political significance, European sovereignty being unhurried on executing its claim of possession, and the mighty Congo River budding into the blood vessel of trade to the Dark Continent.

"Quite impressive," said the captain.

"What is?" replied Dawson.

"Your recollection."

"So I've been told," responded Dawson with a chuckle. "I have the memory of an elephant."

"Precisely," said the captain.

The pair broke into laughter briefly.

"Why Stanley?" said Van Lanterman.

"His work fascinates me. In a sense, Stanley is quite right. There is much interest being shown by King Leopold, with England missing her opportunity." She gazed off, distracted for a moment. "Oh! Look there!" she suddenly blurted from her place on the garden chair.

"Where?" asked the captain, gazing at the garden far away.

"Look at the woodland statue near the palace," said Dawson.

"Indeed, blowing a horn in her half-dressed state, highlighting the curves of her right breast, apparently needing assistance," said Captain Van Lanterman.

"Isn't she beautiful?" said Dawson.

Van Lanterman smiled.

"I remember being told by my professor as a child that I would become a journalist or writer, which turned out to be correct. I now pen articles of life and individuals, amongst other things," stated Dawson.

Van Lanterman watched her without speaking a word. Dawson had the looks of a goddess.

"How about you, Captain? Tell me about yourself. How did you become an army officer?" asked the journalist.

"It's a long story," said Van Lanterman.

"I'm all ears," she smiled.

"To be brief," Van Lanterman continued, "I am from a troubled family. My father, who held an officer position, died in battle. It was a fierce battle.

The French had withdrawn, but alas, my father was amongst the fatalities. My mother made the decision to move our location near the Ncome River. As the years passed, I began to harbour a deep unsettlement—an anger determined to see that the death of my father was punished. That was how I came to be thrown into the Battle of the River Blood. There was much blood. I, myself, murdered countless Zulus. Then, upon being old enough, I joined the army and have ever since been completely committed to my cause."

"Would you say this is about revenge?" asked Dawson.

"What?" asked Captain Van Lanterman.

"This expedition. What is it to you, Captain? Revenge? More Negro blood? A thirst to avenge your father's death at the hands of Negroes?"

"Reasons of my own, Miss Dawson," responded the captain.

"You did not answer my question, Captain." Her eyes sparkled.

"Negro deaths are a casualty of war. Any other questions, mademoiselle?" asked Van Lanterman.

"I'm sorry, Captain. Please excuse my insolence. I surely did not intend to upset you," said Dawson. "Sometimes I'm just too inquisitive. My journalistic instinct, I suppose."

"Apology accepted. I really don't mind your questions, and I fancy your company, Miss Dawson," countered the captain.

Dawson blushed and evolved their chat into something else. "So what became of your mother after you left her and joined the army?"

"I've been travelling a lot, and I lost touch. I have not seen her since. I don't know if she is still alive, and I do not really like to talk about it."

"My apologies," said Dawson. "I fathom you were strong enough to get over it."

"Yes, but it took a while," said Van Lanterman.

"Interesting pendant you're wearing. Is that half a cross?" asked

Dawson. "Any significance?"

"Yes, a half-cross, it is," he replied, "but one of no consequence or significance. I just like to wear it to keep my neck busy."

Dawson was once more distracted. "Do you hear that?" whispered Dawson. "What is it?"

"Negroes. Every night they worship their gods," said the captain.

"How do you know?" asked Dawson, sipping her wine.

"I witnessed similar rituals in the Congo, and I—"

"Capitaine! Mademoiselle! Please join the rest of the guests in the reception room. Sir Charleroi is prepared to deliver his speech," interrupted Le Renard, emerging from the garden whilst trading a cold stare with the captain.

"More drink, Mademoiselle Dawson?" Captain Van Lanterman questioned.

"Gladly, Captain. A glass of champagne, thank you," said Dawson.

Meanwhile, somewhere near Beloeil palace, in the fenced natives' quarters, the ritual progressed. Negro men, women, and children all gathered at the ritual ceremony; the men, bare-chested with white and black paint on their dark faces, formed a dancing circle around a young fire. Nsala caressed Mpende's braids; their friendship had strengthened over the years of captivity. Weeping on the ground in a foetal position, Mpende mourned the death of her child, *Nzazi*, slain almost two decades past.

Nsala rose, her character grew stronger in judgemental maturity, and she stood near her friend, holding her shoulder, and addressed the assembly. "It is time. It is time to strike now."

She looked to the men who proceeded to play the khoko, a folkloric instrument, and beat drums made of antelope skin, whilst the women and children danced around the growing huge fire, barefoot. Their masters had gifted them with some of those instruments on days when their labour had been favourable or when they were tasked to please a casual amicable guest.

Amongst the group of dancers, Yambi was performing a rain dance. Drumming provoked excitement, making those attending the ceremony more susceptible to Yambi. A while later, she fell into a trance. A fire ceremony ensued, during which purifying flames were passed over Yambi's arms and legs. She fell on the ground, and the bare-chested men in white and black colours escorted her into a small tent.

Yambi, in her state of trance, turned to the Ndoki, the sorcerer, who had survived a deadly voyage aboard a slave ship from the Congo and only just arrived at the natives' quarters as Charleroi's freshly allotted servant, like many before him. His captives had made a blunder now known only to the natives—one that would play in their favour. Slave traders had always been careful in their captures of slaves, slaying sorcerers in the process. This time, the mistake was theirs to bear when this man carried his cargo undetected, bringing with him magical herbs that he carried in his anus, where they had not thought to search.

After almost three decades in lawful captivity, Negroes were ready to strike, and the unexpected sorcerer's arrival was perceived by all as their destiny path to freedom—their way back to their homeland, should they succeed.

"Sorcerer, I see the man!" proclaimed Yambi.

"Tell me about him. I will carve his body through this piece of wood, the product of his death. I will cast a magic curse upon him. I will also carve the nail and hair of this *muntu*, along on this wooden statue. It should be adequate to inflict hurt," said the sorcerer.

Those standing around him listened as he carried on.

"Then, one by one, we shall take them till the very last one. Once they're all dead, we will escape this cursed and cold, dark and gloomy territory, and find our way to the mouth of the ocean and capture one of their ships. Over the years, you have all become wiser to live with them on this land, but our gods will see us safely back to our beloved kingdom. Have patience, and the gods will surely see us through."

A moment later, Yambi passed out.

"She needs rest," said the sorcerer, completing the carved statue. "Nsala will take over."

The sorcerer emerged from the tent dressed in red, leaving behind Yambi and a support unit to tend to her. He placed the statue in front of the fire. A live hen had been positioned on the statue's head. The statue was then put in a sitting stance, and Nsala consulted the hair and nails of the quarry to determine how to kill him. A spell ceremony was underway; someone would soon die.

Back at the Château de Beloeil, a speech had started. Sir Charleroi stood in front of the audience and began, "Mesdames et messieurs, a civilising mission is recognised as providing justification for the presence of the European Imperialists in Africa, with the verb 'to civilise' recognised as meaning 'to improve.' Of course, the colonial effects in terms of reforming the European mould is clear," stated Charleroi.

In the meantime, the supernatural basis at the natives' quarters amounted to a significant degree of disassociation. There was much unease felt by Nsala, who heard the strangest of sounds during the chanting and dancing, the drums having an almost hypnotic effect on the participants.

"Spirits of Darkness, listen to our voices, we plead you," said Nsala. "We plead for destruction of the evil man that robs our people and plagues our lands. Oh, Spirits of Darkness, entrust me with the power to curse their crossing to our beloved kingdom. Flood the gates open to my paranormal instincts as intercessor of the living and the dead. Flood the gates open, oh Gods of Destruction."

Nsala convulsed, facing the growing fire. "Oh, Spirits of Darkness! No further suffering," pleaded Nsala. "Now we ask you, Spirits of Darkness, to fulfil your duty to your dearly loved."

Shortly thereafter, from above the statue, the black hen was taken and sacrificed, its blood subsequently smeared across the figurine, believed to hold magical influences.

At that point, Nsala found herself in a more dreamlike state; her eyes were wide, but she remained in a mystic stance, with few people succeeding in holding her. She saw the inside of Château de Beloeil.

"*Khambi…*" said the sorcerer. "Tell me, daughter…tell me…"

"I see! I see them all," said Nsala. "In a large room, hundreds of them, like a cluster of ants… Someone speaks. It's the master," said Nsala, fainting, then returning to life. Her eyes turned bloodshot as she regurgitated Sir Charleroi's speech.

"…I think, mesdames et messieurs, this expedition is important and unique. It will be remembered throughout history. I hope those involved in the journey will perform to the best of their abilities to achieve the objectives. Let us all raise our glasses to the explorers and long life to our king. Vive le Roi! Vive le Roi!" declared Charleroi, raising his glass high and toasting to the clap of his audience.

"Vive le Roi! Vive le Roi!" cheered the audience.

"Now, Nsala. Now!" said the Ndoki, imploring the spirits.

"*Fua!*" shouted Nsala. "Die!"

A glass of champagne shattered into a million tiny pieces on the floor as Sir Charleroi collapsed. His hands went around his neck as he gasped for air. Sanguine fluid surfaced from his nostrils. A crowd of shocked guests quickly ran in a panic and hovered over him. His body was strongly rolling side by side, as if fighting with himself.

Pacing through the horrified crowd, Sir Antoine rushed to Charleroi and securely and firmly immobilised him on the lustrous, glistening parquet, smearing in blood. "Breathe. Breathe," shouted Sir Antoine, baffled.

"Guards! Guards!" called out Major General Bosco.

In rapid succession, Sir Antoine unbuttoned Charleroi's shirt and performed mouth-to-mouth. "Come on, Jean. Breathe. Breathe!" yelled Sir Antoine.

"Let me through! I'm a doctor. Let me through, for heaven's sake," shrieked Dr. Lapierre as he finally came into sight from the throng.

"Please hurry," bequeathed the Major General.

Sir Antoine unwillingly moved out of the way as the doctor lobbed himself onto the inanimate body and performed resuscitation checks. His body was warm, and the smell of alcohol was no longer exhaling through his nose. Lapierre put one hand on Charleroi's hairy chest near the heart and the other along the neck, just under the ear.

"Doctor?" posed Major General Bosco.

"Bear with me a second, Major," nervously said the doctor, still examining Charleroi's upper body. Dr. Lapierre spread open Charleroi's eyes and looked at his hands, which were strongly clasped in claw fashion. He inspected his mouth, which was now vigorously closed due to the incurred pain. At once, the good doctor urged "Messieurs, Sir Charleroi is certainly not well. Quick! Have the carriage ready to transport him to Saint-Pierre, or he will die."

"This is just so awful," cried Madam Charleroi.

"It is difficult to say, but whatever the cause, your husband's heart stopped beating," added the doctor as guards rushed in.

"Are you certain your husband does not have a history of heart disease?" asked Dawson.

"Yes, I am certain. This is just…bizarre," concluded the agonised spouse of Sir Charleroi.

"Guards, hurry! To Saint-Pierre!" ordered Major General Bosco.

Guests consoled Madam Charleroi as they trailed her husband's frail body, hauled out by royal guards. Following Madam Charleroi's exchange with the doctor, Captain Van Lanterman left as well.

"Where are you going, Captain?" asked the journalist.

"The natives' quarters," said Van Lanterman in a pointed tone.

"Why?" asked the journalist.

"A hunch," the captain replied. "Sergeant Lekens, fetch a few guards."

"Aye, Captain," said the sergeant.

"I am going with you," Dawson interjected.

"No! It might be dangerous. You wait here," said the captain.

"Captain, I'm a member of this expedition and an experienced journalist, which makes this my problem—whether you like it or not," she added in a huff.

"Very well, but I don't want any of this matter to be put on the front page of your newspaper. Understood?"

Dawson nodded her acknowledgement.

The team, along with imperial guards, marched towards the natives' quarters.

"Captain, you mentioned you had a hunch. What exactly did you mean by that?" inquired Dawson.

"You remember the mantra from the natives' digs?" asked the captain.

"Sure. Chanting, beats of drums, wood burning into a fire. But they do it all the time. You said so yourself. Nothing unusual there."

"Yes, but this time, a high-ranking peer of the realm nearly dies," said Captain Van Lanterman.

At the natives' base, they rummaged around in all quarters. Guards moved in and out of every tent and wooden house, but they found nothing.

"Awkward," said the journalist. "There's no fire, no ash—not even a trace that a ritual had taken place," said Dawson. "Captain, you were there with me. You saw the small fire."

"You were not hallucinating. It is most certainly abnormal," concluded Captain Van Lanterman.

"Sir, nothing in the tents," said one of the guards. "I'll alarm the brigade."

"Hold that thought," said Van Lanterman, taking back the path they had forsaken.

"Guards, back to the palace," ordered Sergeant Lekens.

Dawson's foot made a cracking sound when her eyes gazed down. "A statue," she exclaimed as she picked it up. "Captain! Sergeant!"

Van Lanterman and his men stormed over to catch sight of what she had discovered.

"Traces of blood on it," said Dawson, holding out the statue for the captain.

"There! More traces of blood on the ground leading down that path," advised the sergeant. "Guards!"

They followed the path, and Dawson gasped at the sight of corpses.

"An execution," said the captain, scanning the grim sight before him.

At the back of the camp, on a path leading to small vegetation, children and women had been tortured and left to die. Hands and feet had been severed.

"Captain! Miss Dawson! Over here!" called the sergeant.

"Footprints—most bare, from the natives. But look at those. Boots! Not sure what happened here, but there was an execution, without question." Captain Van Lanterman examined men and women hanging from trees and checked on some of the cadavers. "This place is to be sealed, and no one is to know about it," ordered the captain. "Dawson, are we clear?"

The reporter nodded.

"Good Lord! The woman who tried to kill me," said the captain when he spotted Mpende dead, lynched. Alongside her were Nsala and Yambi, also dead. Mpende had died from a gunshot to the head, whilst Nsala and Yambi had suffered a most brutal beating and had then been hung like road kill. Nearby were the remains of Ndoki, burnt to ashes. "We are too late," said the captain.

Van Lanterman ordered the men back to the palace, where the festivity had been brought to a halt and guests had been dismissed, leaving the place empty except for close associates of the ill-stricken noble.

Charleroi's top advisor, who had also been overseeing his master's transportation to the medical establishment, upon Van Lanterman's return summoned him to a corner near the double-gate entrance door, almost whispering to his ears like one who talks to his friend, "Van, it goes without saying that the mission must go on. Whatever has happened here must not be a stumbling block to our plan."

"Understood, sir. We will leave right now for Antwerp. There are, however, more mutilated dead bodies in the slaves' quarters. They have been murdered. It's not clear to me how all this unfolded under our very eyes, but see to it that all traces of incrimination to the house be dissolved," replied Van Lanterman.

They then parted each other and during the sombre night, they travelled to Antwerp, somewhat puzzled about those last events. Once in Antwerp, they checked into a lavish hotel. At the reception desk, the team gathered to procure their room keys.

Bushed from a long day and ready to retire to his room, the captain bid goodnight to the team. "Goodnight, Miss Dawson, Dr. Lapierre, Sergeant Lekens."

"Goodnight, Captain. Sweet dreams," offered Dawson.

"Indeed, we do need rest now, Captain. Rest well, for tomorrow's big day," said the doctor.

"Certainly. Travelling to the Congo is not child's play," said Captain Van Lanterman.

"Let us hope the weather will cooperate," said Sergeant Lekens.

"Just get up early and don't be late," said the captain.

Hotel porters rallied 'round with luggage and guided Miss Dawson and Dr. Lapierre to their respective rooms.

Van Lanterman opened the door to his room and stepped inside. He dropped the keys on a chest that had been crafted from butternut wood and let himself fall onto the bed.

The echo of an impostor's voice seated in the dark spooked him. "Time for a night breather, Captain?" asked the man.

Startled, the captain jumped to his feet. "Who are you?" he demanded, reaching for the light.

Before he could switch it on, the man continued, "No need for that, Captain Van Lanterman." He lit a cigar in the shadows. "You don't know what could hurt you, and I love to sit in the dark."

Hesitantly, the captain decided against switching the light, not sure if a gun was pointed in his direction. "What do you want?" asked the captain, standing now and facing the voice.

"A great question—perhaps your best query thus far. I will be straight with you, Captain. I *will* accompany you on your voyage. I find the Dark Continent most fascinating, and I am sure you have no choice but to accept my proposition," offered the uninvited guest.

"If I refuse, what then?" asked the captain.

"We shall not make a big scuff about it," said the mysterious man in the shadows, snapping his fingers, "but if you refuse, you may be too tied up to take the trip yourself, I'm afraid."

"I'm not following. Speak plainly," said the captain.

"You will be detained for the murder of hundreds of Congo natives. It's as simple as that," said the man.

"That's a lame accusation, don't you think?" asked the captain.

"Don't be so stupid, Captain. Your sword and gun were at the scene, used to slay the natives. Whilst you schmoozed the ladies and elites at your soirée, you may have failed to consider that you were disarmed at your entry. Your sword and gun were left at the reception, were they not?" The visitor smiled, making himself comfortable by crossing his right leg.

"Nonsense!" offered the captain as he charged towards the man hidden in obscurity.

A second man emerged from the darkness and shoved a gun in the captain's neck.

"Le Renard!" said Captain Van Lanterman. "I should have realised the horrid stench of the dead belonged to you."

"Captain, you and I both are of the same make," offered Le Renard.

"Nonsense! You are a man of such lower character. What was it then? The contract from the Assembly was unsatisfactory, so you killed the natives to frame me?" said the captain.

Angrily, Le Renard pressed the tip of his gun harder and deeper into the captain's neck to intimidate him more. "There is no need to try and be clever, Captain. I do not even bother to clean mud off my boots. I'd like to think the idea of framing you was utterly—shall we say—incidental?"

At these comments, the man in shadows laughed at the captain's dismay while ghastly smoke evaporated from his mouth in chokes. "You want to know what happened to Sir Charleroi, don't you?" asked the man in the shadows while flicking his cigar ashes into the ashtray on the chest.

"Why kill the natives?" asked the captain.

"I'm surprised at your sensitivity, coming from a man known to brutally murder Negro infants," said the man in the dark behind the red light illuminating the thick end of his cigar.

"If not to frame me, then why? Why them?" asked the captain.

"I understand you haven't been back to the Congo for close to a decade. You've been pushing orders behind a desk, so I'm sure you hadn't noticed—" said the man in the shadows.

"Noticed what?" interrupted Van Lanterman.

"A sorcerer made his way to Charleroi's servant roster," said Le Renard.

"A sorcerer? They're killed when captured. Besides, am I to believe some superstitious stories?" queried the captain.

"The noble nearly died, did he not?" asked the man in the shadows.

"So you murder a sorcerer and a bunch of natives? Congratulations! You've saved the imperial crown," said a sardonic Van Lanterman.

"Wrong. The murder was to get to you, as you've so eloquently put it. If not to frame you, we'd let you and your pack rot in the hands of the sorcerer's curse," said the stranger, standing and moving just before Van Lanterman.

"You see, we needed a pass onboard the ship to partake in this expedition. The German government finds it to be of high interest, an expedition that is to provide vital information about the Congo."

Reflection from the street lamp shone through the window and revealed the man, who had now edged his way near the captain.

"Baron Von Schweintzler?" the captain questioned.

"Indeed," said the baron.

"I thought you were dead," said Van Lanterman. "I was there... I saw you...Your troop fell at Maqongqe, and—"

"Sorry to disappoint you, Capitaine, but I was only slightly wounded. My physician tells me I have the lungs of a stallion and I'll live to be 120 years young—long enough to witness the entire African continent under German dominance and imperialism at the height of the century. It is correct that our troops suffered attack from tribal cannibals, their screams and squeals piercing our ears. Unfortunately, many of my men died from the venom arrows, but I managed to survive. Besides, this is all history," said Baron Von Schweintzler.

"And now?" asked Van Lanterman.

"Well, let's just say I thirst to once again explore the most impenetrable forests on Earth. And you, dear old friend, will allow me to join. On the chest, you will find the contract. I expect it to be signed, sealed, and delivered by morning. Now get some good sleep, my dear captain. You will need it for our journey," concluded Baron Von Schweintzler, laughing as he exited the room with Le Renard in tow, wildly pointing and circling his gun at him.

"I promise you, it doesn't end here," said the captain bitterly.

# CHAPTER XVI

# JOURNEY

In the morning, in his hotel room, Dr. Lapierre was displeased to read about the sudden death of Sir Charleroi in *The New York Herald*.

There were alarming stories in the press about the torture and killing of Negroes and rumours suggesting that the deaths were related. Under the heading "African Exploration," *The Times* had delivered a story relating to the departure of the group as they initiated their mission bound for the Congo basin. The article was detailed on the "Home News" page, with edits linked to His Majesty's humanitarian effort.

Many hundreds of people gathered to watch the departure of *La Caprice* at Antwerp Port, which was busy with the crewmen's families and friends and a number of merchants. Onboard the vessel was no calmer, with army engineers, observers, officers, and sailors, all in excited conversation. On the highest deck, Master Loinseach, the ship master, provided the sailors with their orders, emphasising his task of ensuring *La Caprice* made it through the perilous waters and achieved safe passage to the Congo.

Furthermore, in addition to being responsible for all the seamen onboard, the ship master was also required to work closely with the captain. At the quarterdeck were twelve cannons, with the ship's sail controlled at the main deck from the forecastle. The responsibility of stores was assigned to Sergeant Lekens. The busy ruckus of sailors and officers signalled that everyone was working hard in preparation for the voyage, and throughout the docks was the bustle associated with a ship's imminent departure: the whistles of sails, the clanging of chains, and the cracking of ropes.

A while later, Baron Von Schweintzler and Le Renard arrived at the port.

"Schweintzler?" queried Lekens. "I thought he—"

"So did I, Lekens," interrupted Van Lanterman with a thoughtful muse. "So did I."

"Give the order, and I'll have him thrown overboard," said Sergeant Lekens.

"I'd be inclined to," said Van Lanterman, "but the bastard has me by the balls."

"Pardon me, Captain?" said Lekens.

"Never mind," said Van Lanterman walking past a mob of reporters who were putting questions to Dr. Lapierre.

"Doctor, can you tell us about your views on this most important expedition?" inquired one of the journalists.

"In the position of a scientist, I hold the belief that such a venture will bring with it a number of new discoveries, in terms of cures for diseases or other things. But I also believe we will come across a number of other new diseases, things we cannot fathom as Europeans. After all, this venture is remarkable—the most profound of the century," Dr. Lapierre said, looking at the excited faces of the press.

From the hotel nearby, Susan Dawson arrived at the port by stagecoach. On her way to the dockyard, the boat's amazing and beautiful splendour caught her eyes. She began to pen notations in her journal…

*Whilst making my way to the port, I am overwhelmed by the breathtaking beauty of* The Spirit of Darkness, *the vast vessel that has, thus far, taken twenty long and perilous voyages to the Dark Continent. Regardless, the ship maintains its stature. Acknowledging this, I recognise how appealing it is to consider* La Caprice *as the final sail progression.*

*Looming ahead is an intricate but nevertheless impressive ship, comprising a vast amount of rigging providing the poles with much-needed support and ensuring the sails—notably adorned with bulky rots—are restrained. The mizzen main surpasses the entire vessel, supported by an arena of space.*

*Without question, a number of other vessels could surpass this in various ways, such as in terms of the loads it can carry. But, I stand by my opinion that no other ship could ever be* La Caprice; *she is the ultimate craft. She somehow manages to achieve a combination of speed and power alongside manoeuvrability, and weighs 300 tons, spread across 140 feet.*

*It is in mind of such thoughts that I can acknowledge the fact that my being seduced by this ship is completely rational; it is beautiful and powerful and has the potential to explore every corner of the Earth.*

*The sheer loveliness of the craft is further augmented by the wooden carved lady figurehead. Her inclination to begin her journey is apparent when considering the tidiness and order of her decks, the good order of the armature; everything in its rightful place.*

*The many suitcases and bags belonging to the crew all ready and prepared for departing. The small boats fixed on the upper gun deck, positioned on their cradles, fixed to the beams.*

*Everything is positioned and loaded, and everyone awaits the commencement of the voyage...*

At the ship's main topsail yard, a young sailor gave the final signal to Master Loinseach.

"The ship's prepared to take us to sea, with the exception that there's one missing," said Sergeant Lekens, reporting to the captain. "Your dear friend, Monsieur Heinrich, has yet to arrive—the only one missing by my count. What says the captain? Do we anchor off?"

"Give him a minute," said the captain, waving to people at the dock.

"This is out of the question. He is late, Captain. We shouldn't wait," argued Baron Von Schweintzler.

"We will wait. He'll be here," said the captain.

"Baron Von Schweintzler, Heinrich will be here," supported Dawson.

"My apologies, Lady Dawson, but we are anchoring off," countered the baron, leaving the canvas and heading towards the control cabin.

"I'm the captain! Perhaps you're forgetting this."

Sergeant Lekens restrained Baron Von Schweintzler. "I must insist you stay here, Captain's orders."

Baron Von Schweintzler lunged at the sergeant, knocking him to the deck floor.

Van Lanterman swiftly evened the score, drawing his sabre.

"Hold, Captain," commanded Le Renard, cornering him and shoving a three-barrel flintlock pistol at the nape of his neck.

Sergeant Lekens was on the ground, bleeding from his mouth, and Lapierre and Dawson congealed as the crew looked on.

"Master! Master!" shouted the young sailor from the top of the sail yard, "someone's approaching the dock! It's Heinrich, fast on his horse."

Everyone on the ship regained their position following the skirmish, disappointed at a missed opportunity to make bets on the averted squabble. The doctor and a soldier helped Sergeant Lekens up to his feet.

"You have a small cut that should be dealt with, Sergeant. Come with me to the dispensary," offered the doctor.

"I'll be all right, Doctor. Thank you for the offer," said Lekens.

"Baron, there will come a time," threatened the captain, returning his sabre to its place.

"Perhaps I should remind you of something," hinted Baron Von Schweintzler.

"Perhaps I should," said the captain. "I have many men at my disposal."

"Of course. You're the captain," said Von Schweintzler, walking away. "Le Renard, come with me."

Jurgen Heinrich joined the crew, and the young seaman gave the clear. "Master, there is not a ship in sight. The route is clear."

"Anchor off the ship, Loinseach. We're ready to sail," said the captain.

"Anchor off! Anchor off!" shouted the shipmaster.

The heavy anchor was lifted by a handful of seamen, all working the pulleys and ropes. With their combined muscle and adrenalin, the ship anchored off, slowly heading for open waters, leaving behind the safety of the port. Observers and spectators stood on waterway edges, waving the ship off; crewmembers' wives and children waving with sadness in their eyes but smiles on their lips.

Quickly, the crew grew accustomed to the habit of the daily routine for the couple of days they had been at sea. Each and every morning, the cleaning of the decks would take place, announced by the familiar cracking sound of plaque wood on decks. Sailors offloaded stacks of holystones and scrubbed the ship away. Once clean, the upper decks sparkled and shimmered, whilst the lower cabins remained damp for lack of sunlight. Lazy sailors were quarantined to wash hammocks and clothes in the much-preferred rainwater collected in buckets, for fabric washed in seawater dried very slowly. A number of other handy men cleaned the manger, where the livestock of the ship were held.

Back at the quarterdeck, Heinrich and Loinseach looked out to sea, coveting the sunshine and watching as a vast sea monster neared the surface, basking in the sunrays. Its strong, grey body would periodically emerge from the waves, swimming against the waters, feeding on the smallest of platoons positioned nearby. But in its ignorant bliss, the basking shark neared the sailors' trap, and soon it was breathing its last as it was dragged onto the ship and harpooned through its belly and body. The magnificent carcass was ripped open, its blood flowing overboard, turning the beautiful marine ocean a sickly crimson.

"What a terrifying kill," said Heinrich. "How atrocious."

"Sir Heinrich, one's got to eat or make a living," responded Loinseach coolly.

"A big kill for liver oil," said Heinrich. "Such a waste."

"A waste?" questioned Loinseach.

"Surely. We're not sailing back to Antwerp. We're sailing to the heart of Africa. Liver oil?"

"Oh, trust me," said Loinseach. "You'd be surprised how many natives you can buy with a few droplets. Anything of perceived value is a form of currency."

"Interesting, I reckon," said Heinrich, "but the way they gutted the animal... Horrendous, wouldn't you agree?"

"Surely we are the caveman's offspring. Our dying fate perhaps," said Loinseach.

"Undeniably," said Heinrich, whom Loinseach patted on the shoulder as they fell into a silence, watching the men at work.

Late in the afternoon, back in the day cabin, Loinseach navigated the ship. After their onboard cleaning duties had been completed for the day, sailors would spend their time partaking in games of chess or cards, whilst others would lounge and laze in the sunshine, sprawled across hammocks or even on the open decks.

"Doctor!" shouted a patient at the sick bay, where Dr. Lapierre consulted the infirmed. "It's been days, and I feel no better, sir. My gums remain sore, my eyes are hollow, my face is gaunt, and the pain in my muscles is worsening. What is wrong?"

"Scurvy," said Dr. Lapierre. "I don't have a handle on why it's spreading so rapidly. Soon as I find out, I'll inform the captain."

"I don't want to die," said the patient, clinging desperately to the doctor's arm.

"You'll survive. I promise," said the doctor. "For the time being, lots of lemon. You'll feel better soon."

Meanwhile in the stern, Captain Van Lanterman, the sergeant, army engineers, and observers had been engrossed in a heavy discussion on the expedition. Dawson rested on an outdoor reclining chair and writing a report to the members of the Assembly of the International Association:

*Monday, 14, Day 21*

*Dear Members of the Assembly,*

*In consideration to the deliberations in which I partook with the*

*Assembly concerning my agreement with your society relating to my own part in this voyage, which notably involved my keeping you informed of voyage-related developments, please find attached a detailed account of the journey thus far.*

*Primarily, I wish to report with sadness and regret that Sir Charleroi has apparently experienced a sudden death upon the society's first anniversary. This has surprised and saddened me greatly. Thus, I would like to communicate my most sincere condolences and best wishes to Madame Charleroi.*

*Secondly, at this point, we are three weeks into our voyage and, after much delay, are crossing the Breton coast. The journey has been somewhat treacherous, owing to the rocky coastlines and southwesterly winds. I, along with the ship crew,*

*have been waiting for a change in the winds to something more preferable, but we*
*remain positive and are all doing well. As was established before the onset of this*
*voyage, the ship has great capacity; thus, we have a great many cattle, fowl, goats,*
*and sheep, as well as swine, all stored in our manger.*

*It remains that there is a varied and nutritious diet enjoyed by all onboard* La
Caprice: *meats, porridge, wine, prunes, onions, fish, cheese, bread, figs, hazelnuts,*
*apple pips, grapes, walnuts, rye seeds, plum stones… The list goes on and we are,*
*indeed, very fortunate. It is pertinent to highlight that we are all well, although*
*it remains that*

*Monsieur Le Renard is unwell—a combination of voyage sickness and the*
*bullying ways of Shipmaster Loinseach, who is known to be a tormentor, widely*
*acknowledged by the vessel's men. There is no defence by the crew; it is rumoured*
*he cannot be bettered.*

*One interesting moment was the capture of a sixteen-foot shark, the incarceration*
*and subsequent slaughter of which was commanded by the shipmaster. The beast*
*thrashed around on deck following its capture, smashing the skylight positioned*
*above Loinseach's day cabin who, notably, markedly seemed well hidden shortly*
*after. The shark subsequently destroyed much on deck before being put out of its*
*blind panic with a harpoon.*

*This evening, I expect all will be revealed in terms of whether our shipmaster*
*relishes shark-fin soup.*

*Sincerely yours,*
*Ms. Susan Dawson.*

.

"Miss Dawson!" called out Moran, the cook, pointing to the captured
great white on the deck.

Dawson walked cautiously nearer to feel the shark, and it jerked sharply.

"Careful!" advised Moran. "It's still alive and lethal. It will attack."

"Death by beestings does not have the same emotional charge as being eaten alive by a shark. Do you see this pegleg? The work of a great white—a beast much like this one," said Moran.

"I'm sorry," said Dawson.

"I used to be a proper seaman. Now, to feed my family, I work as a cook, one of the few jobs a disabled seaman can do. This is my first trip to the Congo."

"I'm sorry," said Dawson.

"Yes? Well, so am I," said Moran, "but I hear the Congo is filled with riches—forgotten and hidden treasures that even the natives aren't aware of."

"Sounds like a fairytale, don't you think?" said Dawson.

"The only fairytale is forgetting to dream," said Moran. "You see, Miss Dawson, I have hope. I might be a poor, filthy beggar of a cook, but I hear in the Congo we have room to become kings."

"You should stop believing in stories, Moran," Dawson said, smiling.

On the forecastle, Le Renard threw up overboard. He had been sick but refused to make use of the sick bay.

"Pull it together," commanded Baron Von Schweintzler.

"I hate the ocean," said Le Renard.

"It's been three weeks," said Von Schweintzler.

"Lie down. It'll do you some good," encouraged Heinrich, enjoying his cold swim.

"Mind your manners," chastised Le Renard.

"Join me. A cold swim will relieve your angst," said Heinrich.

"In the water! In the water!" chanted laughing sailors.

"I'm not getting in that filthy water."

"I bet he can't even swim," laughed Heinrich.

"Foolish!" barked Le Renard.

"In the pool then. Show them you've got guts," challenged Baron Von Schweintzler.

A gang of seamen shoved Le Renard and hurled him into the pool, setting off a raucous cacophony from the men below, clapping in enthusiasm.

"Get me out!" shouted a drowning Le Renard.

The crowd cheered like a chorus of tickled, white-headed capuchin. Out from the stern, the captain and the crew joined in the laughter.

"Get him out. He's clean enough," laughed the captain.

"Right, Captain," said Heinrich, amused and chortling with everyone on deck. "Come on, Le Renard. I'll see you off to the deckhouse."

Captain Van Lanterman watched below. The crew dispersed as he pressed on the silver pendant around his neck and returned it inside his chemise.

At the other end of the ship, Dr. Lapierre investigated scurvy that affected the crew. Upon making his way to the hold, positioned at the bottom of the ship, Dr. Lapierre noticed the great white, hanging upside down on the fish tackle. He watched as they removed the shark's internal organs, cleaned the animal, and cut it into large shanks.

"Is shark meat on today's menu?" asked the doctor.

"Yes, sir—an exceptional meal," said one of the sailors.

"Never had it. I'd have to seriously consider it," said the doctor.

Meanwhile, the sergeant joined Loinseach at the day cabin. "How are you doing?" the sergeant queried.

"Much better," responded Loinseach, watching Dawson who, away from the crew, at the forecastle, sunbathed and listened to the sound of sea waves pounding at the ship as it ploughed through the water.

"That shark took us by surprise. I never would have imagined it could have smashed the skylight over the cabin," said the sergeant.

"Indeed. I have repaired some of the equipment, but there's more mess to clean up," said Loinseach.

"Not to worry. We're having shark-fin soup tonight, and I hope you are kind enough to share with us your opinion of the recipe," laughed the sergeant.

"Indeed. The bastard must pay for the damage," Loinseach said, returning the laugh.

"Indeed, Loinseach," said Lekens. "Indeed."

"Sergeant, see the lovely mermaid?" said Loinseach, staring at Dawson through the cabin's window. "There, at the top of the deck."

"I know what you're thinking," said Lekens. "She's beautiful."

"Indeed she is," said Loinseach. "I wonder how she feels to be in the company of so many men. Is she not frightened?"

"I've watched her carefully, I might say. She has the strength of an African lioness," said Lekens, admiring Dawson's good looks. "I'm afraid she's already caught the captain's eyes."

"We've arrived late at the gate," Loinseach said with a laugh. "I don't remember when I last saw such a beauty."

"Indeed," interrupted Captain Van Lanterman, entering the day cabin. "How are we doing, besides spying on the seductive journalist?"

Loinseach grinned.

"Still on track, Captain."

"Good to hear," replied the captain. "Hope we encounter no foul weather this time."

"Weather's great," said Loinseach. "We're making rapid headway."

"And our trajectory to the Congo?" queried Van Lanterman.

"The compass indicates south, so we're heading in the right direction. Furthermore, when one considers the position of the sun at noon, within four days at sea, we can expect to reach the Congo coast, as long as speed is maintained," stated Loinseach.

"Good," said the captain.

Meanwhile, Baron Von Schweintzler had joined Dawson and was busy behind a drawing board.

"Baron, you have been gazing at me for almost an hour," said Dawson, frozen in a French model stance.

"I am almost there," said Von Schweintzler. "I am curious though…"

"About?" said Dawson.

"Why a stunning woman like you is on such a chancy expedition."

"I could ask you the same," said Dawson.

Von Schweintzler grinned. "If I tell you, I'd have to kill you."

"Funny," responded Dawson.

"Really. Why this?" said Von Schweintzler. "You could be tanning at a private beach in Venice in the arms of a rich beau. Why the Congo, of all places?"

"I want to discover Africa, the ends of the Earth, the glamour that Africa and her tribesmen can provide—to see the people and their culture. I find it utterly exciting," said Dawson.

"Discover the Negro land? Are you kidding? Come on! You must be bluffing. The Congo? Why, it's merely a deep forest infested with cannibals, uncivilised natives, and wild animals. This is what you want to see? Take it from me, mademoiselle, you are wasting your time."

"I interviewed Dr. Livingstone once. There was such excitement in his voice when he spoke of the Congo…and a true passion for Africa," said Dawson.

"So what do you make of his sudden death?"

"Not at all surprised. It was clear to me during my interview with him that he was seriously ill. I remember servants had to help him with his every move, even holding his watch whilst he wearily turned the key. The interview was often interrupted," said Dawson. "Yet, in spite of his illness, he was so determined to return to Africa. It was his true love, his prized possession. I remember clearly what he said to me…"

"And what was that?" asked Von Schweintzler.

"He reminded me of my grandfather, with those strong and deep eyes. Very focused…and burning with such passion," said Dawson.

"Quite the man," said Von Schweintzler.

"Yes," Dawson replied quietly.

"And you said?" said Von Schweintzler.

Dawson smiled, "In the same way, Doctor, I could very well have suggested you spent your life unknown. Considering your primary objective, which was to labour amongst the Chinese, you ultimately provided great contributions in terms of great discovery."

"And at that?" asked Von Schweintzler.

"He simply laughed."

"Fascinating!" said Von Schweintzler.

"Yes. Quite the man," said Dawson.

"My dear, I have been on that Dark Continent several times. Honestly, if not for its rich abundance of free labour, I'm not sure anyone is telling the truth."

"How do you mean, Baron?" said Dawson.

"Don't play naïve with me, Miss Dawson. You know what I mean," said Von Schweintzler.

"You mean the natives make excellent servants and slaves, and they are the world's greatest discovery and money-maker?"

"Precisely!" said Von Schweintzler. "And I am sure you have seen the evidence yourself. So don't tell me about all this nonsense that the good doctor told you."

"Well, believe it or not, there's more to it than the savagery and greed."

"And that would be…?"

"Beauty, in essence. It was voiced by Livingstone that the middle third of the country gave them their opportunity, considering its white settlements in the south and its tropical belt in the north.

Essentially, this portion also delivers some of the most incredible country," Dawson commented.

"Rubbish," dismissed Von Schweintzler.

"I have been witness to various proofs of the most expansive river basins, surrounded by the most incredible vegetation, mountains, valleys, breathtaking lakes, exotic peoples," Dawson mused. "His explorations were undeniably magnificent and impressive. My own role in this venture was much decided by him and the motivation he inspired in me. As such, I strongly hold the belief that the Congo basin is the most tempting piece of Africa yet to be explored. It remains relatively unchartered, and therefore all the more enticing and vulnerable."

"And I bid you luck," said Von Schweintzler.

"You're such a pessimist, Baron," said Dawson.

"I'd settle for opportunist," responded Von Schweintzler. "It fits me well."

"Anyhow, enough for now," said Dawson. "I've been lying like a redhead lizard for over an hour. I'm sorry, Baron, but the sun has vanished," said Dawson, rising to pack her belongings. "This breeze is sure to provoke a cold."

"Come and see my *chef d'oeuvre*. Come on," said the baron, "Look at this! Isn't this magnificent?" he asked. During their conversation, the baron had been working on a palette of watercolours.

"That is the most astounding watercolour picture, depicting myself with the albatross," stated a stunned Dawson.

"Well, that is what I do in my spare time. I've always had a passion for it—wild animals in particular," the baron said proudly, "Contrary to popular belief, I'm not all evil."

"I reckon you're not, Baron," said Dawson. "I have discovered a new you."

"Indeed, mademoiselle," said Von Schweintzler.

"Well, I give you credit for this beautiful drawing. It's perfect. Words cannot describe the loveliness."

"Then say nothing," said Von Schweintzler.

"May I keep it?" said Dawson.

"By all means, my dear. A gift," said the baron.

"Thank you," said Dawson.

"Pleasure's all mine," said Von Schweintzler.

"Well, I should be off to my deckhouse to prepare myself for the evening party. I hope to see you later at the shark meal, Baron," said Dawson.

"Certainly, Miss Dawson. Goodbye," Baron Von Schweintzler said with a nod.

"One more thing, Baron," said Dawson.

"Of course. What is it?"

"My acceptance of this gift," said Dawson, "doesn't render your deeds unpunishable."

"I'm not following, Dawson."

"The death of Charleroi's black servants," said Dawson. "If the good Lord sees to it that we have a safe return to Belgium, we will have this conversation again."

"I know nothing of it," countered a bewildered Von Schweintzler.

Dawson smiled courteously and walked away.


Back at the stern, in the day cabin, Dr. Lapierre paid Van Lanterman a visit. "Captain, I'm sorry to interrupt, but we have a problem."

"What is it, Doctor?" said Van Lanterman.

"As you are aware, my diagnosis indicated some of the crewmembers suffer from strong fever and scurvy," said Dr. Lapierre.

"Yes," said the captain. "I'm aware. And we're working around the clock to make sure the men are properly cared for. Is there anything else, Doctor?" said Van Lanterman.

"The sick bay is overcrowded with patients. The disease kills slowly, but we have already lost almost twenty crewmembers," said Dr. Lapierre. "Père Raymond conducts funerals almost twice a day now, and the dead are buried at sea. If we do nothing, we will have an epidemic on our hands."

"I understand, Doctor," said the captain. "We need everyone in good health if we are to succeed."

"Precisely," said Dr. Lapierre.

"One of the lesser-enjoyed tasks of the sailor is wrapping their deceased comrades in sailcloth, with cannonballs. It is indeed the worst request to be made of a sailor," commented Dr. Lapierre. "Am I not correct, Loinseach?"

"You're on point, Doctor," said Loinseach.

"So they'd rather let the dead rot than have them properly disposed of?" said Dr. Lapierre. "This is turning into a major irritant."

"I've ordered a few men—soldiers—to take over the task," said Van Lanterman.

"Very well," said Dr. Lapierre. "That should alleviate some of the problem then."

"What else could cause the persistence of the plague?" inquired the captain.

"There are various elements to take into account, such as the overcrowding of the vessel, the dirt and moisture, the lives and works of the crew in their airless conditions. In particular, the lower decks are worse in terms of ventilation and the grotesque scent of old sweat. In addition, the barrels are lacking fresh water, and there is very little soap.

The only water remaining must be reserved for cooking, so now our men are unable to carry out basic washing of their clothes and their bodies. In actual fact, they are forced to clean their garments in urine and rinse them with the water of the sea." The doctor looked grave. "It is my hope that we make it to land soon, before it becomes too late. Billy, the purser, can tell you all about the problem with supplies." The doctor pointed to a young man to his left.

"I can't say more than what the good doctor has said. My responsibility, as you know, is the supply of food, clothing, and bedding. Since we left port, I've been keeping track of how much everyone uses and, at the moment, I can confirm that we have run out of soap. In a few weeks, if we are not careful, we will be completely empty of everything," said the purser. He continued, "I have ensured the adoption of a rations system to ensure the lasting of supplies for as great a period as possible, but I must admit I am not popular following such implementation. It is considered that I may be a thief, looking to earn my fortune through selling foods to the sailors. But it must be recognised that, without such a rationing system, supplies will last but a few days, at which point we'll all starve if we have not reached land."

"Billy, sometimes it's a necessary evil to be unpopular. The crew will have to accept this strategy for the time being," said the captain.

"Doctor, reaching land is not an immediate option, and at this rate, by the time we reach the natives' coast, half the crew will be dead. We need a solution right away."

"Is there anything we can do to prevent the disease from spreading so rapidly?" said Loinseach.

"Maybe the gun ports can be opened to allow some fresh air to filter in. Also, we need some form of disinfectant—potentially vinegar," suggested the doctor.

Loinseach responded, "I'll implement this immediately. The men are currently assigned with the full-time task of trapping starving rats, which we've come to see. They've been gnawing through barrels in search of our food. They're even attacking the hull."

"I believe fumigation may be a viable option," Captain Van Lanterman suggested.

"Vinegar and brimstone should be scattered across the hot coal buckets, which will ensure the ballast smells will be less damaging as a result of the poisonous fumes. Now, is there anything else?"

"I'd like to suggest we change the crew menu," added the doctor.

"What do you intend to accomplish by that?" queried the captain.

"At the root of scurvy is the absence of essential nutrients and vitamins. The crew needs to be fed a lot of fresh fruit," Dr. Lapierre explained. "Lemons or limes would be wonderful, and vegetables, such as sauerkraut. This will keep scurvy away."

"Very well. I assure you that your advice is taken in high regard," said the captain, "and we will do all we can."


Late evening on *La Caprice*, a fiesta ensued. The crew had something to celebrate—the catch of the great white shark. In the captain's dining cabin, the table was laid out. Van Lanterman enjoyed the luxury of a bath; his servants heated the rainwater on a portable stove since the little bit of soap left worked poorly with seawater.

The sailors positioned up on the poop deck used pulleys to retrieve casks of rum and wine from the hold. "Steady! Steady!" they shouted to one another.

On the lower deck, the party had started. Sailors and officers were busy too—dancing, drinking, gambling, and playing games. Those suffering from a number of different ailments—bronchitis, rheumatism, and yellow jack fever—were kept in the sick bay and continuously complained of the noise disturbing them from upstairs, although their grievances were not considered.

Instead, those crew who were well sang rhymes and verses, all containing some degree of insult for their officers.

Another popular way of passing the time were fistfights, which further enabled the men to partake in a spot of gambling, regardless of the fact that it was against the law. And much to the displeasure of the crew, smoking was banned to ensure a decreased risk of fire safety, and so the men were instead forced to chew on tobacco, spitting the remnants into buckets.

Later, most of the expedition-leading crew arrived in the dining room, ready to devour the evening meal. Entertainment was provided in the form of soldiers playing the flute and others singing.

Moran, the one-legged cook, made sales to the crew, selling slush to be spread across biscuits, following the stale, rancid state of the butter. The cook entered the dining room followed by two assistants carrying a large dish.

"What have you got for us today?" ranted the crew in a ruckus. Some drummed their plates with utensils, and others applauded.

Moran gazed at the crew and straightened his posture in a proud manner. "Lady and gentlemen, Officers…today's à la carte menu is shark-fin soup, a specialty of the ship," said the cook, elated to deliver the great white.

The crew whistled.

"Have you had shark before?" Dr. Lapierre addressed Captain

Van Lanterman.

"No. This will be my first, and I am very much looking forward to it. And you, Doctor?" questioned the captain, appearing distinguished in his uniform.

"I have not, Captain, but I, too, am looking forward to this culinary adventure," he responded, fiddling with his thumbs, waiting to be served.

At the other side of the table, Jurgen Heinrich wore an appalled expression, not at all looking forward to nibbling on the beast. As soon as Heinrich's plate was filled, he was overcome with nausea.

"What's the matter, Heinrich? Aren't you hungry?" joked Le Renard, much sarcasm dripping from his voice.

"Tell me something, Le Renard. Are you amused by all this?" said Heinrich, who seemed troubled and uncomfortable.

"I don't know," said Le Renard. "I'm wondering if your disgust of shark-fin soup is as amusing as my eventful ocean swim this afternoon."

"Come on, Heinrich. Chow down," said Loinseach. "Then puke at sea."

The crew broke into hysterical laughter.

Although the meal was presentable, Dawson was never convinced: She struggled to swallow even one bite whilst gazing around at her shipmates, all chewing with delight and hearty appetites. Baron Von Schweintzler, much to her surprise, requested a second helping.

"You've outdone yourself, Moran. Absolutely delicious," said Sergeant Lekens.

"Miss Dawson, at least swallow the first spoonful," beckoned the captain, returning his greasy spoon into the bowl of soup. "You will like it if you give it half a chance."

"How can you be so certain?" asked Dawson, frowning.

"You haven't a choice," said the captain, lifting up his spoonful of soup into his chops. "You'll starve to death. Go on and eat."

Dawson had her mouth full of soup. She closed her eyes with a grimace, trying to swallow. As soon as the slippery liquid slid down her throat, she stormed out to the poop deck, vomiting the shark bits out into the sea from whence the creature came.

"Come on, Dawson! It's just fish," shouted Loinseach, laughing hysterically, along with the rest of the crew.

"It's horrible," retaliated Dawson.

"Heinrich, I neglected to address that the sack of biscuits contained barge men, so they were added to the soup."

"Barge men?" laughed the scientist. "And what, may I ask, is that?"

"Well, the biscuit represents the barge, and maggots are said to be men. Essentially, everyone has been eating maggots," Le Renard laughed.

Heinrich stormed out to join Dawson at the poop deck and puked his bulging mouth into the sea.

The crew burst into laughter, some of them having to spit their soup out as they were overcome with giggles and chuckling.

"Juvenile, aren't they?" said Dawson to Heinrich, acknowledging that the farce had been amusing and effective. Even the captain had found it amusing, sharing a chortle with his crew—a night of carousing and fete.

Whilst festivity and laughter lingered aboard *La Caprice*, somewhere in the middle of the ocean, something cruised towards the ship in the far distance—something large, something big, something heading directly for the unsuspecting ship...and heading there fast.

Back on deck, Dawson checked on the scientist. "Are you okay, Heinrich?"

"Not to worry. I will be okay," groaned Heinrich.

"Take this spare handkerchief and wipe your mouth," said Dawson.

"That was the most atrocious soup I've ever had. How those men managed to eat it without a fuss, I don't know," said Heinrich, wiping the fishy spew from his mouth.

The crew had gulped down the meal and moved on to wine and rum. They enjoyed themselves, drinking, dancing, and singing like loud fools, without a care in the world.

Dawson and Heinrich, meanwhile, left the party. They walked near the lady figurehead on the far front of the ship.

"Are you feeling better now?" asked Dawson, reassuringly patting her right hand on Heinrich's back.

"Much, thank you," said Heinrich with a little cough and feeling the soft tap of Dawson on his back, which was enough to help him clear his throat.

"I love the full moon. Isn't it beautiful?" said Dawson.

"Yes, magnificent, but you know what they say," prompted Heinrich.

"What?" said Dawson.

"Bad spirits thirst at the hour of the full moon—vampires in particular. They like to fly around in search of fresh blood," said Heinrich.

"Do you believe in such fairytales?" said Dawson. She moved towards the edge of the deck.

"You mean spells and curses?" said Heinrich. He plunged his right hand in his left pocket and pulled out a smoky pipe.

"Yes," said Dawson.

"Why do you ask?" said Heinrich, retrieving tobacco, which he crammed into the pipe.

"The article written about Sir Charleroi claimed his death was inconclusive," said Dawson. "Surprisingly, the writer ventures to theorise about the prospect of a spell, possibly by the African natives Charleroi employed."

"Well, I am an open-minded person. I look at spells or curses from two perspectives," said Heinrich, clamping the pipe in his mouth.

"And those being?" said Dawson.

"First, from a religious perspective. I was raised as Roman Catholic, educated on both good and evil. As much as I hold the belief that people may be cured through spells, they can also destroy lives. And, following many years in Africa, I can say, in all certainty, that curses do, in fact, exist," stated Heinrich seriously. "Spells are carried out in a variety of ways in eastern Africa, although knowledge and understanding of such remains restricted. Essentially, curses are believed to stem from negative energy, which is a belief held as a direct result of poor understanding. However, importantly, a witchdoctor will manipulate magic so it is individual and unique to the person and their own circumstances."

"So what you're saying is that if I believe I am cursed, for example, in a sense I have premeditated a series of negative outcomes as I journey through life?" asked Dawson.

"Exactly. I was once told by an African witchdoctor that much spiritual power is contained within the continent. It can be felt the moment one's foot touches the ground. It is almost tangible," said Heinrich, taking a few drags from the smoking pipe. "I was quite terrified to learn that. She told me if someone imagines they are cursed, the first step to overcome the curse is to think otherwise," continued Heinrich.

"By that you mean one must think the opposite," said Dawson, at rest and enjoying the conversation, "that they're not cursed."

"Bingo!" said Heinrich. "One has to empower oneself. The cursed must gather all his strength in order to stand strong and firm and believe he is well. In other words, he must regain control of his own mind."

"And then?" probed Dawson.

"The secondary phase comprises the utilisation of cleansing or spiritual ointments, applied to the limbs and the face with the aim of eradicating any negative energies," highlighted Heinrich. "On the odd occasion, herbs or essences may be used. For example, sage is believed to heal and cleanse, so it is simmered in the presence of the cursed individual in a ceremony dedicated to eliminating the curse."

"Does it really work?" asked a cynical Dawson.

"To be quite frank, I have no personal experience with such a situation. And more so, from the perspective of a scientist, I must say that it is difficult to rationalise its success. Then again, having said that, I have never before been cursed myself."

"If you don't mind me asking, why are you involved in this expedition?"

"I am dedicated to my cause in my field of academic specialisation, and I have an example to set in terms of being a scientific traveller. I was one of the young men chosen as a paid volunteer to attend courses at Munich University, representing The African Association, which is concerned with endorsing the unearthing of Africa."

"And then?"

"During the course of my education, I developed an interest in Africa, which stemmed from the consideration of plant artefacts brought back from the region by German travellers. Subsequently, upon the completion of my education, I was somewhat of an expert in African studies, so I chose to become involved in The African Association of Brussels. Henceforth, I spent a great deal of time in Muslim Africa, which gave me great insight into a number of wonderful fields, like anthropology, botany, geology, history…"

Whilst Dawson and Heinrich chatted on the deck and the party continued late into the evening, the crew remained blissfully unaware of the lurking danger. A large object was heading towards *La Caprice*, now ever so slowly and delicately directing its war behind the ship.

"Both the captain and Baron Von Schweintzler hold the view that Africa is hazardous. Do you believe any such opinions?" queried Dawson, making her way towards the deck edge, closing her eyes momentarily as a warm breeze ruffled her face and danced across her cheeks.

"In complete honesty, my dear—and I can only go off my own personal experience, which involved much time exploring some of the wildest, most dangerous parts of Sudan—I found so many of the people were very good to me. My own encounters were spread over several months, covering vast expanses of area," Heinrich offered as he moved near the edge of the deck.

"You have spent much of your time in Muslim Africa. One would think that's where your heart is," observed Dawson. "So why Central Africa? The Congo basin in particular? A change of heart perhaps?"

"Not really," said Heinrich shifting his pipe away from his maw.

"Why else?" said Dawson.

"Dr. Georg August Schweinfurth," said Heinrich, hunting for something in his pouch.

"Schweinfurth?"

"Indeed. A German botanist, ethnographer, and colleague explorer—a top-ranging one, I might add—who had just come from Central Africa. He held a conference in Berlin around a time when rumours were rife about people located in the deepest jungles of Africa—the pygmies. The people were eventually confirmed by Dr. Schweinfurth, and he even purchased one from the cannibal king—in exchange for a small dog, no less. Unfortunately, however, their *proof*, as it were, did not survive the journey back."

"Tell me more," bid the prying journalist.

"Dr. Schweinfurth, during his conference in 1873, gave a speech on the fascination of his boatmen on the Nile," Heinrich responded.

"What is that?"

"His account. Here…I'll read you something," said Heinrich. He spread open an old tome, holding his pipe in his left hand, and read of Dr.

Schweinfurth's crusade and his quest for the pygmies and of many men who had personally witnessed some of the most immortal myths.

"Did he finally—" said Dawson.

"Yes," interjected Heinrich. "Staying by the palace of King Munza of the Monbuttoo, whose territory spread across the easternmost tributaries of the Uele River, Dr. Schweinfurth eventually met his first pygmy. Do you care to hear more?"

"By all means, Heinrich. Please," offered Dawson from the edge of the deck. She turned towards the sea and gazed at the stars from a distance.

"Fine then, Miss Dawson. Let me see…" Heinrich again referred to his book, frowning as the pipe's stinging smoke traversed his eyes momentarily.

He read of an account that spoke of one morning, which took Dr. Schweinfurth's attention, when he learned that one of the pygmies had been taken by surprise and was, despite much resistance, being transported to the doctor's own tent. Thus, Schweinfurth was able to verify his existence with his own eyes—living proof of a myth some 1,000 years old. The pygmy was asked to answer many questions: an intense interview, if you will. Dr. Schweinfurth established his position as a leader of a small colony.

Dawson returned to face the scientist. "He was first to confirm the existence of the pygmies?"

"Yes. He is the inspiration for my wanting to go to the Congo and for my joining this expedition. I want evidence and, where possible, I want to do what Dr. Schweinfurth failed to achieve—to bring living proof to Europe of the existence of the pygmies," said Heinrich.

A sudden breeze rolled a few more pages from the manuscript.

"I see," said Dawson with a nod.

"Essentially, Dr. Schweinfurth personally admitted that the privilege of being the first European to have met a pygmy was an honour taken by Paul du Chaillu, a French-American explorer in West Africa. He wrote his many explorations and discoveries in his book, of which I also have a copy."

"You're a roving library, Heinrich," chuckled Dawson.

"Do you mind?" said Heinrich, puffing again then turning pages and settling on one.

"Not at all," she responded with a smile.

Heinrich continued his recital, reading from Dr. Schweinfurth's Account… "….and henceforth are provided details of my journey through one of the wild forest territories spanning the country's highway, where I came across a small collection of unusual, small huts, which undoubtedly I should have passed by, considering that they could have been some type of fetish-house. I have *been previously warned of dwarf Negroes…but I have afforded such reports no credibility, and thus not considered such a reference should have been made in any former account. However, curiosity filled me upon seeing such huts… I thus commenced forward with the hope of discovering at least someone, but the jungle positioned adjacent had provided them a safe hiding place upon my arrival. The shelters almost resembled gypsy tents; low and oval-shaped. They stood no more than four feet high and were no greater in width. They were made from supple tree branches and large leaves. And they would burn fires in the middle of the floor…"*

"Fascinating!" commented Dawson. "It seems these dwarf tribes live peacefully within the jungle. So I wonder why this continent is as dangerous as people claim. Is it an exaggeration or some dark fairytale or simple speculation?"

"I'm not sure why there is so much ill speak of the Dark Continent. The picture painted by Du Chaillu is somewhat interesting and does give one the inspiration to discover the people. I, myself, cannot wait to see them, having held a fascination of the dwarf Negroes since Dr. Schweinfurth's discussion of them. And, as you can see, Du Chaillu has provided his own evidence of their existence, which has thus spurred my own interest, as he is acknowledged as the first to have ever reported anything specific on them and their lives. Now, let me read you this passage. It's really moving," said Heinrich flipping more pages.

Heinrich then described how the Ashangos appreciated the company of such strange individuals as the Obongo men—professional and well experienced in their fishing and snaring of animals. He reported on the Obongos fulfilling their own needs first and that any surplus would be exchanged with or sold to their neighbours—all which they felt they could make use of. "Without question," Heinrich continued as he narrated on the group being extremely nomadic, relocating whenever they felt the need whilst ensuring they did not venture too far, "Obongos are believed to be admiringly humane," concluded Heinrich.

"You're quite the knowledgeable man, Heinrich," said Dawson, "I'm impressed."

"Well, that's not all," said a proud Heinrich. "Furthermore, it is believed that the pygmies' first writings were approximately 1200 BC and set in stone—a notable 1,000 years before the building of Stonehenge. Furthermore, there is much history to support the presence of the pygmies for a great many years."

"Now that I think of it, I do recall a mention of pygmies from Dr. Livingstone's tales, but I wasn't aware they dated back quite so far. Surprising, I must say," said Dawson.

"Well, even more surprising is the fact that pygmies are known to have been on our planet since the beginning of all time," stated Heinrich. He finished his smoke and returned the pipe inside his pouch. "But there is more to the story. Herkhuf, an administrator of Egypt, had something of great historic significance inscribed in his waiting tomb."

"I bet you have it somewhere in that book of yours," said Dawson. "I'd love to hear what it says."

"Surely, Dawson," said Heinrich, flipping pages. "You're a fast learner. Voila! This is quite good."

"Enlighten me," said an intrigued Dawson.

Heinrich narrated on an account of a number of gifts prepared for the person of Nefrikare by Hator, the Goddess of Iman. A tale of a pygmy in the Land of the Legend, that never before had anything so valuable been brought home by one of the majesty's servants, thus bringing joy to the heart of King Nefrikare. It spoke of the majesty's desire to see the pygmy, ensuring it was brought safely to his realm.

"Truly amazing," said Dawson. "Finding the inscription on the tomb must have been one of the world's greatest discoveries."

"Absolutely, Dawson," agreed Heinrich. "However, it seems this story remains a legend, with various Egyptologists stating that there is no acknowledgement of the Land of Yam or Iman and that the reported pygmy may not have actually been a pygmy."

"Still, to me, Herkhuf and Pharaoh Pepi II would have known the difference between a pygmy and a dwarf, even if the Egyptologists did not."

"That's right," offered Heinrich.

"If you successfully deliver a live pygmy to Europe, I may be the first journalist to write on them to support your evidence. We would make a lot of money."

The two laughed.

"Well, I'm glad you find my company to be entertaining, Dawson," said Heinrich.

"I surely enjoy speaking of Africa."

Heinrich studied his book, feeling his palm over the aged pages.

"Sir Heinrich," said Dawson.

"Yes, Dawson?"

"I've been meaning to ask—"

"By all means," said Heinrich. "I'm all ears."

"What do you make of the captain?"

"You mean Van Lanterman?" said Heinrich.

"Yes," said Dawson.

"A bit of an odd ball, isn't he?" offered Heinrich.

"Quite so," said Dawson.

"You find him attractive, don't you?" said Heinrich.

"Heinrich!" Dawson blushed. "Aren't you the bold herald."

"I only choose to speak the truth, Dawson," stated Heinrich.

"Well, I reckon he's an interesting fellow," said Dawson.

Heinrich laughed loudly.

"What?" questioned Dawson.

"You avoided my question," said Heinrich.

"I'm a journalist, sir. That is what I do best—avoid questions," said Dawson as they fell into laughter.

Late at night, life onboard the ship was slowed. Following the merrymaking, the crew could no longer stay on foot to celebrate; far too many of the seamen and officers were drunk. Sailors were required, in adherence to rules, to be in their hammocks at eight o'clock—the commencement of the first watch; however, owing to the party and its unusual circumstances, they were each permitted to remain a little longer and continue on with the celebrations. For those who were not on duty, however, it was bedtime.

Dawson and Heinrich left the deck after the long tete-a-tete and groped their way down the wooden stairs, into their respective deckhouses. Dawson removed her day clothes, pulled her nightgown over her head, and got into bed.

Still queasy from the fishy meal, she quickly got out of bed after a bit. She unpacked stomach pain tablets from her small bag and filled a glass with fresh water from a bottle in a corner shower. She drank the water and swallowed the pill, retreating to bed and hoping it would dissolve quickly and calm her belly whilst she read the prized book Heinrich had passed on to her about the puzzling pygmies.

Later on, in the hours of darkness, sailors, officers, and members of the crew slept on the deck. Onboard *La Caprice*, all was quiet. A select few officers and sailors continued their watch, until the commencement of the second watch, when eight bells were rang by the timekeeper—known as the Master of the Glass—upon which the two teams exchanged.

At second watch, a shadow moved in the forecastle. Le Renard, quiet and clandestine, loomed in the dark. The forecastle was the ideal place for him to plot. "Listen carefully," he said, addressing a pigeon. "Take this message and deliver it. No one else must get it but the intended receiver, for it contains vital information." He placed the note in a small container tied to the bird's leg. "Fly! And tell them the message comes from Scarredface. This time, Van Lanterman will meet his maker before we anchor off this ship."

The pigeon flew up and away, into darkness.

On the deck, lanterns lit the ship's two compasses. The quartermaster had a clear vision of where the ship headed, so as to ensure that no other ships or rocks were in sight, with which they might have collided.

In the darkness of the expanded ocean, danger loomed and, sadly, the crew, still unaware, slept until a night watchman perceived motion at sea from the quarterdeck.

"Something's in the ocean!" pointed the watchman as he paused from a concerted card game with the quartermaster. "Over there," warned the watchman, still pointing in the direction of whatever he perceived.

"I don't see a damn thing," said the quartermaster. "You've had too much rum, methinks."

"I drank nothing. Captain's orders. I stayed off the booze," said the watchman. "I saw something."

"All right. Don't panic," said the quartermaster, peering through his night glass. "Show me."

"Right there, sir," said the watchman, pointing his index in the direction of the wave at sea.

The quartermaster moved the telescope across the horizon, glanced through it, and then gazed back at the watchman. "Nothing there," he observed nonchalantly. "You must be drunk. Are you certain?"

"Certain as my Irish blood, sir," said the sailor, widening his bright eyes. His eyebrows lifted. "This telescope brightens up the view, and I'm afraid I can't see a thing. Let's wait till tomorrow. Probably just a shark…"

"Can't be. It was large—as large as this ship, floating with bulging lights," beckoned the sailor.

"Don't be a fool," said the quartermaster. He shoved the telescope back into his box. "Are you trying to be funny?"

"No. I am certain of it, sir," said the sailor, uneasy now.

"At this time of the night, it can only be a large creature. You had an illusion. And you did drink in spite of the captain's order, didn't you?" said the quartermaster. "I am no fool. I can smell it on your breath."

"I had a little rum," admitted the sailor, "but I'm not drunk."

"Enough of this," said the quartermaster. "Back to your post." The quartermaster laughed. "A sea monster with shiny lights for eyes? Indeed!"

O'Gowan grabbed the game from the floor and made his way to the lavatories.

The watchman, with the telescope pressed against his eye, scanned the area where he had spotted the large, dark entity. *Maybe an illusion*, thought Ben, doubting himself as he moved back to his post.

Just then, a shadowy figure, veiled in the darkness of the night, snatched him and, slowly, the startled sailor saw himself hauled off the deck. Ben vanished into the water, abandoning the telescope and his hat on deck.

The deck was forsaken when O'Gowan returned, whistling and content to be Van Lanterman's most illustrious quartermaster—a job that took guts. "Ben!" called out O'Gowan when he saw Ben had deserted his post. "Ben?" he called out a second time, growing frustrated with the boy's insubordination.

There was no response but the eerie pounding waves of a darkened ocean.

"Damnable young lad. Never obeys orders," He shook his head, frustrated. "I'm going to wring his neck." He failed to notice the telescope abandoned on the deck before he walked off.

Sunday morning was a new day, and new life awaited at sea. The sun had risen above the horizon. A vast number of brown pelicans scoured for food, dipping low to the water surface, hunting out their food like well-trained fishing boats, their bills used like fishing nets. They plunged into the waters, emerging moments later with their scoop-like bills brimming with their catch. However, upon arising fruitful, they would be hounded by the common terns—the sea swallow, taking the prize of the pelicans straight from their bills, distracting the large birds with a shrill cry. Hence, pelicans fished not only for themselves, but also for those that stole from them, so their work was long and laborious.

Morning work commenced aboard *La Caprice*. At the quarterdeck, a Sunday chaplain service was on the way.

Standing atop a barrel covered with the flag of the International Association, a yellow star on a blue background, Père Raymond, known among the crew as 'Holy Ray,' conducted his divine service. Seamen and officers gathered to listen. "Reading from St. John, '*God is love.*' For those who have the Bible, we are going to read in I John 4:7-10," said Holy Ray. "*Beloved, let us love one another, for love is of God; and everyone who loves is born of God and knows God...*"

The verse was read by Holy Ray, adorned in black wool cassock, trimmed in black silk. He held on to the Bible and the holy rosary, whilst a sailor and officer continued on with their in-depth conversation.

"How can the Lord possibly love us when we kill innocent men, rape their women, and smash their children's heads against hulking trees?" asked the officer.

"Where does your faith come from?" asked the sailor.

"A battle," said the officer.

"A battle?" inquired the sailor. "Your faith comes from a battle?"

"Face to face with the enemy," said the officer. "Then there is no choice but to kill."

"Tell me," said the sailor.

"A battle, West Africa, long ago. I faced a young boy, about fifteen, a warrior from the Wabembe people. When I looked into his eyes, I hesitated to shoot. He was afraid. He was there in the bushes, sitting still between trees, holding another young boy in his arms," said the officer. "There was blood on the face of the boy he held in his arms. I could see a firearm wound in his chest. I shooed at him to run away, but he could not understand me. He must have been afraid I might kill him when he turned his back on me. He panicked and reached for a spear. I had no choice. I shot him dead in the face."

"God will forgive you," said the sailor.

"I should have saved that Negro boy. I could have saved him, let him go," said the wistful officer.

"Ask for forgiveness. God will listen," said the sailor.

"I don't think He's listening," said the officer. "He hasn't since that day."

"Where's your faith?" said the sailor.

"I've asked for forgiveness, yet I still have nightmares every night. I never sleep. The curse has never left me," said the officer.

"Why are you here then?" asked the sailor.

"This has been my life for as long as I can remember, but I'm afraid to die," said the officer. "I'm afraid of what's coming, afraid of what will be when we set foot in the Congo. Many will die. This time, the natives await us. They await our return, to avenge their dead fellows."

"We have armaments, machinery, and the Good Lord on our side. Negroes must die if it be the will of God. Listen to Holy Ray," said the sailor, comforting the officer. "This is a prize mission of the King of the Belgians, a faithful servant of the holy church. We won't fall."

"Sailor, my nightmares are little compared to what awaits us, I'm afraid," said the officer.

"Rubbish! Have faith in God's righteous. He'll protect us," said the sailor.

"*...this is love, not that we loved God, but that He loved us and sent His Son to be the propitiation for our sins.* This is the word of the Lord," said Père Raymond, closing the Bible and holding it close to his heart.

"Thanks be to God!" said the crew.

"Let us now pray for the forgiveness of our sins, the sick on the ship, the good weather, and also for good fortune. Let us pray," said the long-bearded priest.

At the ship side, sailors' heads were shaven to reduce the potential of an infestation of lice, whilst officers ensured their weapons—swords, muskets, pistols—were cleaned.

Le Renard had not a good night's sleep. Still seasick, he found himself on the quarterdeck at early dawn, forever puking over the side. He cast a gaze at the sea, and a devilish smirk lit his scarred face; then he dashed to the upper deck. "Sailor," said Le Renard, "sound the alarm!"

"Yes, sir!" shouted the sailor as he stormed off.

At the sound of the alarming call, Loinseach was the first to turn up, still in his checkered shirt. "What's the matter?" he asked, troubled.

"On the horizon! Do you see it?" said Le Renard.

"Hardly. The mist..." said Loinseach, his hand above his eyebrows as he peered into the distance. "Bloody hell! It looks like…it's a ship!"

"A ship?" said Captain Van Lanterman, tucking in his shirt when he joined the group.

"What kind of ship?" said Sergeant Lekens.

"Telescope," said Loinseach, leaving the deck to fetch it.

"It's been trailing us for some time," said Le Renard.

"Sergeant, find out who was on duty," said Van Lanterman.

"I'm on it, Captain," said Sergeant Lekens, leaving the deck.

Loinseach appeared with his telescope, which he poked against his eye. "Sir, a vessel comprising three masts, a square rigger," observed Loinseach.

"A vessel of that type must be a merchant ship," said the captain.

"Why is a merchant ship so far out at sea, in the middle of the Atlantic Ocean? No merchant vessels do business so far out in these waters," said Le Renard.

"Possibly an underground slave ship travelling to the coast," observed Van Lanterman.

"Captain, there seems to be much alteration to the vessel," stated Loinseach, watching the vessel through his telescope.

"In what way?" inquired Van Lanterman.

"The vessel is almost a sea rover. She has been made flush, flattening her stalls," said Loinseach.

"Flush?" asked Le Renard.

"The platform is a clear combat type," commented Loinseach.

"Captain!" boomed the voice of Sergeant Lekens from the quarterdeck. "It is reported that the sailor on duty last night has since gone missing. He was apparently last seen on this side of the deck, and his telescope has seemingly been smashed."

"Quartermaster O'Gowan was also on duty last night," said Loinseach.

"Pace yourselves, gentlemen," said Van Lanterman. "We need to know what we're up against." The captain then beckoned Sergeant Lekens and the quartermaster to a secluded corner, away from the group and privately said, "O'Gowan, you're one of my best men."

"I'm always honoured to serve, Captain," said O'Gowan.

"Tell me, did anything peculiar happen last night?" said Van Lanterman.

"Sir, Ben reported seeing something at sea, but I looked and saw nothing. I then left for the lavatories. When I returned, Ben had vanished, and I haven't seen him since. He's been caught stealing provisions at night. I assumed he was at it again," said O'Gowan.

"I'll order the crew to search again," said Lekens.

"Very well, Sergeant," said Van Lanterman.

They walked away from the barrel-filled corner.

"Loinseach, anything else?" asked the captain.

"It's difficult to see anything through the mist, and I'm unsure if I can actually give any further insight at this stage. I would guess they've got fifty-two guns onboard, with much space to operate the firepower of the craft. Thus, it should be considered that the ship is extremely powerful," stated Loinseach.

"There would be no need for so many guns if it were a slave ship," Van Lanterman observed. "With that in mind, I would state that this is something far more dangerous. I doubt we can rule out the potential of the vessel being a battleship."

"Perhaps Arabs?" said Le Renard. "They're known to wander these waters."

"Hard to say," said the captain. "Loinseach, any flag of sort?"

"None that I can see through the fog, sir," said Loinseach.

"This makes the matter more difficult to resolve," said Van Lanterman. "We've got a missing sailor and a large far-side seafaring vessel heading straight at us."

# CHAPTER XVII

# PIRATES

O n the mystery ship, a conversation continued between the shipmaster and some of the crewmembers in the vessel stern.

"Captain Kunda, we received the note Scarredface sent through the bird. It contains plans to capture the young sailor and secure the unmarked pistols, as grandly effected," said a tall, bald-headed black man wearing a long, heavy canvas coat.

"Marvellous, Diarabi," said the shipmaster, Captain Kunda.

Both men were *Kisúndi* tribesmen from deep in the heart of the Congo Kingdom, stripped from their heritage at an early age and taken into slavery. Kunda, broad-chested and big-boned, was the son of a *Kisúndi* chief, Súndi Kunda. Diarabi, born Kasongo Nkole, inherited his nickname after the death of a Mali co-pirate, Diarabi Ali Farka Ibrahim, who had great influence on him. Both men had faint memories of their homeland, but one element they held on to was their ability to speak in Kongo language, yet in their own way, which turned out to be sort of an odd Bantu Créole by reason of their mixed use of French, English, and Dutch.

Furthermore, they had come to know the sea quite well. All their adult lives, they had been as pirates at sea, in search of riches and freedom they could never have had inland. At sea, they felt like men they could never be on any one of the continents; a reality they understood early on and one they cherished.

"What happens next?" queried Diarabi, a bloke with a large nose, high cheekbones, and substantial lips. White chalk painted on his lips and ashen strips on his cheek established his power and high status amongst the crew. The man also wore a necklace made of lions' teeth, tightly tied around his enormous neck.

"According to Scarredface, their watchman has been detained," advised one of the older seamen. Calixte had been the overseer of the affairs aboard the ship.

"Good, Calixte. So everything is progressing according to plan. I am pleased. Anything else?" asked Kunda, seated at his large wooden desk.

"Do you want the bad news, Captain?" said Calixte.

"So we have bad news?" said Kunda.

"I'm afraid so, Captain," said Calixte.

"Well, don't keep me waiting," said Kunda, speaking in a deep authoritative voice and distinctive African accent.

"Just tell me what bastard's head I'll be adding to my collection," Kunda added.

"Alfonso, Captain," said Calixte.

"Vangu Vangu?" said Kunda, gazing at Diarabi, his eyes wide and glaring, then back at Calixte.

"Yes, Captain," said Calixte.

"And what is he accused of, Calixte?" said Kunda, plunging his hand into a wooden ball of nuts on the table—a practice that tempered his tension. He clutched an assortment and gobbled.

"Phase 2 of our plans is in jeopardy. We can't get further intelligence on the ship," said Calixte. "We have been cut off from Scarredface."

"How so?" probed Kunda, crushing shelled nuts with his strong teeth.

"The pigeon is dead," said Calixte, lowering his voice and fearing the most evil castigation. "Alfonso snapped its neck. Thought it was a bird spy."

Kunda gazed away and sighed in silence whilst he tried to maintain his composure. That, in truth, was bad news: Alfonso was the son he had with a signares woman on Île de Gorée, before he fled the island, yet pirate code had to be honoured and followed. One like Kunda and captains before him could never show any weakness. It had to be done. "Bring him!" shouted Kunda, angered by the countless faults of an adolescent and mistake-ridden son.

Soon, fear spread amongst pirates. Calixte motioned to one of the men, and two pirates hauled Alfonso Vangu Vangu, who fell to his knees.

"I'm sorry, Father," said the pigeon-chested, Afro-French Métis boy.

Kunda approached and wrapped his arms around the boy. "My own flesh and blood…my boy…my only son. You know our laws. This is your last offence. I have loved you, and I have shown you mercy, but protecting you is a burden I can no longer bear." As he continued his rants on previous misfortunes by the boy, he slowly and gently pulled him to his chest and embraced him in a reassuring manner. Kunda then unsuspectedly slipped and gently rubbed his hands around Vangu Vangu's neck. The contact was warm, but the neck knuckles felt fairly hard.

As the boy lifted his eyes to understand his father's action, his young body suddenly collapsed to the floor, inanimated in response to the *snap* his father's hands had just administered to his neck.

All gasped, silence on their lips and fear in their eyes.

"Feed him to the sharks," said Kunda, his back turned on his deceased son before falling to his knees at his colossal chair—a moment of weakness.

Diarabi swiftly remedied by placing his hand on Kunda's shoulder. "Master, not in front of the men," said Diarabi in Bantu Créole.

"What of the young sailor?" said Kunda, finding his strength as he sat back on his regal base. "And it better be good news."

"The watchman has been made to answer a great many questions," stated Ansel, the youngest of the crewmen. Despite his age, he was regarded as the trusted sailing master, afforded the task of navigation and recognised as an extremely valuable crewmember. He was also understood to be the only literate individual onboard the craft. He was also known to be the right-hand man of Kunda, so he commonly took the position of quartermaster, attempting, upon the clearing of the smoke, to shoulder the role of the division of spoils. In the absence of Kunda, he was placed as second-in-command, afforded with the vessel's entire supervision. For instance, after a battle, he would make decisions of what plunder to take and which to burn. "…but it amounted to nothing. The watchman won't speak," he stated.

"Sacrilege!" shouted Kunda, slamming a fist hard on the desk, smashing everything around him, including glasses and bottles of wine. "What are you saying? None of you can make the white man talk?" Kunda, captain of the unidentified ship, spoke with authority. He would kill any member of his crew who failed to follow his orders without question, but they were still within the pirates' decree, so he restrained himself. "As for the boy, we have no choice but to use other means. Believe me when I say, he *will* talk." He walked to the stern windows.

Diarabi walked alongside Kunda, as if he was the shadow protecting him.

"Make him suffer," demanded Kunda, leaving the stern with the crew.

"Captain, allow me. He will speak or die trying," said Diarabi as they headed to the prisoners' chambers.

Kunda and his men soon arrived on the quarterdeck where the prisoners were held. "Is this the stubborn prisoner?" Kunda asked.

"Yes, Captain," confirmed Ansel.

"So, kid, don't feel like spilling your guts?" prodded Kunda.

"Coward!" replied Ben amongst ill-fated captives. He spat on Kunda's garment, forcing the pirates to restrain him.

The watchman of *La Caprice*, young Ben, had metal rings positioned and locked around his legs; he was shackled in leg irons.

Kunda stared at the captive. He raised his large fist and smashed it repeatedly in Ben's face. "You're not that tough after all. You don't know who I am, do you?" Impatience seared through the captain's voice as he let off the pounding. Kunda motioned, ordering Diarabi to continue with torture.

"Take off those irons," said Diarabi, "and tie him to a grating."

Ben had been chained quickly, whipped with knotted ropes, bound, face down, to the grating, his limbs all spread wide. His shirt had been torn from his body, leaving the quivering man beneath exposed.

"Now, boy, do you wish to speak?" asked Kunda.

Ben spat.

"The boy's stubborn," said Kunda. "Have you heard of the chicotte? White man's curse to my people. Many lives destroyed by greed and terror. A true poison to the people I once knew!"

Diarabi stretched the chicotte and held it firmly, ready to engage.

"A whole village killed, raped. Then my people sold into slavery," seethed Kunda. "I don't remember my village, but I do remember the chicotte, as you will." Kunda nodded to Diarabi, ordering him to whisk the boy with the chicotte whilst the rest of the prisoners gazed on in horror.

Diarabi enjoyed his role of torture man and gunner, charged with overseeing the prisoners and gun crew. Diarabi's men took turns whipping the boy. Ben screamed in agony as one of the pirates squirted brackish sea water on the cuts plastering his back. Blood gushed in all places on deck.

"Hang in there, kid!" shouted captives emphatically, watching from their places in the leg irons.

"Are you prepared to tell us something, watchman?" said Kunda, lifting the boy's head with the tip of his sword.

"Go...to...hell!" said the boy, bloody saliva pouring from his mouth, "You'd better...kill me."

Prisoners cheered him by stomping their feet. "Hang in there, boy!" screeched the captured mob.

"I want to see blood. I want to hear him scream so loudly that angels from hell take heed. Whip him till his death!" ordered Kunda.

Diarabi and Ansel commenced the beating. Ben bore hundreds of gashes and cuts, enough to take his life. He had reached the depth of hell, a place of no return. The beating was so extreme that his skin peeled off like that of a boiled fowl. Shreds of his flesh stuck to the chicotte and parachuted on the dirty, blood-spattered deck.

"Mercy," begged a captive. "Mercy!"

The rest of the prisoners protested, screaming and yelling in outrage. They banged their hands against the deck and kicked their feet against metal rings.

"Calixte, control these men," commanded Kunda.

Pirates flogged at captives with small pieces of hard rope to hush them. "Silence, bloody whores!" they shouted. "Shut up!"

As opposed to living a life brimming with glamour and allure, those aboard the ship of Kunda were widely acknowledged as doomed in all arenas, lacking the skills and general capacity to escape. They put their captives through the most hellish ordeals—torture and humiliation—for no good reason beyond entertainment. Amongst the captives were two American travellers, who'd been Kunda's prisoners for weeks.

"Master Kunda," said James Williams, one of the Americans, "please show mercy on the boy."

"Silence, cracker," said Calixte. "You will speak only when spoken to."

"And your peers?" said Kunda. "Did they show mercy to my people?"

"Captain, the boy is of no use to you dead," said Williams, drenched in grease and sweat. "Listen to me and stop beating the boy."

"He knows what you want, Captain. My colleague, Jim Williams, can help you," said Wilson Taylor, the other American.

Williams had an irate look on his face. *What the hell?* he fumed.

"Please give us a minute, Captain," said Williams.

"I'll give you half that," said Kunda, "and then I'll start chopping hands."

Williams turned to face Taylor. "Are you mad? You're gonna get us killed."

"Can you think of anything better?" said Taylor, grinning at Kunda, who waited edgily. "We've got to find a way out of here."

"That's stupidly clever. You want us dead? That will not buy our ticket into the Congo," whispered Williams.

"Listen to me. Just tell them anything they want to know about that ship. Make it up. I know you can get us out of here alive—both of us," said Taylor.

"Time's up, white man," barked black-faced Diarabi, thrashing the chicotte at the Americans.

"Enough!" said Kunda, lifting his hand in the air.

"Captain, we need to act fast," said Diarabi. "These men can't help us."

"The watchman can't speak. He's nearly dead. We will rely on the two men to tell us what we seek, should they wish to do so," said Kunda. He then approached the rusted bars separating them from the captives. "May the gods help you, Jim Williams, if you can't help me. Now, tell me your plans."

"Will you meet our conditions?" asked Williams.

"You are in no position to bargain," said Kunda. "Do not test my patience."

"Free the young sailor and the rest of the prisoners," said Williams.

"And us, of course," said Taylor.

"And if the captain refuses?" said Ansel.

"The answer is simple. He won't tell you anything about the ship," said Taylor.

"Either way, you are finished," said Kunda, seizing nuts from his pocket and crushing them in his chops, as if to emphasize his threat. "And not by my hands, I might add, but perhaps the men onboard that ship. However, I pledge to grant you and the other prisoners your freedom once you tell me what I need to know. The young sailor is of no further use to me. You can have his cadaver once he crosses over." Kunda spat nuts on the mucky floor.

The shipmaster directed the crew, at Kunda's summons, to remove the irons from Williams.

"Am I not going along?" asked Taylor.

"I am still the captain of this ship, am I not? You will obey my orders. You will stay here with the captives in case Williams tries anything foolish. If I am not satisfied with him, I will see you hanged and fed to sharks, piece by bloody piece. If I were you, I would say your prayers that your friend Williams does my bidding," said Kunda. "Diarabi, let us regroup at the poop deck. I want a sword on Williams's throat."


Meanwhile, onboard *La Caprice*, tension mounted amongst the crew. The captain directed his men to their posts and told them to hold there until further notice, until his questions about the unidentified vessel were still unsettled.

"Captain, the bank of fog has cleared up," said Loinseach. "The crew on vessel are seamen, early to mid-twenties, I'd say."

"So it's not a merchant ship as we thought, nor is it a formal army warship. A private crew? Hmm," said the captain, speaking to his men.

"Loinseach, how many people onboard the ship?" asked Lekens.

"I'd approximate 200, sir."

On the unidentified ship, Kunda and his men arrived on the poop deck to observe the object of their pursuit. Whilst some busied themselves with removing sails from their storage lockers and airing them during spells of nice weather, thus helping to ensure they would not rot, other pirates filled the decks, hammering unravelled rope fibres and oakum into the cracks and sealing them with tar to prevent water from filtering in through the cracks.

"Williams, here we are. Today I have lost my flesh and blood, and I won't hesitate to have your head chopped off. Don't try anything stupid," said Kunda. "We know the ship carries goods—lots of them. We know from our informant that it lugs clothing, tents, and weapons. What we don't know is what else. So tell me."

"I need a spyglass," said Williams, his hands still bound with a rope.

"Untie him and give him a telescope," said Kunda. "Now, tell me what you see."

Williams worked the spyglass, focusing on the gigantic ship ahead. "*Spirit of Darkness... La Caprice*. It's heading to the Congo," said Williams.

"Tell me something I don't know," said Captain Kunda, looking through his own telescope.

Williams was cautious in his answer: He knew the pirates wanted him to fail in order to grant them an excuse to read Taylor and the rest of the prisoners a death sentence. Williams was careful to make no mistakes that could cost him or the others their lives. "It carries a lot more, contrary to what your informant may have led you to believe," he added. "How about 120,000 gold francs?"

"What did you say?" said a flabbergasted Ansel, "How do you know this?"

"*The Bruxelles Herald*," said Williams, with bullets of nervous sweat streaming down his face. "And there's more. The ship carries medical supplies that will heal your sick." He took a deep breath. "They intend to use the money to bribe tribal chiefs in the Congo. They've been doing it for over a decade. It's nothing new."

Ansel watched him carefully. He wanted Williams's blood, and he was losing his patience.

"Fine," said Kunda after a long pause.

So as to ensure *La Caprice* remained on its correct path, heading into the core of the darkness, Captain Kunda made use of a back staff to establish the position of the ship in regard to the sun. He stood with his back to the sun and measured the shadow.

"Perfect, Williams," said Captain Kunda, spitting yet again.

Williams was relieved.

"You are lucky," said a twitchy-eyed Diarabi.

"Captain, we have run out of goods," said Calixte. "Some of the crew have died from gruelling."

Kunda still watched *La Caprice* through his telescope, playing deaf.

"Drinking water is foul, and whatever food we have left is

Rotten. The crew is slimming down," said Ansel.

"We must attack now."

"Williams, you've heard the wishes of my crew. Is there provision in abundance on the enemy's ship?" asked Kunda.

"I would venture to say there is, Master Kunda," said Williams.

"No guesses, Williams. I need a definite answer. And be careful with your words. I will not warn you again."

"Yes then. A ship that size on an expedition to the Congo must carry an abundance of food—and most likely the best wine and rum," surmised Williams.

"Anything else?" said Kunda.

"The ship is well equipped with big guns—twelve-pounders 'round the ship, and…Christ! It's—"

"What?" said an irate Kunda.

"That's Captain Bison Van Lanterman," said Williams.

"So?" snapped Kunda.

"He's a notorious and skilled officer," said Williams.

Kunda was quick to dismiss Williams's remark. "We attack when ready," he said. "My people want whatever riches are on that ship," said Kunda, "and they shall have it. Now kill him."

"Wait! Please," begged Williams. "There's more."

"Speak," commanded Kunda.

"The ship…it's a special convoy," said Williams.

"Portuguese?" asked Kunda.

"I'm afraid not, Captain."

"Then…?" said Kunda.

"The King of the Belgians sent the ship and its crew on a journey to expand his domain in the Congo," said Williams. "It's lined to be confidential, if you will."

"You mean more of my people killed?" said Kunda.

"Precisely," said Williams.

"Then the ship and those aboard must be destroyed," said Master Kunda, ready to launch the attack. "I will tear down that ship before any more of my brethren are forced into slavery."

"Yet you have your own men as slaves," said Williams.

"Careful now..." warned Diarabi.

Kunda dismissed Diarabi's warning with a wave. "Look around you. Do you see a black man on this ship working as a slave?" asked Kunda.

"I-I'm sorry," apologised Williams.

"Of course, Williams. Only a fool would test my tolerance, but you do have guts. I'll give you that. And I'll answer your idiotic riddle."

"Forgive me. I-I only misspoke," said Williams. "Your crew is of free men, clearly."

"Precisely," said Kunda. "We are of many nations. Ansel, an English, Calixte, a Frenchman. My crew is made up of free men. I welcome Europeans and Africans as equals on my craft. The black fellow there, Diarabi, my tribesman, was born in *Kisúndi* land and sold into slavery by men like you."

Diarabi prodded a sword on Williams's gullet.

"I teach my crew to become sailors without turning them into slaves. This is the way of my world," said Kunda. "I show *white* men that blacks are equal and free men on this ship. We are pirates, blind to colour. If you survive the attack on *Spirit of Darkness*, you will tell your people what you saw. As long as I live, I will rid the world of the likes of those who travel on that ship."

The crew cheered. By the galley, on the main deck, a number of pirates smoked whilst the biscuits savoured throughout long journeys, hardtack, were enjoyed.

"Men, it is time!" barked Captain Kunda. "Are you ready for the battle?"

"Aye-aye, Cap'n!" shouted a mob of pirates on deck, ready to spill and savour the enemy's blood.

"Then let us fight," said Kunda.

The crew roared, brandishing their swords and firearms in the air.

Diarabi rushed to sound the ship bell to prompt the men for battle.

All and sundry onboard the pirate ship dashed to their respective posts.

"Captain, what about the prisoners? And Williams?" asked Ansel.

"Send him back amongst the rest. Let him perish with them," said Kunda, offering no mercy.

"You're nothing but a low-life sham," snapped Williams.

"Take him away. I want him chained and ironed," said Kunda.

"Master, perhaps we should release all the prisoners," said Ansel.

"For what purpose?" demanded Kunda, resting a large sword on his shoulder.

"Master, battle is underway, and it would be wise if they fought not only for us, but also for their own lives. The enemy will fight them without question. They'll assume they're part of our crew," said Ansel.

"Clever," said Kunda. "Release them and give them each a sword and pirate clothes. Tell them to fight or die. Persuade them the enemy will show no mercy to anyone aboard this ship."

"Master, permission to raise the pirate flag?" queried Calixte.

"Patience," soothed Kunda. "Raise the friendly flag. Let's see if they'll bite."

"Aye-aye, Cap'n," said Calixte.

"Master, we've concealed the gun ports with canvas screens," advised Diarabi.

The helmsman on the pirate vessel at the wheel steered the ship on the proper course.

"Full speed," ordered Kunda, aiming at *La Caprice*.

CHAPTER XVIII

# BLOODBATH

The pirate ship gradually increased speed, sailing faster toward *La Caprice*. In an effort to increase speed, all the pirates were assigned to their own roles: ensuring the sails were correctly rigged and utilising the best combination to protect the mast whilst achieving speed. Pirates trimmed the sail into a large area; some had climbed to the yard and accordingly rolled it out to better performance. Soon, the pirate ship was cruising fast through the water towards *La Caprice*.

"Captain," said Loinseach, onboard *Spirit of Darkness*, "I see Negroes aboard the ship. Considering their garments, they can't be slaves. They're finely dressed, sir."

"Pirates," said Le Renard. "They're pirates."

"How sure are you?" asked Captain Van Lanterman.

"Pretty sure," said Le Renard. "Only pirates would allow Negroes to work freely onboard and to dress so richly. These men must be escaped slaves from the West Indies plantations."

"Captain, there is a full crew onboard their craft, and her captain is a muscle-bound Negro," said Loinseach.

"Africans are considered full crewmembers by a number of vessels. That said, they have much to lose if they are to be captured, knowing they will become slaves. Many Africans have been successful in becoming pirates, even prowling the Caribbean, killing and eating the hearts of white men," stated Le Renard, instilling fear to all who heard his rant.

"What are you getting at?" asked Loinseach.

"The slave trade has reached its peak. A well-defined link between the white world and the Dark Continent is now apparent—and it's lucrative to say the least," Le Renard said. "Slave ship spells are recognised as being extremely rewarding."

"What are you saying, Le Renard?" demanded Loinseach.

"Let him speak," said the captain.

"This is what I'm stating," added Le Renard. "There is a great less wealth and value to physical goods—whether iron or pewter—than

African slaves, who could potentially offer ivory, gold, spices, and more.

Upon the selling of slaves, ships are loaded up with a number of treasures, like sugar, rum—"

"Ridiculous!" interrupted Lekens. "All juvenile foolishness."

"Primarily," responded Loinseach, "these are African waters and not the Caribbean sea. Secondly, there is no gun port visible to my trained eyes. Thus, I believe it to be a merchant vessel and nothing more. In fact, I would wager their inclination to trade with us for fresh food. We could benefit."

"What a foolish thought," Le Renard chastised. "I would state with certainty that the only food to be garnered through such a meeting would be our crew being flung to the ocean's beasts."

"I hate to admit it, but Le Renard's dead right," said Captain Van Lanterman.

"And how can you trust this man?" Lekens questioned, furious.

"He's a rogue."

Meanwhile, Kunda's ship cruised towards *La Caprice*. Upon closing the distance between themselves and the enemy, Kunda and his men began to develop hunger for the ship's destruction and the garnering of all contained upon *La Caprice*.

Pirates were anxious for battle, and they were always determined.

They had the ferocity to slaughter the enemy at the call of duty. Already, Kunda and his crewmembers had plotted as to how best to defeat the target vessel.

"Gunfire could damage the prize," said Diarabi.

"Perhaps we should board the vessel, Captain," suggested Ansel.

"From the size of the ship and its crew, I say we attack by gunfire," said Kunda.


Onboard *La Caprice*, Van Lanterman continued, "It's not that I don't believe this man. I have my share of suspicions about him, yes, but my military intuition says this is not a friendly ship. It's headed directly towards us at an unusually high speed. We must ready ourselves."

"I concur, Captain," said Baron Von Schweintzler, observing the pirate ship with a telescope. "If I were you, I would immediately order the crew to take speed."

"Isn't that slightly premature?" said Loinseach. "We haven't even confirmed a threat thus far."

"Well, that ship belongs to Royal Africa Company, clearly a raided and captured vessel," said Von Schweintzler.

"What makes you the expert?" said Sergeant Lekens.

"I believe the Royal African Company symbol to be apparent when considering the figurehead of the ship. The ship is known as Onslow and is regarded as being the last ship of Black Bart—one of the most dishonourable and infamous of pirates ever to have sailed waters for the past hundred years. Without question," Von Schweintzler mused, "Black Bart is a legend."

"Captain!" called Lekens. "The ship has raised her flag. It depicts a pirate clasping an hourglass and a skeleton holding a spear."

"Clever—a kind of psychological warfare," said Von Schweintzler.

"Perhaps you gentlemen will now pay heed," said Le Renard.

"How do we know you're not one of them?" demanded Sergeant Lekens furiously.

"I am a child of war," said Le Renard, "but I'm certainly not a brute."

"By my account you are," countered Sergeant Lekens.

Le Renard rushed up heatedly before the sergeant. "I demand an apology."

"The only apology I'll give is to your remains for not killing you earlier if you don't venture off my face," said Lekens, his fists clenched.

"Enough!" said the captain. "I know we don't like each other very much, but now's not the time for a duel. Now's the time to unite and put aside our differences. Otherwise, we are guaranteed a quick death. Enough of these trivial spats, gentlemen."

"Everyone knows Black Bart's dead," said Loinseach. "Otherwise, he'd be over 200 years old."

"His spirit lives," said Le Renard, "and he's commanding that ship heading straight at us. Either we surrender or—"

"I demand such idiocy come to end," Loinseach demanded, "*Onslow* was seized, and that is a well-known fact."

"If it was seized, then what do you make of that ship?" said Le Renard.

"There is only one explanation," injected Van Lanterman.

"And what would that be, Captain?" said a frustrated Heinrich,

"Because I feel pretty dumbfounded."

"*Khosi yi Afrika*," said Van Lanterman.

"Who the bloody hell is *Kossi ye Africa?*" asked Loinseach, undoubtedly mispronouncing.

"The African Lion," said the captain. "Kunda."

"One of Bartholomew 'Black Bart' Roberts's faithful disciples—one who keenly sought to be just like him. It is known that, upon the capture of the fleet of Black Bart—which was achieved by Captain Ogle—a number of prisoners from both the Americas and West Africa, as well as Kunda's adopted father, a Wolof named Bubacar, were not made to face trial. Instead, they were made to become slaves, with the profits split amongst Captain Ogle and his men, as per the sale of the private ships," stated Le Renard.

"How do you know so much?" questioned a suspicious Sergeant Lekens.

"I'm well read. As I've said before, I had my reservation about that ship," said Le Renard.

"Anything else we should know, Le Renard?" inquired Loinseach.

All eyes gazed at Le Renard.

"Better you speak now," said Van Lanterman.

"The last of the white crewmembers were forced to face trial, with a number subsequently hanged whilst others were acquitted," Le

Renard stated. Then whilst slowly glancing back at his listeners, in turn, he continued, "Twenty or so were forced to work several years' hard labour, I believe in the African Gold Coast mines. The punishment was a death sentence in itself. But Bubacar escaped, and he was successful in freeing the crewmembers enslaved at the mines. Bubacar established an unruly crew of cutthroats with the objective of avenging the death of Black Bart. He apparently became very determined to fulfill his goal and instigated a number of attacks, targeting slave ships. It is believed he managed to recruit hundreds upon hundreds of seamen for his cause."

His confident speech and precise diction about the undoubtedly enemy ship raised further suspiscions about him in Van Lanterman and Lekens. Nonetheless, he carried on unaware. "However, there was a notable decline in piracy following the capture and execution of Bubacar, mainly owing to the presence of the Royal Navy which, owing to such events, were charged with guarding and overseeing the high seas. As such, a number of pirates neglected their cause. Nevertheless, it is known that the pirate golden age and the peak of such was yet to come. Essentially, Kunda personifies the buccaneer to the greatest possible degree. He is almost seven feet tall and has been described as the devil incarnate. He is determined to achieve all he sets out to do. He is black and brave and holds unquestionable authority. And he strictly adheres to the ways in which Black Bart conducted himself—the charter of the Bartholomew Roberts Crew, 1722."

Everyone eyed him, examining his posture in an attempt to determine whether he was telling the truth, all silently questioning how he knew so much.

As silence awashed, Le Renard considered it best to continue, not sure if he'd been digging his own grave, exposing his ties to Kunda, or gaining the trust of an already wary crew. "He is a satanic character indeed and is feared across the pirate world, known to be brutal and terrifying. Any who have survived his wrath or general demeanour describe him as a bald-headed black giant," said Le Renard. Briefly pausing and unable to read their minds, he pushed further. "One specific tale to be told across the seas is of the declining morale of his crew during the journey around the Pacific Ocean, during which a man known as Dzigbode—one of his crew—voiced his unease and displeasure, which subsequently enraged Kunda. As the story goes, upon being questioned on his continuous ranting, the man called the captain a 'dog,' reprimanding him for a broken promise of food and drink during the journey. Kunda, not taking kindly to such criticism, picked up a wooden bucket, complete with an iron bar fixed to its base, and hit the man across the face before shooting him in the leg as all the other pirates looked on—a lesson to them, I hasten to assume. It is said Dzigbode had a fractured skull and, of course, a deeply wounded leg. Consequently, he died the following day. His body was hung from the front of the ship for a long time—some say months—a warning to the other pirates," said Le Renard. He took a breath but felt his monologue required a more theatrical ending. "It has been stated that, upon the death of Bubacar, Kunda cried and subsequently sought revenge," added the man with a scarred face.

Heinrich, who had been listening intently, spoke. "So how did it ever come about that Kunda was adopted by Bubacar?"

"It is said that upon escaping from Île de Gorée, Kunda and

Alfonso, his newborn, were taken in, and Kunda was taught all of his ways, with Bubacar recognising that his days left were limited and he would need someone to replace him and pursue his cause. Kunda was sworn to maintain and endorse the vengeance of Black Bart by raiding ships, much like the many pirates before him. And that," stated Le

Renard, to his own satisfaction, "is how a villain was born from an escaped slave."

"Gentlemen, are we done with the fairytales?" demanded

Sergeant Lekens. "That ship is cruising fast. Captain, we must prepare for battle."

"Tell the men to hold their fire," said the captain, addressing the sergeant, finally aware that the incoming ship carried bloodthirsty pirates. "Although Le Renard's account seems vividly engaging, I have no intention of starting a war."

"For Christ's sake, Captain!" objected Loinseach. "Why not?"

"This transport is not a warship," said Van Lanterman.

"We've got 100 cannons, sir, with all due respect. If it's not a warship, then what is it?" retaliated Von Schweintzler.

"What I mean is that we are not here to wage war but to conduct an expedition," said Captain Van Lanterman.

"Captain, again with all due respect, we will be killed if we don't fight back. Pirates care not about expeditions and will show no mercy," said Von Schweintzler.

"Then we surrender," interjected Le Renard.

"No, the captain's right. We're sailing under the auspice of His

Majesty, the King of the Belgians. No war, no surrender. If any man has a problem with that, he should abandon ship now," said Sergeant Lekens, pointing overboard.

"Captain, I suggest you think about this carefully," said Baron Von Schweintzler.

"You no longer have me by the balls, Baron," said the captain,

"Might I remind you that we're miles away from the Port of Antwerp?"

"Indeed, Captain. Acknowledged. But I mean this in all earnestness," said Baron Von Schweintzler. "These pirates will not give up until the ship is in their possession. They're well armed and experienced for sea battle. We have no chance of survival unless a miracle occurs. I implore you to make a wise decision—and swiftly, before it is too late. I refuse to die on this ship."

"Gentlemen, it is worth repeating that I have no intention of engaging the enemy in war. Under strict orders of the International Association, I am to defend this ship but not to engage in warfare," stated Van Lanterman unswervingly. "I will not disobey the code of conduct to which I have pledged allegiance. For the time being, our strategy is to ditch the pirate ship. If there comes a point when we have no further choice, I won't hesitate to engage."

"Well, we don't have much of a choice now, do we? Captain, I will have better luck abandoning ship," said an antsy Von Schweintzler.

"Sorry, but no one leaves the ship—not now. We all stick together. We must preserve all lifeboats in the event that we're forced to abandon ship. Either you stay onboard this vessel or trust your fate to the sea," said Captain Van Lanterman. "We can spare deserters no lifeboats."

"Captain, neither you nor your band are in a position to tell me what to do. My request is simple. I want off this ship. Either you order your gang lower a lifeboat, or there will be blood on this deck before pirates board the vessel," said Baron Von Schweintzler, aiming two pistols at Captain Van Lanterman and his men. "Le Renard, it's time to leave this bloody floating coffin. Lower one of the boats and take some bread and wine."

"Right, sir. On my way," said Le Renard. "Anyone joining us?"

Four sailors joined the small group of deserters. They rallied 'round Le Renard and lowered a boat onto the roiling surface of the ocean.

One of the deserting sailors saluted. "I'm sorry, Cap'n, but I don't want to die."

Hastily, two junior officers attempted to hoist Baron Von Schweintzler whilst he aimed his pistol at the captain. Alas, one of the two was killed with a knife that pierced his back, which Le Renard flung from a far distance.

"Next time, I won't hesitate to shoot. Captain, it's not too late for you to change your mind and fight. I wish you a pleasant journey on this ship, and may the great Lord save you all," said Von Schweintzler, gazing carefully around him for an ambush.

Le Renard and the deserting sailors saluted the lodged crew.

"Take the boat and leave," said Van Lanterman.

As Baron Von Schweintzler neared the lifeboat that had been lowered to the sea, a loud blast ricocheted. *La Caprice* was roughed. Seamen and officers dispersed in all directions on the deck. A second blast erupted, followed by two huge explosions and two blasts on *La Caprice*. The ship rocked sideways on both impacts. On the decks, sailors and officers were wounded. Tables, chairs, and equipment scattered far and wide on the ship. Crewmembers tumbled as the ship rocked back into position after impact.

"Sailor, report!" ordered Sergeant Lekens, struggling to get up from deck.

"The pirates! They're reloading, sir!" shouted one sailor.

"They've damaged the ship's hull," said another on the side of the deck.

"Captain!" called out Loinseach, assisting Van Lanterman as he recovered from the shock.

"I'm fine, Loinseach," said the captain, rising and grasping his head.

Van Lanterman pointed to Baron Von Schweintzler at the base, unconscious.

"Take him away to his cabin for medical attention," said the captain.

Le Renard rose to his feet, bleeding from his head. Sailors and officers died on impact from the cannon blast.

"A battle is unavoidable. It's clear they want our blood and to seize control of *La Caprice*," said the captain. "Loinseach, have the sailors deploy the sails. We need speed to distance the ship from the enemy. Move! We don't have much time."

"Aye-aye, Captain," said Loinseach.

"Sergeant, ready all onboard officers for battle," said Captain Van Lanterman.

"Sir, I've ordered the gunner to distribute to each officer small hand weapons. All 100 cannons are ready for the battle. We await your order to fire," said Sergeant Lekens.

"Excellent, Sergeant. One more thing..." said the captain from his position on the poop deck. "I want Miss Dawson and the rest of the crew to stay on the lower deck."

"Consider it done, sir." Sergeant Lekens rushed down to the lower deck with the orders.

Meanwhile, on Kunda's ship, a plan was in motion for a fierce battle.

"Fire!" demanded Diarabi, responsible for the artillery aboard the pirate ship.

Following the gunfire, the cannons were quickly reloaded by the crew, who worked tirelessly each time to clean, load, aim and fire.

"Reload!" commanded Diarabi.

The gun was cleaned and the sparks dampened by the crew, ensuring that explosion did not follow the reload. The gun was loaded with gunpowder, with a fuse made from a quill, filled with powder, which was inserted into the gun.

"Get into position and maintain," commanded Diarabi. "Target the hull."

Ropes and handspikes were used to lever the gun into position, with the pirates waiting for the roll of the ship into the water before the gun would be shot at the hull of the enemy.

"Ready...set...fire!" shouted Diarabi.

The gun captain ignited the fuse, the men jumping from range and covering their ears with their hands. The cannons sounded large explosions, with the crew again retaking their positions for reload.

*La Caprice* was badly damaged from gunfire, preventing the sails from being deployed. As the sailors struggled to loosen them. The crew was becoming agitated, needing more wind and the release of the sails.

"Left fall!" said the top man, who struggled to hold the sail against the strong wind.

At this point, an unfortunate soul was hit; he fell from his position at the yardarm and was subsequently thrown into the rolling ocean.

Down on the main deck, sailors controlled the sails. The lines controlling the set of the sails were organised carefully as the men loosened them, with Captain Van Lanterman giving officers orders to release gunfire on the pirate ship.

Two stern chasers were being used, with cannons positioned at the gunroom stern, firing shots at the enemy vessel behind.

"In position!" shouted Kunda. "The enemy ship has retaliated. All in position!"

"Master Kunda, our target is deploying its sails. We need to restrategise," said Ansel, carrying a large pistol wrapped with a long red silk looped ribbon.

"They're attempting an escape, Captain. No surrender," said Calixte.

"We need to slow them down," said Kunda, carrying a large sword, an axe, and a pistol tied with silk cords, hugging his waist. He was a ferocious man, determined to assume command of *La Caprice*. "Diarabi, aim all cannons up at the rigging of the enemy ship.

Bring out all four twenty-four-pounder cannons."

Much damage had been sustained by *La Caprice*, a number of round shots having inflicted injury to the hull, with her riggings suffering chain shoots, disabling the ship. The riggings were completely destroyed.

There was also an abundance of structural damage, although *La Caprice* remained navigable. But, ever focused on their objective, the crew repaired the damage, risking their own deaths whilst in the line of gunfire.

Loinseach was terrified. "Captain, there's much trouble. The likelihood of escaping the pirates is becoming slimmer. The riggings have been destroyed, and the crew is unable to move upwards. There have been a number of fatalities, and the sails are difficult to loosen, much less repair. The pirate gunfire has inflicted much damage on the sails, and they can no longer capture the wind. We're losing speed, Captain. It's only a matter of time."

"Our sailors will do fine," said Van Lanterman. "They were born for this. Focus on navigating the ship. You're doing swell, Loinseach."

"Aye-aye, Cap'n," said Loinseach.

The entire experience was terrifying, with comrades, wounded in battle, sobbing and moaning, the sounds only momentarily drowned out by the loud cannon fire. The once fresh salty sea air and comforting smell of tar were now undistinguishable amidst the blood and burning gunpowder.

At times, Kunda's ship would be perilously close, with Captain Van Lanterman, officers, and sailors positioned on the upper decks, lying alongside, waiting for the enemy to come that little bit closer.

Meanwhile, various crew maintained protection by hiding beneath a breastwork wall, comprising rolled-up hammocks, positioned within nets.

"Gentlemen," Captain Van Lanterman commanded, "the enemy ship is within close range. Each of you aim at your own bloody pirate and make them pay for the king's ship. Upon my order, fire will commence."

The crew became tense and alert, watching as the sails of the enemy vessel drew ever closer.

Then, upon being positioned at close distance, Captain Van Lanterman barked the order: "Fire!"

Across one side of the ship, an eruption of gunfire could be heard, all sounding in synchronisation, crippling the enemy by the massive broadside power. A large number of pirates were immediately killed.

Following the first blast, the pirates sought to connect the two vessels, throwing grappling hooks and struggling to link the two ships together, stern to stern.

Quickly, the pirates onboard Kunda's ship climbed onto *La Caprice*, with a fierce battle initiating. Captain Van Lanterman's crew fought bravely and courageously, seeking to debilitate the pirates by wrestling away their hatchets, knives, pikes, pistols, and swords. But retaliation followed, with the pirates throwing grenade shells, powder flasks, and stinkpots, injuring and killing a number of crew.

Meanwhile, positioned at his stern, Kunda advised his crew of the next step. "A ship of such size is undoubtedly home to a number of treasures and valuable loot. I would imagine there to be clothing, munitions, portable huts, tents, scientific measures, weapons, and more. I would estimate the loot to be worth in excess of 120,000 francs, so this is an opportunity not to be missed. As such, take everything. I trust all of you to do your job. Utilise your experience and infiltrate the ship at the enemy's stern without recognition. Do so in memory of my father and Bartholomew Roberts."

"Aye-aye, Cap'n," they shouted.

"We haven't much time," said Kunda, watching his men exit the ship stern through exposed windows.

Ansel had walked out and cleared the window when Kunda was ready to make his exodus.

"Where's the pigeon?" asked a man in the shadows.

Kunda paused briefly before he turned. "Come out of the shadows, I command you."

Le Renard stepped forward. "You've kidnapped my bird and heedlessly attacked a heavily armed ship. This was not part of—"

"A plan we never received," interrupted Kunda. "Alfonso killed the pigeon, and he's paid his debt. Cut out from you, we had no choice."

"The plan was to be delivered in stages," said Le Renard,

"Capture the sailor, have him reveal the location of the swag—'

"The boy's dead," said Kunda.

"Dead?" questioned Le Renard. "You were to secure information.

He was the only one other than the captain who knows of the location of the Assembly funds onboard the ship."

"Kiss it goodbye," said Kunda. "We had no choice. The boy was mulish."

"Then pay me what you owe me, Captain," Le Renard roared.

"Return aboard *La Caprice* with us," said Kunda. "We'll find the riches and destroy the ship. My men, you know them. They're very good. They'll find it."

"Had you protected the bird, you would have known the plan was to demand surrender. *La Caprice* has the strength of 10,000 men. You're losing men—and you're losing ground fast." Le Renard moved around the cushioned bench seats lining the open windows.

"Sorry, friend, but our partnership ends here," said Kunda.

"This is still *my* plan," said Le Renard.

"Of which we were denied intricate detail," said Kunda. "Particularly regarding 120,000 gold francs onboard *La Caprice*. Seems your habitual avarice has once again got the best of you."

"Did you say 120,000 gold francs?" Le Renard gasped. "Then someone has once more duped—"

"Duped me?" said Kunda. "*You*'ve duped me."

"Enough!" boomed Le Renard. "You owe me for bringing you this close… and you'll pay me now."

"I'm afraid we have yet to reach a milestone based on your predictions. The battle ensues…and, in your own words, I'm losing ground fast," reminded Kunda, headed for the stern window.

"Hold it! One more step, and you'll be savouring the lead from this flintlock," said Le Renard, pointing the pistol at him. "You'll pay me now, and then I'll dispose of you."

Kunda paused. "Let us unite. Together we can form the mightiest pirate gang. Consider for a moment Studland Bay, with men travelling far and wide, seeking out deals and making negotiations. Think, Scarredface, of all we achieved. You remember the gold, hawks, ivory, jewellery, parrots, wines? We garnered goods from Crete, Norway, Brazil, West Africa. Come, dear friend. Don't you remember?"

"Unfortunately, old days stay old. Things change. *I've* changed," said Le Renard. "This is not a social call. I know you keep a little loot here."

"Be wise," warned Kunda.

"Put your hands where I can see them," said Le Renard in his most demanding voice.

"My men are waiting. Don't be a fool," said Kunda. "Drop your pistol and let us speak like men."

"I want my bribe now," said Le Renard.

"Very well, but you'll find my vengeance inferior to a scorpion bite," said Kunda.

"Spare me," said Le Renard. "You'll be dead. Now move."

"My desk drawer," said Kunda. "Your riches are there."

"Nothing brash, Captain," said Le Renard, "or I'll shoot."

"It is there," said Kunda. "I only need the key."

"No," said Le Renard. "Tell me which drawer and toss the key."

"Second drawer," said Kunda, eyeing a bottle of ink. He moved slowly.

"If this is some trick," said Le Renard, making his way to the desk, "I'll kill you." Le Renard checked the drawer for traps.

Kunda moved closer to the ink bottle.

"You're in luck," said Le Renard, taking United States bank notes and stuffing them into his pockets. "Now where's the rest?"

"With my men," said Kunda.

"Then why do I need you?" said the scarred-face man who fired when Kunda pitched ink at his face.

Le Renard fired when Kunda pitched ink at his face. "Bastard!" shrieked Le Renard, firing at will as spatters of blood coated the floor.

Kunda, hit, bolted and tackled Le Renard, and both men balled up into a fight, rolling back and forth on the floorboards. Le Renard clocked Kunda's jaw with his pistol, and the two separated.

"On your feet!" demanded Le Renard, rising and disposing of his Pistol, then drawing his long sword.

Equally wounded, Kunda drew his sword. "Die!" he boomed as he struck.

Le Renard struck back, wiping the ink from his temple.

Kunda thrust his sword at his lad-turned-villain, slicing a hole through Le Renard's pocket.

"Are you mad?" shouted Le Renard as currency escaped his bulging pockets and scattered across the floor.

"There's always more, Scarredface," said Kunda, bleeding from his left shoulder. "Put down your weapon and let's unite."

The wrestling match prolonged. Kunda assailed skillfully, bending Le Renard's cartridge box to the hilt. But the captain, weak, struggled to fight. He lost little blood and held his ground.

Le Renard wounded Kunda's agile fingers, disabling and tossing away the man's sword. Kunda jumped back, falling loudly, in excruciating pain. Le Renard scarred Kunda's neck with his blade in one swift motion. Kunda choked, retreating from the sword.

"So long," said Le Renard as he lifted his sword, but a small knife found its mark on his shoulder. Le Renard dropped his sword and pressed the fresh wound on his shoulder. "Ansel?"

"Scarredface," Ansel greeted, emerging from the stern window, firing.

"Kill him!" screamed Kunda, regaining strength.

Le Renard made a swift escape as Ansel's shots missed. Le Renard barricaded the stern door with a piece of wood, hindering the progress of the pirates trailing behind. He then headed towards the gunpowder storage room located deep in the hold. There, he encountered two pirates guarding the door. He shot quickly and precisely, sending both pirates into a lifeless heap on the floor.

Quickly, Le Renard sneaked into the magazine, stumbling across two unarmed captives, who were taking powder to the filling room.

Moisture was apparent in the air, with darkness thickly draped. The only sounds to be heard were a constant dripping and orders being boomed by the enemy in the adjacent room, with a number of sobs and cries echoing around the ship, the shrills of wounded comrades.

"Boys, I will blow this ship. If you want to live, you'll leave now," said Le Renard, setting explosives.

The two young captives nodded in gratitude, making their exit.

Le Renard dropped a barrelful of powder to the floor, using a sharp knife to gauge a hole in the cask and delivering a straight line of powder straight from the door, leading towards the vats. Le Renard observed the movement of wet curtains, which were commonly used to lessen the chance of explosion. "Come out of there slowly, with your hands up," ordered Le Renard.

The hushed retort of the place supported Le Renard's postulation that he wasn't alone.

"Step away from the curtains," pressed Le Renard. "I will light this powder and lock these doors. You'll go up in flames with this godforsaken ship!"

"How do we know you won't kill us?" asked a voice.

"You'd be dead by now," said Le Renard.

"We don't want trouble," said the Americans, emerging from behind wet curtains. Williams clutched a French dagger and Taylor, a buccaneer cutlass.

"Who are you?" Le Renard asked.

"James Williams…and this is my colleague, Wilson Taylor. We are travellers—"

"Explorers from America," added Taylor.

"What brings you aboard this ship?" asked Le Renard. "Are you benefactor of these pirates?"

Williams began, "Well, monsieur—"

"Le Renard!" boomed the scarred-face man.

"Swell," said Taylor, with a goody smile. "Monsieur Le Renard, my partner and I were travelling to Africa when we fell under Captain Kunda's attack."

"He confused our ship for a Portuguese caravel. We lost all twenty members of our crew in the pirate raid," said Williams.

"He slaughtered all black priests onboard our ship," said Taylor.

"He called them all sorts of wicked names—"

"*Mundele ndombe*, 'black white man,' apparently," interjected Williams.

"And we've been under house arrest ever since," said Taylor,

"We've lost everything."

"Why are you hiding here?" commanded Le Renard.

"We escaped during the squabble," said Williams.

"Have you seen a young sailor?" asked Le Renard "About yay high and yay—"

"We witnessed his death," said Taylor.

"He died in the torture chamber," said Williams. "Kunda assured our freedom, but he backed out on his word."

Cleverly hiding his contentment and feeling no emotional remorse about the boy, Le Renard was satisfied; the dead boy could no longer betray him. "Poor lad. I came late to spare his life. Gentlemen, I'm about to blow this ship. I can help you. *La Caprice*—"

"*Spirit of Darkness*, I presume?" said Williams.

"Indeed. It's headed to the Congo," said the crafty man. "I take it you'd want to join that expedition?"

"We would be enchanted," said the two men. "You'd be doing us a great service."

"I can take you. I'm one of the guides onboard *La Caprice*. You can trust me," said Le Renard, quickly earning the men's confidence.

"We can't thank you enough for your kindness," said Williams,

"How can we be of service to you?"

"Well, my work as your guide will cost money. Can you afford to pay me now?" asked Le Renard.

"Oh, monsieur, we thought you'd never ask," Williams said cheerfully.

"We know of Kunda's treasures. They lay hidden in a wooden barrel with a blue dot painted on the top. If you don't want to be paid in cash, we can pay you in gold dust."

"I'd prefer gold dust," said an eager Le Renard, shaking both men's hands. "You remember the location of the barrel? We must secure it and get out of this ship."

"Surely," said Williams. "It's stocked away in my head. Kunda spoke of it to one of his men before battle."

"I've got a lifeboat on the far end of the ship that'll take us to *La Caprice*," said a salivating Le Renard. "No one will ever suspect a thing, as long as we take it back before the battle ends."

"Great plan, monsieur," said Taylor, now energised.

"The gold's kept in Captain Kunda's sleeping cabin. We best hurry," said Williams, urging both men.

"We have half an hour to get out of here. That's tight, but it'll do," said Le Renard, pressing on with the plan. Positioned deep within the darkness of the hold, Le Renard took a small lantern, which he quickly positioned in the lamp room behind the windows, highlighting the way to the gunpowder storeroom positioned next door. Subsequently, he transferred fire to the trace of powder scattered across the floor, before shining the lantern to light the way.

Meanwhile, on the upper decks of *La Caprice*, the battle raged on. Pirates, officers, and sailors fought for liberty more than anything. The idea of sustained or newfound freedom gave both sides strength. There was the ongoing noise of killing, shouting, and the clanging of swords, with both vessels navigated side by side, tied and adjoined by pirate hooks.

Those responsible for guns took their position, abolishing the riggings and masts of their enemy, firing at the broadside; low as they rolled downwards, high as the ships rolled upwards. Huge blasts were fired between the ships. All and sundry were busy doing all they could to defend *La Caprice* from the pirate invasion.

Heinrich and gunners ran up and down between decks, moving from the upper gun deck, middle deck, and lower deck. Heinrich assisted carpenters in filling holes whenever a direct hit was scored by the enemy, commonly at the waterline, having established a dedicated corridor to provide ease of repairs.

"Sir Heinrich!" an officer cried. "A direct hit was inflicted upon the gun deck. Flying splinters, officers are dying… The holes are vast and huge. Carpenters are needed immediately… Badly damaged timbers are in urgent need of repair, sir."

"Right away," said an exhausted Heinrich. "Has anyone seen Von Schweintzler?"

"No, sir," replied a junior officer.

"And Le Renard?" said Heinrich.

"Nowhere in sight, sir," replied the officer.

"We need everyone to defend this ship," said Heinrich, dashing to where carpenters had banded.

On the other side of the ship, in the operating theatre, Dawson lent a hand to Dr. Lapierre. It was an awful ordeal, complete chaos. Injured seamen and officers were rushed to the emergency ward. Dawson watched as crew members carried in the wounded. In the corridor, red blood soaked the timber floor, and cut arms, fingers, and legs flooded the doorway to the emergency ward.

No one cared to clear the mess; they were all much too busy trying to save lives. The horrid smell of blood attracted hungry vampire rats that fed on human parts abandoned on the gory floor.

Dawson dumped sand on the deck and companionway to soak up blood and prevent the crew from slipping as they hurried into the emergency ward. One by one, wounded seamen and officers crossed the threshold into the operating theatre—undoubtedly the most horrifying place on the ship. It was overcrowded with wounded, lying down on the floor, covered by sails. Those who could not be placed in the theatre were left in corridors, awaiting treatment or eventual death.

Sobs of wounded comrades and the screams of patients undergoing surgery overshadowed the piercing gun blasts outdoors.

Dr. Lapierre operated at the aft of the orlop deck, below the waterline, where they were less susceptible to enemy fire.

Through the chaos, Dawson still found time to record what she saw in her diary…

*It seems that the only valuable operations to be carried out in the operation theatre are those of amputation, and I maintain that Dr. Lapierre is in the most difficult position with the hardest of job roles to fulfill, dealing with the wounded and the dying. Although there remains some degree of humour and joviality, I must admit that it is difficult to bear the sights I am having to behold.*

*Time is of the essence, and Dr. Lapierre acknowledges this, recognising the speed at which infection can set in and take the lives of our crew. The number of wounded is ever increasing and, as the only surgeon onboard, the task of dealing with all patients falls to him.*

*There are four assistants, and around them are a number of baskets, all holding the amputated limbs of the patients, as well as fresh water and bandages. There is also a cask of boiled water, wherein the amputation tools are stored and disinfected.*

*One of the assistants, I believe to be named Adelbrecht, has the job of holding a lantern in position just above the head of the patient, his other hand armed with rum, used for drugging the patient, either providing pain relief or facilitating unconsciousness so work can be carried out. If rum is to run out, there is also brandy to be used. There is also the use of a tough leather gag, onto which the patients bite when the pain becomes unbearable. It is our hope, in such situations, that the patient passes out with the pain and is not made to endure the experience.*

*It is a frightful thing to take a position as an assistant, as I have done, and to watch the pain and anguish of men; helpless and willingly cut so their lives may be spared. I try to show compassion and empathy whilst, at once, feeling helpless and out of control, lost in a minefield of emotion and screams and gunfire.*

*The smell is something else I must acknowledge and, in regard to such, I can only state it is overwhelming. We are engorged in it and never seem to become accustomed. It is a smell of death—looming and passed.*

"Knives please, Miss Dawson," Dr. Lapierre requested, exhausted and covered in sweat. "The right leg has suffered many gunshot wounds, and there is no way it can be saved. It requires immediate amputation."

"Any other way to save his leg? I remember speaking to this young officer. It's his first combat. He just joined the king's army. It'll be hard on him, remembering his first battle with a missing leg," said Dawson, hoping the good doctor could change his mind.

"I'm afraid the injury is too deep. The only other option is to remove bullets from his leg, but that would take several hours. Time is a luxury we don't have. There's a long line of patients waiting, and I don't have much of a choice. We have to save as many lives as we can, even if that comes at the expense of this young man's leg," said Dr. Lapierre.

A seaman, assisting, leaned next to the doctor and wiped the sweat from his face with a wide cloth. Reluctantly, Dawson passed razor-sharp knives from the sea chest to the doctor. Dr. Lapierre cut through the patient's skin, muscles, and ligaments, spilling blood, and finally reached the bones.

The young officer wailed. He stirred, but the officers had him pinned down to the operating table. He screamed, but the gag in his mouth held him quiet. His eyes fell blank and absent, like one in a trance. Dr. Lapierre finished his work using a bone saw.

Dawson wrote on…

*Following the amputation, I take the bloodied stump and seal the wound to stop the bleeding by dipping it in boiling pitch. There are countless body parts and pitches, all of which are subsequently thrown overboard, along with the dead and the badly injured. It is a watery grave—one no man should bear.*

*I can no longer take such visions; the memories and the experiences themselves. The moments are unbearable, and I have asked to be relieved several times. The dead, the limbs, the blood… It is a nausea far worse than any seasickness or shark-fin soup.*

*Upon running out of the operating theatre, I vomit.*

Nothing she remembered more keenly than the embroidered crimson from her dead comrades' blood, concealing all floors on which she travelled.

*La Caprice* rocked back and forth from compound discharge and the battle endured within her walls.

# CHAPTER XIX

# DISASTER

I visit the sick bay, wherein those wounded are left to recover and rehabilitate in peace. And it is here that a Belgian Priest, Père Raymond, is located. Although he has played no role in any of the battles, he is now busier than ever before, acting as a messenger, helping with fetching, putting out fires—anything and nothing.

He might provide the sick and healing with wine or lemon juice, sometimes to distract them and ensure their spirits are kept high. The operating theatre has, of course, far more to endure than the sick bay, which is much less ghastly and painful, although there is still the high chance of death, yet somewhat more peaceful. Essentially, it is the only place onboard the vessel to offer any degree of refuge away from the battle.

"Pirates are retreating!" announced an officer.

A mob of officers hailed, firing at will at the tyrants.

"Oh, bless the Lord," Dawson said, sighing.

"He's always on time, my child," said Père Raymond.

From a distance, not far from where they were conversing, sudden shrieks echoed through the air. Dawson quickly hid behind a caging stack of crates, thinking to herself that the cries were from men freshly hit by lost bullets or gunshots and that some could be heading in her direction. She shielded her ears from the noise, but then noticed that Père Raymond did not for a moment hint from that sudden outcry. Somewhat embarrassed, she inquired, "Is that—"

"Patients," said Père Raymond. "They awake every other minute to the reality that they've been amputated."

Right then, two shots were fired nearby. Père Raymond and Dawson ran to the other end of the sick bay.

"My God!" said Dawson, her palm on her mouth.

"Seaman suicide," said Raymond. "He had been here for an hour, and I prayed with him. Poor lad. Such a strong disciple he was, but with two of his legs amputated, gangrene was claiming his life. Sad to see that he gave up." Père Raymond blessed the dead with the sign of the cross, "He was another of those who believed this ship is cursed."

*La Caprice* and its crew kept firing at the escaping pirates, when a jarring, heavy, loud explosion caused a shockwave, sending all the crewmembers onboard *La Caprice* flying to various parts of the deck to violently land on their floors.

Dawson's fall sent her sliding to a cornered post right under the main sail boom. As she went past some secondary shrouds, she firmly hooked her hand on a lump of ropes and reeled her still-moving legs around the post to stop her trajectory. "For crying out loud," she said, "What was that?" She tapped her head with her free hand, as if trying to fix a brain damage. She was flat on the floor and struggled to regain her balance.

"Dear me. Could it be a collision?" asked the priest, rising to his feet, a little shaken by the compassing blow. He held on to a rail to heave himself up. At the touch of the rail, he felt a mix of debris, ash, and dust; nonetheless he pushed up and arose sane. Slightly bent forward as if awaiting a subsequent attack, he examined the surroundings with a mild degree of disorientation and discontent.

All around, the crew was gathering, and everyone appeared to be covered in a thin layer of abrasive dust.

Air suddenly seemed hot and hard to breathe, he wiped his face while leaning his right shoulder on the bay wall, which had lost much of its aesthetic polished grease. He flicked his eyelids a few times to force a clear view and gazed at Dawson.

On her knees, trying to get herself up, she looked at him and at his overall direction and tried to utter something, but minor bits obstructed her lips.

"It's not a collision, Dawson. We're not sinking, but the air—"

Dawson hastily managed to rid her lips of stuck wooden bits and immediately warned, "Père, careful!"

Père Raymond, without hesitation or questioning and understanding the urge, dodged back down onto the floor and then looked up. One of the pieces of timber supporting two lanterns parted and smashed nearby.

"Are you all right?" asked Heinrich, helping Raymond to his feet.

"I'm fine," said Père Raymond, agitated. "Thank you, Miss Dawson. Kind of you to warn me."

"Dawson, any injuries?" queried Heinrich, joining the crew past the sick bay.

"Lucky enough, I've managed," said Dawson.

"We heard the *bang*. Pirates have escaped. They've ceased firing," said Heinrich.

"Any crevasses through our hull?" asked Raymond.

"None such, Père. Loinseach says she is still solid and will hold. However, I have sent carpenters to check for smaller holes, open cracks and pots," said Heinrich, plastered in bruises.

"And the captain?" questioned Dawson.

"He's all right. They're securing the captives," said Heinrich, "He worried you might have been injured. I promised him I'd check on you."

"Thank you," said a blushing Dawson.

"Come on. Let's gather the dead," said Heinrich.


At that moment, huge balls of fire erupted on the pirate ship *The Royal Fortune*. Great pillars of water and shattered wood planks rose high into the sky. All sorts of other objects could also be seen breaking past. Explosions were so powerful they were felt onboard *La Caprice*. *The Royal Fortune* rushed uncontrollably through the sea.

"Lower the boats!" screamed Ansel.

"Lifeboats are stuck," Calixte replied, working with the pirate crew to release lifeboats and rafts whilst the ship slowly sank. "They're smashed pretty good."

Flames raced through the wood panel of the ship, licking into the air. The ship's framework and cannon metal toppled into the sea after buckling under intense heat. Trapped pirates were guaranteed a slow, brutal death. Thick, dark smoke stretched into the air. Fire spread wildly and rapidly, engulfing the mass. Those who could escape abandoned the ship to save their lives, jumping into the sea anywhere that offered safety from the sinking inferno.

At length, lifeboats hit the surface of the water. Despite the limited seats on boats and rafts, pirates found their way out of the ship, jumping into the water by the hundreds. They swam away from the wreckage towards *La Caprice*. Kunda remained on the bridge of *The Royal Fortune*, giving his last orders for the safe evacuation of his men. He stayed with his ship to the last, whilst those already on lifeboats struggled to remain afloat.

Pirates watched as *The Royal Fortune* tilted by the last blast burst into flames; the ship keel emerged and rose high resembling a disproportionate

Leviathan, but due to its own weight a horrible creaking sound ensued, and the anticipated crack came.

Running along the keel's half- and releasing remnant cargo, the serpented large crack provoked a sinking vicious pool to form, swallowing further distressed pirates. The keel partitions then submerged, imprisoning those trapped between the severely damaged rudder and a dislocated bulkhead.

Unforgiving, the ocean swallowed them whole. Various flying jibs, now with loose tacks and burning red fumes on the bowsprit, followed and disappeared last. Large gaps of smoke spun from the pool centre into the air, and the hurtling sound of many waters concluded the victims' critical disaster.

Back at *La Caprice*, on the quarterdeck, Captain Van Lanterman and Sergeant Lekens took in some surviving and panicking pirates from the busy sea.

"Hold on to these ropes!" shouted the captain.

A series of ropes were cast into to sea in order to help the surrendering and desperate crew.

"You're honourable," said Diarabi, stepping onboard.

"You'll work to pay for the deaths you have caused onboard my ship," said the captain.

Diarabi looked at the captain, and in his shame, he respectfully nodded.

"Help these men aboard," instructed Captain Van Lanterman.

"Are you mad?" Le Renard quizzed.

"They'll work," said Van Lanterman. "We've lost many men. Perhaps you care to share where you wandered whilst we defended our ship."

"Playing Good Samaritan, saving lives, Captain," countered Le Renard. "Whilst you, Captain, save the devil in the name of the king."

"Careful," said the captain. "You are treading shallow waters."

"Look around. Look what they've done to us. They've killed our men, destroyed our ship," said Le Renard. "Show no mercy. They haven't shown any, and they must die."

"Are we savages or king's men?" asked Van Lanterman.

"They're ruthless brutes. They've killed our men. We've lost lives, Captain. You take them in, and they'll start a mutiny," emphasised Baron Schweintzler. "They're nothing but murderers and thieves—and they've proven that here today."

"Look around you! The dead want vengeance," Le Renard said, pointing at the chaos around them.

"People of *La Caprice*!" Diarabi interrupted, "I am Diarabi, born Kasongo Nkole of the Kisúndi people, gunner aboard *The Royal Fortune*. We have been sailing for months without food and drink. Our crew has been dying from spells of near starvation. We saw a ship—your ship—as an opportunity to endure."

"Are you suggesting we should feel remorseful, Pirate?" asked Le Renard. "That *we* should feel sorry for the likes of you?"

Diarabi eyed Le Renard with a look of warning, yet Diarabi knew revealing Le Renard's failed plan would only make matters worse when Kunda had to be rescued at sea.

Le Renard winked discreetly at him, aware that he was treading thin water. *Van Lanterman's rescue of Kunda would be of grave concern*, thought Le Renard; the vengeful Kunda could then expose Le Renard's failed plan, rendering worthless his future schemes with the Americans.

"You say your people fight for food and drink? Then explain this," said Loinseach, displaying a handgun to the crew. "An unmarked army pistol. I recovered it from a dead pirate. What say you about this?"

"One of hundreds of weapons specially made for the expedition. They're all sealed in cases. No one has access to the chamber except me," said Van

Lanterman, but when he found that his keys had vanished, he exclaimed in face of his crew, "Guts and gore! There is a turncoat amongst us."

"Captain?" said Sergeant Lekens. "We must flush the rat."

"By all means, quickly continue to rescue these pirates and seek Kunda off the waters," said Van Lanterman. "We'll offer him safe haven onboard in exchange for the double agent."

"Captain, I assure you that Master Kunda *will* cooperate," said Diarabi.

Le Renard's eye twitched; his ruse had failed. *Nowhere to escape*, he thought, and he knew any brisk attempt would render him blameworthy.

"No one leaves this ship until we get this sorted out," said Captain Van Lanterman.

The crew helped survivors of *The Royal Fortune* reach *La Caprice*.

"Captain!" shouted Diarabi, "there, on the lifeboat! It's Master Kunda."

*Bloody hell!* agonised Le Renard as more rescued pirates climbed onboard.

"Soon as they're within reach, I'll order my men to rescue your captain," said Van Lanterman. "Sergeant, handle all prisoners."

"Sir, they are many," advised Sergeant Lekens.

"Yes, a worthwhile investment. There must be bounties for those pirates, and they could add up to quite a large take for us. They'll trade places with the dead and work harder at the lashes of our chicotte," said Captain Van Lanterman.

Sergeant Lekens saluted the captain and walked off.

"Loinseach, let's have a report prepared on the ship damage and on the crew," said the captain. "Ten minutes."

"Aye-aye, Captain," said Loinseach.

Under attack, Baron Von Schweintzler had been elected in charge of fire-fighting.

The fire of cannonballs resulted in not only major holes in the vessel, but also the explosion of fire, with the crew required to race with bucket after bucket of water, dousing the burning timbers. Quickly, chains were formed, comprised of able-bodied crewmembers, with Baron Von Schweintzler supervising as the leather, water-filled buckets were passed one at a time, hand to hand, ensuring minimal spillage.

Meanwhile, on lower decks, Dr. Lapierre operated on his last patient. Dirt and dampness triggered infection of even small cuts and scratches. At the sick bay, Dawson carefully dressed ulcers. Heinrich and Père Raymond watched after the sick.

Abruptly, there was a *bang*. The ship was violently shaken, along with her crew.

"Here it comes again," said Dawson.

"And again," said Heinrich, falling about as a second bang shook *La Caprice* and all onboard, causing everyone in the quitter deck serious concern.

Powerful tremors were followed by clicking and clopping sounds, alarming the livestock located in the manger.

Captain Van Lanterman asked, "Where are these sounds coming from?" anxious to be without answers.

"Below the waterline, from the copper plating on the ship side," answered Loinseach. "Water will soon get through the timber with the force of such waves. Then, Captain…well, you don't need me to tell you the ship will sink."

"I disagree," commended Lekens. "I believe the ship would be sinking if it were the cracking of copper plates. It must be something else."

"Well, whatever it is, we need it resolved at once," said the captain.

"From the deep," said Baron Von Schweintzler, emerging from the lower decks. "I heard the banging down below. There are echoes of clicks and squeaks underwater."

"I heard the same, and it grew louder down into the hold," added Dr. Lapierre, joining the crew with an apron drenched in human blood.

The banging resumed, shaking the ship once more.

"Summon Heinrich," ordered Van Lanterman. "Have him join us on the bridge straightaway."

 Heinrich and Dawson turned up on the bridge momentarily.

"Heinrich, what do you make of the sounds?" questioned Captain Van Lanterman.

"I-I don't know, sir. It could be anything," stated Heinrich, uncertain.

"Captain, over there! In the water," said Dawson, now at the side of the deck.

"*Balaenoptera musculus!*" said Heinrich.

"A blue whale," concurred Dawson, gazing at the dinosaur-sized mammal ploughing through the stressed ocean.

"Harmless," said Heinrich.


Meanwhile, at sea, survivors of *The Royal Fortune* were much closer to *La Caprice* but struggled to keep afloat. They bawled in horror as the whale swam nearer and then disappeared over the horizon. Captain Kunda and his pirates rowed as fast as they could, but strong waves insisted on thrusting them back, in spite of their grand efforts to make strides.

The rest of the pirates, taken as prisoners, called out to them to scull faster.

Survivors, moving towards the ship, ran into groups of porpoises. Hundreds of the creatures moved swiftly, crossing the ship and the survivors.

With some of her topsails needing attention, *La Caprice* was veering farther off course by strong waters and winds, with the ocean rolling upon the dictation of the gusts. Slowly but surely, small waves gained height and momentum, becoming topped with large crests, spraying foam across all in their path. Crew and survivors looked on as the ocean rulers, its mightiest beasts—poisonous lionfishes, bone-crushing sharks, stingrays—flashed by; dolphins avoiding their predators, swimming playfully by.

"Kunda's drifting away," Le Renard noted with a smirk, pointing to a wafting boat struggling against burly waves. "Why rescue men prone to unleash a mutiny? Captain, you will see us killed if you bring those men onboard."

"We are entitled to the truth," responded the captain. "We have yet to resolve the matter of unmarked pistols and the mole onboard this vessel. Once Kunda is rescued, we shall find out."

"They're pirates, for Christ's sake," barked Le Renard.

"We have many mysteries to solve," said Captain Van Lanterman.

Le Renard countered, "The bloody ship is cursed—"

"Then by all means, I intend it to be uncursed," said Van Lanterman.

"Officers, help me get to Kunda," said the captain.

"I'm afraid that won't be possible," said Baron Von Schweintzler.

"Baron, careful," said the captain in a raised tone.

"I mean well," said Baron Von Schweintzler as gushing winds thrust the crew around deck. "Have a look at the sea. There are high waves with overhanging crests. The sea is white with foam, and visibility's poor. It's much too risky, Captain."

"You must do something," pressed Diarabi, anxious. "If we don't, the ocean will swallow them dead."

"Row! Row!" hollered pirates onboard *La Caprice.*

"Baron's right. The winds are far too strong," said Captain Van Lanterman, standing against strong, blustery weather.

"If you don't, we will," said Diarabi.

"Are y-you mad?" stuttered Dawson.

Diarabi and his pirates leaped off into the gusty sea, some quickly drowning as they willingly plunged to their own watery graves.

"Nothing we can do," said Van Lanterman, restraining Dawson. "If they can save Kunda, let them."

Van Lanterman eyed Le Renard. "You must be delighted."

"*Au contraire*," said Le Renard, with a smirk that made his permanent scar more pronounced.

Sergeant Lekens and Loinseach returned to the main deck, where the crew was busy counting the dead and piling them, one on top of another.

"Captain, we couldn't find anything on the ship that could create such a racket," said Sergeant Lekens, joining the crew on the upper deck.

"The crew thinks the ship's cursed," said Loinseach.

"Then tell them otherwise," demanded Van Lanterman.

"Looking at the horizon, I see dark clouds forming," said Dawson, pointing.

"Looks like a killer storm's approaching," said Loinseach, his eyes wide, astounded at the hasty storm in the far distance.

All was happening so quickly: the sky was overcast, blowing dark and rolling clouds, whilst gushing wind lashed out at the deep blue sea, delivering an ominous sound and electrifying lightning.

"We best leave the deck. It's getting icy," advised Baron Von Schweintzler.

Just as they were about to leave, Dawson hinted, "Oh! I think I know now. The animals down in the hold must have felt the storm. By instinct they clopped and clicked those sounds we have been hearing."

"Well that explains it, some kind of a natural warning. Very well, Miss Dawson. That is definitely one mystery solved," acknowledged the captain. "And to my reckoning, others we shall write off as mystery. Loinseach," said Van Lanterman, "control the ship."

"Aye-aye," said Loinseach, departing the deck.

Bursts of static trailed electric, shimmering lightning. An increase in static intensity proved to those onboard that thunderstorms were nearing.

From a short distance away, significant turbulence could be seen swirling in the thunderclouds. Draughts and currents induced, causing charged particles to swish around. Thunder and lightning erupted from the clouds, illuminating them with intense light. They zigzagged through the air and lower parts of the clouds. From the ship, the crew witnessed only their flickering reflection in adjacent clouds. Significant flashes created incredible cloud snapshots, lasting up to half a second in visibility.

Dr. Lapierre, returning, provided a stark reminder. "The storm's headed this way. We've saved the lives we can. The wounded are all cared for in some way or another. Now, how do you suggest we care for the dead, Captain?"

"Bury them at sea. We need room for the living," Van Lanterman responded quickly.

"Very well," said Dr. Lapierre, motioning to a sailor.

"Throw them overboard," ordered the sailor in a sombre fashion as cadavers were disposed of at sea.

Fervent updrafts pursued thunder and lightning, triggering water droplets to brush against one another. Heavy rain reached the deep.

"Evacuate the deck! All crew vacate the deck now," shouted Van Lanterman. "Everyone to lower decks."

Even in poor visibility, Sergeant Lekens guided the crew.

Dawson, along with Dr. Lapierre, rushed to the fireplace.

"Storms with lightning. One still finds many people who have yet to conquer a childhood fear of this awesome phenomenon," Dawson observed, a tremor in her voice.

"Fear stems from the unknown," observed Dr. Lapierre. "I felt much the same as a child, but as I came to understand the mechanics of this marvel, my fear graduated to avid fascination."

In the daily cabin, Loinseach struggled to steer the ship from the dreadful weather whilst, drenched, Captain Van Lanterman and Heinrich helped sailors and officers replace damaged sails, working laboriously in the ghastly rain. The bad storm and poor visibility made for an impossible task as the ship struggled to stay afloat.

*La Caprice* rocked back and forth in the burly winds and waves, making the lines controlling the set of the sails impossible to manoeuvre. Officers chased goats and poultry that broke free and roamed the deck; others worked tirelessly to secure lifeboats strong winds shoved around. And, from the top of the ship, sailors struggled to control the sails. Stun sails were fastened to the booms by crewmen, but during their attempts to save the ship from its doom, many fell and died. In the distance, clouds could be seen tightly spinning, cone-shaped, hanging from the bottom of a thundercloud. A powerful spinning motion occurred when high-level winds blew over the sea in different directions than low-level winds, sending the giant monster system into a violent rotation. Vast, more keenly revolving air cyclones progressed fast and strong, moving quickly over the ocean.

By far, the sea monster was the most notable and devastating of all whirlwinds, creating havoc, lapping up everything in its course. The funnel-shaped cloud rotation, complete with its powerful twisting effect, caused devastation wherever it journeyed. Pirate lifeboats, fish, aquatic mammals, and vegetation of the deep were lifted and hurled, imposing a life-threatening storm for all that stood in its path.

Van Lanterman and his crew realised the giant sea monster was headed straight for the ship. "The giant w…waterspout moving f…fast!" shouted the captain, struggling to keep up with the rest of the crew on the poop deck.

The stubborn storm caused severe waves to rock the ship sideways.

"Navigate away from the spout now, Loinseach."

"Impossible! I-I can't control the ship. The storms are too strong," shouted Loinseach. "She struggles to keep up with weather conditions."

"Work with her! Keep her steady," demanded Van Lanterman, exiting the daily cabin. "I've got to check on the others." Young crewmembers who had never before ventured out to sea and were still virgins of long voyages such as that aboard *La Caprice* were fearful as they wailed and prayed for the Lord's grace. They witnessed the powerful sea monster approaching at a terrifying speed, causing intense devastation along the way.

"God save us," beckoned Heinrich, indicating the sign of the cross.

"Dawson?" asked the captain of Heinrich.

"In her cabin," said Heinrich. "She'll be safe there."

"Stick together," said Van Lanterman, "and keep an eye on each other. This is life or death."

"Père," said Heinrich, "a benefit prayer would be most welcomed."

"Everyone," said Père Raymond, "kneel."

"Kneel," ordered Sergeant Lekens.

"*Pater noster qui es in caelis, sanctificétur Nomen…*" recited Père Raymond, shifting rosary beads in the hollow of his hand.

"Brace yourselves!" shouted Van Lanterman. "This is it!"

A mammoth waterspout struck against the once-elegant, majestic, beautiful *La Caprice*, which bore the brunt of gallons of salty sea water crashing down on her decks as the remaining crew made use of buckets, trying to rid the ship of the abundance of an unwanted stream onboard the ship.

From her sleeping cabin, Dawson, in despair, undernourished, on her knees, composed a memo to the International Association…

*Friday, 21; Day 70*
*To the Assembly of the International Association:*

*Dear Members of the Assembly,*

*Since La Caprice and her crew were navigating across the Atlantic, in excess of two months have passed. Three weeks ago was when the incredible, yet devastating weather storms hit; although we are lucky to have survived, the vessel has nevertheless experienced much damage and now, when things are at their worst, I advise that we are almost out of fresh food and livestock.*

*Food and grog rations—notably, three parts water, one part rum—have been given to each of the crewmembers, in addition to those pirates we have taken as captives.*

*Considering such insufficient rations, there has been a great deal of theft across the vessel, with water even so sparse that they simply consume whatever they can find. A great many murders have been committed, the dead discovered in the hold, with such instances undoubtedly inspired by the fact that a dead seaman's supplies are auctioned amongst his mess mates. With this in mind, even Monsieur Le Renard has been found guilty of stealing goods, which he was to give to two American travellers subsequently found hiding in the lady's hole of the hold's stern—recognised as being the safest location onboard the vessel.*

*A great many hundreds of pirates have been taken as prisoners, with noisy drinking and negotiations made following the completion of their daily work. Undoubtedly, all aboard are strange and unusual in their own ways; some play games or fight, some wear the garments of those they murdered, others mock lawyers. It is a strange circumstance to be a part of.*

*For two weeks, the crew has been struggling to simply survive. Following the strong waterspouts that hit the ship, however, we were provided with an abundance of frog legs and fish; those of us fortunate enough to circumvent starvation for the* time being have celebrated only in the short term, knowing only too well that our ordeal has only just begun. We now face hunger as the cause of death, despite having survived a perilous battle.

In specific consideration to the pirates mentioned, we came across a small group floating on small wreckage, so we rescued them, shocked to find they had survived, despite being at sea since the battle. Those recovered state that there are more survivors, amongst them Captain Kunda, strong winds apparently having separated the groups. They notably faced shark attacks, poor weather, the prospect of drowning, and undoubtedly a number of other life-threatening circumstances, and many lost their lives to such causes. But perhaps the most terrifying and mocking of all deaths is dehydration when surrounded by an ocean.

Without question, life onboard La Caprice is difficult, hard, and wearing, a situation all the more keenly emphasised by the lack of food and drink. A number of crew are being lost at regular intervals, with dead bodies continuously deposited into the uncaring ocean. Such suffering is enough to drive anyone mad, not least of all so many men trapped onboard a vessel without supplies, watching as what they fear will kill them causes the deaths of their comrades.

In regard to the above—and I am unsure whether or not I should report this without evidence—there are rumours that some of the crew have taken to cannibalism, forced to consume the bodies of their dead crewmen to stay alive. Less in need of evidence is the belief that rats are also being caught and eaten. In this same vein, I am a little disheartened to even write this letter, uncertain as I am that it will reach you, as I have been informed that even the messenger birds are being eaten by onboard sailors.

In spite of all we have endured and what is yet to come, I continue to pray to God each and every day, never allowing my faith to waiver. I am determined that I will see it through, in whatever form. I believe and hope we will reach Congo coast, despite acknowledging that there are so many obstacles still in our way.

*Consider the significantly damaged sails and the destroyed rigging; the weather; the lack of supplies… Moreover, there is the compass, which is markedly damaged, and is the only tool we have at our disposal to guide our way to our destination. Essentially, it could be stated that we are lost at sea, although Captain Van Lanterman maintains that his knowledge in terms of charts navigation will see us through, although this is problematic, owing to the inaccuracy of sea maps and the fact that any small degree of error could cause us a longer journey—and death.*

*Nevertheless, as I pen this report and detail my thoughts, I acknowledge that I maintain faith that myself and the crew will continue to see another morning, each and every day.*

*Ms. Susan Dawson.*

Their gun was fired to signal the sunrise. It was time for the crew to carry out the daily routine work, but nobody seemed to care. On the lower decks, sailors and officers remained asleep in their hammocks. The mass of sleeping bodies made the lower decks stuffy. The air was thick and vulgar, so much so that it felt to the sailors that they had passed the night asleep, with their mouths full of copper coins, referred to as 'fat head.'

On the outside of the ship, all was quiet, and still nobody was out to sort out the early morning work. The sun was at its peak, and the sky was clear. It was dry and hot.

At the lubbers' hole, Quartermaster O'Gowan lay on the platform halfway up the mast. He was just about to open his eyes from the gunshot, but the sunrays in his face made him feel lethargic. He had been on the platform watching the sea for days and nights, enduring both the heat and the cold, watching for danger whilst hoping for a miracle.

At the surface of the seawater, the air was undoubtedly thicker and colder than that directly above it, with warm layers heading skywards and back down again. The air behaved in much the same way as a lens, diverting and flexing light, creating an unrecognisable, upturned, augmented vision in a different position. And just above the cold seawater, above the level but close to the young sailor, a false image was produced.

O'Gowan was disturbed by flies attracted to the salty sweat on his face. He shooed them away with his hand. "Damn flies," said a maigrichon Quartermaster O'Gowan. When he opened his eyes to kill the pesky insects, he pointed. "Lord Almighty!" He was thrilled to catch a glimpse of a distant land. He readied himself to shout—despite his weak limbs and caked dry mouth; his body had been dehydrated for days. *A floating forest? Damn. I'm hallucinating. A bloody mirage*, thought the quartermaster. He fell to the platform, hopelessly shutting his eyes to make the false vision go away, wondering if the ship had ever crossed the equator.

Sunlight slowly consumed whatever vital water he had left in his body. He had been starving. It had been almost two weeks since he had eaten a much-savoured decent meal. He appeared almost anorexic: a burgeoning gigantic head; a skeleton protruding the side of his ribs; a depression where a potbelly the size of three human heads used to be. He no longer had the energy to induce him to wake up and watch over the sea. But despite his weakness and disillusionment, he rose to his feet and looked out over the sea just once more.

He was the crew's hope for renaissance—and he reckoned it.

"God, I will not despair. Père Raymond says, 'Anyone who believes in the Father must have faith.'" He trembled, his legs failing to support him any longer, but he didn't give up so easily. He cupped his feeble hand above his brow to shield his tired eyes from the sun so his view would not be obstructed. And, as he moved around the platform, he perceived something in the distance. *My eyes are weak, and the sun's so high*, thought the quartermaster. He shaded his mug with his hat and took a second look.

A vast plateau, covered with green bushes and dense vegetation, rose to its highest point in the mountains, the spine of the Dark Continent.

*Dear Lord! The Great Basin!* thought Quartermaster O'Gowan.

He struggled on his feet as he hastened to the bell and banged it loudly with all his might. He stood firm, staring with hope at the land that rose before him—a strange land somewhere on the west coast of Africa.

It was the most magnificent, breathtaking experience of his life. If he were to die in that moment, his mission would be complete. But nevertheless, Quartermaster O'Gowan longed to set foot on the Dark Continent before he took his last breath.

# EPILOGUE

Below the deckhouse, locked up in the ship hull, Le Renard, Taylor, and Williams had heard the pompous sound of the ship horn above decks, signalling the sighting of the Congo. A scraggy Van Lanterman appeared on the upper deck next to Susan Dawson, and into view came Sergeant Gérome Lekens, Dr. Lapierre, Jurgen Heinrich, Baron Von Schweintzler, Master Loinseach, and the rest of the crew.

Dawson's watchful eyes had seen the captain squeeze the half-cross, silver-tone pendant in his palm, a distressing glance crossing his face before a relieving thought invaded his mind.

Below, at sea level, the even, murky water banged at the boat hull as *La Caprice—The Spirit of Darkness*—traversed into an open cove of brownish waves.

"At last!" said the captain, addressing his crew, weakened, the dead carried off by the sea. A frail smile lit up his features. "We have found the Congo."

Bison Van Lanterman and his crew believed, in Europe, that they were commoners. In Africa, they were…kings.

***To be continued…***

# POSTSCRIPT

*London, United Kingdom*
*Saint Bartholomew's Hospital*
*December 20, 1938*

**H**ence it was that we had found the Congo, yet the story does not end here but only begins. However, Elizabeth, my faithful nurse, had stopped reading.

Her sweet voice had faded to the impermanent stillness of my heart. Physicians had rushed in when Liz called out. I had collapsed; a fading out that left me comatose whilst I recuperated. And so it was that I was forced to pause before I could hear Liz's soothing voice once more and the account of a secret journey to the Heart of Darkness, that of Captain Van Lanterman, aficionada of the King of the Belgians with his band of travellers. Till then, I bid you good fortune, in the hopes that we shall together continue to explore my tale another day.

Godspeed to you!

Sincerely,

Susan Bailey Dawson

# AUTHORS' NOTE

Here, we try to do what is ethically sound by means of a disclaimer in adherence to the law of the land and in respect to those who have made it possible for us to impart this tale and to whom much credence is bestowed.

This work was inspired by the lives and works of many to whom we attribute much credit in our bibliography acknowledgment. Any failure of a mention is purely an omission and by no means deliberate or otherwise intentional.

Although there are a vast wealth of historical events and personalities presented in this novel, this work is purely fictional, as may be an alternate history or historical fantasy, and therefore should not be construed or otherwise used as a source of factual accounts. Truth and fiction have been merged harmoniously to create this captivating tale through the eyes of two inventive authors—the Ngwala brothers.

Importantly, it should be emphasised that this work is one wholly intended for entertainment purposes.

Thus, we hope you have enjoyed your reading!

# ACKNOWLEDGEMENTS

## ALLAIN'S THANKS

I wish to express my thanks, first and foremost, to my Lord God, through Jesus Christ, my saviour, for the life He has given me and the opportunity to complete this novel.

I also wish to thank the following people, all of whom have helped in the manifestation of this dream and to whom I am indebted.

Susanne Ngwala, for her moral support in the completion of this piece; for reading our story, and for her criticism and encouragement to the end.

My thanks go to my brother, collaborator, co-author, and publisher, Mayi Ngwala, for pressing on and writing during the course of many late nights and weekends, spending time away from his loved ones, and for giving me the inspiration to write.

My thanks are also extended to my brother Bodi, for supporting me spiritually in overcoming life's obstacles. My thanks go further to my brother Junior, my twin sisters Benonia and Nawita, and my wonderful family in Africa for their constant source of strength and support. My thanks are also extended to my 'brother' and friend, Mr.

Ken Ward, and his family, for their encouragement and support during our student years.

I especially thank the following dear friends for their moral support as I struggled through life: Mr. Anthony Douglas, who reminds me there's always a bright light at the end of the tunnel; my loving friend Miss Iona Cree, who has been a sister to me for as long as I can remember; Mr. Ola Ajayi; and Mr. Ketan Ghelani.

I am eternally indebted to my lovely parents, Dr. Faustin Ngwala Ndambi and Ma' Paku Bodi Alexandrine Fifi, for their support and encouragement in my studies abroad and in achieving my dreams and ambitions in life.

Finally, I thank all the readers for appreciating our work and taking the time to read our novel. Remember always: Good things come to those who wait!

Thank you—and God bless you all.

## MAYI'S THANKS

I want to thank my beloved brother, Allain Ngwala, for inviting me to collaborate and co-author this amazing tale. This has been an amazing adventure and, by far, one of the most fulfilling experiences of my entire life. I welcome the opportunity to co-author many more novels with such a brilliant mind in the future. Allain is one of the most creative minds and storytellers I have ever known, and I am certain our relationship will continue to grow as we continue to collaborate on future works.

I would also like to thank my lovely parents, Dr. Faustin Ngwala Ndambi (aka Docta, the Grand Wizard) and Ma' Paku Bodi Alexandrine Fifi (aka Madame Ngwala, My Goddess), for their unconditional love. Neither has ever ceased to encourage us to reach high and realise our wildest dreams. Thank you so much. This is for you. I love you forever.

Further, I would like to thank my siblings for their relentless support: Guyguy Jean-Remi Bodi Ngwala and his lovely wife Samantha Bodi-Ngwala; Ndambi Ngwala Jr.; Benonia N. Ngwala; Nawita N. Ngwala; and the loving Susanne Ngwala.

To my wife, partner, and co-publisher, Nakia T. Ngwala, the queen in my life, and my two boys, African princes, Xavier and Xander M. Ngwala, I thank you from the bottom of my heart for giving me the opportunity to do what I love: write. I love you always.

Finally, what can I say? I saved the best for last! I thank my savior *Yezu Klistu* (Jesus Christ) for redemption. Glory to Almighty God for strength and the gift of life. I am eternally yours.

# SPECIAL THANKS

Warm thanks go to our language translators and manuscript editors and tireless contributors who have made this enterprise a work of art and a reality. None of this would have been possible without your great effort and constructive input.

Finally, we thank our devoted readers for their continued support, primarily for reaching out and giving back to humanitarian causes and charities through their purchase of this novel.

Many thanks!

# BIBLIOGRAPHY

The research for this novel was conducted over several years, dating back close to two decades to the present, through the use of a variety of sources. Notably, every effort has been made to ensure the accuracy of the information, research, and resources used. Any failure to accurately credit a source is by no means deliberate. Hence, here we list the sources and research used to add to the authenticity of the historical time invoked in the book for artistic reasons (in alphabetical order):

Afrika, L. O. *African Holistic*. A&B Publishers Group, 1998. Print.

Allen, C, & Fry, H. *Tales from the Dark Continent: Images of British Colonial Africa in the twentieth Century*. Time Warner, 1990. Print.

Ashley, L. R. N. *The Complete Book of Magic and Witchcraft*. Barricade Books, 1995. Print.

Biesty, S. & Platt, R. *Stephen Biesty's Cross-Sections: Man-of-War*. Dorling Kindersley, 1993. Print.

Davidson, B. *The Africans: An entry to cultural history*. Penguin, 1973. Print.

Defoe, D. *A General History of the Robberies and Murders of the Most Notorious Pyrates*. Ch. Rivington, J. Lacy, and J. Stone, 1724. Print.

Delpar, H. *The Discoverers: An Encyclopedia of Explorers and Exploration*.

McGraw-Hill, 1979. Print.

Du Chaillu, P. B. *Explorations and Adventures in Equatorial Africa; with Accounts of the Manners and Customs of the People, and of the chase of the Gorilla, The Crocodile, Leopard, Elephant, Hippopotamus, and other Animals.* Harper & brothers, 1871. Print.

Du Chaillu, P. B. *Adventures in the Great Forest of Equatorial Africa and the Country of the Dwarfs.* Harper & brothers, 1890. Print. Harper & brothers, 1890. Print.

Evans-Pritchard, E. E. & Gillies, Eva. *Witchcraft, Oracles and Magic among the Azande.* Clarendon Press, 1963. Print.

Everett, S. *History of Slavery.* Chartwell Books, Inc., 1992. Print.

Hameso, S. Y. *Development, State and Society: Theories and Practice in Contemporary Africa.* iUniverse, 2002. Print.

Haws, D. *Ships and the Sea: A chronological review.* Crescent Books, 1985. Print.

Hochschild, A. *King Leopold's Ghost: A Story of Greed, Terror, and Heroism in Colonial Africa.* Mariner Books, 1999. Print.

Hutchinson, G. *Medieval Ships and Shipping (The Archaeology of Medieval Britain).* Leicester University Press, 1997. Print.

Hyland, P. *The Black Heart: A Voyage Into Central Africa.* Ulverscroft Large Print Books, 1992. Print.

Jeal, T. *Livingstone.* London: Heinemann, 1973.

Keith, A. B. *The Belgian Congo and The Berlin Act.* Oxford at the Clarendon Press, 1919. Print.

Konstam, A. *Elite 67: Pirates 1660 – 1730.* Osprey Publishing Ltd, 1998. Print.

Konstam, A. *Pirates: Terror on The High Seas.* Osprey Publishing, 2001. Print.

Konstam, Angus. *Scourge of the Seas: Buccaneers, Pirates & Privateers*. Osprey Publishing Ltd, 2007. Print.

Making of America Project. *The Living Age*. The Living Age Co. Inc., 1890.

O'Hanlon, R. *Congo Journey*. Penguin UK, 2005. Print.

Pakenham, T. F. D. *The Scramble for Africa: White Man's Conquest of the Dark Continent from 1876–1912*. Avon Books, 1992. Print.

Robertson, Stuart. *Pirates Pocket-Book*. Anova Books, 2008. Print.

Roome, W. J. W. *Apolo: The Apostle to the Pygmies*. London: Marshall, Morgan & Scott, 1934. Print.

Schweinfurth, G. A. *The Heart of Africa. Three years' travels and adventures in the unexplored regions of Central Africa, from 1868 to 1871*. London: S. Low, Marston, Low, and Searle, 1874. Print.

Severin, T. *The African Adventure: Four Hundred Years of Exploration in the Dangerous Continent*. E P Dutton, 1973. Print.

Stanley, H. M. *The Congo and the founding of its free state; a story of work and exploration*. New York, Harper & Brothers, 1885. Print.

Steele, P. *Pirates*. Kingfisher, 2000. Print.

Taplin, S. *Pirate's Handbook*. Usborne Publishing Ltd, 2006. Print.

Van Gennep, A. *The Rites of Passage*. Textbook Publishers, 2003. Print.

Webb, E. J. *Africa: as seen by its explorers*. London: E. Arnold, 1899. Print.

Williams, N. *Sea Dogs: Privateers, Plunder and Piracy in the Elizabethan Age*. Littlehampton Book Services Ltd; 1st US Edition edition, 1975. Print.

# TRANSLATIONS

These unedited translations (selected words, expressions, and phrases) from English to Kikongo (Kongo language) and English to Flemish (Belgian Dutch) from the earliest manuscript did not make the final cut for inclusion in the novel for editorial reasons. They are provided here, courtesy of Dr. Faustin Ngwala Ndambi and our Flemish translators, for educational purposes.

## ENGLISH TO KIKONGO

i. "Palm wine" translates to "*Tsamba*" or "*Malavu ma ngazi.*"

ii. "Look," translates to "*Tala,*"

iii. "Elder Ngoma." translates to "*Yaya Ngoma.*"

iv. "Farewell, Elder Ngoma... Mother of our kingdom. Mother of our nation. Don't forget about us." translates to "*Wenda mbote wedi yaya Ngoma... Ngudi kipfumu kieto. Ngudi mvil'etu. Kadi kutuzimbakana.*"

v. "I don't know!" translates to "*Ndikadi zaba!*"

vi. "Burnt-face" ("Arab") translates to "*Nkanda uvia mbazu.*"

vii. "Shut up!" translates to "*Kanga munu'aku!*" or "*Ba dio sui!*"

viii. "Move and keep your mouth shut!" translates to "*Botuka ayi kanga munu'aku!*"

ix. "PLEASE!" translates to "*NDEMVUKILA!*"

x. "NOW!" translates to "*MUTHANGU YAYI!*" or "*BUABU!*"

xi. "Don't be afraid." translates to "*Bika mona wonga.*"

xii. "It is time! We strike now!" translates to "*Thangu ifuene! Tufuete hanga mambu muthangu yayi!*"

xiii. "Cassava root" translates to "*Didioko'*" or "*Khayi'*" or "*Phanza.*"

xiv. "Yambi, tell me about him." translates to "*Yambi, khambi mo zebe mu yandi.*"

xv. "Through your own eyes." translates to "*Mu meso maku.*"

xvi. "I will carve his body through this piece of wood." translates to "*Si nabanda nyitu'andi mu tini kinti bene kioko ki nkisi mosi kafua.*"

xvii. "A product of voodoo. The product of his death." translates to "*Kima ki nkisi. Kima ki lufua.*"

xviii. "I will cast a magic curse upon him." translates to "*Si nansiga te yi kuna lufua*" or "*Si nankomila mianda te yi kuna lufua.*"

xix. "The person's hair, nail clippings, and this wood carving will be enough to cause harm." translates to "*Ayi tsuki zandi, ayi zingongolo zandi, ayi tini ki nti bene kioko bifueni kuandi mu kumhanga or kumonisa phasi.*"

xx. "Then one by one we shall take them all out till the very last one." translates to "*Buna ma tubimisa mosi mosi te yi kuna utsuka.*"

xxi. "Once they're all dead, we will escape this camp and find our way to the mouth of the ocean and capture one of their ships." translates to "*Bawu mana fua, ma tubotuka vava ayi tomba nzila yi tudila ku mmbu.*"

xxii. "And the gods will see us safely back to our beloved kingdom." translates to "*Ayi minkisi mietu ma mitusadisa mu fiela vutuka ku tsi'etu.*"

xxiii. "Have patience and the gods will surely deliver our freedom." translates to "*Tuvunganu moyo ka minkisi mietu ma mitusadisa mu baka dipanda di tsi'etu.*"

xxiv. "She needs rests." translates to "*Kafuete vunda*" or "*Mfunu vunda kadi.*"

xxv. "Nsala will take over." translates to "*Nsala ma kavinginina.*"

xxvi. "We plead for destruction of the evil man that robs our people and plagues our lands." translates to "*Tuzolele Vonda mutu mbimbi unzola kutuyiba ayi kutubotula ntoto'etu.*"

xxvii. "Oh spirits of death, entrust me with the power to curse their crossing to our beloved kingdom." translates to "*Oh minkisi mi lufua, phanianu ngolo yi bebisila kuluzu'awu mu tsi'etu.*"

xxviii. "Flood the gates open to my paranormal instincts as intercessor of the living and the dead." translates to "*Thondisanu zngolo zi zingisila ayi zi vondila.*"

xxix. "Flood the gates open, oh gods of destruction." translates to "*Thondisanu, oh minkisi mi lufua!*"

xxx. "Oh, Spirits of death! No further suffering." translates to "*Oh minkisi mi lufua! Manisanu ziphasi zietu.*"

xxxi. "Now we ask you, spirits of death, to fulfill your duty to your adored people." translates to "*Mu thangu yayi, oh minkisi mi lufua, sadisanu mvila'etu.*"

xxxii. "Nsala. Tell me…" translates to "*Nsala. Khambi…*"

xxxiii. "In a large room. Hundreds of them like a cluster of ants. Someone is speaking." translates to "*Mu vinga kinnene ki nzo. Badi zikhama buna biniona. Umosi ulembo tubi.*"

xxxiv. "Wait… It's the Master." translates to "*Vingila… Nyandi Pfumu'awu.*"

xxxv. "Now, Nsala! Now!" translates to "*Mu thangu yayi, Nsala! Mu thangu yayi!*"

xxxvi. "I'm sorry father." translates to "*Ndemvukila tata.*"

xxxvii. "My own flesh and blood… You know our laws." translates to "*Nsuni'ama ayi menga mama … Zebi kuaku minsiku or minkaka mietu.*"

xxxviii. "This is your third offense." translates to "*Yayi yawu nzimbala'aku yi ntatu.*"

xxxix. "I have loved you but I can no longer protect you." translates to "*Ndibekuzolanga, hangi buabu phodi bue kukengidila ko.*"

xl. "Master, not in front of the men." translates to "*A Pfumu, bika hadi batu batelimini.*"

## ENGLISH TO FLEMISH

i. "The Negroes won't stop running, Captain!" translates to "*De negers wiln nie stoppen van weglopen, Kapitein!*"

ii. "Capitaine! Four hundred women." translates to "*Kapitein! Vierhoenderd vrouwn.*"

iii. "Five hundred men and forty children." translates to "*Vuufhoenderd vinten en veertig kinders.*"

iv. "We can't fall short. We contracted for ten thousand. We've only got half. We need more. Children will not fetch enough. They're too weak. Preferably men. Strong men. Ones that can survive the long voyage." translates to "*We kunn der gin tekort komn. Wen der tienduust beloofd. Wen mo den helft. Wen der meer nodig. Kinders gon nie genoeg zien. Ze zien te zwak. Het liefste vinten. Sterke vinten. Types die de lange tocht overleevn.*"

v. "Take a hundred men. Stick up competing convoys. Bribe village chiefs if you have too. Those that resist, you know what to do. The rest of the platoon will join me. I'll take these back to the ship." translates to "*Nimt hoenderd man mee. Schakelt de schepen ut. Koop de dorpsleiders om als da nodig is. Voe degene die under verzetten, weet je wa da je te doen stoat. De rest van de platoon goat me mien mee. Ik gan met under were keren nar het schip."*

vi. "You and your regiment come with me." translates to "*Gie en joe mensen komen met mien mee.*"

vii. "Move!" translates to "*Komaan!*"

viii. "Get from under him!" translates to "*Pakt hem van onder!*"

ix. "Flemish bastard! Fight him!" translates to "*Vlaamse eikel! Vecht met em.*"

x. "Sissies!" translates to "*Mietjes!*"

xi. "Negroes can punch better than that!" translates to "*Negers kunn beter slaagn dan da!*"

xii. "Cuff the fucker in the jaw, Dietger!" translates to "*Neemt dien eikel in zen kake, Dietger!*"

xiii. "Dammit! We have lost men! Many men. If this is your idea of honouring their memories then I'm appalled. Get these Negroes on their feet and let's march! Is it understood?" translates to "*Godverdomme! Wen vele man verloren! Veel man. Et da joen idée is voor under herinneringen teeren zienk geschokt. Lat die negers lopen en vertrekt! Ej da begrepen?*"

xiv. "You heard the Sergeant!" shouted a superior officer. "Pick up your weapons. Get the fuck back in line! We march, now!" translates to "*Jet de sergeant gehoord. Schreeuwt de opperleider. Pakt je wapens. Pakt je positie in! We vertrekkn nu!*"

xv. "Into the bushes!" translates to "*Nar het bos!*"

xvi. "Right behind you!" translates to "*Achter je!*"

xvii. "Found anything?" translates to "*Etwuk gevonden?*"

xviii. "No! Nothing in here!" translates to "*Nee! Niks hier!*"

xix. "Nothing at all." translates to "*Helemaal niks.*"

xx. "Come on! Maybe just an animal." translates to "*Kom we zijn weg! Misschien ist nen dier.*"

xxi. "Capitan Van Lanterman will have our heads if we're but a minute late. Let's get out of here." translates to "*Kapitein Van Lanterman is nie bliede als we nen minuut later zen. Kom we zien weg.*"

xxii. "Move! Bitch!" translates to "*Komaan! Trutte!*"

xxiii. "March!" translates to "*Vertrekt!*"

xxiv. "He said march! Old witch!" translates to "*Ne zegt daj moet deure doen! Oede hekse!*"

xxv. "The old wench is dying?" translates to "*De oede vrouw gaat dood?*"

xxvi. "She was slowing us down." translates to "*Ze vertraagt us.*"

xxvii. "Wait! I've got to take a piss." translates to "*Wacht! Kmoen efkes pissen.*"

xxviii. "At my command." translates to "*Op mien teken.*"

xxix. "Shut up! Fucking nigger! Shut up, whore!" translates to "*Oed je moend! Klote neger! Oed je moend, hoere!*"

xxx. "Sergeant, find out who was on duty." translates to "*Sergeant, et uitgezocht wien dat er verantwoorderlijk was.*"

xxxi. "I'm on it, Captain," translates to "*Kweet et, Kapitein.*"

READ ON FOR

ALLAIN NGWALA'S

SHORT STORY

# CHILDREN OF THE NIGHT

IN COLLABORATION WITH

MAYI NGWALA

# CHILDREN
# OF THE NIGHT

**I'M PEDRO PEREIRA**…and I've been saved…

It was February 13, 2000. I turned on the television set, and there it was: *The Oprah Winfrey Show*—"How to Discover the Best of Yourself by Finding the Courage to Give."

This notion had a great impact on me; I was younger at the time, but I remember it to this day. I wanted to give back to others what I had received.

I owe a debt of gratitude to my adoptive parents. They once taught me: "The hand that gives gathers," and, "He who can give has many a good neighbour," taken from a French proverb.

During my lifetime, I have sought to live by such guiding principles. I was born in a suburb of Rio de Janeiro in Brazil. One day, like every other day, I returned home; however, this time I found my mother dead in her bed. I never managed to find out how or why she had died, but I imagined she had killed herself because she felt she could no longer cope with the suffering of this turbulent life.

In regard to my dad, well, he left me and my mom decades ago, without so much as a hint as to where he was going. And, to make matters worse, I was only ten years old at the time when my mother died.

Alone and struggling to survive, I became homeless, caught up in a gang, shooting up drugs. Many times I was scared stiff. I saw my friend die of an overdose, but I just couldn't stop. I wouldn't say I was an addict, but whenever the world's burden felt so heavy, I'd go for it again.

But I was one of the lucky ones: I was taken to an orphanage and a touring British couple, on their wedding anniversary in Brazil, settled on adopting me. They flew me to England with them, where I grew up and became someone. But I could never forget the suffering in my home country, so I went on to work as a youth street worker.

On the streets, I met amazing people who shared incredible stories of survival; "To live is to see," teaches a Bantu proverb.

These are the stories of homeless young people and their daily struggles to survive. Each young homeless person has to get money in order to survive— by whatever means necessary. Many become involved in illicit activities and harlotry. So I devoted my life to getting these broods off the street.

These are the stories I'd love to share with you. They are the stories of the *children of the night*.

First is an account I shall never forget about a young woman who had been on the street for as long as anyone could remember.

**I'M DESTINY.** I had been on my own since I was about seventeen years old. I lived on the streets because I could no longer live with my *folks* at home.

My real father left when I was young, and my mother remarried. She must have been crazy to be fond of him, for he beat me terribly on no justifiable grounds. When he was intoxicated he would beat my sister and I bloody—just for being in his way.

It seemed to me that anyplace would have been healthier than living at home. At seventeen, I didn't know that living on the streets could be so trying.

They say life is a battle—and they're right. You may or may not believe it, but I went to school and held a job before I left home. When I became heavy with child, my stepfather went nuts and threw me out. I was on my own, with nowhere to go. After I miscarried, I never saw the baby's father again.

I don't speak to my stepfather now, but I ring my mother when I have a little money.

I went from selling weed to crack and acid. I spent my days and nights tripping and piping, just hanging out, with nowhere to go and nothing else to do. I did it to live to tell the tale. I slept in an old shed at a derelict train station surrounded by rubbish. Twenty or more people shared the shed, depending on who needed somewhere to be dead to the world each night. There was never enough space, but we had no choice but to share the place with other groups of children. There was no power, and doors were replaced with pieces of cardboard and wood. We all shared the same tank of stagnant water, and we cooked on a rusty grocery cart we had turned into a barbecue grill, lighting a fire with old newspapers and tiny branches. We would boil water for coffee or heat up some soup if we had any change.

The shed was infested with mice, rats, and cockroaches. I slept in a puny space I shared with a few other girls. The space was pretty revolting: Graffiti covered all of the brightly coloured walls where obscenities found a home when the girls were bored. We'd hang out most of the time, doing nothing really, but roaming forsaken streets like starving hyenas. There was no purpose to our day—just sniffing and smoking. We were out of it most of the day. It got us by.

At night, we would hang out on the streets, looking for ways to get currency. A corner street under a congregation of trees alongside a street light marked the spot where all sorts of men would drive by, looking for girls to pick up. We had no choice. Besides, we were high most of the time. We knew each hour of darkness could be our last; we knew what we were doing was risky. I knew of girls who had been murdered, but it remained a chance we took. What other choice was there? Of course, when we had cash, we had food in our bellies.

Each night men would drive past us. We hiked up our skirts and squeezed our feet into stockings and pointed stilettos or thigh-high boots. When a car slowed down, one of us would walk over and talk prices through the open window. If he accepted our terms, we took a chance and got into the car. That was the risk we were willing to take.

Most patrons who drove down those streets were men, young and old, with riches. Mostly, they wanted sex, but on occasion they got really forcible; girls got beaten up. Again, it was the chance we took or we'd die playing cute with no money in our pockets. If you thought the guy looked creepy, you'd raise your prices and walk away.

With £5 and £10 notes stuffed in our purses, we knew we could get drugs and sell them back at the shed to the other kids. We'd buy food from the twenty-four-hour shop and crawl homewards in the early hours; drained, ready to slumber, telling each other stories about the men we'd met, laughing at how we'd duped them, charging markedly excessive rates. We would somehow manage to justify what we did—not only to them but to ourselves. After all, we needed the money.

How else would we survive?

We couldn't talk about how afraid we were or how inexperienced we were. We wouldn't discuss the fear of being violated, beaten up, or wasted. We knew everyone felt the same, even the older girls who'd been doing it for years.

I remember the day I first met Brenda. She started to hang around with me for protection. She looked at me warily, very nervous.

"How long have you been on the street?" I flicked my cigarette to the floor and stepped on it.

"Too long," replied Brenda.

I could have turned and walked away, but I felt sad for her; she looked so young. "How old are you, kid?" I asked.

She looked at me, afraid to tell me the truth. "I'm nearly fourteen," she said ultimately, moving on quickly, nervously. "I just couldn't bear to live with my old man. I had enough of his beatings. My mother wouldn't listen to me. She'd say she didn't believe me."

"You know, living in the street is hard. It's not as easy as you think. You'll have to work hard. Haven't you got other family or friends you can stay with?" I muttered.

"I don't want to go back home," came Brenda's reply, her voice rising and agitated. "You won't persuade me to go back. My old man's a bastard."

I knew she meant it. Sadly enough, I could relate. "Well, it's your decision, but I'm warning you that it's not easy. To earn money, to survive, you'll have to be prepared." I said.

Her eyes were wide. She bit her nails nervously.

"Look, don't worry, kid. I'll look out for you. I'll set up the first customer for you, but you'll have to give me a cut of what you make. That's the way things are done here. Okay?" I offered.

"Okay. Thanks, Destiny."

An hour later, Brenda arrived back on the street. She was walking with no sign of the car that previously took her. As she approached, I could see she was in tears, and as she got nearer I could see her blouse had been ripped.

"What happened?" I asked, beckoning her forward, taking out a cigarette and passing it to her.

She couldn't talk at first. She was just sobbing.

"Come on, Brenda. Have you been hurt? Tell me what happened," I said.

She sucked hard on the cigarette, wiping her nose with the back of her hand. "Look." She lifted her skirt, and I could see blood on her knickers. "That bastard!" she said and began to cry again.

"Brenda, what happened? Come on. Tell me," I said.

The other girls could hear that something was wrong, and they began to walk over to us.

Brenda was shivering all over. "I refused to do what he wanted. He started to lash at me. I thought he was going to kill me. I just wanted to get out of his car, but I couldn't. He held me down. He did terrible things to me. I screamed. I thought I was going to die." Brenda wailed, sobbing again. She continued, "He told me if I made a sound, he would kill me. And then he threw me out and gave me twenty quid."

Brenda didn't stay with us. She left a couple days later. She had a shocking experience the first time, but that's life on the street. I wake up every morning wishing it could be different, but where would I go? I'd been here too long now. I knew nothing else.

I never imagined that one day I would be homeless, putting my heavenly gift to shameful use in exchange for money. I had ambitions, hopes, and dreams like everyone else: One day I would be with a man, living in a lovely house, working in a decent profession, driving a fly car, and I'd have children. Even now, I want that life. I want people to know that I'm normal and I deserve a chance at living like them.

My best friend, Fiona, died three months ago from a heroin overdose. She always told me, "Destiny, if one day you see an opportunity to get out of this life, go. Take that chance. Fall in love. Have lots of children. And don't ever think about us, or you'll never leave. Just go."

Being homeless is a funny game; there are no rules. Once you're in the cycle of drugs and money, it's hard to get out. People say, "The fowler's pipe sounds sweet till the bird is caught." Fiona knew she was in a trap, traveling the path of her own demise.

I loved her so much.

Seems I'll be a prisoner of this life till I die, unless I make my mind to walk away…


It is difficult to grasp how dangerous the streets can be until you listen to homeless people like Destiny. Walking in the night and living in the cold; Try to imagine how scared they must have been, trying to survive in the dark, filthy, fetid streets.

I'm Pedro Pereira, and my next story is about a young couple, Victory and David Jr. They live in fear and don't have any idea about what tomorrow will bring.

I'M DAVID, and I married Victory. I was twenty-one years old. I'd been on the street for seven years. I didn't have money. I shoplifted in stores nearby. I stole money from people, and I sold drugs. Life was hard, but I had to care for my wife. She'd suffered a lot in her past, and now I wanted to look after her.

We did not have a proper place to sleep. Many nights we slept at the bus stop, and sometimes, if we were lucky, we slept in a squat. It was a risk but worth it when the weather was cold. More often, we stayed in forsaken, derelict houses and factories. We never stayed at the same place for long; we were always on the move in search of food, clothes, and money. If we were hungry, all we could think about was finding food. If we were freezing, all we thought about was getting warm.

I'd met a lot of people and made decent friends. The majority of us came from broken families. When we were homeless, there was no class; no difference between us. We were all broke, down, and out. There was no rich, no middle class; just plain, poor, and filthy, defined by the environment surrounding us that treated us like a plague of shunned bastards.

For the past four months, I'd been worried about my beloved wife Victory. We had discovered she was about to become a mother, and I now had a duty and commitment to look after her and to prepare for the arrival of our unborn child. The good news—or perhaps I should say, the worst news, if I could call it that—was that Victory was expecting triplets, and I was worried sick. The street was no place for a child, let alone three. The streets had broken me emotionally, physically, and spiritually. I found myself depressed, feeling less of a man because I could not work. The only way I could provide for us was with the money I earned on the street, which I had to rely on.

I reflected on my life to a time when I was well off, earning good money, when I was comfortable and stable. I knew I had responsibilities. It was my choice to become what I was. I felt disliked by society and feared I might never be able to fit back in. On a daily basis, I wondered if I would ever make more of my life for the sake of my wife and my children.

I first became aware of a place called Carrefour some years ago. Carrefour simply means "crossroads" in English. It's a place situated somewhere in London. The name was given to this particular place because the majority of customers were French lorry drivers who used the area as a resting place during their long journey through the English country. As time moved on, the area became a popular place for harlotry.

Some miles away, there was a park where, during the early months of summer, fairs would come and gypsies would camp. These people would take us in and feed us. We knew the camps were a meal ticket.

One day at the fair, I met an old lady friend of mine, Amber. I was pleased to see her after all the years that had passed. Later, Amber asked me to give her a lift on my motorbike to where she was working. I picked her up and took her to Cross Avenue in London. As we arrived, Amber said, "Not this Cross Avenue, but to Carrefour. Follow the traffic."

I remembered that particular day: It was Saturday early evening and, as we crossed this little bridge, I thought we had arrived in a war zone. It was like another world. There were call girls all along the boulevard, half-stripped women revealing their ample bodies. They donned long boots, short boots, leather jackets, fur coats, and lacy bras. You name it, they wore it—any item of clothing that would show off their curves. Here I met women and girls, many underage, working year round, in the cold of the winter through the hot summer.

I remembered looking at a younger girl once as she turned down a customer. She wore a tight cherry mini skirt and an equally tight black leather jacket. She held a tiny mirror in her left hand and a tube of lipstick in the other, pursing her lips and painting them with the scarlet stick. She knew she was being watched. She was playing with her hair, running it through her fingers and shaking it back, then holding up the mirror again to have another look.

Amber gave me ten pounds for the lift, and I didn't go home straightaway. I drove around for maybe an hour, watching a group of adolescents known as *children of the night* work their lure. As I drove past my own reality, I recalled Amber saying, "They think we can do anything they want, anything they ask. They're wrong. Most of us want to be loved, as would any normal person. But I get it in their eyes that we're just tramps."

Later that year, Amber was found dead in an abandoned factory. I didn't attend the funeral. I wanted to remember her as she was, pretty as she had always been.

Flashing back to even happier days, an earlier and most virgin image of Victory appeared in my mind. I first met Victory at Carrefour. It was early afternoon. She looked very much like a schoolgirl in her school uniform and her big blue pair of glasses. She was so young and beautiful, with her black curled hair. She was always holding a cigarette in her right hand in her own strange way. I always saw her in the early afternoon, when school was just let out.

Being homeless had been really difficult. I wasn't proud about what I had done on the street, but it made me wiser and stronger.

What kept my wife and I alive was our faith in God and our prayers each day. If I had three wishes, first was to get my family out of this misery; second was to help those who shared my fate; the last was to thank God personally for putting my wife and me in His hands.

Is this wishful thinking? I don't know...


**I'M VICTORY**, and I'm twenty. I've lived almost all my life as a streetwalker at the Carrefour. It all started when my friend Lisa, who lived in the area, introduced me to the Carrefour. She told me she had been working for a while and to try it out first. I just couldn't come to terms with accepting that everyday life. I remember telling her, "No way! What will my friends think of me, a bloody whore?"

"Listen, Vicky," she said, "your parents are dead, and with no close relatives, no place to live, nowhere to go, and no money, you'll die. You must survive. You must work. This is work and nothing else. Focus on the money."

And so I consented. We agreed to meet one day in front of an old building in the Carrefour. I was there a few minutes earlier than Lisa. Rolling up in the streets of Carrefour, I later saw Lisa walking towards me. She had a Gazelle-like figure. She was all in white, from her long fur coat to her shiny silk pair of leggings, down to her high-heel shoes.

She asked that I watch the way she hooked up with clients. She floated across the boulevard against the heavy sound of the traffic in the night and shadows from the flickering street light; against flashing lights from passing cars and lorries; against the backdrop of a noisy late train crossing over the bridge. Her exhibition resulted in a luxury limousine coming to a halt in front of her.

"What's up, babe?" said the money man in the limo.

"Are you buying or faking?" said Lisa, showing off her perfectly aligned pearly whites.

"Buying," said the man, dressed in a chic tuxedo.

Lisa went straightforward. "I'm feeling generous."

The black man smiled, moved by Lisa's quirkiness. "Well, I've got champagne…Loran Perrier…Paul Letrier."

"Put me in your limo. Take it or leave it," said Lisa, blasé.

"All right," said the client waving to the driver. "Get the door. Will you?"

A chauffeur who resembled a nightclub bouncer propped open the door, and Lisa climbed in. I watched alone on the boulevard, shocked to see how quickly Lisa got in a total stranger's car, never putting to question his integrity. But that was the life. Who had time for a background check? Each night these girls played Russian Roulette.

One never knew if we entered the car of a maniac or psychopath. We just had to take that chance. I hung out on the boulevard until I met a client. When his car pulled up to the curb, I went up to his passenger's window.

"How much is around the world?" asked the man, who was dressed conservatively and spoke in a polite tone. It was odd to see someone so different. I had never heard anyone speak so proper. I was told most of the time it was obscenities, and I was new to all of this and wondered what the hell 'around the world' even meant.

Yet I had to act in response, so I said, "Ten pounds."

The man threw an odd gaze. I must have said the wrong thing. So he asked again, "Are you certain?"

"Yes," I said. "It's what I charge."

He never asked a third time and let me in his car. That was my first, and I never looked back.

Weeks later, I was knee-deep in the business. I would climb in just about any car that stopped in front of me. First I thought this happened because I was a newcomer. I hadn't realised what I had been doing.

Lisa had noticed clients pouring in for my service. She bluntly asked, "What are you charging your regulars?"

"Ten pounds for everything."

"Are you insane? That's a dead giveaway," barked Lisa. "You're underselling yourself. No wonder they're flocking to you."

I wanted to make money, but somehow, I'd also wished for company; keeping the price low assured me of a constant flow of companions. But Lisa's words hanging in the air reminded me just how stupid I'd been. I was a lady of easy virtue—not a housewife.

"Listen. Forget it. It's in the past now," said Lisa. "You're a beautiful girl. You've got the charm. Use it. Charge them an arm and a leg. If they're going to be with you, make them pay."

Gosh, was I naïve. I'd come to Carrefour to survive—earn a living, make money. Surely that would get me out of my misery and off these cursed streets. Reality always set in; to evade, it I'd use drugs. I'd float whilst my pain went away, only to return when the drugs wore off. I hated descending from the high that kept me in La-La Land, where my dearest fantasies endured.

All good things come to an end, and so did all my highs.

I later left hustling—not for long—although it wasn't easy to get out of the business. You get passing joys, cash, and meet people who think you could never be: physicians, attorneys, even a high court judge. You're trapped in a devious world of wishes and dreams. Worse was that every time we quit, we were reminded that we had no other skills but the one we knew best: hooking—a reality that was best dealt with by returning back to the streets we dreaded so much. After all we were working girls and, above all, *children of the night.*

Might I remind you I was married to David, who loathed me running the streets to make ends meet, but it had to be done. And he reminded me just how careful I had to be. The truth was, there were too many unsolved murders—and David worried.

Each moment I'd climb into a car, David was right there, following behind incognito on his motorbike. He took great care in taking the plate number of the car. We had gone through the routine several times over, and I had instructed him that, in the event I was not back in time, he'd rush to the police station. He'd say these words: "My wife was last seen in (where he'd describe the car), and here's the plate number." Each night before I joined my equals on the hellish streets, we'd rehearse, and he'd remind me a thousand times that he understood. Each time I read his emotions: He hated sharing me with other men—and women, on some occasions. But he never complained, and he always followed behind.

He was my only safety net. At least if I was to end like many before me, David would know my killer. Every single night when I was out in the Carrefour, David prayed with me. I'm not sure why, but we'd do a prayer as soon as we arrived.

He never failed to pep me up. "I love you, Victory. Don't you ever forget that. And be careful. You get in the car and get out in one piece."

He said it often enough that I'd fall down in tears. Each time was like the last goodbye, as we never knew if somehow I'd come back alive. The streets were simply too rough and dangerous. One couldn't be too careful.

After some time, our relationship had begun a downward trajectory.

David became almost intolerant of me; he wouldn't touch me as he had in the past. Often, David would ask if I'd been like one of his patrons—just another *man*. He became irate, sad, and disillusioned. I never saw that coming: David had always been so understanding. I tried to make him understand that we needed the money and that I had to work. Every single night I had to be with ten, perhaps more: do or die. I had no skills and, candidly, I had been working in this way for so long I couldn't think of any other way to earn a living.

Things went from bad to worse when we found out I was expecting triplets.

When I first heard the news from the nurse, I felt miserable. I wanted to get rid of the babies. I was a fallen woman, for Christ's sake, without a *normal* job. How could we live a stable life? Then again, when I later walked past the Church of Christ near the street where I'd hook, I thought twice of terminating my babies. Have I mentioned I had already given up a bastard child to my grandparents, one I had conceived decades ago with my first love?

But despite our differences, David and I could work things out, so one night we sat down and talked about it. It was the most productive sit-down we'd had since we first fell in love with each other. And David pledged to look after me and our children.

David sold his motorbike for a few thousand pounds. We hoped that would be enough to support us for a few months, until he got a chance to secure a job. Some of my friends also pledged to chip in as much as they could. Somehow, though I'd been enslaved to my own flesh and fallen from grace, I trusted in God that one day all this would be behind us and things would get better. Surely it must be, if there is a God…

*Olá novamente…*

**I'M PEDRO PEREIRA**, born in the suburb of Rio de Janeiro in Brazil. These stories and experiences of today's juvenile homeless touched me deeply. My experience working with youth for nearly a decade helped me understand the depth of youth homelessness in England.

When I joined Youth and Community Services, the first thing I had to do was gain the young people's trust. The sincere bond between us allowed them to show me their closets full of bones and share their darkest stories of anguish with me; otherwise, my work would have had no purpose.

Once more, I recalled *The Oprah Winfrey Show*. The words played over and over in my mind.

On several occasions, I brought food and drink when I first walked the streets to chat with some of the teens, but none came to me; no one was interested in talking to me. It took me a long time to show the kids that I was there to help them.

I really cared.

Brazil, my home, reminded me each passing moment of the power of giving. The most challenging task for any youth worker is to gain the kids' trust. Once trust was established, you'd graduate to the next step—inquiring through courteous talks, finding out where problems lay, and discovering the best ways of assisting and resolving them. Truthfully, most issues seemed insurmountable—almost impossible to resolve. How does one get a sixteen-year-old hustler off the streets, one who's been selling her body most of her teenage life, with no motivation other than money?

I saw more death, pain, and atrocity than I could ever have imagined.

At the start of homelessness, youngsters typically heavily depended on those already living on the streets; like an apprentice-type system where experience led ignorance. To find food and a roof above their heads, most homeless juveniles were forced to steal or undertake otherwise illegal activities, with those successful leaving the drifter circuit by finding a 'regular' job as a professional harlot. Victory was an example—a drug dealer, burglar, and thief.

I remembered my first stride on the street and the secret life it sheltered. Secrets hidden behind each corner, secrets that lurked behind the shadows of boys and girls walking up and down all with a common goal—making fast money. I asked myself why and how they became who they were. Why was Victory a prostitute? Why and how had she chosen that life? Why had Destiny absolutely no choice but to hook? Why had Fiona been a victim of a heroin overdose? Why was David his own wife's pimp? Why had Amber been killed? And the whys never ceased to end.

As I worked the streets, I found that many juveniles had already been engaged in delinquent acts before they became permanent dwellers of the streets. Parental control, conflict, school involvement, and commitment were some of the participating factors in their delinquency, all of which eventually led to theft, burglary, vandalism, and prostitution. Even with that, I also found that many simply had no choice in the matter and had been de facto victims simply because of a variety of circumstances devoid of delinquent acts.

On each street corner, I witnessed homeless juveniles using hard drugs, and the much younger using lesser addictive substances, like marijuana and ecstasy. Cocaine, crack, stimulants, and LSD/PCP were typically those used amongst the eldest.

Beer was a favourite more so than wine and hard liquor. I remembered how, on some nights, I would watch young kids falling drunk after bottles of beer. Our conversation seldom proceeding anywhere as they spoke like fools at night, believing they were victims of our society.

When I spoke to Fiona and Amber before they passed, they all told me that, very often, they'd had to run away from home to avoid victimisation by their parents, yet they got caught in circumstances that made them more vulnerable; their newly adopted lifestyles attacked the very fabric of their livelihood.

Christians believe that if you have faith in God, you can move mountains. Little gestures of giving you do from the heart, which are pure and loving, are like mustard seeds that swell into mustard trees; tall and wide.

I've witnessed much propaganda promoting that kids stay off the streets, warning them to stay off drugs, but failing to teach them how to fish. If the streets were all they knew, how would they survive outside of the only world known to them? Teach them! No child, man, or woman deserves to be homeless.

Our children are our future.

It broke my heart when I once watched a starving child eating out of a waste bin. Standing on the street corner, staring at that child, I had run out of food and had no money in my pocket. I spent sleepless nights trying to clear my mind of that sight, knowing I could have done better, that more could have been actioned: I could have found a way to feed that child. But there's only me and them, so many nights I cried myself to sleep.

A few years passed, I left my post as a youth street worker, determined to establish a benevolent group to help young people get off of the streets. My homeless links dubbed it Children of the Night, in remembrance of those that had passed and in knowing that, although they struggled, they'd one day return home victorious.

Much to my surprise, the charity had great success and brought about the greatest sense of awareness in high places. Money poured in from pole to pole, in the hopes of saving those whom I'd learned to call friends.

Programmes specially designed to prevent the development of juvenile behavioural issues were set up. Our key aim was to intervene and resolve matters of those already on the streets.

Amongst essential services, we had emergency shelters run by Destiny, which involved handling the basic needs of the homelessness, such as a place to stay for the night, a meal, or food stamps. The shelter became so known in the area that each night youngsters fought for limited space. We could hardly serve those on our rosters, and the volume required that we expand; only we lacked the finances to open new shelters.

Destiny became our main coordinator and never returned to the streets; rather, she'd only return to speak out and encourage those who came after her, assuring them that there was life beyond the streets. As suggested by her name, her dreams, ambitions, and hope became true: After a few years working as leader of the emergency shelter, she was stable and settled with the car she had always dreamed of—a Mercedes-Benz. Go figure.

She found herself a good man, a respectable barrister, and soon after they met, they tied the knot. Happily married, they were living amongst the elite in one of London's most expensive neighbourhoods. Last known news was she was expecting. She brought me such pride.

David struggled for some time. He'd ignore my frequent visits, putting down any idea I brought to the table. With everything, his question was always, "When do I get paid?" I understood money was his main concern—especially with triplets on the way. I had to be consistent and, with much perseverance, he finally opened up.

We had convinced him that he was a natural and that he'd do really well with my help. And so we agreed to set up a youth employment programme. I thought his experience, having been a drug dealer and a pimp, was appropriate enough and that he'd transition well into running the programme operations. I reminded him that it was much the same—only this was legit. So he went for it.

Boy, was I right. He was, simply put, a natural. He had great marketing, contact and management skills. We'd laugh when I'd remind him that his past life was his boot camp and that the good Lord had finally made a way.

He really cherished our chats.

A year after the start of this programme, David excelled as its leader. He became the busiest person in the organisation. He had grown so much and enjoyed his job, travelling across the country like most business people do. He even went as far as making profitable deals with several blue-chip companies, willing to provide basic financial security to working with homeless youths and funding for the prolongation of positive vocational learning—something to be exceptionally proud of.

And I was proud…

REMEMBER ME?

**I'M VICTORY**. How did my story end? Well, I received thousands of letters from people all across England and even more letters from abroad, asking me questions and wondering if I had finally given birth and whether I had to put them into adoption or if I was still with David.

Well, I always had faith in God, and that proved rewarding. David and I were happily married.

With the support and the help of Pedro, we both had found work at Children of the Night. I was involved in the Street Outreach programme; I followed in Pedro's footsteps. I would go to areas where homeless kids congregated. I'd hand out cards, phone numbers, or addresses of our health clinics or our drop-in centres, where they could reach us for food, clothing, and a shower, crisis-counselling, and all kinds of help.

David and I bought a four-bedroom detached house in the suburbs of London. I gave birth to three babies: two girls, Lynette and Ronda, and one boy we named Pedro. They're all beautiful children. I later reunited with my first son, who came to stay with us permanently. With a complete family, David and I would do our best to ensure a good upbringing for our children.

You might be asking yourself what happened to Pedro, the youth worker. Sadly, late one evening, Pedro was found dead in his automobile somewhere on one of the streets known for its booming prostitution in Scotland.

Inquest from the Scotland police was inconclusive.

Four months earlier, Pedro went missing after failing to attend a project launch. We knew something was wrong because he never rang and never returned, which he had never done before, but that was normally when he went underground to earn the trust of those he wanted to help off the streets.

That was the method he had used in the past, but this time everything felt wrong. In his flat, the police found two bodies in the lounge—a female and a male.

Drugs and alcohol coated the dining table. Again, no traces of substances were found in the bodies. The footsteps found by the window never matched Pedro's or any of the victims'. The local coroners stated in the newspaper: "These sudden deaths are a mystery and until now remain an unsolved mystery..."

Yet strangely enough, we had learned that prior to his sudden death, Pedro had renewed his faith in God.

Today, we continue Pedro's work, and his memory will forever be celebrated through our good works, for he was a true angel among the living...

**I'M PEDRO PEREIRA**...and I've been saved.

# ABOUT THE AUTHORS

## ALLAIN NGWALA

ALLAIN NGWALA is Congolese-British. He was born in Kinshasa, Democratic Republic of Congo, formerly Zaire. He's a graduate of The Abbey College and the University of Hertfordshire and has worked for nearly two decades as an IT and Clinical Data Consultant. *Congo: Spirit of Darkness* is Allain's joint debut novel with co-author and brother Mayi Ngwala. He lives in Cambridgeshire, United Kingdom, and enjoys the company of his two children and his nephew.

Visit Allain online at www.allainngwala.com

## MAYI NGWALA

MAYI NGWALA was born in New Orleans, Louisiana, and grew up in the Democratic Republic of Congo. He's a graduate of the University of Maryland, College Park, and the former *Hollywood Scriptwriting Institute*.

Mayi was trained in the art of storytelling and screenwriting by mentor, noted writer, and Iowa Walk of Fame inductee Earl D. Blakesley, Jr. *Congo:*

*Spirit of Darkness* is Mayi's joint debut novel with co-author and brother Allain Ngwala. He lives in Maryland with his wife, Nakia T. Ngwala, and their two sons.

Visit Mayi online at www.mayingwala.com

*A portion of the proceeds from*

*all book sales is donated to*

*humanitarian causes and charities.*

*For more information visit*

www.genetpress.com

20335049R00203

Printed in Great Britain
by Amazon